DEVIL'S ADVOCATE

ALSO BY MICHAEL A. BLACK_

Chimes at Midnight

Trackdown Series

Devil's Dance

Devil's Fancy

Devil's Brigade

DEVIL'S ADVOCATE

TRACKDOWN

BOOK 4

MICHAEL A. BLACK

ROUGH
EDGES
PRESS

For all my fallen brothers and sisters
in law enforcement

I am a man whom Fortune hath scratched.
Praising what is lost
Makes the remembrance dear.

All's Well That Ends Well
- William Shakespeare

DEVIL'S ADVOCATE

CHAPTER ONE_

THE BUBBLE AT THE MGM GRAND
LAS VEGAS, NEVADA

The arena beyond the cyclone fencing was shrouded in darkness, making the vague figures look like ghosts moving in the shadows. In contrast, the numerous floodlights illuminating the octagon almost made Wolf feel that he was once again experiencing the contrast of the brightness of the Sandbox and it brought back a flash of memory of Iraq. He paced back and forth, allowing his bare feet to become accustomed to the rough texture of the padded mat. His opponent across the way, Marcus "Blood" Ford, was bouncing on his toes with a wide grin that exposed the flash of white vampire-like teeth painted on the black mouthpiece.

An attempt at intimidation, Wolf thought. Ain't gonna work.

It would have been more effective if the guy had kept his mouth shut and then parted his lips during a moment of close-in combat. Now the initial shock effect was minimized.

In Iraq, Wolf and his squad had done something similar, putting skull-like renderings on their body armor and helmets to signify to the indigenous personnel that they were the death dealers. It was hardly a new idea. His friend and mentor, Big Jim McNamara, had told him about leaving playing cards with the ace of spades on the dead bodies of the VC back in the day. And the tons of propaganda leaflets that had been dropped in virtually every conflict since World War II were testament that psychological warfare was all about making your enemy feel unnerved, inadequate, second best. This was the same principle, only on a much smaller scale.

Marcus Ford stopped bouncing and cast a baleful stare in Wolf's direction as he smacked his gloves together. Reno had told Wolf this wouldn't be a cake-walk. Ford had been a collegiate wrestler and had a record of 8 and 3, with 5 wins by way of knockout. He was taller than Wolf and Ford's arms were huge but, as he bounced, Wolf saw something: a barely noticeable layer of suet around his waist. It wasn't excessive but might be an indication that Blood hadn't taken the match as seriously as he might have. Then again, maybe he didn't think he needed to. After all, Wolf was just a last-minute replacement in what was considered to be the pre-contender match-up. Reno Garth, his erstwhile sponsor and trainer, had assured him the winner would go on to contender status for the world title.

Just like déjà vu all over again, Wolf thought, remembering that Reno had said the same thing a little over a month ago back in Phoenix. That bout had ended in a draw which hadn't been that much of a disappointment on Wolf's part. He was only in it for the money with no real plans to keep ascending the staircase of the Mixed Martial Arts world. But that was before the pandemic slowed the court system to a virtual halt and, with it, the bounty hunting business. So when Reno had called him, his voice brimming with excitement about a chance that "just opened up to fight in Vegas, for some real decent money," Wolf figured the paycheck would be nice and he also didn't want to turn his buddy down. In some strange role reversal, Reno, the man whom Wolf had regarded as an obnoxious and dangerous rival in the bounty hunting business a few months back, was now a friend who was trying to regain his own lost dreams of contender status in the MMA world. So, Wolf had agreed, despite not having had the time to do extensive training.

He owed Reno that much but this was definitely going to be his last fight.

Of course, he'd told himself that the last time as well. Still, this was a fight where he'd be on equal footing, unlike the other one that dominated his life. This one he had a chance of winning. The other made him feel like he was Bambi being stalked by Godzilla.

Maybe not Bambi, he thought. How about Batman?

Ford's lips pulled back in a grimace displaying the imitation vampire[1] dentition once more, as he smacked the gloves together harder.

Save it for after the bell, Wolf thought, and kept his expression neutral.

"Don't let his bullshit bother you," Reno said, leaning close to Wolf's ear. He spoke in a low whisper, even though the arena was only sparsely populated due to the pandemic restrictions that were still hanging on in these uncertain times. "Remember, you win this one, you're the USA champ, and the number one contender. It's almost unheard of to get a chance like this without being in the game for a couple years."

Wolf nodded. He was, actually, amused by Ford's antics as if choosing the ring name of "Blood" and a fierce-looking mouthpiece were going to make any difference.

George Patton, Wolf's main trainer, massaged his neck a bit and asked how he was feeling.

"Ready, willing, and able," Wolf said. The mouthpiece was making his word sound sloppy.

"Ladies and gentlemen," the announcer yelled into his microphone. He continued through his exaggerated spiel about the co-main event of the evening being for the interim, USA light-heavyweight championship, and guaranteeing the winner a shot at the world title. He went on introducing the fighters and hyping the importance of the match for the benefit of the cable TV crew who were filming everything.

Wolf raised his arms when the announcer barked out the particulars: "Standing at six foot-one inches, and weighing in at two hundred-twelve pounds, fighting out of Phoenix, Arizona, Steve, 'Airborne Ranger,' Wolf."

The appellation was bittersweet. Wolf had earned his jump wings and Ranger status during his time in the army but had to forfeit it all as part of the plea agreement that sent him to Leavenworth for a four-year stretch for being involved in the deaths of some Iraqi civilians. His tour in the Sandbox had almost been up, too. Not that it would have made any difference at his court-martial. A blow to the head had left him with eight missing minutes that robbed him of a chance to mount a proper defense. He knew he was innocent and he also knew there was a video of another man's confession out there somewhere that could help him clear his name and he wanted to find it.

Easier said than done, he thought. And first things first.

Marcus "Blood" Ford danced around when his name was announced. There was that hint of jiggle around his waist again but his arms looked as thick as tree trunks and the guy was going to be trying to take Wolf's head off in a little over a minute.

"Seconds out," the ref called as he motioned the fighters to their marks.

Reno and George both clapped Wolf on the shoulder as they walked to the gate, Reno using his cane as he limped along. Wolf glanced up into the dark, sparsely populated stands and thought he caught a glimpse of Mac and the P-Patrol and wondered what Yolanda would be seeing in about two minutes.

"Are you ready here?" the referee yelled at Wolf.

He nodded.

The ref turned to Ford. "Are you ready, Marcus?"

Ford's lips closed over the vampire teeth and he nodded as well.

"Then let's get it on," the ref yelled and dropped his arm to the accompaniment of the blaring air-horn.

————

PRIVATE ROAD OF THE VON DIEN WINTER ESTATE SOUTH

BELIZE

Lancelot returns to Camelot, Richard Soraces thought with a smile as the limousine turned onto the paved side road which he knew led to the massive sliding gate. The vehicle's headlights washed over a white sign with black lettering proclaiming this to be a private road.

The paved surface curved through a maze of tall trees and verdant greenery so dense that it probably required a small army of peasants with machetes once a week just to keep the ubiquitous plant encroachment from overwhelming the roadway. They whizzed past another sign warning *DANGER—NO TRES-PASSING/PELIGRO—NO ENTRADA.*

In English and Spanish, Soraces thought. Both in all caps.

A second bilingual sign advised not to touch the fencing, which Soraces knew was electrified, and a third posting stated this was private property. All that was missing was another proclamation that violators would be shot. Of course, that would most likely be done inconspicuously.

Soraces smiled again. He'd enjoyed his past stay there about three and a half weeks ago in this sunny country south of Mexico.

Especially the ladies, he reflected lasciviously.

An incredibly rich man, Dexter Von Dien, and the fat man's attorney, Anthony Marco Fallotti had previously hired him to obtain a plaster statue of a Mexican bandito that was in the possession of some disgraced army ranger. It supposedly contained some kind of priceless Iraqi artifact that Von Dien was jonesing about. The damn thing had practically fallen into Soraces's lap, or so he'd thought, and he'd raced back down to Belize to present what he'd assumed was the Holy Grail to his employers, figuring they'd be ecstatic.

They weren't.

The scene unfolded again in Soraces's memory like the real-life replay of *The Maltese Falcon*. Von Dien, who was morbidly obese and almost a look-alike for Sidney Greenstreet, except with less hair, became totally devastated as he quickly realized the artifact he sought was not inside the plaster statue that Soraces had brought from the States. It had been reminiscent of that climactic scene in that old movie where Casper Gutman, the fat man, chipped away at the black bird and suddenly discovers it to be an ersatz copy of the original. Soraces would have laughed out loud, in appropriate Bogart fashion, if he hadn't been a bit concerned about retribution from Von Dien's oversized bodyguard. The fat bastard had practically collapsed and had to be helped out of the room, a sobbing, collapsing, flabby mess with the bodyguard on one side and the attorney, Fallotti, on the other.

Since Soraces had already received half of the agreed upon fee in advance, and knowing the fat man's penchant for ordering harm to those who displeased him, Soraces figured it was time to make a quick exit rather than face the fallout. Without further ado, he walked out of the mansion and got into the waiting limo that had picked him up from the airport.

"*Lleve me al aeropuerto,*" he told the driver. "*En seguida.*"

The driver looked perplexed and Soraces realized he might not speak Spanish.

"The airport," he yelled. "Now!"

A look of alarm swept over the driver's face as he nodded and shifted into gear.

Soraces kept his ninja pen stiletto in his hand in case he had to stab the driver in the neck, toss him out of the car, and ram through the gate himself, but no one attempted to stop them. He'd gone straight to the airport and got on the first commercial flight back to the States. After so many years working for the Agency, he knew when to make a tactical retreat.

The fat man had a low tolerance for failure and was always moaning about "troublesome loose ends." Soraces didn't want to take the chance of becoming one of those, like the lawyer, Cummings, he and his partner had dispatched back in that ghost town in Arizona. Von Dien had made it clear from the onset that he wanted it done and, from all accounts, the guy had it coming.

Terminate with extreme prejudice.

Another fond Agency term, he thought. Just like the good old days, except way more lucrative.

He hadn't expected to hear from Von Dien again, assuming that failure to deliver was grounds for termination, but after a few weeks, the call, surprisingly, came from Fallotti, Von Dien's lawyer, inviting him down to Belize to discuss "further dealings."

"I got the impression you were less than satisfied with our last dealing," Soraces said.

"Nonsense," Fallotti said, his voice cordial and welcoming. "It was unfortunate, to say the least, but Mr. Von Dien firmly believes that you're the man for the job. In fact, we're ready to double the previously agreed upon amount and send half of it to your Cayman account."

Soraces agreed to take another trip to Belize, but he kept his ninja pen handy. That was all he needed thanks to a lifetime of specialized Agency training. He was very adept at both throwing and stabbing with it. If push came to shove, he could, deftly, hurl it into to eye of Von Dien's oversized bodyguard or jab it into the man's jugular. Then it would be a small matter of retrieving the big Walther Q4 Steel Frame semi-auto from the dead bodyguard's pancake holster and using the fat man as a bargaining chip to get the hell out of there. The pistol had red dot sight attached and an extended, suppressor adapter on the front end of the barrel and Soraces was curious as to how it would be to fire.

Hopefully, it won't come to that, Soraces thought. Perhaps the fat man really does realize what happened wasn't my fault.

But it did bring up the concern of an insurance policy of some sort, something that he could have to ensure he'd be home free and untouchable after this new transaction had been completed. So just in case, Soraces had two pens with him on this trip: his ninja knife blade and his spy pen. Those two items were the particular reason he'd chosen to wear a short-sleeve dress shirt with a pocket.

The limo slowed and Soraces saw the emerald green canopy of trees gave way to the well shorn grassy area leading up to the high, fifteen-foot fence topped with triple strands of barbed wire. The painted skull and the words again in both English and Spanish: *STOP. DANGER. DO NOT TOUCH THE FENCE. NO ENTRY/DETENER. PELIGRO. NO TOQUES LA CERCA. NO ENTRADA* graced the sign on the big gate. Although the estate was in an area that predominantly spoke English, the bilingual signs, Fallotti had previously explained were meant not only for the local populace but the estate employees as well.

"Most of them are imported from Costa Rica or Guatemala," Fallotti said.

It made sense to Soraces. Import foreign help which would not have that much of a base in the local community, the land outside the castle gates, that was in a section of the country that predominately spoke English. It would also ensure loyalty based on dependence and make it easier should any of them "disappear." He remembered the luscious girls that had pleasured him the last time. Costa Rican, if he remembered correctly. Please the boss and whomever else he tells you to please or you'll find yourself part of the garden.

A man of extreme caution and means, Soraces thought.

A fat security guard ambled out of a guard shack and came to the driver's side. The window lowered with electronic ease and the driver said in Spanish that Mr. Von Dien was expecting them.

"¿*Quién es*?" the guard asked.

"*Señor* Soraces," the driver answered.

The guard immediately straightened up and scurried back to the gate shack. Moments later, the large gate retracted to the side leaving the path open before them.

Lancelot welcomed back to Camelot, Soraces thought.

He considered that comparison for a moment and then reconsidered.

Well, not quite. It was more like welcome back to tropical Oz.

———

THE BUBBLE AT THE MGM GRAND
LAS VEGAS, NEVADA

Wolf extended his left hand to do the customary glove-touching as he advanced to the center of the octagon. Ford ignored the gesture and kept advancing with a determined look on his face.

So much for good sportsmanship, Wolf thought. But neither of us is here to dance.

He pulled his arm back into his standard guard position and began a slow rotation to his left. Ford was apparently left-handed, or at least preferred to stand in a southpaw stance. This threw Wolf off a bit. Usually, southpaws were more difficult to fight due to most fighters being orthodox, or right-handed. Everything was virtually thrown in reverse, which was why preparing for a left-handed opponent required a bit more diligence in training. Due to the short notice, Wolf had little more than nine days to prepare. Luckily, there were a couple of guys at Reno's gym who were reasonably competent at affecting a southpaw stance but neither was truly left-handed. Ford seemed to be naturally inclined that way. He shot out a quick right jab that slammed into Wolf's left forearm and felt like an electric shock.

It was a common tactic in the boxing ring: beat on your opponent's arms until he has a hard time holding them up and then the head becomes more vulnerable. But it was, basically, a tactic meant for the long haul—a systematic beat-down meant to inflict damage over an expanse of rounds. Ford tossed a flurry of punches as he moved forward again.

A man in a hurry, Wolf thought.

He backpedaled away and only one of the punches landed, this time on his left shoulder.

Wolf concentrated on moving in a clockwise pattern, trying to keep his left foot on the far side of Ford's leading right, placing more distance between his power side and Wolf. It required more conscious thought than was desirable and had a tendency to throw a fighter's timing off. Even a fraction of a second could make a difference, as Wolf found out when Ford's left foot shot out and smacked into Wolf's left inner thigh.

It was too close for comfort and Wolf danced out of range instead of engaging. So far, he had yet to land a blow.

Apparently, thinking that his kick had hurt Wolf more than it had, Ford lumbered in and began tossing overhand punches. Wolf countered with a quick one-two punch of his own and then pushed the bigger man to the side. He slammed into the black cyclone fencing that had been strung between the octagon posts. Ford's lips curled back in fury, displaying the vampire fangs on the painted mouthpiece once again. Bouncing off the cage, he rushed at Wolf who sent a quick jab to the other man's jaw, then slammed home a right.

Ford shook his head and backed up a step. Wolf stepped in and delivered another combination, but the close proximity allowed Ford's arms to snake outward and grab him. The man was strong and Wolf felt like he'd been snared by an anaconda. Reno had told Wolf beforehand to try and avoid being taken down to the mat by Ford so Wolf spread his feet apart and pushed back. The two of them danced around, each trying to throw the other, but Wolf judged that they were evenly matched as far as strength. If anything, being an inch or so shorter gave Wolf a lower center of gravity, thus making him harder to lift upward.

Ford tried to snare Wolf's lower leg but Wolf sensed the bigger man had suddenly become off balance. Surging forward, Wolf pushed Ford into the fencing and then both of them tumbled to the mat. The impact broke the vise-like hold that Ford had on Wolf's body when they landed on their sides. Both men kicked their legs, trying to gain a dominant position. Ford shoved away, rose to his knees, and then got an arm around Wolf's neck, trying for a guillotine choke-hold. Wolf shifted his jaw downward, so Ford's wrist wasn't in the right position.

Wolf heard Reno's frantic yell: "Get outta there, Steve."

With only the sparse crowd Reno's voice was strangely audible.

Wolf smashed two hard rights into Ford's side, aiming for the liver. He felt the other man's grip lessen slightly.

Two more rights ... Ford's grip slackened more.

Wolf gripped Ford's encircling arm with both hands and pulled it away. Their sweat-slicked bodies came together and then rebounded allowing Wolf to get to his feet. Ford did the same but Wolf stepped in and sent a left hook to Ford's temple. He dropped to his knees, recovered, and made a crab-like move toward Wolf's leg, grabbing it with both hands and pulling.

Wolf felt himself slam down onto the mat on his back as Ford started to scramble over him raining down punches on Wolf's body. He brought his left knee upward and interposed it between himself and Ford. Twisting to the side, Wolf slid out from under and rolled away. Ford was still on the mat on all fours. Wolf thought about delivering a kick to Ford's side but hesitated, the thought of striking a downed opponent still anathema because of his boxing background.

The hesitation was costly.

Ford lashed out with a backhand blow that struck Wolf squarely in the groin. Hunching over, he stumbled backward, out of range of another blow, cognizant that Ford was now on his feet and coming toward him.

The nauseating pain was laced with anger.

So that's the way it's gonna be, huh?

Just as Ford was within striking distance, the ref was there between them, shoving the other man back.

"You fouled him, Marcus," the ref said. "Get over there."

Ford grunted something and walked to the other side of the cage.

The ref turned to Wolf and placed his hand on his shoulder.

"You okay?" he asked.

It was Wolf's turn to grunt. The pain was subsiding but the accompanying nausea was still circulating in his gut.

"You got fouled," the ref said. "You got up to five minutes to recover. Take all the time you need."

Wolf grunted again. He knew he should take the

full five but doing so would also give Ford a chance to recuperate, and Wolf was beginning to feel like the other man was getting arm-weary. The guys with the overinflated muscles usually did. He took a few steps around and heard Reno yelling once more.

"You go back out there and do the same to that motherfucker, Steve. Don't let him get away with that. You had him."

Wolf agreed somewhat. He had felt like he was on the verge of knocking Ford out. Ford must have felt it, too, which might mean that the foul was intentional, in which case, the man needed to be taught a lesson in sportsmanship. Wolf had been in a lot of matches, both in and out of the ring and octagon. Sporting events had rules for a reason. Violate those rules and things degenerated into a street fight.

He took a series of small steps, enlarging his stride with each one. The pain had pretty much dissipated now, but Wolf didn't quite feel that the strength had fully returned to his legs. He glanced across the way and saw Ford taking in deep breaths, his cornerman yelling at him to "Concentrate on breathing."

He was recuperating, getting his second wind.

Can't let him do that, Wolf thought, and signaled to the ref that he was ready.

As the ref signaled for them to start fighting again, Wolf glanced up at the round clock, which had been activated again.

4:05.

Almost a minute to go before the round ended ...

Fifty-five seconds of hell, Wolf thought, and his arms felt like they weighed fifty pounds each.

Ford took in another deep breath and moved

forward, this time extending his long right arm in to signal he was apologizing for the foul.

Too little, too late, Wolf thought, but he slapped the other man's hand anyway.

They circled one another and this time Wolf reversed his circular pattern, going counterclockwise. It put him in more danger of receiving one of Ford's power-punches, but Wolf saw the other man's breathing was still ragged, his punches a bit slow.

Ford threw a lazy right jab and Wolf slapped it away with his left, then went over the top of Ford's arm to deliver a jab of his own to Ford's nose. It was more of a snapping, annoyance punch than one to deliver maximum damage, but it served its purpose well. Ford's head snapped back minutely and then a blast of crimson droplets spread over his dark face. The dribbling flow continued as he moved forward, and Wolf doubled up on the jab again.

More blood from *Blood*, Wolf thought, dancing to the side a bit.

Ford followed, angry and lurching now, swinging looping punches of his own which Wolf blocked with ease.

Ford took another step forward and Wolf shifted his weight to his right side and brought up an uppercut that connected with the tip of Ford's jaw. He made an involuntary jerking motion and crumbled like a six-story building that had been imploded, his arms flailing at his sides, his legs twisting against each other as he collapsed to the mat.

"Follow him down, Steve," Reno yelled. "You got him. Ground and pound him till the ref stops you."

Reno's voice sounded almost frantic but Wolf took a

step back. He'd knocked out men before and knew the signs. Ford now lay on his side, eyes half-open slits, his mouth agape displaying the bloody mouthpiece with the painted-on vampire fangs.

There was no need for any ground and pound.

This one was over.

————

THE VON DIEN WINTER ESTATE SOUTH BELIZE

Two of the yellow-shirted security guards had ushered Soraces into one of the anterooms in the big brick mansion. This was different than the last time in that they both wore face masks and blue latex gloves. They did the same frisk search and metal detector wanding that he'd been subjected to the last time but this time they did something new. They told him to sit down and then one of them rammed what looked to be an extended Q-tip up Soraces's nose, wiggled it around inside the nasal cavity, and then withdrew it and placed it in a plastic tube.

A fucking COVID test?

Soraces shook his head. It appeared as though the fat man had become a germaphobe.

"*Queda aqui,*" one of the guards said. "Ah, stay here."

"Not a problem," Soraces said. The man's English was heavily accented.

"And you will put *dis* on, *por favor,*" the other guard said, handing him a mask.

Soraces thought about saying they were taking precautions to the extreme but saw two PTZ cameras mounted on the wall and figured he'd been under additional surveillance the whole time. He recalled them from his last trip and suddenly wondered if all of his activities had been videoed, including his bedroom interlude with the two Latin cuties.

Maybe I'm already a local porn star, he thought as he put on the mask. In which case, this thing will come in handy this time. He remembered the video of Cummins that he'd been shown, a fragment of which he'd shown Wolf back in Phoenix to get him to play ball. Von Dien seemed to have a habit of filming his employees without their knowledge or consent. It was like working for Big Brother or like being on assignment in the old Soviet Union or Mainland China—always wondering if there was a camera behind that bedroom mirror.

Which reminds me, he thought. This might be an opportune time to do some camera work of my own.

He turned away from the PTZ camera mounted on the ceiling and casually brought his right hand up to his breast pocket and flicked the tiny black cover down, exposing the pin-hole camera and activating it. The spy pen took excellent video and audio recordings.

Insurance, he told himself. Just in case.

The two guards left and Soraces found himself alone to admire the fat man's art collection. It consisted of oil paintings, bronze and marble statues, and a glass case containing a variety of crude stone figures that looked like the products of a third-grade art class. There was a gold bowl with a blue sapphire jewel affixed to it and a black stone carved to resemble a duck.

He didn't touch the cabinet, which Soraces assumed was alarmed, but one of the items near the top immediately caught his eye. It was a stone about the size of a halved cantaloupe with an intricate baroque design carved onto the outer shell. A mother-of-pearl inlay covered the flattened portion, upon which two black onyx figures, a man and a big jungle cat, struggled in a death match. But the rendering of the big cat showed no mane.

"This must be the lioness," he said aloud for the benefit of the recording. "Obviously, the distaff portion of the most sought-after artifact, the Lion and the Lioness Attacking the Nubians."

He'd only seen a photograph of the artifact on his last trip here, to give him an idea of what they were seeking. The other half of the intricately carved stone featured the male lion, which was considered the more valuable due to the head and neck intricacies.

It had supposedly been concealed in the plaster bandito which was now, allegedly, in the possession of Steven Wolf.

Although the intricate design of the figures did have a certain fascinating elegance, Soraces felt an amusement that someone as rich and powerful as Dexter Von Dien would go to such lengths to possess a couple of carved rocks that had been around since before the time of Christ.

But Soraces had seen men killed for less. He'd even dispatched a few of them himself, some in the service of his country, and the others, well ...

He smirked. Who was he to question the motivation of the private sector? He shut off the spy pen and waited.

About fifteen minutes passed before the door opened and the same huge Hispanic in a butler's uniform, whom Soraces recalled from the last time, stepped inside.

"Good evening, "*Señor* Soraces," he said, entering the room. His words were muffled by the mask that he wore. He had on blue latex gloves as well.

"*Buenas noches*," Soraces replied. "*Está bien a verlo otra vez.*"

The butler smiled, apparently appreciating the greeting in his native tongue.

"*Señor* Von Dien is ready to receive you now," the butler said. "But first, *por favor*, you must put on your mask and gloves."

Soraces nodded. The guy was so massive he looked almost like a gorilla in black tails, but he still had the familiar bulge under the left armpit of his jacket of a small-caliber semi-automatic pistol.

"*Por supuesto*," Soraces said, and strung the mask attachments over his ears. Whether the butler was smiling was impossible to tell. "*De donde es usted? Corozal?*"

He'd mentioned one of the predominately Spanish speaking sections of Belize.

The butler shook his head slightly.

"*Estoy de Guatemala.*"

Another Guatemalan, Soraces thought.

And a very trusted employee. Specially imported. It would be good to stay on this big fucker's good side, impress upon him that we're both part of the brotherhood of workers, the imported help.

"*Coma se llama?*" Soraces asked, slipping the gloves

over his hands, then pretending to scratch an itch while he activated the spy pen again.

"My name is Gordo, *Señor*. Please, step this way and please keep your mask on in the presence of *Señor* Von Dien. Is that clear?"

Not knowing how to say, "Crystal," in Spanish, Soraces instead said, *"Claro."* He couldn't resist adding, *"Su patron es muy cuidadoso, eh?"*

The butler said nothing, but Soraces caught sight wrinkling around the eyes. Nothing overt, nothing stated, but still a tell. He wondered if it would show up on his recording. The loyalty of the crew depended on Von Dien paying them well, which opened up the possibility, should the need ever arise, that they could be bribed. It also called into question the degree of fidelity that they would be willing to provide in an emergency.

Soraces followed the man down a hallway and into another room with a large stone fireplace. Bookshelves filled with leather-bound volumes lined both walls and a long mahogany table with similarly fashioned chairs sat in the middle. The chair at the head of the table, however, was a huge black sofa-cushion type and in it sat the fat man himself, his massive bald head sitting atop his expansive, soft-looking body, which was encased in a light blue terrycloth robe, which matched the blue gloves. Despite the mild temperature, Von Dien had a scarf around his throat and the room smelled faintly medicinal. He also had on one of the most elaborate masks that Soraces had ever seen. It was rubber and had what appeared to be two breathing filters on each side. His equally massive, but exquisitely proportioned bodyguard stood next to the chair in his usual tight-fitting black T-shirt and black cargo pants. His mask was solid black and fit over his nose and jutting chin. Soraces saw the man was also wearing that Walther Q4 Steel Frame semi-auto. The bodyguard wore the same blue plastic gloves, but Soraces didn't think they would interfere with his ability to draw and shoot.

Soraces let his fingers trace over the ninja pen ever so slightly. He'd forgotten about the bodyguard's big tanto knife, positioned for easy withdrawal, that he wore on the left side of his belt.

Across the table and several feet away from the fat man, in one of the regular wooden library chairs, sat the lawyer, Anthony Marco Fallotti. He was clad in a double-filtered mask similar to his boss's, a tan polo shirt, and, of course, the ubiquitous blue latex gloves.

The butler halted and pulled out a chair at the opposite end of the table. Soraces glanced at the chair, shrugged, and sat in it. He didn't like the fact that he was now seated with his back to the door, but he also figured that he'd be safe enough for the time being. If Von Dien had planned to kill him, he'd had plenty of opportunities prior to this. Plus, the seating arrangement gave his spy pen's camera an unimpeded view.

Anyway, he thought. The fat son of a bitch wants something ... The other half of that Iraqi artifact and he knows I'm his best bet at getting it for him.

"Nice to see you all again," he said and added, "That is, what I can see of you." He realized that none of them could see his grin beneath the mask.

Von Dien's brows knotted together slightly, but he said nothing. His big head was hairless and resembled an enormous egg that, despite being down here in sunny Belize, hadn't seen the sun in ages.

Fallotti spoke first.

"Richard, so glad you agreed to come down. How've you been?"

"You tell me," Soraces said. He was conscious of the mask slightly muffling his words and hoped they'd be audible on the recording. "I assume my virus test came back negative?"

The lawyer laughed. "Well, you know. One can't be too careful nowadays."

Soraces gave a slight nod. In reality, he'd been in so many tense situations, faced death so many times, that the thought of some new virus hardly bothered him. He'd noticed that same tendency among people who were accustomed to putting it all on the line. But he filed the information away for future use. It was definitely a crack in the Von Dien foundation that might be exploited, should the need arise.

Fallotti seemed ready to engage in more small talk, but the fat man was having none of that. He leaned forward slightly and spoke.

"You left rather abruptly the last time."

"Yes," Soraces said. "I did. I got the impression you were upset over the circumstances, so ..."

He let the explanation trail off.

Von Dien stared at him. "You were aware that the statue you brought here was a useless fake?"

Soraces had stayed for the unveiling, and the pathetic almost theatrical collapse of the rich bastard, but he felt it best not to mention the fat man's foibles.

"Yes," Soraces said. He offered nothing further. An apology might be construed as a sign of culpability and he didn't want that. "It was, however, the same one that I recovered from your man, Cummins."

"And you killed Cummins?" Von Dien asked.

Soraces wasn't about to reply in the affirmative when he was recording the conversation, and there was a distinct possibility that Von Dien was recording as well. Was that the fat man's intention? Get him on video admitting to a murder?

There were no indications of a camera system in this room but that didn't mean there wasn't one. He recalled the video of Cummins relating his part in the framing of Wolf. Cummings probably hadn't thought he was being recorded either. But then again, Von Dien would be a fool to record himself asking direct questions about a murder. He suddenly felt better.

I've got to be the only one recording this now, he thought. As careful as this fat prick is, he's not going to create a video record of anything implicating himself.

"Actually," Soraces said. "As I told you in my initial phone conversation, before I arrived, he was killed by my associate, Werner Gunther. In self-defense, I might add."

"Naturally," the fat man said. He turned his head away. "So, we have no way of knowing where the artifact is now or even if Wolf ever had possession of it."

Soraces did a quick review of the options. If he wanted to extend this rather lucrative deal and get the rest of the money that had been agreed upon, it would be best to prolong things a bit, to feed the rich man's vainglorious fantasy of obtaining the second half of the artifact.

"I'm pretty certain he does," Soraces said. "The bandito he gave to Cummins was a copy."

The fat man turned and looked at him, the rich man's blue eyes almost piercing above the edge of the mask. "A copy? And you know this how?"

Soraces took his time answering.

Feed the fantasy, he thought, just like stoking a bonfire.

"If you recall," he said finally, "I was in negotiations with Wolf to obtain the statue when Cummins interceded. We'd paid Wolf a substantial amount of money, and I'd shown him that partial video clip that might clear him."

The fixed stare continued.

Wait for it, Soraces thought. Wait for it ...

Finally, Von Dien broke the awkward silence by speaking first.

"Of course, I recall that," he said. "But what makes you think he still has it?"

Again, Soraces took his time in answering.

"I did a little digging through some informal sources to find out what exactly happened between Wolf and his partner and Cummins." He paused to adjust himself in the chair before continuing. The fat bastard edged forward slightly, like a horny teenage boy about to get his first look at some female genitalia. His breathing was sounding a bit more sonorous.

"Wolf was about to deal with me," Soraces said. "Then he received a phone call and abruptly left. It turns out that call was from Cummins, who'd kidnapped Wolf's partner's grandson." He was filling in some blanks with his own speculation now but figured it would suffice to advance the narrative. "Cummins then contacted you and claimed he would be in possession of the bandito, correct?"

Von Dien nodded briskly.

Soraces resisted the temptation to tell him to speak up so his response could be audible for the record. His lips stretched into a sly smile under the cloth of the mask. The camera would capture the nod.

"So, Wolf obviously had a copy made before-hand," Soraces said. "He used that to turn over to Cummins for the boy. Which most likely means, he still has the original because he intended to do business with me."

"Then he knows about the artifact?" Von Dien asked.

Soraces shrugged. "Possibly. He hinted at its value during our negotiation but didn't specifically name anything."

Von Dien blew out a heavy, frustrated breath that rattled his mask.

"You're saying he definitely knows then?" Fallotti asked, inserting himself into the conversation.

"At this point," Soraces said. "More than likely he does. But that's not such a bad thing. I think we still have the dominant hand."

"How so?" Fallotti asked.

"We still have something he wants very badly," Soraces said. "That video of Cummins admitting that he set Wolf up to take the fall back in Iraq. And you'll note that even with his friend's grandson at stake, he still didn't want to give up the original bandito. That tells me he'll still be willing to deal."

Fallotti and Von Dien exchanged glances. The fat man gave a fractional nod.

"So you think that despite all that's happened," Fallotti said. "Wolf is still amenable to a deal?"

Soraces smiled, then realized once again that the mask had obscured his expression.

"I can bring him around," he said. "But it'll be tricky. At the moment, as I said, we're both holding a pair of aces, and the joker's wild."

"Spare us your inane metaphors," Von Dien said. "Just get me that artifact, if he still has it."

"I can do that," Soraces said. "But it'll be a bit more convoluted and difficult than before. Not to mention some additional expenses."

"You want more money," the rich bastard said. "Is that it?"

Soraces hooded his eyes a bit, letting his silence and the visible portion of his face provide the answer without mentioning the money still owed to him. And not knowing if he'd get another face-to-face opportunity like this, he decided to stack the deck a bit more.

"I'm worth it. Look at all the trouble you've gone to already," Soraces said, holding up his hands and began ticking off one point after another with his gloved fingers, careful not to interfere with the view of the camera lens. "You originally hired Jack Cummings and Vince Eagan to get the artifact in Iraq almost five years ago, right?"

Von Dien said nothing.

Come on, come on, Soraces thought. Let's speak up for the video, please.

"And those jokers ended up killing some Iraqi nationals in getting you one half of the artifact," Soraces continued. "The Lioness Attacking the Nubian. The female section. But the male second part, the more valuable part, was still missing." He paused to allow for the dramatic tension to build. "And Cummings and

Eagan managed to frame Wolf for the murders. Then four years later, the second half resurfaces, but that reprobate, Accondras, gets arrested before he can give it to you, and then absconds with it to Mexico."

"Which we already know," Fallotti said. "You're belaboring the obvious."

"Bear with me," Soraces said, desperate to get Fallotti and Von Dien to incriminate themselves. "I'm trying to give you a proper perspective." He took in a deep breath and continued talking as fast as he could, pulling the mask away from his face for better enunciation. "The Mexico venture ends up a complete fiasco, Wolf gets the artifact, and you then send Zerbe and his South African goon squad to Phoenix to get the artifact and kill Wolf. But that doesn't work out either."

"That damn Wolf," Von Dien said. "He's proven to be a most formidable adversary."

Good, Soraces thought. At least I've got him in an admission of non-denial.

"Like I told you before," he said, trying to sound nonchalant. "Let's offer him some money and the flash-drive and get it that way. Without any violence."

"Without any violence?" Fallotti broke in. "You say that after you killed Cummins and still didn't get the artifact?"

"I told you," Soraces answered. "Werner Gunther killed him. And I did fulfill my end of the bargain by bringing you the bandito statue, did I not?"

Fallotti snorted, causing his mask to bulge away from his face slightly. "You were also supposed to—"

"Fine," Von Dien said, his voice sounding angry as if struggling to burst free of the affixed prison. "Just get me that artifact. I'll pay you whatever you want."

Of course you will, Soraces thought. Through the nose, and then some, for stiffing me before.

Von Dien's words sounded wheezy and he began coughing, each intake of breath becoming more labored than the last. His hands fluttered at the elaborate mask and he frantically gestured to his bodyguard.

The big man reached behind the ornamental, high-backed chair and came up with an oxygen tube and a translucent plastic mask. He twisted the valve-release on the top of the tube and the soft hiss of oxygen became audible. Von Dien ripped off his mask and placed the translucent, oxygenated one over his nose and mouth, taking in several deep breaths before trying to speak again.

When his breathing had returned to normal, more or less, he pulled the mask from his face and said, "And after you do get it. I want you to kill Wolf. No loose ends. Understood?"

Soraces nodded, thinking, Smile, you're on candid camera. You've just given me everything I need.

CHAPTER TWO

MCCARRAN INTERNATIONAL AIRPORT
LAS VEGAS, NEVADA

Wolf noted that his right foot was somewhat swollen and tender as he slipped his running shoe back on, but that was the least of his concerns at the moment. The rest of him was pretty bruised and tender as well. During the fight he hadn't been cognizant of Ford connecting with that many punches, but today he realized that he must have. Sitting down on the metal bench, Wolf waited as the TSA screener did a wand test and then a full-fledged pat-down of McNamara, who had set off the airport metal detector despite having emptied his pockets.

"You ain't gonna find nothing on me, sonny," McNamara said. "It's just a lot of residual shrapnel that they never picked outta me."

The TSA agent completed his task and nodded. "Thank you, sir."

"Don't call me 'sir,' sonny," McNamara said. "I work for a living."

The TSA agent seemed confused and Mac grinned and clapped him on the shoulder.

The mask had concealed the smile Wolf knew had to be there. "It's an old army saying."

"Army?" the TSA agent said, his head swiveling back and forth from McNamara to Wolf and then back again. "You were in the military?"

"Back before you were born, sonny," McNamara said. "And long after you were copping your first feel under the bleachers, too."

"Thank you for your service, sir," the TSA agent said.

McNamara grunted something, grabbed his carry-on luggage, and strode over to where Wolf was sitting.

They'd declined Reno's offer of a ride back to Phoenix in the van. With Reno's girlfriend, Barbie, doing the driving, and trainer George and cut-man Willie both in the vehicle, Wolf and Mac had felt the crowded conditions would be too much. Plus, their celebration party with Ms. Dolly and the P-Patrol had extended into the wee hours. With an eleven o'clock flight to catch, they had barely made it through the security checkpoints.

Wolf got to his feet and grabbed his two bags, one of which contained his newly awarded championship belt. It was thick black leather and handsomely adorned with a gold-plated crown and the words *USA LIGHT HEAVYWEIGHT MMA CHAMPION*. Wolf really had no place to display it so he figured he'd tell Reno that he could keep it in the gym to inspire the younger fighters. The way he was feeling, he didn't even want it now. The fight had, more or less, been for the money and as a favor to Reno. It had been hard, and he'd taken a few lumps, some of which were expressing themselves more this morning than they had last night. But all things considered, it had been a cakewalk compared to some of his other battles.

When you have a foe intent on putting a bullet between your eyes, or slicing your head off with a knife, getting into the octagon and facing a near-naked opponent was easy.

But it had been what occurred after the fight, and after the celebration at the Peppermill, that had felt like a severe gut-punch to Wolf. In the wee hours, as he and Yolanda had lain in the tangle of damp sheets in his hotel room, she'd casually mentioned to him that she might be leaving the P-Patrol.

"What?" he said. "Why?"

She rolled over onto her side, the white sheet slipping off the dark skin of her exquisite shoulder.

"I told you before, doing this bounty hunter stuff was just a pit-stop for me," she said. "Didn't I?"

"Yeah, I believe you mentioned it."

"So back before I got hooked up with Ms. Dolly, I put in an application with the police department."

Wolf rotated his head on the pillow. "Las Vegas Metro?"

"Right. I took the test, passed and got on a list."

"And your number came up?"

She nodded. "I'm starting in the Police Academy Monday."

"Wow. Congratulations."

A slight smile graced her lips, but her eyes looked away.

He considered the ramifications of this. He knew she had some college classes in law enforcement and she was a black female, which in today's policing world put her in the prime candidate category. She knew how to handle herself, too, as an investigation into her bounty hunting background would surely show, which further enhanced her marketability. So why was she looking so glum? Then it dawned on him: her background investigation.

Everything would be put under a microscope as they looked at her personal life. They'd do a comprehensive investigation, and finding her being involved with an ex-con with a dishonorable discharge who was under investigation by the FBI wouldn't exactly be listed in the plus column.

So this isn't just a talk, he thought. It's *the* talk.

Wolf got up on one elbow. The movement caused a wave of pain to sweep upward along his torso. It appeared that Ford had landed more than just a few of those body blows he hadn't felt during the actual match.

"What's wrong?" Yolanda asked.

"Just a bit of soreness from the fight," he said.

Her forehead crinkled with concern, so he forced a smile.

The pain he was feeling in his heart was the real clincher. The prospect of not seeing her again was devastating. But what did he expect? He couldn't very well ask her to give up her dream, if that's what it was, of becoming a police officer, of a new career choice where she could go someplace, and he was like a twenty-pound dumbbell around her neck in a triathlon.

"Don't worry," he said. "In the rare instance they

might come knocking on my door, I'll tell them that our relationship was strictly professional."

She frowned. "I'm not worried about that."

"You should be."

"Hey, if they can't accept that I have special people in my life, then that's too bad."

"Special people aren't ex-cons with dishonorable discharges."

"Oh, babe, I didn't want to tell you, but I figured I had to—"

He reached up and put a finger to her lips. Her eyes closed and a tear wound its way down her cheek. He drew her to him and kissed her softly.

"I think you're going to make a dynamite cop," he said.

The memory of their second turn of lovemaking drifted through his memory as they walked toward their gate.

"What you so glum about?" McNamara asked. "You won, didn't you? The championship. And you hardly broke a sweat. I ain't never seen a guy beat up another one so bad, even on the street."

Wolf snorted and shook his head. Mac was making it sound a hell of a lot easier than it had been.

"What fight were you watching?" he asked. "I feel like the kissing cousin to a punching bag."

McNamara laughed. "The way you kicked his ass was a work of art. And that walk-away after he went down for the count ... Pure class."

Wolf thought about the end of the fight and was again glad he hadn't chosen to follow Ford down to the mat to inflict more punishment. It was one aspect of the MMA sport that he didn't like.

"It was just like the Frenchies say," McNamara continued. "Insouciance. Swag without the fucking conceit. Pardon my French."

Wolf glanced at his friend. "I'm impressed. I didn't know you were bilingual."

McNamara laughed. "Nah, I'm not. I just picked up a few phrases here and there, mostly from my time in Nam. The French were there damn near as long as we were, until they got their asses handed to them at Dien Ben Phu."

Wolf remembered reading about that battle in the history books. It effectively ended their involvement in what had been known as French Indo-China.

"And we had some French Foreign Legion guys attending some of our training when I was in one of them damn police actions in the Middle East. Those guys were pretty good. Turns out their white hats, the *kepi*, are held in pretty high regard. They get them in a special ceremony, just like we get our berets."

Wolf recalled a similar ceremony when he'd completed ranger training. It meant something, and he understood what Mac was talking about. As they passed one of the shops, McNamara slowed and bumped Wolf's arm.

"Let's stop in there," he said. "I want to buy a couple of souvenirs for Chad and Kasey."

They went in, with Wolf checking his watch. They were cutting it close to get to their gate on time, but he knew Mac wouldn't go home empty handed.

"Pick out a sweatshirt for Kase while I get something for my grandson," McNamara said.

Instead of a sweatshirt, which would have about as much use in Arizona as a lead-lined jockstrap, Wolf instead picked out a purple T-shirt that said *Whatever happens in Vegas, stays in Vegas*. He thought about Mac spending the night with both Ms. Dolly and Brenda in one of their customary hook-ups and put that T-shirt aside in favor of one with the Las Vegas sign on the front. He remembered reading that the woman who'd designed it never applied for a copyright.

Lots of money lost, he thought. But I'm sure she regretted it at her leisure. Hindsight's always twenty-twenty.

McNamara came to the counter with a toy police car, a toy army Humvee, a miniature lamp in the shape of the Las Vegas sign, and a couple of other items.

"Maybe I should buy him something, too," Wolf said.

"Nah. Don't want to spoil the kid."

Wolf hesitated, and then recalled the violence that the little boy had witnessed in recent weeks.

Spoil the child and spare the rod, he thought, and picked up a small, cartoonish, plastic purple dragon holding some type of silver globe.

"You think he's old enough to appreciate the lamp?" Wolf asked.

"Hell, if he's not, I'll keep it in my room," McNamara said shoving his credit card into the slot. "You mind putting a couple of these things in the bag with your belt? Mine's packed kinda tight."

Wolf paid for the dragon and stuffed the items into his carry-on.

When they got to their gate, the A group was already starting to be called. Wolf and McNamara assumed their positions by the window and took out their boarding passes. On board, they found seats near the front, with Mac telling Wolf to take the one by the window. The middle seat was vacant due to the virus precautions.

"It'll give you more room to stretch out," he said.

"The flight's only about an hour or so."

"Yeah, but you're the champ now," McNamara said with a wide grin.

Once they were airborne, McNamara unbuckled his seatbelt, slipped off his mask, and got into the middle seat next to Wolf.

"I been thinking," McNamara said.

Wolf took off his mask as well and smiled. "I thought I smelled rubber burning."

Mac barked a laugh and then squinted at Wolf. "All kidding aside, you think you want to keep on fighting?"

"Probably not," Wolf said. "I only took this fight because I felt I owed it to Reno."

"Shit," McNamara said. "You don't owe him nothing. In fact, it's just the opposite. We saved his bacon down in Mexico, and he knows it."

The brutal scene of what had happened down in Cancun replayed itself in Wolf's mind once more: the hot, Mexican night, the three members of Eagan's Private Military Company, the Vipers, standing guard over him, Mac, Reno, and Reno's buddy, Herc. Black Hercules, he called himself, aka Henry Preen. All four of them with their arms handcuffed behind their backs, waiting to be executed by the Private Military Contractors, Wolf struggling to retrieve the handcuff key he'd secreted in his boot, and Herc using his tremendous arm strength to break the steel loops of the cuffs. And the son of a bitch did it. He was a powerful man, but even he couldn't withstand the 7.62 mm round that pierced his massive chest. Reno had taken one in the leg and Mac sustained a through-and-through to his abdomen. Wolf had managed to take out the three Vipers. Reno's MMA career had been short-circuited when the bullet shattered his femur, and now was trying to regain his former status through a surrogate— Wolf.

Ironic as all hell, he thought.

"And the money was real decent this time," McNamara said. "Wasn't it?"

"Decent enough."

"Not that Trackdown, Incorporated is exactly hurting for money at the moment," McNamara said. "Thanks to all that you gave me, not to mention what was in that money-belt that your late, not-so-great lieutenant so graciously bestowed upon us."

That scene flashed momentarily through Wolf's mind as well: former army lieutenant Jack Cummins, one of the men who'd set Wolf up for those war crimes in Iraq, lying dead on the dusty street of the ghost town, the bald-headed black guy who'd, apparently killed him, pulling the money-belt off of Cummins's recumbent form, Richard Soraces holding what he thought was the real-deal bandito statue ... The rest of it had taken place in a matter of seconds, but in Wolf's mind it had played out in slow motion. The black guy raised his arm and took a shot at Wolf who had returned fire in a lethal response. As the black guy fell, Soraces jumped into a waiting bronze-colored Blazer. Soraces, the same man who'd shown Wolf a minute portion of a video that might clear his name, disappeared into the night.

"I still think you should take it," McNamara said. "Put it in the bank or something."

Wolf shook his head. "I already told you. It's yours."

"No need for you to keep giving me money like you been doing."

Wolf shook his head again, as much to clear out the troubling visions as to decline Mac's offer. It was blood money, that was for sure, and while that didn't bother Wolf so much, he wasn't about to forget that Mac had picked him up from Leavenworth and helped him get back on his feet.

"Bullshit," he said. "I owed it to you. You lifted me up off of the floor, gave me a job, free room and board ..."

"Which you've officially repaid in spades," McNamara said. "Especially giving me the purse from your previous MMA match."

"I owed it to you for all you've done for me," Wolf said. "Besides, we needed to get the company back in the black."

"Trackdown's back in the black, all right," Mac said. "After me leading us into the Mexican misadventure. And you insisting I keep the cash in that money-belt."

"I don't need it," Wolf said.

He thought about the large sum of money that Soraces had given him which was still untouched in Wolf's bank account. One hundred thousand dollars. Well, technically it wasn't from Soraces but from Dexter Von Dien, the rich asshole behind the scenes. Or behind the schemes. It was time to do something about that.

"Hey," he said. "I been meaning to talk to you about the money. I'd like to set up a college trust fund for Chad."

McNamara's brow furrowed. "Damn, you don't need to do that."

"I want to."

Mac blew out a long breath. "That's mighty generous of you, Steve. I appreciate it, but we can talk about it later. Right now, we got some other things to discuss."

Wolf wondered what that meant. He waited.

"In case you haven't noticed," McNamara said. "This damn virus thing is slowing the courts, and hence the bounty hunting business, down to a crawl."

Wolf had noticed, all right. He nodded.

"And," McNamara continued, "with some of them asshole, liberal politicians talking about ending the cash bond system all over the country, it's gonna effectively kill the bondsman business. And with it, the need for us bounty hunters."

Wolf had thought about the ramifications of that possibility but hadn't mentioned it to Mac.

"So," McNamara continued. "We got to start thinking outside the box."

"Meaning I should seriously reconsider my retirement from MMA?"

McNamara laughed. "Nah, not if you don't want to, although I think you could go all the way to the top if you wanted to. No, I'm talking about expanding our horizons, maybe us diversifying a little bit."

"Diversifying?"

"Right. We're experienced trackers. We could maybe get our private investigators licenses, or maybe even become salvage consultants, like Travis McGee."

"Who?"

McNamara's brow furrowed again. "Don't tell me

with all the reading you been doing for those stupid lit classes you been taking that you never heard about John D. MacDonald."

The name did ring a faint bell for Wolf, but he didn't think he'd read any of the man's books.

"Hell," McNamara said. "That settles it. I'm gonna have to have a talk with that damn professor of yours when we get back."

"I'd rather you didn't," Wolf said. "All I have to do is turn in my final paper and the class will be over."

"A paper? On what?"

"Shakespeare."

"Well, I'll still send him a nasty email then."

Wolf laughed. The thought of Mac attacking a college professor's choice of assignments was incongruous at best.

"No," Wolf said. "Don't do that. I may want to take another course from *her* down the road."

"Her? Figures. She's probably another one of them liberal asshole professors that doesn't know her ass from a hole in the ground."

Wolf recalled the rather stout professor and told Mac he might have a hard time beating her in an arm-wrestling contest.

"All the more reason for me to suggest some good literature to her," McNamara said. "I suppose she doesn't like Raymond Chandler, either." He got a wistful expression on his face as his gaze moved upward. "I can remember finding one of his books on a USO table back when I was in Oakland at the Overseas Replacement Center waiting to be shipped out. A paperback. *Farewell, My Lovely*. I almost passed on it, except there was this real big, tough looking son of a bitch on the cover. Took it with me and read it on the plane. What a writer. When I came back to the world a couple of years later, they'd made a movie of it with Robert Mitchum starring as Marlowe."

"Who's he?"

"A great actor."

"I'll have to see if I can find it on the nostalgia channel."

"Read the book instead," McNamara said. "I have a copy. I'll loan it to you."

"I'll look forward to that. But reading about a PI in some novel is a lot different than doing it in real life. It's like watching Rambo take out a whole company single-handedly only using a bow and arrow. We'd be playing catch-up trying to do something we don't have the slightest idea how to do."

"Exactly," McNamara said. "Which is why I've been seriously considering another possibility."

Wolf raised his eyebrows in expectation.

McNamara smiled. "Mercenary work."

The thought of the Vipers and the team of South Africans who'd tried to kill him and Mac sprang into Wolf's mind. His face must have reflected his discomfort because McNamara seemed to read his thoughts.

"Yeah, yeah," he said. "I know those Afrikaans guys we dealt with were all pieces of shit, but I ain't talking about that kind of mercs. I got a buddy, an old buddy, who's setting up this special shooting, combat, and tactics school over in Mesa. He's got his own facility and everything. Calling it the Best in the West Tactical Training Institute."

"Best in the West, huh?"

McNamara nodded. "And not only that, he's got a

side gig traveling around giving seminars to teach courses in firearms, dignitary protection, urban combat techniques, all sorts of that stuff. His name's Buck Mason."

"Was he Special Forces too?"

"Well, no, he was a marine, but don't hold that against him." McNamara smiled. "He was with Force Recon and he saw a ton of action in a whole lot of shit-holes around the globe. Good guy."

"So you thinking of joining him in doing some teaching?"

McNamara grinned. "Already set up. You and me got a spot as instructors down the road at his next semi-nar. If we want it, that is. All we gotta do it go through some tactical training so we're all on the same sheet of music, is all."

Wolf considered the offer. It wasn't like he had anything else pending, at least something he could act on. He nodded, then asked, "You sure he wants both of us? I don't want to be a deadweight for you."

"Are you kidding? You'd be a natural, with all your training and experience."

Wolf compressed his lips.

And what about my prison time and DD? he thought. I'm a liability, just like with Yolanda.

"What's wrong?" McNamara asked. "Don't you like the idea?"

The flight attendant, a tall, statuesque black woman, stopped at their seats and cleared her throat loudly.

"I'm sorry, gentlemen," she said. "But new regula-tions during the pandemic require that all passengers must wear their masks at all times in-flight."

McNamara shot her a wry look. "Masks? You must have us confused for the Lone Ranger and Tonto." He grinned and jerked his thumb toward Wolf. "Even though he's half Indian."

"No mistake, sir," she said. "It's the new regulation."

"Aw, hell, ma'am," McNamara said, the grin still stretched over his face. "Me and him are both veterans. You think we're afraid of some little Asian flu bug?"

Her dark eyebrows arched. With the mask on it was impossible to tell how she was reacting to Mac's contrariness.

Wolf put his hand on McNamara's arm and said, "Mac, the mask." He picked his up.

"Shucks," McNamara said. "You know how many times we put our butts on the line in different places around the world? I bet I got more scars from getting shot than you've got birthdays."

"I'll bet do," she said. "And I'll have to take your word for it. But that still doesn't change things. You'll have to put your masks on, please."

McNamara seemed ready to say something else, but Wolf slipped his mask back into place and said, "We're always ready to oblige a pretty lady."

Actually, Wolf couldn't tell how pretty she might be with the blue mask covering the lower portion of her face, but her dark eyes looked good.

McNamara slid his mask on again as well.

"Thank you, gentlemen," the flight attendant said. "And thank you for your service."

She continued down the aisle and McNamara snorted.

"Hot damn," he said. "She was a bit of a pistol, wasn't she? There was no dealing with her."

"She was just doing her job."

"Yeah, but I was just wondering what she looks like without her—"

"Mask?"

"Yeah, right." McNamara chuckled. "Seems like there's always some babe who comes along to spoil our fun." He turned and glanced after her then turned back to Wolf. "She kind of reminds me of your little gal, Yolanda."

Wolf had thought about that too and wondered how she was doing.

"Well, whaddaya think?" McNamara said.

"About what?"

"About you and me maybe doing some stuff with the Best in the West Tactical Institute."

"Sound's great," Wolf said, although he was feeling just the opposite. He wasn't really eager for a new gig. What he really wanted was to figure out a way to clear his name, and to do that he'd need a new lawyer, a new trial, and some new, exculpatory evidence.

And the only way he could get that would be to get hold of that video confession that Soraces had shown him, which meant he'd have to get it from Von Dien.

Batman vs. Godzilla, he thought, then smiled.

No, maybe Bambi was the more applicable choice after all.

———

THE VON DIEN WINTER ESTATE SOUTH BELIZE

. . .

Just like old times, Richard Soraces thought as he set his iced tea down and lit up one of the hand-rolled cigars that the servant girl had brought him. He was riding the crest of the wave with a lucrative new assignment, the new deposit in my Cayman account, and my insurance policy duly recorded on my spy pen.

He sat in the gazebo in the exterior garden surrounded by creeping lines of bougainvillea, symmetrical rows of bright flowers, and all sorts of other immaculately trimmed vegetation. It was almost a shame to ruin the natural fragrance with the heavy tobacco smell, but Fallotti had assured him it was a pure Havana. The servant girl was young and pretty, perhaps no more than eighteen, if that. She was more slender than his usual preference, and a bit younger, too, but he looked forward to watching her melt under his tutelage. She'd scream, too, and not only with delight. But that would wait until later.

Business before pleasure, he thought, as he rotated the cigar in the flame of the match, puffing copiously to get the tobacco ignited.

The smoke tasted heavy and hot. Cuban cigars were a bit overrated, in his opinion, but there was something to be said for the defiance factor. Knowing that he was violating the U.S. boycott edict, even though he was technically on foreign soil, made the bitter taste almost sweet. Especially after all those years with the Agency having to justify every expense on a Department of Defense form.

Yes, he thought, blowing out a smoky breath. It was good to be back in the private sector.

The girl stood by holding an ashtray, her luscious brown face frozen in a smile.

He'd have to see how long that lasted tonight.

Dropping the extinguished match in the glass ashtray, Soraces took it from her and said in Spanish that he'd need her services later.

"*Sí, Señor,*" she said. "*Yo sé.*"

"*Tome un bano y aféitate,*" he said, telling her he expected her to be clean and shaven. "*Traiga algunas profilácticos. Muchos profilácticos.*"

The smile flagged a bit with a slight twitching at the corner of her mouth at the mention of the rubbers. Perhaps word of what he'd done to the last two Latina sweeties that had been provided for him had spread. She turned and scurried off, no doubt contemplating what was to come.

No matter, he thought. Lancelot has returned and is once more in good graces with the king. And the rich bastard doesn't even know that I've got him by his short hairs. He thought about the video recording which he hadn't yet taken the time to review. That could wait. It was best to set his new plan in motion.

After taking a few more puffs on the cigar, he set it aside and picked up his cellphone. They'd given him a burner to use but he had most of his old contact numbers on his smartphone. He scrolled through them and found the one he'd been looking for: Cameron Dirk, or just Dirk, as he preferred to be called. Since Wolf had proven to be a tougher customer than Soraces had originally thought, it was time to pull out the biggest gun. Gunther had been good, one of the best Soraces had ever worked with, but Wolf took him out with one shot. Dirk, however, was a Superman capable of handling any and all comers, always competing, even with himself, to be the best. He didn't come cheap, but he could take Wolf out six ways to Sunday. It would be interesting to watch.

And since money doesn't seem to be an object, Soraces thought, I might as well make sure I've got the A-team.

But Dirk was always in demand. The best of the best usually were. Soraces hoped he'd be able to get him. That way, when the time came, Dirk would crush Wolf like a bug underfoot.

He continued to scroll, thinking about who else he might need to round things out. Dirk would be the muscle, but he also needed a bit of finesse. But who?

"How you enjoying that Havana?" Fallotti asked, walking up to the gazebo.

Soraces set his cell phone down, surreptitiously activated the recording device on the spy pen, and picked up the smoldering cigar. It had gone out. He reached for the packet of matches but the lawyer stepped forward with a silver-colored lighter.

"Allow me," he said and flicked the wheel, igniting it.

Soraces leaned forward to guide the tip of the cigar into the flame. He squinted as he drew some of the smoke into his mouth.

"You know," he said. "I don't even like cigars. Don't know why I'm bothering with this one."

Fallotti laughed and held the lighter to the end of his own cigar.

"Perhaps, as you said, it has to do with the accompanying satisfaction of defying the U.S. trade embargo," he said. "Sort of symbolically giving the finger to the government, or something."

"Yeah," Soraces said. "Or something."

He sat back and placed the phone on the wire table.

"Come to check on my progress?" he asked. "Or just to check up on me?"

Fallotti smirked as he pulled out the chair across from him and sat down.

"I would like to get an idea of how you plan on proceeding," he said. "Mr. Von Dien's getting a bit anxious. He is a man who likes results."

Soraces purposely took two long drags before he answered, pausing to blow out a smoke ring with the second.

"Is he all right?" Soraces asked. "That coughing fit seemed a bit disconcerting."

Fallotti frowned and waved his hand dismissively.

"He's all right," he said. "Just petrified of the virus. He'll probably outlive us all."

"Well," Soraces said. "I will need your expertise and connections in resetting the game a bit in the Phoenix area."

Fallotti's brow furrowed. "Resetting the game? You mean with the law firm? Do you think that's wise?"

Soraces puffed on the cigar. "The plan was a good one. I'll just need to tweak it a little bit," he said. "But first, I'm going to need to assemble some reliable back-up. To keep an eye on things, and for when we take Wolf and company out for good."

"Okay, but how do you plan on getting the item?"

The item, Soraces thought. Euphemism for the bandito, or more particularly, for the stolen Iraqi artifact —The Lion Attacking the Nubian.

"Much like I intended to handle it before," Soraces said. "Everything was set in place and going well, until your man, Cummins, threw a monkey wrench into the works."

"He was hardly *my* man," Fallotti said. "I told you, he'd gone rogue. Now what exactly is your plan? Mr. Von Dien will want to know."

Soraces toyed with the cigar. "Simple. Approach Wolf and offer him a deal he can't refuse."

Fallotti looked contemplative. He took a couple of puffs and then said, "What makes you think he'll go for it?"

"He'll deal," Soraces said. "Everybody always does. We have what he wants."

Fallotti raised an eyebrow and edged forward slightly.

"You think he'll trust you again? After what happened?"

Soraces smiled and let some of the smoke leak out between his teeth. The taste was too hot, too bitter. He wasn't enjoying it at all.

"Like I said, he'll deal. It's all in the setup. We just have to tweak our approach a bit." He crushed the half-smoked cigar into the glass ashtray. "And I know just how to do it."

Dirk for the heavy lifting, he thought. My rook, so to speak, but who else?

Then it came to him as the words to the old Sinatra-Sammy Davis tune echoed in his mind.

Just me and my shadows.

CHAPTER THREE_

CARACAS, VENEZUELA

Darkness was his friend, and it merged with the black fatigues he was wearing to allow him to melt into the shadows. But in a few more hours it would be light. It was time to get moving on this.

Cameron Dirk, or just plain Dirk, as he liked to be called, flattened his body against the wall and moved with silent efficiency to the corner of the building. The structure across the way, a seedy-looking hotel, was on the fringes of the slums that merged with the concrete mountains of the once prosperous and thriving down-town area. In recent years the area had seen a vast depreciation, as had most of Venezuela. Shimmering skyscrapers, some of the tallest in Latin America, now stood like lonely vestiges of a more prosperous time. The side of one building was adorned with a large, brightly painted mural depicting former president Hugo Chavez, his red beret cocked defiantly on his head, his right fist elevated, and the words *SIRVAN LA REVOLUCION*.

Good to see that they have their priorities on straight, Dirk thought with amusement. Making sure there was money to maintain a painting of a dead dictator while the people starved.

Bags of uncollected trash had been piled next to the curbs and those rodents that had escaped the dwindling meal plates scurried about with a desperation that seemed to mirror the vanished middle class. A series of anemic streetlights, half of them broken or inoperative, cast a shadowy pall over the front of the building across the wide avenue. Three bored-looking National Guard members who were supposed to be on guard stood next to their antiquated army Jeep and the black Cadillac limousine. One leaned over and lit the cigarettes of his two companions and then his own.

Sloppy work, Dirk thought, thinking that if he were in a sniper's position, he would have been able to zero in on all three of them after a move like that.

But he much preferred to work up close and personal anyway, just as he preferred to work alone, when he could manage it. Being on foreign soil made that somewhat problematic, especially in a country as tumultuous and crestfallen as this one had become. So, he had to do the next best thing: assemble some locals whose loyalty he could buy with a few thousand bolivars and use them to run interference. The main thing he had to be sure of was a solid exit plan to get out of this shit-heel country.

He turned to Carlos, the local pimp who had led him to the site of the general's liaison and reconfirmed the location.

"*Sí*," Carlos said. "*Está ahí*"

"*Bueno*," Dirk said. And soon it'll be time to pay the piper.

He'd only been here three days and already he was sick of it. It had taken him that long to tag up with the other Agency contact who had laid the groundwork for what was to come: a termination request, with extreme prejudice.

The target was a Venezuelan army general whom they wanted to be replaced by another, allegedly more pro-American, general. It was deck-stacking at the highest level, hoping that the US would draw the ace on the next deal. Dirk couldn't care less. To him, one sanction was pretty much the same as another. He'd done so many over the years that he'd come to realize that loyalties and presumed fidelity were as vacillating as the wind and, more often than not, ended up being wrong.

Not that any of that mattered to him as long as he got paid.

Although any record of his fingerprints had long since been flagged and suppressed, he didn't believe in being careless about even the tiniest of details. He pulled out a pair of black latex gloves and slipped them on. He estimated this would take seven and a half minutes to complete. Ten at the far side, should any unexpected problems arise.

The three guards laughed and one of them pointed to the building behind them.

Obviously, they were alluding to the general's clandestine activity. Dirk had no doubt that it would remain a veiled secret even afterwards. Maduro's goons were very adept at sweeping things under the rug, especially those things that might tend to tarnish the dictator's strongman image.

Latinos, Dirk thought. Even the most privileged of the current ruling class were prisoners of their own cultural machismo.

He removed the silencer from his pocket and began screwing it into the end of the barrel of his Caracal Enhanced F model 9mm semi-auto pistol. He hadn't used this particular pistol before but found the removable barrel thread protector, which allowed the silencer to be attached to the threaded end, efficacious. It certainly lived up to its reputation as being "suppressor ready."

Carlos's eyes widened at the sight of the gun.

"*Señor* Dirk," Carlos said. "*Pagame ahora, por favor. Tengo que salir antes algunas fuscilamientos.*"

So he wants to be paid before the fireworks start, Dirk thought.

It made sense but something else was evident. Payment would have to be quick, expedient, and most of all, silent.

"*Por supreso,*" Dirk said, then added in English, "I don't blame you."

He smiled and watched as the pimp smiled back reflexively. Dirk finished screwing the silencer onto the barrel of the pistol and then secured the weapon temporarily under his left armpit. Cocking his left forearm, Dirk pressed one of the two buttons on his wristwatch that started the stopwatch.

All right, he thought. The clock's ticking.

When his right hand was free, he lowered it downward, toward his pants pocket, as if he were reaching for the wad of cash that he'd kept there. But instead, his ring finger caught the end of the clip securing the butterfly knife inside. In one fluid motion, honed by continuous practice to the point of making the movement one fluid gesture, he disengaged the knife from his pocket, gripped the handle as his thumb flicked the clasp on the base. Gripping the inside handle, he flicked his wrist sending the outer handle and the blade swinging outward. The top edge of the blade straightened in a flashing moment and then his fingers wrapped around the outer handle securing it and leaving the four-inch steel erect and ready for action.

Dirk's arm shot upward driving the point of the poniard into the pimp's throat. He waggled it to make sure he hit the carotids as well as the spinal cord. Carlos's jaw drooped and a cascade of blood came pouring out as he made a slight gurgling sound, collapsing to the ground. It would have been more enjoyable to have used a knife-hand chop to the windpipe. Dirk meticulously conditioned his hands striking them one thousand times on the *makawari* board almost every day, causing a calloused thickness on both his knuckles and hardened ridge along the outside edge of the palm. But enjoyment was always superseded by efficiency when he was working.

The blade was surer and quicker and the clock was ticking. He watched Carlos's final body spasms in the narrow expanse as the dark puddle spread on the ground beneath his neck.

Another tally for the high homicide rate of Caracas, Dirk thought as he wiped the tapered steel on the dead man's pant leg, snapped the knife closed, and replaced it in his pocket. Flipping the blade open had caused a slight tear on the thumb of his latex glove—an error.

Number one, he thought. How many more?

He always kept an ongoing tally of the mistakes and mechanical failures on each mission. Then, in retrospect, he'd assess his overall performance by providing a numerical rating and subtract each mistake or setback. Now he was already one in the hole even though this was more like equipment failure.

One of the guardsmen was leaning over now, saying something in a hushed tone as the other two laughed.

A dirty joke perhaps?

Or maybe another snide comment about their *comandante*'s fractious proclivity.

It didn't really matter. They were about to become three more in the latest statistics in Caracas's rising unsolved homicide rate.

Dirk held the Caracel down by his leg as he walked across the street without looking. There were hardly any cars to worry about during the day and one of the city buses sat in a state of broken, dilapidated neglect, missing all six tires and all of its windows.

"*Quién es el cófer?*" Dirk said as he approached them, gesturing conspicuously with his left hand toward the limo.

All three of the guards glanced at him questioningly their eyes widening in surprise.

It was the typical reaction of most people. Although he was relatively tall at six-three and impressively built with wide shoulders and a narrow waist, it was his eyes that people tended to notice above all else. They had an uncertain aberrance to them. If the lighting conditions had been better, or if the guards would have had a chance to study his visage more closely, perhaps they would have noticed that this stranger who approached them in the wee hours of the morning with such alacrity, in the same uniform as that of the *Policía Nacional*, had one brown eye and one blue one.

But timing was everything. Dirk raised the Caracal and squeezed off three perfectly timed shots to each man's center mass. The sound suppressor made a plinking sound each time, accompanied by the three consecutive grunts.

No body armor, he thought.

Dirk then stepped over and delivered three more shots, one to the back of each fallen man's head.

Ten shots left, he thought, as he slipped the Caracal back into the bellyband holster and fastened the Velcro flap across it. He hated to waste the time but decided it was prudent to resurrect the three guardians a bit. Placing each one in a sitting position against the side of the limo, he frisked each man's pockets for car keys. None had any. Dirk assumed the old-style Jeep didn't require a key but merely had an ignition switch lever. That meant that the general either had kept the keys to the limo himself, or there was a driver waiting inside the building.

Either way, it was time to find out.

Rating thus far: plus three, minus one.

Dirk turned and walked to the door of the hotel. As he pushed open the door. A musty smell assailed his nostrils. A weasel-like clerk was perched behind a Plexiglas barrier paging through a magazine. A glass of amber liquid sat beside him. His eyes widened as he saw the gun.

"*Policía*," Dirk said, figuring the clerk wouldn't notice the absence of a police badge. Apparently he didn't because his eyes remained fixated on the gun.

"*Cual cuarto está el general?*" Dirk said.

The clerk didn't answer.

Is my accent that bad? Dirk thought with a grin and raised the Caracal.

He repeated his question.

This time the clerk's head elevated, and he looked Dirk right in the eyes.

"*Dos ciento y tres,*" the clerk said. "*Numero dos ciento y tres.*"

"*Y cuantos de mis amigos están arriba?*" Dirk asked.

The weasel's brow furrowed, and he didn't answer. Had he grown suspicious? Why would this "police official" be asking how many men were upstairs? Wouldn't he already know?

The jig's up, Dirk thought, and he fired two rounds through the Plexiglas. One struck the clerk in the forehead and the other hit the man's throat.

Eight rounds left.

Rating: Plus four, minus two.

Glancing around and assuring himself that he was alone, he moved to the adjacent stairway. He longed to check his watch to see how much time had elapsed but he resisted the temptation. An elevator was next to the stairway. Dirk assumed that any of the general's guards who were competent would have it disabled on the second floor to prevent being surprised.

But the guards in front had been lax and they paid for it. Perhaps these guys were so used to no one confronting them, or having the numerical superiority to administer a beat-down with overwhelming force, that they didn't keep their drawers up. He crept up the stairs with the grace of a big jungle cat. At the half-way point he caught sight of the first door on the second-floor landing.

Number 205.

The clerk had said the target was in room 203.

Glancing to the right, he saw the next consecutive room was numbered 206.

Pausing at the top of the stairs, Dirk gripped the Caracal with both hands and did a quick peek. Two men stood in the hallway smoking and talking. Both had rifles, M-16's from the looks of them, slung over their shoulders.

The weapons had probably been supplied by everybody's favorite uncle once upon a time when the U.S. and Venezuela had gotten along.

Before Chavez, before Maduro.

But back to the hall guards ...

Dirk edged partially around the corner to squeeze off two head shots.

As both men slumped down onto the dingy, threadbare carpeting, Dirk covered the space between them

Six rounds left now.

Rating: plus six, minus two.

Stepping over both bodies, Dirk positioned himself in front of the door, trying the knob.

It was locked.

Naturally, he thought, then brought his leg up and delivered a hard kick to the section just below the doorknob.

The door burst open, hitting the wall, and then swinging back toward Dirk as he entered.

Two naked, sweating bodies were busy in the tangle of sheets on the bed. One of them, a dark-haired slender youth, was perched on his side, his face near the other man's groin. The supine man, dark-haired, middle-aged, and with a flaring mustache and an air of authority, immediately sat up in outrage, his brows knitting in a mixture of surprise, anger, and, suddenly, fear.

"*Buenos dias*," Dirk said and shot the older man first.

His eyes widened in shock as the neat, round hole appeared in the center of his forehead. Twin streams of blood gushed from each flaring nostril coloring the bushy black mustache crimson. The other one, who looked barely pubescent, twisted his face in an agonized scream that was truncated by Dirk's second shot. The boy's right eye disappeared inside of a dollop of blood. His body jerked once, then collapsed onto the general's legs.

Four rounds left.

Dirk stepped over to the bed and delivered two more shots to the general's temple and one to his unlucky lover's head.

Rating: plus eight, minus two.

The slide on the Caracal locked back and Dirk dropped the magazine and inserted a fully loaded one. He went to the general's folded uniform, which had been draped over a chair, and checked the pockets. There was a set of car keys inside. Dirk retrieved them and went back to the bed, He gazed down at the dead man's face. The startled expression was frozen on it. He used his cell phone to capture the image, and then snapped a few more to show the nature of the assignation, just in case the Agency would want to leak a few photos to discredit the regime.

The Latino machismo would never be the same.

After pocketing the cell phone, Dirk pulled out his knife and plastic tube.

The right index finger would do nicely, he thought, and took it off with a deft chop. After depositing the verification of his work in the plastic container, he wiped the blade of the knife, leaving a crimson spoor on the tangled white sheet. The Agency always preferred proof in addition to the pudding.

Dirk then walked briskly to the door, stopping to peep up and down the corridor.

Not a creature was stirring, he thought.

Stooping down, he retrieved one of the rifles from the fallen guard, just in case, and checked the selector switch.

Fully automatic. Definitely U.S. Government property at one time.

It had an old fifteen-round magazine in it so he disengaged the mag from the other guard's rifle and then trotted down the stairs.

No need to police my brass, he thought with a smile.

Outside, the street was still dark and, basically, unoccupied, unless you counted the three guards whose bodies still leaned against the limo and two rag-tag beggars who were now going through the trash bags down the way. Dirk pressed the key fob unlocking the doors of the limo. The taillights blinked on and off quickly.

Striding around to the driver's door, Dirk opened it, tossed in the rifle, and slid behind the wheel. The limo's engine started right up, and Dirk decided to use it instead of the motorcycle he'd stashed in the alleyway to ride to his departure point down by the marina.

But first, he thought, all the loose ends needed to be tied up.

He pulled out onto the street, stopped, and then shifted into reverse.

Stopping adjacent to the two scavengers, he lifted the Caracal as he lowered the passenger side window.

"Hey," he yelled.

Both beggars looked up, their grimy faces registering shock and trepidation.

Dirk squeezed off two more rounds, both center-mass hits, and then shifted into drive, raised the window, and set off down the street.

Rating: plus ten, still minus two.

He retrieved his satellite phone from his pants pocket and hit the transmit button.

A voice answered and Dirk said two words: "En route."

"Roger that," the voice said. "We're waiting."

Dirk terminated the call and then hit the stop button on his watch.

8:59

About a minute and a half over, he thought.

But he'd dallied to pick up the rifle and the extra magazine. And he was still under the ten-minute mark. He gave himself an extra point for finishing under the high-end mark.

Overall rating: plus eleven, minus two equals nine.

Close enough for government work, he told himself, and then momentarily lamented at how sparse the wet work assignments had become in recent years.

More red tape and fewer opportunities as the bureaucrats continued to take over the Agency. He was overdue for a string of good luck.

He lowered the driver's window to let in some of the cool night air, but the odor from the omnipresent floating fecal matter on the *Guaire* River that ran through the center of the city was too pervasive. He raised the window back up.

Sometimes life's just a bowl of shit, he thought. But maybe something better will come along.

THE MCNAMARA RANCH
PHOENIX, ARIZONA

Despite the lingering soreness from the fight, Wolf got up at his usual pre-dawn time and dressed in his running clothes, a T-shirt, sweatpants, and a handkerchief tied around his forehead. When Mac had once called attention to it, Wolf had replied that it was in homage to his American Indian heritage. His mother was full-blooded Cherokee. His father had been white and a drunk. He'd ended his life crashing his pickup truck into a cement porch at about ninety miles-an-hour. At least that was what the sheriff's department had estimated the speed to be. He'd been an absentee father most of the time anyway and Wolf's life had been hard. Half-Indian, half-white, and the son of a drunk who'd essentially killed himself.

But before his father had been a drunk, he'd been a soldier and a good one at that. This he knew for sure because Mac had told him so.

He stepped out onto the asphalt driveway and watched as the first vestiges of light began to crest the distant mountains. The heat of the day wouldn't be far behind. He started his run, trying to ignore his still-sore body and pushing the disturbing thoughts of his current troubling situation out of his mind.

But that was easier said than done.

Mac had picked him up from Leavenworth and brought him here, giving him free room and board and a way to make some money. He'd slowly been working his way back and intended on repaying Mac for his largess. While he'd pretty much accomplished that now, he'd also brought a whole load of trouble to his friend and mentor. Conflicts from Wolf's past kept twisting around with the unpredictability of a pissed-off rattlesnake. First, there'd been the Mexican fiasco, where McNamara was wounded, and then the band of South African mercenaries who'd invaded the ranch and taken them all prisoner. They'd also murdered Kasey's fiancé. It was all over the statue of a Mexican bandito, or rather what was inside of it. Wolf still hadn't yet determined exactly what that was but he hoped to know soon. He did know that a very rich and powerful man coveted whatever it was. And he was obsessed with getting it.

Dexter Von Dien ... Wolf knew the name and also that the man behind it had unlimited money, power, and influence. One hundred thousand dollars sat in Wolf's bank account now—a gift from the rich man or, rather, supposed compensation for the multiple attempts on Wolf's life. Or so Von Dien's mouthpiece, Soraces, had stated.

Wolf trusted Soraces about as much as a smiling politician and Von Dien, whom he'd never seen, less than that.

But how does Bambi fight Godzilla?

The question kept echoing in his mind as his feet skipped over the pavement with rote skill as he made his way to the mountain. He paused at the beginning of the trail that led up the side of the first and smallest of the massive structures.

In times gone by he'd taken the trail up to the top. It was an intense workout even in the relative coolness of the nascent dawn. He'd done it many times in the past when he was honing his body for one of his matches or just trying to find solace in the joy of physical exertion.

But not today, he thought, and did the swooping loop that set him on the road back to the ranch.

After his last encounter with Soraces, it had been Wolf's plan, his vow, to go on the offensive, to track down this Von Dien character and put a stop, once and for all, to the incremental disorder that had overtaken virtually every aspect of his life. Von Dien had been behind it all, from the setup in Iraq, to the shootout south of the border, to the South African contingent. He'd also paid Wolf all that money, which to him was, apparently, nothing more than a tip left for a waiter or bellman.

The bandito statue that Soraces had ended up with had been a fake and Wolf wondered how that had turned out.

The speculation brought a smile to his lips.

Von Dien couldn't have been pleased and probably figured that Wolf still had whatever it was that the rich man was seeking. But he had what Wolf really wanted as well: a video of Cummins confessing that he'd set Wolf up in Iraq, that he really wasn't guilty of the war crimes he'd been convicted of committing.

The question now became how to obtain it.

Maybe Garfield will be able to give me some answers, he thought.

As he neared the familiar two-mile marker on the back side, Wolf was thinking about sitting down with his laptop after he'd showered and pounding out that final English lit paper. The on-line classes had been compressed into a work-at-your-own-pace sort of thing, and Wolf just wanted to get it over with and grab the three credits. He quickened his pace and then saw McNamara jogging toward him. Mac wore his usual baggy sweat clothes and Wolf knew his friend had one of his stainless-steel semi-autos in a shoulder holster under the shirt.

"Don't leave home without it," McNamara always said.

He turned as Wolf got to him and they fell into step together. Wolf had to slow his pace a bit but the company made it worth it.

"I didn't think you'd be up this early," Wolf said.

"You know better than that," McNamara said. "Especially when my pard's got something on his mind that he's not telling me."

Good old Mac, Wolf thought. Always able to read a man like a book. That came from leading men all over the globe, not to mention facing down others in hostile lands and instantly being able to figure out if they were going to fight or quit.

"What makes you think that?" Wolf asked.

"You hardly said two words last night at dinner. Kasey went out of her way to fix you your favorite. Meatloaf and baked potatoes."

He remembered that she had gone the extra mile

with the meal and regretted that he hadn't shown the proper appreciation.

"Sorry. I should've said something but my jaw was a little sore,"

"Horseshit," McNamara said, his feet making skidding sounds on the gravelly shoulder adjacent to the rough asphalt highway. "You gonna tell me what's really bothering you?"

"A lot of things."

"Like what?"

"Your stride, for one thing," Wolf said. "Is that how they taught you to run at Bragg? Pick your feet up more."

"Shit," McNamara said. "These old feet have logged more miles than you can even imagine on your best day."

"I believe you."

"Good. Now tell me what's really bothering you."

Wolf didn't answer.

They ran about ten yards in silence and then McNamara said, "Well, there's only one thing that'll make a man clam up like you're doing. Woman trouble." He was huffing a bit more heavily now. "It's none of my business, but is everything okay between you and your gal?"

Again, Wolf was silent.

How the hell did Mac know?

But it was a moot point. Wolf didn't know if Yolanda had discussed her upcoming departure from the P-Patrol with Ms. Dolly and, if not, he didn't want to risk spilling the beans too soon. He didn't want to ruin things for her.

Ruin things ... He was getting to be an expert at doing that, and in so many different ways.

"Either you're gonna answer me, or tell me it's none of my business and to shut the hell up."

The sun behind them had begun to crest the mountains and Wolf and McNamara's jerking shadows extended out before them.

"Let's just say she doesn't need me dragging her down in the dawn's early light anymore," Wolf said.

———

After the run Wolf had proceeded into the garage and went four three-minute rounds on the speed bag and then the heavy bag.

Or, he thought. He tried to.

His thoughts intruded each time, crowding out his concentration and destroying his rhythm.

Bambi versus Godzilla. He needed some way to even the playing field between him and the rich, powerful adversary who held the key to salvation.

One step at a time, he told himself as he pounded the last series of punches into the canvas surface. One step at a time.

By the time he'd finished showering, his cell phone was ringing. He looked at the screen and saw it was Mac.

"You coming over here for breakfast, or what?" McNamara said. "Kasey's whipped up a bunch of scrambled eggs and bacon. Just the sort of thing for a fighting man."

Wolf looked at his own kitchen and the meager

supplies he knew were in his refrigerator and told Mac he'd be right over.

"Okay," McNamara said. "But shake a leg. Today's Chad's first day of kindergarten and she has to drop him off."

"I thought they were doing that remote learning stuff?"

"Remote learning bullshit you mean," McNamara said. "It's what they're calling a hybrid class. A couple days in the school and a couple watching on a computer. This partial lockdown horseshit is sure cheating the kids out of a decent education."

Wolf recalled his own elementary school days and how much he'd hated them. Little Chad had already been through more trauma than a dozen children his age. Maybe this modified school setting and schedule would help the kid ease into learning. Wolf hoped so.

He finished dressing choosing a tan Polo shirt to complement his regular blue jeans and running shoes. They were the same pair that he wore on his morning runs and were covered with reddish-brown road dust so he grabbed his shoe brush and ran it over them. The beam of sunlight was streaming through the window and illuminated the minute particles as they floated toward the floor and he realized he'd have to vacuum later.

But to do that, he'd have to borrow the vacuum cleaner from Mac.

Not too much different than my Sandbox days, he thought. Dust everywhere, no vacuum cleaner, and staying in somebody else's abode. I really need to start thinking of getting a place of my own.

He trotted down the stairs of his apartment and into the lower floor, which was the garage with his workout equipment: the speed bag and heavy bag that he and Mac had put up, a set of weights, Mac's riding lawn mower, which he never had to use, and various tools and items in storage. Wolf had used some of the money from his last MMA match to buy himself a laptop, a relatively small TV, and an old used Jeep. The vehicle was about fifteen years old and had well over a hundred thousand miles on it, but it got him where he wanted to go. Wolf had given the remainder of the money to Mac to cover the room and board that he'd accumulated over the several months. McNamara had initially refused to take it but then relented after Wolf's insistence: "The only reason I took the chance of getting my ass beat," he'd said, "was to put Trackdown, Inc back in the black."

With this new paycheck coming from this most recent bout, and the still untouched money he'd gotten from Soraces for past injuries and inconveniences, Wolf figured he was financially very comfortable. He still was mistrustful of the payoff that the sleazy lawyer had arranged but he left it in there. It was more money than he'd ever had in his life, not to mention the cash in the money-belt they'd recovered from Cummins.

I'd trade it all for a decent shot at clearing my name, Wolf thought. But that's probably not in the cards, video confession or not.

But a hundred thousand would go a very long way in hiring some new, fancy lawyer, like Andrew Taylor, the one who'd represented him and Mac after the last shootout. But guys like Taylor didn't come cheap, and Wolf still planned to use the money to set up a college trust fund for Chad.

The kid's been through the mill because of me, Wolf thought. It's the least I can do.

And the kid did call him "Uncle Steve," which made him feel too much like the surrogate son that Kasey had originally accused him of being.

Kasey, he thought. She'd really come around, doing a three-sixty reversal since his initial appearance.

Looks like he's finally got the son he's always wanted, she'd said about her father when Wolf had first gotten there. To say that she resented him then was an understatement. It had sure been a rough few months.

He was on his way across the asphalt driveway when his cellphone rang again. He glanced at the screen.

Yolanda.

After letting it ring several times, he finally got the courage to answer it. The temptation to hear her voice, even though she was in Las Vegas, was too great.

"Good morning," she said. "For a minute I thought I was going to go to voicemail."

"Yeah, I'm kinda slow on the draw this morning. What's up?"

"Just wondering how my boo was doing, is all."

"Still kicking," he said. "Mac and I did a few miles this morning and I'm heading over to the house now to eat breakfast."

"I'm starting the academy this morning," she said.

This stopped him. It was hearing something that you already knew but had purposely not been thinking about.

"How'd Ms. Dolly take you leaving?"

Yolanda laughed. "Like she takes everything.

Wished me well and then asked if I could talk you into coming to work for her in my place."

It was Wolf's turn to chuckle. "I'd never fit in with the P-Patrol. I'm not Bruce Jenner, you know."

"That's Catlin Jenner now, and you should never say never."

He slowed his pace across the driveway and was almost at the door.

"So I need you to do something for me," she said.

"Name it."

"Tell Mac about this police department thing for me. I listed him as a reference."

"I'm sure he'll give you a good one," Wolf said. "And I'll tell him to keep any mention of me out of it."

"What? Will you stop?"

He said he would and they exchanged a few more pleasantries. Wolf was standing outside the door now, talking and waiting, and suddenly McNamara opened it and glared at him.

"You coming in, or what?" McNamara said.

"I got to go, babe," Wolf said.

"I know. I heard him. Tell big boo daddy I said hi," she said. "And about the other stuff, too."

Wolf said he would, wished her good luck, and terminated the call. As he slipped the phone back into his pocket, he said, "Yolanda says hi."

His eyebrows rose. "Damn, that's good to hear. I should've yelled something."

"We'll talk later," Wolf said, stepping inside. Kasey waved to him from the kitchen. She had on an apron over a blue business outfit. Wolf saw she was wearing heels, too, and appreciated the triangular musculature of her exposed calf.

"Kasey going somewhere?" he asked.

"She's got some kind of thing at the university," McNamara said.

Chad came running up and started throwing punches in the air.

"Hey, Uncle Steve," he said. He was holding the purple toy dragon. "Where's my belt? You told me yesterday that you were gonna bring it this morning."

"He can show it to you later," McNamara said. "He's gotta eat breakfast now. And you gotta get ready for school."

The boy's face puckered up. "But you promised."

"That's right," Wolf said. "I did. Just let me run back and get it."

He turned and sprinted across the driveway, shuffling his door key out as he went. It was ironic that Chad had seemed to like the dragon better than the police car or army Humvee his grandfather had bought him.

Perhaps the dragon connotes more pleasant memories.

After unlocking the door, he trotted up the stairs and retrieved the belt from his travel bag. He also found the purple T-shirt that they'd picked out for Kasey. Mac had forgotten to give it to her yesterday. He grabbed both and went downstairs again. As he was locking up, he saw a cloud of dust stirring on the access road.

Someone was coming.

———

THE VON DIEN WINTER ESTATE SOUTH BELIZE

. . .

Soraces was packing his suitcase when he heard the quick knock on the door of his huge room and Fallotti came waltzing in. The lawyer was wearing a green polo shirt, tan, knee-length shorts, and white gym shoes. He held a tennis racquet in his right hand and a large, 8 x 11 manila envelope in his left. The two of them were alone in the room.

"Good morning," he said, smiling. "How was your breakfast?"

"Fine," Soraces said, zipping up the case and setting it on the floor. As he picked up the spy pen from the table next to the bed where he'd used it the night before to record his amorous adventures, he once again activated it to capture this interlude.

"And how was the girl?" Fallotti asked, his grin turning a bit lascivious.

"She was fine too."

"I've got a pilot standing by to take you to the airport."

"Pilot?"

Fallotti nodded. "Mr. Von Dien's helicopter. His Lear Jet is being prepared as we speak to get you back to the States."

"I appreciate you setting up such an expeditious departure," Soraces said and glanced around the plush room wondering where the camera was.

How else would they know that he was almost ready to go?

Perhaps the rich bastard had videos of Fallotti getting laid as well. It made sense, especially in view of the video he had of the late Jack Cummings confessing to setting Steven Wolf up for the killing of those Iraqis. It was the best form of insurance to ensure total compliance in place of loyalty. Or maybe he was just a real wealthy voyeur. Von Dien wouldn't be the first rich son of a bitch with a few kinks. Plus, anybody willing to pay a couple hundred thousand and kill a lot of people just to get a pair of carved rocks from the fourth or fifth century had to be a little off his rich rocker.

Or maybe he intended to use the video for something else ...

"I'm considering a second career as a porno star, you know," Soraces said.

Fallotti's brow furrowed. "What?"

"You heard me. I was wondering how you and the old man enjoyed the video of me balling that chick."

Fallotti looked a bit shocked, then his expression of surprise changed to one of mirth.

Artificial mirth, Soraces inferred. It confirmed what he already had surmised. Somewhere in this massive mansion, that looked like it had been transported from the antebellum South, was a recording of him doing the nasty with the girl last night, and most probably the other two *bonitas mujeres* from his previous trip. He was pretty sure those two had been professional hookers though.

But so what, Soraces thought. Let the rich bastard think he's got something to hold over my head. When it comes time for the final negotiation, he'll be in for a little surprise because I'm nobody's patsy.

Just the same, he was doubly glad he'd been discreet when setting up his own recording last night.

"What video is that?" Fallotti asked, the forced smile still framing his mouth.

"Never mind," Soraces said. "I'm not going to make

an issue of it at the moment. But I will expect a copy to be included along with my final payment."

Fallotti kept smiling but his tongue darted out and went over his lips.

For a big shot lawyer, Soraces thought, this fucker doesn't know shit about maintaining a poker face. Or maybe he's just not used to somebody being a step ahead of him.

"Whatever," Fallotti said. His mouth twitched as the smile went away. "I just came by to tell you that I've taken care of those legal matters you asked me to."

"Any problems?"

"None. All taken care of," Fallotti said, handing him the envelope. "Additionally, the funds have been deposited in your personal account in the Caymans, and a separate operations account has been reopened in your name in the States. The credit and debit cards are in here, along with some expense money and that thumb drive with the portion of the video."

Soraces pressed the metal clasp hands together and glanced inside. He removed the cards, slipped them into his wallet, and partially unzipped the suitcase and shoved the envelope into it.

"It's a good start," he said and zipped it back up.

"I'd like to have an update on what you've done so far," Fallotti said. "So I can convey your progress to Mr. Von Dien. And we'll need periodic reports from Phoenix."

Soraces thought about replying with a wise crack about Fallotti's nose being so far up the rich man's ass that he must have trouble breathing but remembered the now almost certain probability that their conversation was being secretly recorded. Appearing overly deferential would make him appear weak nor did he want to evoke the rich man's ire by being defiant or disrespectful. Soraces knew the fine line he had to walk to milk the situation for all it was worth.

"I've contacted a few of my old compatriots," he said.

"They're dependable?"

"Dependables that I can trust and who know how to get the job done discreetly and efficiently. I've left a message for one and I'm waiting for him to call me back. He's the muscle."

"That fellow Derek you mentioned?"

"Dirk," Soraces said. "Cameron Dirk, but don't try finding him on the Internet anywhere. Technically, he doesn't exist."

"You're certain he'll be able to deal effectively with Wolf when the time comes?"

"More than certain. I'd stake my life on it."

Fallotti raised his eyebrows as if to say, *And you will be.*

"I've already got some men in place in Phoenix now," Soraces said. "Experienced survcillance men."

"Surveillance men?" Fallotti frowned. "Is that wise, in view of what's already happened? What if Wolf notices them?"

"He won't. They're good. I've worked with them before. Both pros. Their nickname is the Shadows."

"The Shadows?" Fallotti said, his brow wrinkling. "What the hell kind of name is that?"

"An appropriate one," Soraces said. "Charles and Clyde Perkins. Two identical twin brothers. Experts at disguise. They can look exactly the same or totally different, depending on the nature of the assignment."

"I don't know about this," Fallotti said. "You're sure about them?"

"Take it from me, there's nobody better for surveillance than them. That's why they're called the Shadows."

Fallotti smirked. "How appropriate. And what do you call that Dirk fellow?"

"Just Dirk. He prefers it that way."

Fallotti compressed his lips and took in a deep breath. "And you're sure they can all be trusted?"

Soraces nodded his head. "Absolutely."

Fallotti grunted an approval. "And our plan is still to offer Wolf a deal, using the video as well as some ... financial incentive, to get him to relinquish the item?"

The item ... The lawyer's reticence to spell it out reaffirmed that the videotaping was indeed in progress.

Soraces nodded again.

"And," Fallotti said, "you're absolutely certain that he'll deal with you? Even after the mess up last time?"

"Like I told you and Mr. Von Dien," Soraces said, silently pleased with his exaggerated deference by using the title in case Big Brother was listening. "The last time was a bit of an aberration, thanks to Cummins. But he's no longer in the picture."

Fallotti pursed his lips.

"Like I told you before," Soraces said. "Everybody has a price, and I've got moves in mind that he won't even see coming."

CHAPTER FOUR_

THE MCNAMARA RANCH
PHOENIX, ARIZONA

As Wolf watched the approaching vehicle drawing closer, it became more evident who it was. If the familiar dark navy-blue sedan with the federal government plates didn't give it away, the slender form that became distinctly visible behind the wheel was a sure give-away.

Special Agent William Franker, Wolf thought. Sort of like Opie Taylor from those old Andy Griffin TV shows, all grown up, but still having the air of a naïve schoolboy.

Wolf lifted his hand in a casual wave and Franker waved back as he turned onto the asphalt driveway and pulled the sedan to a stop.

"How's it going?" Wolf said, uncertain about Franker's reason for the visit and also noticing that the agent was alone. They usually worked in pairs.

"Figured I'd stop by before I went into the office," Franker said, smiling and pointing to the championship belt in Wolf's hand. "I heard you won."

Wolf held it up for Franker to see. "I did, and here's the proof."

"Congratulations."

"Thanks," Wolf said. "But exactly where'd you hear about it?"

"It's all over the Internet," Franker said. "They've even posted a clip of you knocking the guy out." His eyebrows rose in unison. "Quite a punch."

"I was lucky," Wolf said. "I didn't know you followed mixed martial arts."

"I don't, but when the guy who promised to give me some much-needed information on an open case I've been working does something that significant, I take notice."

Touché, Wolf thought, remembering his agreement with the FBI man to clear up the Mexico investigation when they thought Chad had been kidnapped.

The deal had fallen through when the real culprit, Cummins and Kasey's ex-husband had been shown to be responsible. Franker had been waiting for Wolf outside the Pima County Jail when he'd been released without charges after the shootout in the ghost town adjacent to where the Devil's Brigade had made its last stand. Wolf had been cooperative up to a point, giving them the location of a couple of dead perpetrators as well as a cache of stolen bank loot. Mac had been brought in for questioning, too, but both of them were released without charges thanks to a high-powered attorney that Ms. Dolly had brought in.

"I thought you guys were able to clear that one?"

Wolf said. "The armored car heist, the kidnapping of Mac's grandson, and a couple of previous bank robberies."

"Those were cleared," Franker said. "And thanks for that. But the one I'm talking about, which I'm sure you know, is the still-open case of those murders down in Mexico."

Wolf clucked sympathetically. "You know, I really don't have anything more to add to what I've already said on that subject. And that's on the advice of my attorney."

"Which one?" Franker asked. "That thousand-dollar suit that represented you in Pima County, or the one who was murdered?"

Wolf thought about Rodney Shemp's untimely demise and felt a twinge of pity. It seemed like everything he touched became blighted. He took in a deep breath and didn't reply.

"Look," Franker said. "I came here today, off the record, so we could talk. You did give me your word. So, are you going to tell me what happened?"

Again, Wolf said nothing.

If you don't cooperate now, I may not be able to help you." Franker said, his voice rising. "Or should I just wait for you to be involved in your next shootout?"

Wolf grinned. "What can I say? Trouble follows me."

"Dammit, Steve. Can't you see that I'm going to get to the bottom of all this eventually?"

It's "Steve" now, Wolf thought. Pretty soon we'll be going out to have a beer together.

He was just about to speak when the door to the

ranch house opened and McNamara came sauntering out.

"Well, well, well," he said. "Look who the cat dragged in. How you doing, Mr. FBI man?"

Franker straightened up. "Fine, Mr. McNamara. I just stopped by to—"

"To say hello to the champ here and see how we're doing?" McNamara finished for him. "Well, come on in. We're just fixing to have breakfast and we'll be glad to set up a spare plate for you."

"I really shouldn't sir," Franker said. "I'm on my way into the office."

"There you go with that 'sir' shit again," McNamara said. "Hell, a man shows up on my doorstep just when I'm having breakfast, the least I can do is give him a plate at my table."

"Well, maybe just a cup of coffee then."

"Sure," McNamara said. "As many times as you've come a calling here, I guess it's time I introduce you formally to my daughter and grandson. He's recovering nicely from that kidnapping, but, just the same, I'd appreciate if you didn't bring it up in front of him. He's only five and I know you wouldn't want to say anything to upset him, right?"

"I certainly won't, sir," Franker said, taking small steps as he fell into step alongside of the other man.

McNamara extended an arm around the thin FBI man's shoulders and ushered him inside.

Wolf grinned.

Good old Mac, he thought. There's nobody better at disarming the enemy.

He followed them in and saw Chad running toward

them. He stopped short when he saw the unfamiliar figure of the FBI man.

"Hey, Kase," McNamara said. "Rustle up another plate, will ya? We got a new guest."

Kasey glanced over and smiled tentatively, the space between her brows furrowing slightly.

"It's one of them FBI fellas that was giving Steve and me such a hard time about getting shot up down in Mexico," McNamara said, his arm still around Franker's back and his big hand clapping the fed on the shoulder. "Special Agent what's-his-name."

"Franker," the fed said quickly, his eyes glued on Kasey. "But please, call me Bill."

"Not Special Agent?" McNamara said.

"Are you really an FBI agent?" Chad asked, running up to him.

I guess he's forgotten all about my belt, Wolf thought, enjoying the look of discomfort on Franker's face.

The FBI man looked like he was caught in a riptide.

"Yes," Franker said, looking down at the boy. "I've been with the Bureau for four and a half years."

"You have a gun?" Chad asked. "My grandpa has one. A real big one, too."

Franker's smile looked forced.

Wolf moved around to the place set for him at the table. A plate with scrambled eggs, bacon, and rye toast sat on the table next to a glass of orange juice and a cup of coffee. The coffee was no longer steaming, Wolf noticed.

"Hey, Chad," he said. "I brought my belt like you asked.

The boy immediately shifted his gaze to Wolf as he

held up the belt. Running to him, he reached up and touched the emblem in the center.

"When you gonna teach me to fight, Uncle Steve?"

Wolf immediately glanced at Kasey, who was busy dishing up another plate.

"We'll have to see, Chad," Wolf said. "But sometimes fighting is the last thing you want to do. Your schoolwork's more important."

"Schoolwork?" Chad said. "What's that?"

You'll be finding that out soon enough, he thought, and looked again at Kasey, who was smiling. He then glanced at Franker; whose eyes were still glued on her.

"Sit down, Bill," McNamara said, pulling out a chair and practically forcing the FBI man to sit in it. "How do you like your coffee?"

"Black's fine, sir. But I really should be going."

"Aw, hell," McNamara said. "You don't want to hurt my daughter's feelings, do you? She'll think you don't think she's a good cook."

"I've already got a plate started for you, Mr. Franker," Kasey said.

Franker smiled nervously and shrugged as he sank into the chair.

Kasey came over and set the plate in front of him.

Wolf was already shoveling some eggs into his own mouth. He bit off a piece of toast and shifted it to his cheek.

"Great breakfast, Kasey," he said. "Thanks."

She smiled at him and then raised her eyebrows as she turned to Franker.

"Would you like some orange juice to go with your coffee, Mr. Franker? Or should I say, Special Agent?"

Franker's nervous smile reappeared. "Oh, ah, Bill's fine. And orange juice would be great. Thank you."

Chad was holding Wolf's belt around his waist now and was prancing around. "I wanna be a champ, too. I'm taking this to school to show the other kids."

Before Wolf could say anything Kasey interceded.

"Give that back to Uncle Steve," she said. "And then go brush your teeth. We have to leave soon."

"Aw, mom."

"No arguments," she said.

The boy's head lowered and he shuffled back to the table and gave the belt to Wolf.

"I was going to give this to Reno's gym," he said. "But maybe I'll give it to you, instead."

Chad's face lit up. "Oh yeah?"

"No," Kasey said. "You have to earn things like that. Now go brush your teeth."

Chad glanced from his mother back to Wolf, who winked.

The boy's grin reappeared, and he ran out of the room taking the belt with him.

"So, is this an official call, or what?" McNamara said as Kasey set a glass of orange juice and a steaming cup of coffee onto the table in front of Franker.

"Actually," Franker said, "I came by on the way into the office. I had a question or two for Mr. Wolf."

We're back to formalities, Wolf thought.

He was enjoying watching the FBI man's obvious discomfort. Things weren't proceeding how he'd planned.

"I thought we already explained that to you," McNamara said. "Our lawyer advised us not to make any further statements unless he was present. You wouldn't want us to not do what he told us, would you? After all, we're paying him a lot of money."

Franker appeared flustered. He sat there staring at the steaming eggs on his plate.

"Now go on," McNamara said. "Eat your eggs before you hurt my daughter's feelings."

"Dad," Kasey said, walking around the table. "Leave the poor man alone." She bent over and kissed her father on the cheek, straightened up, and draped the apron over an empty chair. "I'll have to clean the kitchen later. I don't want to be late taking Chad to school."

"Okay, sweetie," McNamara said. "And me and Steve'll be on KP duty. We'll do the kitchen."

"Okay," Kasey said, smiling at Wolf, who nodded.

It'll give me another excuse not to work on that English Lit paper, he thought.

"I'll see you later then," Kasey said, turning to go out of the room. "Nice seeing you again, Mr. Franker."

Franker, who had a mouthful, shifted the partially chewed food to the side and said, "Bill. Please. Call me Bill." He made a few more attempts to masticate and then added, "Fabulous breakfast, Ms. McNamara."

"It's Ms. Riley," Kasey said, her smile evaporating. "At least until I can get it legally changed back to McNamara."

On that note she walked out of the room without a backward glance. Franker watched her go and Wolf had to admit that her figure looked pretty good in that tight-fitting dress. He wondered for a moment if her fetching looks was what had caught the FBI man's attention, or if he might be considering something else.

Maybe he's thinking about trying to find out more

information about Mexico by questioning her, Wolf thought. If he is, big mistake. Mac'll never stand for that.

McNamara slapped Franker on the back with a bit more enthusiasm than a casual pat.

"That was her ex-husband's name," Mac said. "But he ain't in the picture no more."

Franker nodded and Wolf figured the FBI man already knew that. Charles Riley had been part of the Freedom Brigade militia, which had been responsible for numerous bank robberies. He'd taken Chad, his natural son, and fled south to an abandoned army fort where he'd met his untimely end. The whole sordid chapter was probably common knowledge to the Bureau. They'd been involved trying to track the robbers down.

The door slammed at the front of the house as Kasey and Chad exited.

Wolf took his last bite of toast and shoved himself away from the table. Standing, he finished off his juice and brought the dishes over to the sink.

"I'll get started on the KP," he said.

Franker took a few more bites and stood as well.

"I really should be going," he said.

"You mean you ain't gonna stay and help us with the dishes?" McNamara waited a few beats to watch the FBI man's surprised expression and then laughed. "Just kidding. Steve, why don't you show Bill here out."

"Be glad to," Wolf said.

He and Franker walked to the front door and went through the same living room area where the South Africans had held everyone at gunpoint. Franker and his partner had come at a crucial time and provided the necessary break that Wolf needed to gain the upper hand. The result had been a deadly shootout but it had turned out all right, except for Franker and his partner almost getting shot, and Franker inadvertently having an accidental discharge of his firearm. He paused at the doorway, turned, and stared at the room with a far-away look in his eyes.

"That was quite a night," he said. "Wasn't it?"

"That's putting it mildly," Wolf said. "How'd you make out with that shooting team investigation?"

Franker shrugged.

"A letter of reprimand was placed in my file." He pursed his lips into what passed for a lips-only smile. "But at least I lived to talk about it. Thanks to you, that is."

Wolf passed off the accolade with a shrug.

"I owe you, too," he said. "If you and your partner hadn't come along when you did ..."

The two men stood in silence, each apparently feeling a commonality of appreciation.

"You two gonna be taking a long walk together, or what?" McNamara yelled from the kitchen. "Cause I'm gonna need some help policing up this damn kitchen."

Wolf grinned. "On the way."

Franker turned and held his clenched fist out toward Wolf. The gesture took him off guard until he realized the fed was offering it instead of a handshake. A parting salutation in the age of the new normal. Wolf bumped his fist against Franker's.

The FBI man turned to go, then stopped.

"Ms. McNama—" He gave his head a minute shake. "I mean Ms. Riley ... She was engaged to that dead lawyer, right?"

"She was," Wolf said. "When he was still a live lawyer, that is." He felt bad about joking about Shemp's demise, but the temptation was just too great.

Franker blushed and Wolf wondered again just why the fed was asking.

"Is she pretty much over that?" Franker asked.

Curiouser and curiouser, Wolf thought, remembering that line from one of his lit classes.

"So far she is," he said. "She's a pretty tough kid, just like her dad.

Franker compressed his lips and nodded a thanks.

"Mac's very protective of her," Wolf added, wanting to curtail any ideas Franker might have of trying to interview Kasey. "And of his grandson."

"I'll bet he is," Franker said. "But I can't blame him. She's a doll."

A doll?

The words hit Wolf like a quick, powerful jab ... Like one of those telephone pole jabs that Big George Foreman used to spear his opponents with and knock them down.

Did Franker have the hots for Kasey?

She did look very attractive in that blue suit ...

Or was he, as Wolf had wondered before, merely trying for another angle to get more info for his Mexico investigation?

"Tell her I said thanks for the breakfast," Franker said. "It was really great."

As he walked over to the navy-blue sedan, Wolf wondered what the fed's game was.

Friend or foe now?

Wolf couldn't decide, especially in view of the way Franker had been looking at Kasey.

Whatever he's got planned, Wolf thought as he walked back toward the kitchen, the guy better beware of Mac.

———

SOMEWHERE OVER THE CARIBBEAN EN ROUTE BACK TO THE UNITED STATES

The number on the caller ID hadn't looked familiar, but the voice in the message bank was. Dirk recognized it immediately. It was his erstwhile buddy, Richard Soraces.

"Give me a call back ASAP if you're interested in a lucrative venture," the message said. "And it's right here in the US for a change."

Dirk had heard through the grapevine that Soraces was more or less a free agent now, still pulling an occasional assignment from the Agency but doing very well in the private sector. This one had to be for the latter since Soraces had specifically mentioned it being on U.S. soil. This navy transport plane that had picked him up from the aircraft carrier was way too noisy for him to return the call now, and that wouldn't serve his purpose anyway. Soraces wouldn't have called unless he had something already lined up, and the undercurrent of tension that Dirk had picked up in the voice tone of the recorded message, as slight as it was, spelled one thing: urgency.

Dirk had heard through the informal grapevine about a month ago that Soraces had put the word out that he was assembling a wet work team. The specifics were vague, only that Soraces need someone right away. In fact, Dirk seemed to recall receiving a message requesting that he call the man. With two assignments already lined up, one in the Middle East and this little one in Caracas, Dirk had ignored Soraces's previous query. Now, that same grapevine was reporting that a former agency associate, Werner Gunther, had been killed about three and a half weeks ago in some remote hole-in-the-wall place in Arizona.

Interesting coincidence, Dirk thought.

And he didn't believe in coincidences.

He and Gunther had worked together several times, and Dirk regarded the man as a respected colleague, but they weren't what you could call friends. It was best not to have any friends in this business. Friendship begat complications, like sentimentality, and Dirk prided himself on never being sentimental.

Gunther was a seasoned pro, so Dirk was curious about the circumstances of the man's demise, and if his death were connected to the little Stateside venture that Soraces had been pushing.

That undercurrent of urgency in the phone message flittered through Dirk's memory once again, despite the monotonous thrumming of the transport's twin engines.

The mass of men lead lives of quiet desperation, he thought, smiling as he recalled one of his favorite quotes from Thoreau.

Quiet desperation ... The smile broadened. This could work in his favor and up the price.

GARFIELD AND OLLIE'S CRAFT'S SHOP
SCOTTSDALE, ARIZONA

Wolf and McNamara stood off to the side and watched as Garfield Bellows carefully set the statue of the bandito on the large work desk in the back portion of the shop. The smiling plaster face seemed to stare back at Wolf in some kind of ethereal mockery. Anthropomorphism, his English professor would say—ascribing human characteristics to inanimate things. And that reminded him again about the final lit paper that he had to turn in. Garfield had been a college professor before.

Perhaps he can give me some suggestions, Wolf thought as he stared at the bandito. But first, let's see what kind of secrets you've been keeping.

"I tried to be as careful as I could, Steve," Garfield said. "But as you can see, the excavation did cause some stress cracks to form here. I reinforced them with Superglue."

Wolf saw the faint lines over the bandito's face.

Cicatrizes pequeñitas, he thought. Tiny scars.

Garfield slowly rotated the bandito around so that Wolf and Mac could see the gaping hole in the statue's backside. "Pursuant to your request, I used a tiny chisel and hammer to chip away this back portion here. Very carefully, I might add." He ran his index finger over the black vest. "I had to remove all of this area here, but luckily, I was able to keep the figurine pretty much intact. Stone, which is the type of plaster it's made of, is generally pretty strong and allows for cutting and removal, as long as it isn't too substantial, and you do it carefully."

"Sort of like excavating one of them old Egyptian tombs, or something, eh?" McNamara asked.

"Exactly," Garfield said. "But on a much smaller scale, of course."

"And a lot less valuable," McNamara said.

Garfield canted his head to the side. "I'm not so sure about that."

This piqued Wolf's interest even more. What did that mean?

"But," Garfield said, tapping his fingernail against the bandito's back. "I was lucky enough to have that x-ray I had taken before to guide me. I kept chipping away until it was large enough to remove what was inside without damaging it too much. What do you want me to do? I could whip up another batch of stone and pour it in making it almost as good as new if you want."

"It'd be a damn shame to just toss it," McNamara said.

Wolf said nothing.

"Well," Garfield said. "Like I told you, I could fill it back in. Only take about fifteen minutes to set." He tapped the statue with his knuckle. "It'd be almost as solid as it was before."

"That's good to know," Wolf said. "But what was inside?"

Garfield grinned and held up his index finger.

"That's where I got another 'Eureka moment.' Remember that story I told you before about Archimedes running through the streets naked?"

That had been when Garfield had been making a duplicate of the bandito. He'd noticed a weight difference between the original statue and the newly fashioned one which led him to investigate further. He'd discovered that the original bandito from Mexico contained some strange object buried inside the center portion. An x-ray had disclosed the basic size and shape, which appeared to be something about the size of half of a sliced cantaloupe.

"Like it was yesterday," Wolf said. "But ..."

Garfield sighed. "Please forgive an old, retired professor's addiction to vanity and a flair for the overly dramatic. I miss not being in front of the classroom."

Wolf could envision him in that role, prancing about and delaying the inevitable with a smile and a tease.

"I want you to know that after I saw what it was," Garfield said, "I had my suspicions but wanted to make sure before I contacted you."

"We appreciate that," McNamara said. "But will you get on with it? You're worse than a gal standing in front of the mirror before her first prom date."

Garfield nodded and went to the large safe in the corner of the room. Stooping in front of it, he began to spin the dial as he spoke.

"If you remember back to our misadventure in Iraq," he said. "In April of two thousand and three we invaded Iraq with the intention of toppling Saddam Hussein."

"Yeah," McNamara said. "It was one of the last *misadventures* I was a part of."

Garfield stopped and looked up. "No offense intended. I've always thought very highly of our military."

"None taken," McNamara said. "And don't let me stop you."

Going back to the dial, Garfield twisted it slightly.

"Well," he said. "When Saddam took power in nineteen seventy-nine, he assumed an air of protective reverence over the many antiquities from the region. He doubled his archeology budget and set up numerous museums in the major cities. Archeological sites were also declared as protected areas."

"Well, some dictators will do that," McNamara said. "Hitler was great for grabbing onto works of art, especially those that belonged to someone else."

Garfield laughed, gripped the metal handle of the safe, and twisted it but it didn't budge. He shook his head, adjusted his glasses, and got down on one knee before starting to rotate the dial again.

"This thing has such a sensitive setting," he said.

"You going to continue with the history lesson, professor?" Wolf said. He was feeling anxious about all this being so close to finding something that might provide an answer to this seemingly eternal conundrum.

"Yes," Garfield said. "Forgive me. When the war started, he assumed the National Museum of Iraq in Baghdad wouldn't be bombed, so he moved a lot of the country's antiquities there. What he didn't figure on was how quickly his army would fold in defeat."

"Hell," McNamara said. "It was as much of a cake walk as the first one back in ninety-one. Keeping the peace became the dangerous part." He glanced at Wolf. "A damn shame this country just don't know how to win a war anymore, ain't it?"

Wolf nodded, recalling his days of kicking down doors in house-to-house searches for insurgents, snipers, and IED's. And then, of course, his last little foray that had ended up with two dead Iraqi civilians and a court-martial. If only he could recall those eight or so minutes that had been erased from his memory ... Maybe then he'd be able to make total sense of this ongoing puzzle.

"Once the army fled Baghdad," Garfield continued, "the museum was looted. Priceless antiquities dating back thousands of years were taken." He stopped and pulled up on the metal handle and, this time, it went up with an accompanying thump. Grinning, Garfield got to his feet and swung the heavy, metal door open. Reaching inside, he removed an item bundled in newspaper and walked carefully over to his work table. After setting the bundle onto the center, he slowly began unwrapping it.

"This was what was in the center of your bandito, Steve," he said. "The newspaper's mine. I rewrapped it."

Wolf stared with interest down at the uncovered item on the desk. A dome of ornately fashioned stone about the size of a cleaved sixteen-inch softball lay on the crinkled newspaper. A baroque pattern decorated the exterior shell. Garfield picked it up with both hands, holding it with meticulous care and rotated it. The underside was flat and hollow, the inside showing a shiny gloss of startlingly white inlay—Mother of pearl, perhaps. Two figures of black onyx were pictured on the surface. They looked to be a man and a lion engaged in mortal combat.

"This was inside?" Wolf asked.

"I take it that it's one of them stolen antiquities you were gabbing about?" McNamara said.

"It is," Garfield said. "Or, more precisely, half of

one. The Lion Attacking the Nubian. It dates back to twenty-seventy B.C. and the king of Babylon."

Wolf kept staring down at the beautifully rendered figures, the milky texture of the mother of pearl.

This was over two thousand years old? This was what Accondras had said would make them all rich? This was what so many men had died for?

Then something else hit him like a whistling body blow to the liver.

"Half of one?" he said.

"Yes," Garfield said. "The other half is almost an exact duplicate, except that it features a female lion, that is, one without the mane, attacking a separate Nubian. It's considered almost of equal value as this piece, the Holy Grail to collectors of art from this period, which is a rather moot point since together or separate, they're considered quite priceless."

Priceless, thought Wolf. And paid for with the blood of so many victims, so many lives ruined.

"The FBI's stolen art treasures section has them both on their Most Wanted Art Crimes website," Garfield said. "And therein lies the problem we're facing. Possessing a stolen antiquity, especially one of this value, can bring down numerous charges both domestically and internationally."

"Wait a minute." Wolf held up his hand. "You said something just now ... 'Both of them.' Are you saying the other part is listed as stolen, too?"

"Yes," Garfield said. "I did some substantial checking trying to identify this one, but the other one is missing, too."

"And they both were stolen from the Iraqi National Museum in Baghdad?" Wolf asked.

"That's right," Garfield said. "There was a rumor they were circulating in the black market about four years ago."

Four years, Wolf thought.

He looked at Mac, who nodded and said, "I bet I know who has the other piece."

"And why so many have died," Wolf said. "All for a two thousand-year-old piece of stone."

At last, he thought. This is all starting to make sense.

CHAPTER FIVE

THE GRAND TETONS HOTEL
PHOENIX, ARIZONA

The suite was elegant and included a large dining room area as well as two other bedrooms. Soraces had set up the dining room as his Ops Center and had the hotel move a whiteboard, markers, a roll of scotch tape, and a package of blank paper into it. Right now, it only had a few entries on it: a list of the players, Wolf, McNamara, McNamara's daughter and grandson, and the Shadows. He'd add any others as they entered the picture. All the entries were on pieces of paper that had been taped to the board. On overseas ops he'd taken a liking to the whiteboard displays but always was leery about leaving residual writing on the surfaces, even after it had been erased. Thus, he made the markings on the paper and taped them to the board. It proved to be ideal. Not only did it leave no marks to be found on the board, but the papers could be gathered together and burned very quickly. He knew he didn't need that same level of secrecy on this op here in the States but old habits die hard. Soraces hadn't survived this long by being lax.

While he'd only booked regular rooms for the Perkins brothers, they were still sumptuous compared to the hole-in-the-wall places they had stayed in before when working for the G. They weren't about to complain about the inequity of their rooms compared to his, nor would Dirk, if he ever replied.

Speaking of the big man, Soraces thought, glancing at his watch.

It was nine-fifty.

Why hadn't he called back?

Of course, depending on where Dirk was, the time didn't mean anything.

Soraces had made a few phone calls, after Dirk had failed to call him back, and learned the big man was "on assignment." Knowing the Agency, that could be anywhere from Central America to the Middle East. He hoped it wasn't the latter. The time zone difference, not to mention the distance factor, would make it harder to set up the necessary boots on the ground here. But he wasn't in a hurry, not with that rich, fat clown down in Belize footing the bill and paying for everything. No, for a change, it was a pleasure to be going first class on all aspects of an operation.

He thought about the possibilities of making this one his career endgame. If he could get control of this artifact, he could probably name his own price. But then again, who besides that rich Humpty Dumpty would be willing to pay top dollar for a hunk of centuries-old rock decorated with some mother of pearl and onyx carving? No, let the rich prick have his prize.

Besides, with the little video he had featuring Von Dien and Fallotti, he had his own ace in the hole. Once he'd been paid and was a safe distance away from the hulking bodyguard, Soraces figured he'd arrange for a little snippet to come to their attention. That would foster the understanding that not only was he untouchable from here on out, but he was no longer in need of anything because with what they were going to pay him, he'd already have it all.

Von Dien had multiple estates here in the U.S., in Belize, and even was purported to own his own island somewhere in the Caribbean.

The Caribbean, Soraces thought. That wouldn't be a bad place for an ex-spook to retire. He could go the Ian Fleming route and buy his own Golden Eye and fill it full of fine booze and luscious brown ladies. Well, he'd throw some Europeans into the mix, too.

After all, variety was the spice of life.

The phone jarred him from his reverie and he momentarily chastised himself for letting his daydreams take him out of the moment. That was the sure-fire way to disaster.

Focus, he told himself as he looked at the screen and then smiled.

Dirk was calling back.

"Good to hear from you," he said as he pressed the button to open the connection. "I assume you got my message."

"I'm interested." It was Dirk's unmistakable voice, all right. A man of few words.

"But are you available?" Soraces asked.

"As long as the money's right."

Soraces laughed. "Oh, it is. First class, all the way."

"In that case, count me in."

"Where you at?"

"Base," Dirk replied.

Soraces knew this was code for Agency headquarters in Virginia.

"Good. Meet me in Phoenix. How soon can you get here?"

"I just have to make a drop off at Langley and do a quick debrief. I'll hop on the next commercial flight after that."

Soraces evaluated this new information. A debriefing on the last mission could take hours or even days and he didn't necessarily want to wait.

"Sounds complicated," he said. "Is it going to be involved?"

"Nah," Dirk said. "Be in and out."

This made Soraces feel more at ease. The sooner he had his personnel set in place, the faster the game could get underway. And, since money was no object ...

"I'll tell you what," Soraces said. "I'll set up a private jet for you and have it standing by at Reagan. I need you out here fast. I'll text you everything."

He heard Dirk emit a low whistle.

"I told you it was lucrative." Soraces laughed. "First class all the way, baby."

"I'll be there later today."

"The sooner the better," Soraces said but realized he was talking to dead air.

Excellent, he thought, and started scrolling for private jet services.

The phone rang with an incoming call.

The Shadows, he thought as he looked at the screen. Or Clyde's phone, more specifically.

He answered it immediately.

"They're leaving the shop," Clyde Perkins said. "Appears they've got something with them in a backpack."

The craft shop was where Soraces had assumed Wolf had taken the original bandito to get the duplicate made. Among other things, they specialized in ceramic figurines that people could buy to paint and display. So, Wolf might be bringing the bandito to get another duplicate made, which meant that he might be leaving the original there for the process. Or did he already have the original there? But moreover, where was the artifact? At this point, it was safe to assume that Wolf knew about the artifact. He'd hinted as much in their face-to-face meeting three weeks or so ago. He might have removed it from the original bandito and secreted it in another statue, or even a completely different hiding place.

Dammit, he thought. This was like trying to outguess the scam artist playing three-card-Monte.

Where the hell was the artifact?

"You want us to stay on them?" Perkins asked.

Soraces considered the options. At this point, he was still setting up pieces on his metaphorical chess-board. If Wolf did have the original bandito with him and it still contained the artifact, then he'd most likely be taking it to what he felt was a safe, secret location. He'd also be extra vigilant in looking for a tail. Plus, he had McNamara with him to do the driving. It was way too early in the game to take a chance on blowing their surveillance, but, with the Shadows on the scene, the possibility of that happening was slim to none. They were working in tandem, each with a different car, which they changed periodically. In any case, it was worth the risk to find out where Wolf was taking that backpack. There was still a question of what he was doing in that shop, but that would have to be addressed later. Each possibility, each move, like a chess game, would have to be carefully thought out and evaluated.

"Yeah," Soraces said. "Don't let them see you."

Perkins didn't reply. He didn't have to. Acknowledging the statement would be like dignifying an insult.

Soraces smiled. The game has begun, he thought as he scrolled on his phone.

It was time for his next preemptive move.

———

FIRST FEDERAL PLAZA BANK
PHOENIX, ARIZONA

After the bank employee ushered the two of them into the private viewing room, Wolf slid the backpack from his shoulders and set it on the narrow shelf-like table. The room was so small that he almost felt like he and Mac were trying to share one of those old-time phone booths. Mac placed the safety deposit box onto the chair seat and lifted the lid while Wolf removed the newspaper wrappings from the bandito and flipped it over to test the sturdiness of the patch job that Garfield had done. It felt solid. Wolf grabbed the towel that had been in the safety deposit box and began to wrap the bandito in the soft cloth. The cracked, smiling face seemed to stare back at him in mocking fashion.

No more secrets between us, *amigo*, Wolf thought. I know all of yours now.

He flipped the edge of the towel over the head and put the bundled statue inside the box and closed the lid.

"What I don't understand," McNamara said in a low whisper, "was why you had him put that Lion thing back in there. Wouldn't it be better to keep them separated? I mean, we could get another box."

"Too risky," Wolf said. He spoke in sotto voce too. "If we were to leave it exposed, we'd be acknowledging possession of the stolen artifact. Once Garfield finishes that other copy, we can play bait and switch again if we have to. This way, it gives me an ace the other side doesn't know I have. It gives both of us what you'd call plausible deniability."

"I've always hated them two words." McNamara said. "Reminds me too much of all those politicians with their double-talk."

"Nevertheless, we'll need it if the feds suddenly step in and confiscate everything. We can claim we were never aware of what was inside the original."

"Provided Garfield forgets what he saw."

"I'm pretty sure he will." Wolf recalled the old man's grin as he made the proposal and slipped five crisp hundred dollar bills from the Cummins moneybelt into Garfield's hand.

"Blessed are the forgetful: for they get the better even of their blunders," Garfield had said.

"Shakespeare?" Wolf asked.

"Nietzsche," Garfield said. "From his work, *Beyond Good and Evil.*"

The comment had reminded Wolf that he still had his English paper to complete. Not that it was a precedent at this point but it was something he needed to ask Garfield about.

"You ever read *All's Well That Ends Well*?" he asked.

"Of course. One of the Bard's lesser known efforts, but still an amusing venture. Based on one of Boccaccio's tales from *The Decameron*. Why do you ask?"

"I've got an English paper to do on it," Wolf said. "I was hoping you could tell me what to say so I'd sound smart."

Garfield clapped him on the shoulder. "Then by all means, read the play, write the paper, and I'll be glad to read it, my boy."

"I was hoping you could give me a little bit more help than that," Wolf said.

Garfield tilted his head to the side and pursed his lips. "All right, look for this quote. If she, my liege, can make me know this clearly, I'll love her dearly, ever, ever dearly."

"What the hell does that mean?" McNamara asked.

"Read the play and find out." Garfield smiled. "In the meantime, I'd better get to work on this task at hand."

They'd left him busily working on the duplicate bandito which he said would take him two days.

Wolf felt the vibration of his cell phone in his pocket. Ignoring the signal, he picked up the box and motioned for McNamara to open the door. The bank clerk was seated at a desk about twenty feet away and rose to her feet as they approached.

"All set, gentlemen?" she asked.

"Sure are," McNamara said.

He and Wolf replaced the box in the vault and the

clerk slammed the metal door and twisted both keys, locking it. She then gave Wolf back his key.

As they exited the bank, McNamara mentioned that Manny wanted to talk to them.

"About what?" Wolf asked.

McNamara shrugged. "Maybe he's got some work for us."

"Doubtful, the way the courts have been going during this thing. Everything's either remote or socially distanced and operating at a pace that would make a snail look like Usain Bolt."

"Let's go see what's what," McNamara said.

Wolf took out his phone, checked the screen, and saw that there was a voice mail listed. He pressed the button to check it.

"Mr. Wolf," a feminine voice said. "My name is Dolores Delgato and I work for the Mark Edwards Law Firm. We were appointed to review the cases of your former attorney, Rodney Shemp, after his unfortunate death. I've been reviewing your case and wanted to speak with you about it. Please call me back at your convenience."

She read off a phone number and said goodbye.

"Who was that?" McNamara asked. "Sounded like a female."

"It was. An attorney. Said she was reviewing Rod's old cases and wants to talk to me."

McNamara's brow furrowed. "Well, seeing as how we broke into his office last month and removed that file about the Mexico adventure, you think she's talking about the appeal?"

"We did leave that one there."

"And we got us some money to have her look into it, don't we?"

"We do," Wolf said, although the prospects had seemed dim before when Shemp had reviewed it, that was before Wolf had known the truth about the bandito and how his court-martial was all tied to that stolen artifact. Plus, somewhere out there was a video that just might be able to clear his name.

It was certainly worth looking into.

They got into McNamara's maroon Escalade and he pulled out of the bank parking lot.

Wolf hit the redial number and waited.

"Delores Delgato," a cool feminine voice said after three rings.

"Yes, this is Steve Wolf, returning your call."

"Oh, yes, Mr. Wolf." She had one of those voices that Wolf figured would drive most men crazy wondering if she looked as sexy as she sounded. He put her on speaker. "I'm glad you called back. I assume you got my message?"

"Right." As was his custom, he held back, waiting to sound out the other person.

"Well," she said. "I've been assigned to do follow-ups on several of Mr. Shemp's cases and would like to review yours with you. If you'd be interested in hiring me to look into it, that is."

Wolf considered this offer. Shemp had told him it was all but hopeless, but again that was before he found out about the video clearing him. And he did need another lawyer.

"Yes," he said. "I would be interested in that."

"Would you have any time this afternoon?"

Wolf looked at Mac, who shrugged.

Wolf was intrigued, if for no other reason than he wanted to see what the lady on the other end of the phone connection looked like. But he needed to sort things out in his own mind first, especially in view of what he'd found out this morning.

"I'm kind of busy at the moment," he said. "Tomorrow would be better."

"All right," she said. "Just let me check my calendar." After a long pause of silence, she came back with, "How's eleven o'clock sound?"

That would give him tonight to sort things out and figure out what to say, and what not to say. He agreed and she read off an address which sounded familiar.

"That's the same building as Rodney Shemp's office," he said.

"Yes, we aren't allowed to remove any files until the estate's settled. However, we are allowed to review them. If we agree, I'll order a new transcript and start my own review."

It sounded like more legal mumbo-jumbo to Wolf, but he agreed and said he'd meet her there tomorrow at eleven.

After Wolf terminated the call, McNamara emitted a low whistle.

"Man," Mac said. "I think I'll tag along with you, if you don't mind, just to see if Ms. Delgato looks as sexy as she sounds."

"She does have a sultry voice," Wolf agreed. "But I was thinking of checking to see how much that guy, Taylor, who represented us in Pima last month, might charge."

"Judging from what I had to pay him for just the little bit he did," McNamara said. "It'd probably be quite a bit. Of course, we do have money with what was in that money-belt and the funds in your bank account."

We do have money, Wolf thought, with "we" being the operative word. He'd already decided that whatever was left in the money-belt, minus the expenses of today, which Mac had insisted on paying, belonged to Mac. And as far as the hundred-grand in the bank, Wolf wanted to give that to him as well for Chad's college fund. But now the chance had arisen that he might be able to ultimately clear his name. Should that take precedence?

Wolf blew out a slow breath.

"What's the matter?" McNamara asked. "Things are looking up, ain't they?"

Good old Mac, Wolf thought. Always seeing the glass as half full. There was no way I ever want to let him down.

He figured it couldn't hurt to see what this lawyer with the sexy voice had to say before he made any decisions.

But if only I could somehow get my hands on that damn video that bastard, Soraces, had shown me, he thought. That would provide some traction, give a lawyer something to dig his, or her, teeth into.

He ruminated a moment more and then sighed.

Yeah ... If only.

CHAPTER SIX_

RONALD REAGAN INTERNATIONAL AIRPORT
ARLINGTON, VIRGINIA

Dirk got out of the black Ford Crown Vic and pulled his non-descript carry-on bag from the back seat. After thanking the driver, Dirk walked down toward the last exit. Since Soraccs had informed him that his transportation was standing by, he needed only to get through the TSA screening point and make his way to the private section of the airfield. As he approached the checkpoint, he noticed a man in a black polo shirt walking a big German Shepherd back and forth. The dog sniffed each person and their luggage before moving on. For a moment, Dirk wondered if the canine would recognize that he'd had the general's index finger in the front pocket section of the bag only an hour or so before.

Probably specifically trained to alert on firearms and explosives, he thought. I should be safe enough.

Regardless, he had nothing now in his bag or on his person that could be considered the least bit disconcerting.

Above suspicion, he thought with a smile. The only way for an Agency assassin to travel.

And he was right. The dog walked right past him, giving only a little jerk of its head as his snout came within inches of Dirk's bag.

After showing his identification and the boarding pass on his smartphone, Dirk was ushered through to the scanning line. The TSA screener's eyebrows knitted together above his mask as Dirk lowered his to display his face. He was used to people taking notice of him. At six-three and with the build of a heavyweight boxer, he was an imposing figure, to say the least.

But it was his eyes, he knew, one brown and one blue, that startled people the most.

The screener tried not to show his amazement.

Dirk merely stared back at him in silence and was waved through.

He hated having to go through the trouble of next removing his belt, watch, and shoes, silently cursing every radical Muslim on earth for creating this encumbrance. But he'd killed a good share of them to make up for it and their radicalism was, in his mind, just another guarantee of job security. He knew the G would never run out of enemies that they wanted terminated.

After placing his bag on the treadmill and stepping through the portal, he was ushered over to a special section and told to wait. Another agent came over and did a cursory pat down, explaining where he had to touch Dirk in the course of his search.

Dirk again said nothing but merely nodded. A few of the female TSA agents were kind of hot, and he almost requested that one of them do the touching.

However, he was in a hurry and trying to be cute with security at an airport was a sure-fire way to get flagged.

Once again, he said nothing.

But something else had attracted their attention: the hunk of wood in his carry-on. It was a foot-long piece of wood, a two-by-four, with five slits cut into the width of one end.

"Sir, what's this?" the TSA agent asked, holding it up.

In his haste Dirk had forgotten to remove it and chastised himself.

"It's nothing," he said. "I'm a martial arts instructor and I use it to toughen my hands." He held up his arm displaying the hardened ridge of callus along the heel of his big right hand.

A little levity might go a long way here, he thought.

"Want me demonstrate?" he asked with a smile.

The TSA agent shook his head and said that he was afraid he couldn't allow it to be taken past the checkpoint.

"Not a problem," Dirk said. "I apologize for bringing it, but I forgot it was in there."

After getting his bag back, he made his way to the private gate section.

Mistake number one, he thought. And the mission hasn't even started yet.

OFFICE OF EMMANUEL SUTTER
BAIL BONDSMAN
PHOENIX, ARIZONA

Although Wolf hadn't been in Manny's office for a few weeks, he silently noted that not much had changed except that the front window now had a solid-looking metal netting behind it. Between the netting and the glass, the orange and red neon sign advertising BAIL BONDSMAN was lighted. The small office smelled faintly of the familiar mustiness, but it seemed to have been tainted slightly by some sweet-smelling air freshener. The two big, gunmetal gray desks were still in place taking up most of the space, along with the three large filing cabinets lining the rear wall. The assortment of dilapidated leather chairs, strategically reinforced with layer upon layer of duct tape, were assembled in front of the desks. Manny glanced up as Wolf and McNamara entered and gave a curt shake, his shaggy, bob-style haircut jiggling with the movement. What was visible of his upper body was the size of a barrel, and the metallic portion of his padded leather chair emitted a pitiful squeal as he shifted his enormous bulk. His massive face looked strained and seemed to match the air-conditioning unit which hummed with an equally strained mechanical resonance, but somehow continued to produce a steady flow of cooling air. Manny's nephew, Freddie, whom Manny disparagingly referred to as "Sherman," turned in his chair and pushed up his thick glasses on his hooked nose as his mouth twisted into a thin line. Freddie's bushy crop of red hair looked like it hadn't seen a barber's touch in about a month.

"Hey, Mac," Manny said. "Thanks for coming by." His eyes shifted to Wolf. "Good to see you too, Steve."

Steve?

Wolf gave an acknowledging nod and sat in one of the chairs. McNamara took the one next to him. Manny's greeting had been out of character. He, usually led things off with some kind of off-color wisecrack and normally referred to Wolf as "Wolfman." But today he looked drawn and tired. His jowls sagged and the vigor seemed to have drained out of the man.

"What did you want to see us about?" McNamara asked, settling back into the chair. "You got some work for us?"

"Yes and no," Manny said, then rotated the chair around to face his nephew.

"Hey, Freddie," he said. "Why don't you run over to D and D and get us a dozen or so?" He shifted back toward Wolf and McNamara. "You guys want some donuts or something?"

Wolf shook his head. He was a bit surprised. Not only had Manny addressed his perennially harassed nephew by his proper surname, but he was actually acting rather polite. It was totally out of character for the obstreperous bail bondsman. Mac seemed equally stunned.

"No thanks," McNamara said. "I haven't eaten a donut in fifteen years and that was only one bite to please a lady."

Leveraging his sausage-sized fingers into his pants

pocket, Manny wiggled them around and came out with some currency. He handed it to Freddie.

"Get us some chicken fingers instead," Manny said. "And a couple of soft drinks for our guests here. What kind you want?"

Guests?

Wolf and McNamara exchanged glances. This was getting stranger by the minute.

"Anything's fine," Wolf said. "But you needn't go to any bother."

"Right," McNamara said. "We gotta drive over to Mesa pretty soon anyway."

"Get us three Cokes, then," Manny said. "Make mine diet, of course, and whatever you want for yourself, along with those chicken fingers."

Freddie nodded, his mouth still pulled into a tight line. He started walking toward the door.

"And don't forget your mask," Manny said.

Freddie continued walking and went out without saying another word.

Wolf and McNamara exchanged glances once again. It was like being in one of those old *Twilight Zone* episodes that ran on late-night TV.

Manny placed his forearms on the desk, atop his desk. Wolf was suddenly aware that it looked almost orderly. It usually was awash with paper.

"So how you guys been doing?" Manny asked.

McNamara's face wrinkled with a frown.

"What the hell's going on?" he said. "You been acting like a regular human being since we got here."

"Aw, come on," Manny said.

"I'm serious," McNamara shot back. "You ain't called your nephew Sherman one time, you offered to buy us sodas, and now you're inquiring as to our welfare. What's next? You gonna offer to spit-shine my old jump boots for me?"

The corner of Manny's mouth tugged downward.

"The place even *smells* different," McNamara added. "So, what the hell's going on?"

"Mac," Manny said. "You wound me. We're friends, ain't we? Can't I just ask how you're doing, for Christ's sake?"

"We're still kicking," McNamara said. "Now you better start being straight with us, or we'll get our asses up and out that front door."

Manny closed his eyes and blew out a heavy breath. Wolf couldn't help but notice that his coloring seemed different than usual. He looked paler.

"All right, all right," he said. "I got a lot on my mind, okay?" He took in another deep breath. "What with this virus bullshit causing a major slowdown in all the courts, business has been at an all-time low. It's continuance after continuance with the damn judges are giving out fucking recognizance bonds, and all that kind of shit. I'll be lucky to stay in business once all this is over with, not to mention those asshole politicians talking about doing away with cash bonds nationwide."

"Yeah," McNamara said. "We been lamenting the same thing. But don't try to tell me that's all of it."

The big man looked down, blew out another long breath, and then locked eyes with them.

"It's my niece, Gloria," he said. "She's ... kinda been messing up lately. Fallen in with some bad company."

"Gloria," McNamara said. "That Freddie's sister?"

"Yeah. My sister's kid. She's seventeen and thinks she's got all the answers. Knows everything." He shook his head. "I remember when she was just a little girl, cute as a shiny nickel. Wish she coulda stayed that way."

"What you mean, bad company?" McNamara asked.

Manny compressed his lips and sighed, then opened one of his desk drawers and removed a framed photograph. He held it across the desk toward them.

McNamara reached out and took it, holding it so Wolf could see it as well. It showed a young, pretty girl dressed in a greenish evening gown standing next to an equally young boy in a rented tuxedo. Both of them were smiling and the girl held a corsage.

"That's her prom picture from last spring," Manny said. "She was a junior in high school with her whole life ahead of her."

"And now?" Wolf asked.

"That clown in the picture's her steady boyfriend, Tim Wagner." Manny frowned. "He was a senior, one year older than her."

"He knock her up or something?" McNamara asked.

"Nah, her doctor suggested that she go on the pill to supposedly regulate her menstrual cycle, much to her parents' chagrin." His big shoulders rose and fell in a shrug. "Me, I figured it wasn't such a bad thing, knowing how precocious kids are these days."

The understanding uncle, Wolf thought, thinking back to the painful last years of his own high school experience. He'd never made it to the senior prom and was learning to salute and shoot at Fort Polk, Louisiana shortly after his graduation.

"Anyway," Manny continued. "This virus shut-down and the rest of this shit, kind of ruined her. Instead of going to finish out her senior year, they started doing some kind of virtual class horseshit, and she's pretty much dropped out. And to make matters worse, that little prick, Timmy, has turned into a real piece of shit. His parents bought him a motorcycle, and now him and his shitbird friends have formed a gang."

"Which gang is that?" McNamara asked.

"They call themselves the LO's—the Lost Ones." Manny snorted in obvious disgust. "And they don't even drive Harleys, for Christ's sake. Timmy's got a fucking Honda."

"Not too bikeresque," McNamara said. "It's too bad about her dropping out of school, but these would-be bikers don't sound too serious."

"Serious enough," Manny said. "Last weekend Glory, that's what we call her, came home with a couple of fucking tattoos. A tramp-stamp and another on her forearm. Plus, she's wearing some kind of bracelet that she says designates her as a slave. And she's still a fucking minor."

McNamara visibly winced, apparently sympathizing with the plight of the girl's caring relatives.

"Did her parents make out a police report?" Wolf asked. "Tattooing the body of a minor's an offense without the permission of the parents."

"Yeah, they did," Manny said. "She's run away twice already and is supposedly under some social working mandate, which ain't worth shit. My sister and her husband are at wits end. Even poor Sherman's been down about it. You seen how mopey he looked, right?"

Wolf noted Manny's return to the pejorative nickname for his nephew and wondered if he'd reverted back to it by default.

McNamara handed the picture back across the desk and clucked sympathetically. "Sorry to hear all this. It ain't easy to raise a kid nowadays, especially a daughter. I can sympathize with you."

"So you'll help?" Manny asked as he accepted the framed photo.

"Help?" McNamara said. "What can we do? This sounds more like something her parents and the social worker need to address."

Manny waggled his head nervously. "No, you don't understand. That little asshole, Timmy's trying to hook up with a gang of real bikers. The Satan's Spawn. Those guys don't play."

Wolf had heard about the group. While they weren't on par with the Hell's Angels or the Outlaws, they were loosely affiliated with one or the other of them. Through the wire mesh and filthy glass, Wolf caught sight of Freddie pulling up in Manny's van.

"I can understand your concern," McNamara said. "But like I told you, we ain't social workers."

"Or cops," Wolf said. He wondered if Yolanda would be handling situations like this when she got on the force.

Time will tell, he thought with a twinge of regret. But I'll probably never see her again to find out.

"No," Manny said. "But you're a couple of tough hombres that can run those Lost Ones fuckers off if they come by, ain't you?"

"Run them off?" McNamara frowned. "Just what do you mean by that?"

Manny cocked his head to the side and held both hands outward, palms up.

"All it would take would be for the Wolfman here to kick the shit out of Timmy and his wanna-be biker buddies."

"And get me arrested, too," Wolf said. "I'm not some kind of hired thug."

"I know that," Manny said quickly. His tongue flicked out and swept over his lips. "Look, all I'm asking is you keep a little watch on their house for a couple days. Like maybe tonight and tomorrow night, okay? My sister's making arrangements to send Glory to live with our other sister in Idaho for a while. If Timmy and his friends come by, just run 'em off. Okay?"

"Not okay," McNamara said. "We could be getting ourselves in a real trick-bag doing that."

"Believe me, a show of force is all you'll need." Manny's voice sounded almost like a whine. "These guys are punks. One look at two big guys like you two, and they'll melt into the asphalt."

Both Wolf and McNamara sat in silence. Wolf was thinking it would be best not to get involved, but he knew the situation with the wayward daughter might have affected Mac more deeply given the guilt he felt about not having been there for Kasey's formative years.

"Look," Manny said. "I'm not asking you guys to do it for nothing. I'll pay you if you want. Make it worth your while. Just a couple-two nights. Till she gets outta here. Whaddaya say?"

Freddie had entered the office and was standing there holding a paper bag and a cardboard tray with four large plastic glasses with straws sticking out of the lids. The odor of fast-food fried chicken and French fries filled the air.

"Nights?" McNamara said. "What about during the day?"

"These little fuckers are like vampires. They don't come out till it gets dark. Plus, my sister and her husband are off work and home. I ain't worried until they go to sleep."

"They gonna help us, Uncle Manny?" Freddie said, standing there with a hopeful expression on his face.

Manny raised an eyebrow and stared at Wolf and Mac.

"I don't know," he said. "Are ya?"

Wolf and McNamara looked at each other once again and a silent acknowledgment seemed to pass between them.

Mac's never been the kind of man to turn down a friend's request for help, Wolf thought. Even in a no-win case like this.

"Well," McNamara said slowly. "I guess we could kind of hang around there and keep an eye on things."

Manny and Freddie both grinned and Manny snapped his fingers at the carrier with the soft drinks.

"Great," he said. "Thanks. You guys are the best. I owe you."

"Always willing to help a friend in need," McNamara said. "Or a young girl in distress."

Even if she doesn't want to be helped, Wolf silently reflected.

While he was sympathetic, his doubts about their efficacy were growing.

"Let's drink to it," Manny said, setting the container

with the soft drinks on his desk and then reaching down and coming up with a bottle.

Wolf was wondering if someone had said that to Don Quixote and Sancho Panza before they went after the windmills to defend the honor of Dulcinea.

———

THE GRAND TETONS HOTEL
PHOENIX, ARIZONA

Soraces duct taped the solid square of Styrofoam from the box that had contained the new laptop onto the big whiteboard and then stepped back across the expansive dining room area of his suite. He estimated the distance to be about twenty feet or so.

Good enough, he thought, removed the ninja pen from his pocket, pulled it apart, and hurled it with a backhanded motion toward the Styrofoam.

The blade sunk into the soft surface with a slick sounding thump.

But it was off to one side instead of dead center.

Not bad for first practice throw, he told himself as he strode over to retrieve it. The first of many.

Walking back to his original position, the pen-knife held vertically against the fleshy part of his palm, he rotated the blade downward into his fingers as he whirled suddenly and threw it. This one was a more traditional throw, taking the time to cock his arm back as he pivoted.

The blade had hit the center of the target.

Better, he thought. But still not perfect. Too much time on the positioning.

Soraces repeated the throwing for a solid twenty minutes, varying his stance and throwing techniques, but each time piercing the material with an intentional exactness until the Styrofoam was almost completely destroyed. Going to the whiteboard he pulled the long tapered steel from the mutilated whiteness and dropped the ruined packing material into the waste can next to the desk.

As he slipped the blade into the recesses of the metal sheath and held the contained weapon in his left hand, his burner phone rang.

It was one of the Shadows.

"They left the bail bondsman's office, went through the drive-through at McDonald's, and are now heading east on the seventeen toward the ten," Charles Perkins said.

His inclusion of the definite article in front of the Interstate numerical designation reminded Soraces that the two of them were California boys ... *The ten* ... They talked like that out there. But the LA lifestyle had also allowed them to develop chameleon-like abilities to bend into whatever culture they were dropped into. The Shadows were Anglos but with dark hair and brown eyes. The deep California tans allowed them to pass for Latinos or even Arabs when the need arose. They had the noses for it. And they were multilingual as well; the Agency had seen to that. They were, as Shakespeare had put it, men of many humors.

"Looks like they're heading south on the ten now," Perkins said.

"All right. Continue surveillance. At a distance. And keep me posted."

There was no reply, but Soraces had no doubt this Shadow was thinking, *Don't tell me how to do my job*.

I wouldn't dream of it, he thought to himself, as if replying, and smiled.

"Very good," Soraces said, tossing in what he figured was just enough adequate praise to keep Charles Perkins mollified. In many ways the twins were like schoolboys, always needing positive reinforcement.

It must have worked because Perkins's voice sounded lighter when he asked, "Dirk get there yet?"

"No," Soraces said. "But he texted me. He's on the way."

"Let me know when he gets there. That son of a bitch still owes me twenty bucks from the last time we worked together."

Soraces laughed and said he would, then terminated the call.

The mention of the fast-food drive-through tweaked his stomach. It was getting close to lunch and he might as well order himself some room service.

And maybe later, Soraces thought, when Dirk gets here and the Shadows return for the day, I'll order us all some entertainment for the evening. Girls for him and Dirk. The Gemini twins preferred boys. Soraces wondered about that kind of availability in this city, or if any of the hookers were even working with all these god damn COVID restrictions.

The world's oldest profession stymied by a virus.

At least it wasn't impinging upon the world's second oldest—spying.

In one smooth motion he whipped the blade from

the metal sheath, and then whirled to throw it with a looping motion.

A millisecond later the thumping sound of metal cleaving wood reverberated back to him signifying a nice, solid hit. The blade was wedged into the narrow edge of the open bedroom door about three inches below the top hinge.

Virtually the exact equivalent of an eye-level hit.

Practice makes perfect, he thought.

———

INTERSTATE 10
JUST OUTSIDE OF MESA, ARIZONA

The navigation screen in the Escalade's dashboard indicated which exit for them to take. They'd passed completely through the Mesa city limits and the surrounding built-up area and were proceeding to the more remote outskirts. Wolf, who was driving since Mac had downed both his and Wolf's drinks at Manny's, noticed the black Dodge Charger behind them was still there.

He slowed appreciably to see if it would pass.

The Charger changed lanes and zoomed past them. The windows were heavily tinted, and he noticed it had California plates.

"Hey, Mac," he said. "Write down this plate."

McNamara, who had been talking on the phone to his buddy, Buck, turned his head and said, "What plate?"

"On that Charger," Wolf said. "The one that just passed us."

McNamara told Buck they'd see him shortly and hung up. He reached into the inside pocket of his modified BDU vest and pulled out a pad of paper and a pen.

"Any particular reason?" McNamara asked.

"It's been on our ass since we left Phoenix, is all."

McNamara shrugged and peered at the diminishing vehicle ahead of them.

"You're gonna have to get closer," he said. "Unless you remember it."

The Charger was a good distance ahead of them now and Wolf was no longer sure of the numbers and letters. He pressed down on the accelerator but the Charger continued to out-distance them. The automated voice abruptly told them to take the next exit and then turn right.

"Aw, hell," Wolf said. "Never mind now."

"Too bad I didn't think to bring my ditty bag," McNamara said. "Has my binoculars in it."

Wolf slowed down as the exit became visible. "Probably nothing anyway."

"You think it was somebody tailing us?" McNamara asked. "I was so busy gabbing with Buck that I wasn't even watching."

Wolf put on his turn signal and veered toward the exit ramp.

"Hard to say," he said. "It might just be a coincidence. Maybe I'm being too suspicious."

"Like hell. With all we been through the past couple of months, we can't afford to be anything but suspicious." He put the paper and pen back in his pocket. "Buck's anxious for us to get there. Says the facility's still under construction but it's almost completed."

Wolf said nothing, still mentally trying to evaluate the Charger's lengthy presence.

But it was no longer in sight.

"So, what else is bugging you?" McNamara asked. "You didn't look too happy when I volunteered us for that babysitting detail."

"That's an appropriate metaphor."

McNamara clucked his tongue. "Man, those English classes are doing you a world of good, using two dollars words like that. Maybe you should consider writing a book."

"Maybe," Wolf said. "I could call it babysitting wayward teenage girls for dummies."

McNamara barked out a harsh laugh. "Yeah, yeah, I know, but I figured it would pay dividends down the line, depending on how this bounty hunting business plays out after the election. And who knows, maybe seeing us two white knights out there will put the little girl on the road to the straight and narrow."

"I wouldn't count on that. Plus, I have a play to read and that English paper I have to write."

"Hell, read it out loud to me. And take your laptop with you. I'll be standing guard, and if the bunch of deplorables show up, I'll let you know."

Wolf grinned. "Deplorables?"

"Hey, I told you, you ain't the only one who's read a couple of books."

The computerized voice told them their destination was "ahead on the right."

Wolf slowed down and saw an asphalt road

winding away from the highway and into a large, hilly area. A huge, metallic sign was fastened to two vertical cement pillars by the junction. The block-shaped, black shadowed letters stood out against a tan background: *BEST IN THE WEST—TACTICAL TRAINING INSTITUTE*

The last three words were encased within the drawing of a Spartan helmet.

Clever advertising gimmick, Wolf thought as he steered down the serpentine roadway that wound through the series of little hills in a landscape dry and devoid of trees. Only the indomitable mesquite and a few cactuses seemed to have thrived. After about a quarter of a mile the road turned left and widened into two lanes with an empty gate shack in the middle. Another sign, a duplicate of the one by the highway, was posted in front of the gate shack. Just beyond it a twelve-foot cyclone fence topped by three strands of barbed wire extended in both directions for an interminable distance. Two large gates, one on each side of the roadway, stood open. About a hundred yards away, a cluster of other buildings was visible. There were five in total, with two being fairly large and the others a bit smaller. What looked to be an obstacle course ran along the fence-line. All of the buildings appeared to be prefab, except one of the larger ones, which was cinderblock and still under construction. A cement mixing machine buzzed alongside numerous stacks of bricks on wooden pallets as men worked on three scaffolds amongst the buzzing of saws and the pounding of hammers. The asphalt road wound around the structures and Wolf saw a series of man-made berms forming several consecutive rows of gun ranges, each with a series of flag poles. One of them had a half dozen old cars parked at spaced distances between two berms. Another had a square one-story structure situated in the center of what appeared to be another pistol range. The austerity of the set up almost reminded him of a few of the base camps he'd served at in Afghanistan and Iraq.

He pulled up in front of one of the smaller buildings with an OFFICE sign posted by the door. A third BEST IN THE WEST sign was set up next to the three steps that led to the office. Two metal picnic tables and a dozen or so chairs sat along the front of the building.

"Not a bad set up," McNamara said.

Wolf pulled up next to a tan-colored GMC and three other vehicles. The GMC had two red and yellow bumpers stickers affixed on either side of the license plate. One was the Marine Corps emblem and the other simply said, *Semper Fi.*

As they were getting out of the car, the door to the office burst open and a medium-sized, wiry guy with a well-trimmed beard descended the steps. As McNamara approached the two embraced and slapped each other's backs.

"Buck," McNamara said. "You old son of a gun, how the hell you been?"

"Who you calling old?" Buck said, his grin widening.

Wolf stood by and sized the man up. He looked to be Mac's junior by a dozen or so years and appeared to be in good shape. McNamara stepped back and introduced Wolf.

"Glad to meet you," Buck said, offering his hand.

"Same here," Wolf said as the two men shook.

"Let me introduce you to my partners," Buck said just as a trio of men exited the office building. One was a black guy who looked to be the size of a pro football linebacker.

"Joe Barnes, Force Recon," Buck said as Barnes and Wolf shook hands. The man's massive hand was like a catcher's mitt. He appeared to be around the same age as Buck.

Next was Ron Corbin, a middle-aged white guy, whom Buck said was the best damn helicopter pilot in the U.S. Army.

"Too bad he didn't have sense enough to join the Corps instead," said the third guy, Pete Thornton, a slender, waspish man who moved with a slight awkwardness of gait. Wolf saw that the man's left pant-leg ballooned over a hook-shaped titanium prosthesis.

"We all met in Bethesda," Buck said. "Me and Joe were getting some tightening-up as we got set to retire, and Ron's got so many replacement parts in him that he'll set off a metal detector at twenty-five feet." He paused and winked. "And Pete here was the best damn marine in my squad till he had the misfortune of getting hit by an IED."

The memory of Wolf's own encounter with one of those came rushing back to him and his lips tightened as he thought of Martinez and Thompson. Thompson had lost a leg and Martinez had been killed. The remembrance of their bloody bodies in the ruined Humvee had been indelibly stamped in Wolf's mind. It was something he wished he could forget like those missing eight minutes in Iraq that still eluded him. But he was closer now to remembering or at least to figuring out what had actually happened. It was a matter of arranging all the pieces and connecting the dots.

"Mac says you spent some time in the Rangers," Pete said. "Not quite Force Recon, but a good outfit."

Wolf forced a smile. The inter-service rivalry was nothing new to him.

"Same side, different team," he said, wondering if he should also tell them that he'd been busted down, given a DD, and served time in Leavenworth.

"Well," McNamara said, jumping in and rapping Ron on the chest. "At least you three jarheads had sense enough to invite an army man here to join you and put some brains in the outfit."

This was punctuated by laughter all around and Buck told the two of them to pile into his GMC and he'd give them the tour.

"Just let me grab three beers from the cooler," he said.

"None for me," Wolf said. He'd pretty much given up drinking altogether, especially during his training regimens.

Buck's eyebrows rose. "A Ranger that don't drink? Now that's a rarity."

"He's also a professional fighter," McNamara said. "Mixed martial arts. USA Light-Heavyweight Champion, no less."

"No shit?" Buck nodded his head appreciably. "Maybe you can do some self-defense teaching here, once we get things rolling."

Wolf, slightly embarrassed by Mac's pronouncement, just nodded and said he'd be glad to.

The three of them got into the GMC as Buck's partners went back inside the building.

"Besides the office and the two classroom buildings," Buck said, starting the vehicle. "I've got a pretty good gym in that one over there." He pointed to the large cinderblock structure. "You'll feel right at home, Steve. I've got a bunch of punching bags, some free-weights and machines, and a couple of basketball hoops. And we got a firing house with blacked out windows on one range that we can use for night-vision live-fire training."

He twisted the key in the ignition and the truck came to life.

"That one over there's gonna be a hotel, if and when I can get the license for it," he said, indicating the building under construction. "That way I can eventually offer extended classes where people can stay right here and get tortured the way they did it in Boot Camp and Basic Training. You know, getting them up in the middle of the night to do push-ups and run the track."

McNamara laughed. "Why the hell would somebody want to pay to stay and go through that kind of abuse?"

"You'd be surprised what some of these jokers will do," Buck said. "I'm thinking of offering like an Outward Bound type of confidence course, too. Once we can offer lodging, we'll be raking it in, and we won't lose out to any of the hotels in Mesa."

Wolf had his doubts about prospects of that but again he kept silent.

Let Buck have his fantasy, he thought. He didn't see how they were going to turn a profit.

"You mentioned something about a class coming up," McNamara said.

"Right. We're trying to get this four-day urban combat and dignitary protection class set up for the end of the week," Buck said. "Thursday, Friday, Saturday, and graduation on Sunday. We'll toss in a little celebration party, too."

"Trying?" McNamara asked. "It ain't set up yet?"

Buck shook his head. "So far we got eleven men registered. Well, ten men and a female who wants to be GI Jane. We need an even dozen to make it fiscally sound."

"Well, Steve and me will be glad to sign up," McNamara said. "That'll put you over the top."

Buck shook his head again. "Nah, it won't."

"Why not?" McNamara said. "With us two that'll give you a baker's dozen?"

"'Cause I'm already counting you two as part of the eleven." Buck grinned. "We take Visa, Master Card, or cash, by the way."

McNamara snorted a laugh. "Ain't that just like a jarhead?" He turned to Wolf. "I ever tell you how we met?"

Wolf shook his head.

"It was in Somalia," McNamara said. "A couple of weeks after the Battle of Mogadishu."

"We got dropped into some shit neighborhood," Buck said. "All six foot piles of rotting garbage, junk all over the streets, and tin can houses. Supposed to evac some U.N. aid workers that this one war lord was supposedly threatening. Well, we found 'em and were trying to load them all into their vehicles right before morning prayers. Then, all of a sudden these damn bells start going off signaling *fajr*, the Muslim morning prayer, and then a bunch of fuckers popped out of the fucking woodwork and started shooting. They'd obviously knew we were coming and sprung a trap. We got pinned down and were ushering all the aid workers back into this building that offered about as much cover as a silk nightgown. Rounds were going right through the damn walls. I was in the process of radioing for help when all at once I hear something and a bunch of voices on the radio start barking like dogs and asking, 'Where are you at?' Shit, it was music to this marine's ears." He paused, glanced at McNamara, and grinned widely. "I gave our location and popped some smoke right in front of our building. A couple of seconds later a bunch of explosions start going off, right and left. Bodies of the bad guys are flying around in the street right in front of us. Hell, I thought it was a fucking air strike at first and then, when my hearing come back, I heard the sound of the choppers, army choppers, coming in still barking like dogs. Then those fucking skinnies started scattering like cockroaches when the lights come on. We picked off a bunch of them and then this one chopper starts hovering over us. This big son of a bitch wearing a green beret and five of his buddies come swooping down on a repelling lines, land, shoot a couple more Somali stragglers that us and the Blackhawks didn't get, and then comes waltzing over to us and says, 'I heard you might need a ride.'"

Buck laughed out loud and shifted the vehicle into gear. McNamara was chuckling too.

"I thought it was one of my better lines," he said. "But what I shoulda said was, U.S. Army to the rescue."

"Like he said," Buck continued. "This was right

after those sons of bitches were dragging the bodies of the GI's they killed in the street." He paused, his mouth twisting into a frown as he backed out of the parking space. "The State Department squelched it, so nobody ever heard about it. Unless you were there, it never happened."

"Typical," Wolf said. He had his own experiences with governmental suppression of the facts. Downplay everything, classify any reports, and pretty soon it was gone without a trace.

"Plausible deniability," McNamara said, slapping Wolf on the shoulder. "Didn't I tell you I don't like them words?"

Neither do I, Wolf thought.

————

THE GRAND TETONS HOTEL
PHOENIX, ARIZONA

"The Best in the West Tactical Training Institute?" Soraces said. He put the phone on speaker and started a computer search for that name.

"Right," Clyde Perkins said. "I had to pass them up on the freeway because I didn't want to get made. When I saw them exiting, I pulled over and tracked them with my range-finder. They've been in there for the better part of an hour now. Looks like one of the owners is showing them around the place."

"Where's your brother?"

"Picking up our food. We flipped for it and I got stuck."

Soraces found the site for Best in the West Tactical Training Institute and clicked on it. A web page appeared showing four men, three white and one black, standing next to a big sign bearing the Best in the West name. Each was holding a rifle, AR-15's from the looks of them. They all had holstered side-arms, too, and the site listed available rifle and pistol ranges as well as training in all sorts of tactics. One of the men displayed was missing a foot and had a metal prosthesis.

Must be a disabled veteran, Soraces thought, and continued scanning.

Another section listed them as instructors, along with their bios:

Howard "Buck" Mason, USMC retired

Joe Barnes, USMC retired

Ron Corbin, US Army retired

Pete Thornton, USMC veteran

All were ex-military with purported combat experience in special operations. And Wolf's partner, McNamara, was a former Green Beret. It fit that he might have crossed paths with some of this Best in the West crew.

Another highlighted section advertised upcoming training classes. Soraces clicked on that link and found numerous listings for classes in urban combat, desert warfare, dignitary protection, and war games. *Learn from the best*, the site said. *Experienced combat instructors offer classroom instruction in tactics and principles of warfare and will take you through all the steps of actual field experience. Numerous firing ranges also available for rental.*

He checked the dates and saw that one of them,

Urban Combat Techniques, was scheduled for this week.

Interesting, he thought. I wonder if Wolf and Company are connected to it somehow? Helping to teach it, maybe? But they weren't listed as instructors on the website.

"How near are you to them?" Soraces asked.

"I'm up on the highway about two hundred yards away. There's a lot of open space and I didn't want to get too close."

"Can you see what Wolf's doing?"

"As far as I could tell, some guy's giving them the tour, showing them around. They got a bunch of firing ranges in the place."

Soraces continued to mull over the possibilities. From Clyde's description, it sounded like a sales pitch.

"Continue a loose surveillance," he said.

"Okay," Perkins said. "But I want to turn this car in and get another one. I'm operating on the assumption that they might have noticed this one."

"Fine. Do it later. Once they return. By that time we should have Dirk here to help you two."

After a few seconds of silence, Perkins said, "We don't need any help, especially from him."

Soraces took note of the tone, and wondered, Do I detect a hint of animosity?

His brother, Charles, had joked about Dirk coming aboard. The twins had distinctive likes and dislikes regarding their working partners.

"Whatever," Soraces said, "Just stay on the job and report back." With that, he terminated the call and then went back to the computer screen and the website display. What did it mean that Wolf and McNamara were there? After a few more moments of speculation, he picked up his burner phone and dialed the number listed on the website. After a few moments, a man answered spouting off the company's name. His voice sounded African American. Probably that Barnes fellow.

"Yes," Soraces said. "I saw your ad for the urban combat class later this week. Is it still open?"

"It is," Barnes said. "You interested in signing up?"

His tone sounded eager. Too eager.

"Perhaps," Soraces said. "What type of class is it? Can you tell me a little more about it?"

"It's a combination of lecture, hands on training, and lots of shooting. We cover all the tactical principles involved and then allow the students to put everything into practice."

"Are the instructors experienced?"

"We are, sir. Very."

"I saw three instructors listed on your website," Soraces said. "Are there any others?"

"Not at this time, but as I said, we've all got extensive experience and professional credentials."

"You said shooting. Are personal weapons required?"

"We can provide some," Barnes said. "Or you can bring your own."

Soraces hesitated for several seconds, then said, "How many people are in the class?"

"At this point, we're looking at eleven," Barnes said. "We just signed up two more students today, in fact."

And I bet I know who they are, Soraces thought with a smile.

He had all the information he'd called for, so after a

few more minutes of listening to the hard sell, Soraces said he'd think it over and hung up.

Why would Wolf and McNamara, who each had a vast amount of combat experience both overseas and ironically here in Phoenix, be signing up for some additional instruction when they very well had probably forgotten more than those three yoyos had ever learned? He could just have the Shadows maintain a long-range surveillance of them, but then another idea came to him just as the phone rang in his room. He got up from the table and answered it.

"There's a Mr. Dirk checking in here now, sir," the hotel clerk said. "You left word to notify you when he arrived."

Dirk, he thought. Excellent.

"Tell him to come to my room when he's done checking in, please," Soraces said.

He hung up the phone and glanced at his watch. Dirk had made amazingly good time, but then again, a private jet cut out a lot of the waiting.

After about ten minutes there was a knock at the door and Soraces went and opened it. Dirk's hulking frame was framed in the doorway, his off-color, mismatched eyes staring down at Soraces.

"How was your flight?" Soraces asked, stepping aside to allow the bigger man inside.

Dirk shrugged, said nothing. He walked into the suite, did a quick survey, noticing the whiteboard set-up, and then plucked an apple out of the fruit basket on the credenza.

"Nice accommodations," he said, taking a bite.

"Just like I told you," Soraces said. "First class all the way. But don't get too used to them."

Dirk raised an eyebrow.

Soraces laughed.

"Don't worry," he said. "It's not like you'll be going out in the field or anything. But I have got a little side trip planned for you."

"Oh? To where?"

"Mesa," Soraces said. "You'll be going back to school."

CHAPTER SEVEN

OUTSIDE THE RYLAND RESIDENCE
PHOENIX, ARIZONA

Wolf was struggling to get through the play, as he fought off the incremental fatigue. He and McNamara sat in the Escalade outside of the Rylands' house. The residence was what Wolf called typical Arizona: a one-story tan stucco house with those half-circle green tiles on the roof, sporadic patches of struggling crabgrass in front, next to an asphalt driveway, and an attached garage. All was dark, and had been since about eleven o'clock. They'd arrived at twenty-hundred and set up on the opposite side of the street and about fifty or so feet away. There were a smattering of cars parked on this side along the curb and a few more in the driveways of the neighboring houses. So far, nobody had apparently noticed two white guys sitting in a maroon Escalade, and as the evening wore on, they seemed to be accepted as part of the scenery, except for their occasional ventures down the street to the twenty-four-hour donut shop. It had ice cream, too, and Mac had indulged in a banana split. Wolf had declined, preferring only a cup of black coffee.

McNamara was now snoring in the passenger seat next to him, and Wolf figured it was the ice cream working its mesmerizing magic. Mac allowed Wolf to take the driver's position so he could rest the book on the wheel. Wolf had on a headband with a bright light centered on his forehead and he now switched it off and allowed his eyes to re-accustom themselves to the darkness only broken by the spectral lighting from the overhead streetlight. The powerful LED beam lit up the pages well enough, but the lack of sleep combined with the boredom and the tedium of reading were taking their toll. Both he and McNamara had elected to take naps when they got back from Buck's but, in Wolf's case, it had been an exercise in frustration. Sleep wouldn't come and McNamara admitted the same as they sat down to eat dinner together.

One thing that Wolf had noticed was that Kasey had seemed exceptionally quiet during the meal. Although Chad continually asked them questions about what they were going to do that night that had necessitated the afternoon naps, Kasey had barely said anything beyond the perfunctory.

Wolf wondered what was bothering her and hoped she was all right. She'd been through a lot in recent months with the death of her fiancé and Chad's horrendous parental abduction. Wolf had also begun to feel better about the relationship between the two of them. What had originally been a faux sibling rivalry, as Kasey kept referring to the "freeloading" Wolf as "the

son" her father had always wanted, had gradually softened into an almost friendly tolerance.

McNamara snorted and shifted his position
slightly.

Wolf was somehow reminded of pulling guard duty
in the army, or being stuck on a static-post standing
watch. He'd always been pretty successful at staying
awake, even with little or no sleep beforehand. And
four years of sleeping with one eye open at Leavenworth had further honed his abilities.

Better put them to good use, he thought.

Nothing moved in the ambient lighting and he
switched on the headband light again and went back to
reading. It wasn't like he was expecting a sapper, or
anything.

He found the play tedious and virtually incompre-
hensible. He wasn't sure if this was due to the sophisti-
cated verse being too much for him or the
predominance of personal baggage he'd been carrying
around. Regardless, he felt constantly interrupted by
the disquieting comparisons that came to mind whenever he came across a fetching line.

*That I should love a bright particular star, And
think to wed it, he is so above me.*

That one somehow seemed eerily to his current
situation with Yolanda. Not that he was thinking about
matrimony, but the fact that he, like Helena, the poor
girl in the play, sought the favor of the higher born
Bertram. The Bertram character wasn't much of a prize,
in Wolf's opinion, or that Yolanda was some kind of
royalty, but the fact that he, an ex-con with a DD,
would be an undesirable factor for Yolanda in the
pending police background investigation established

the unlikely parallel. There was nothing lower than an ex-con.

The professor would probably call it personal projection, or something, he thought. But it doesn't change the fact that she's way out of my league. Always was.

He'd managed to call Garfield that afternoon to inquire about the status of bandito number two. The conversation came floating back to him.

"Working on it," Garfield had replied. "I have to wait until closing and then run over and get some more paint. But not to worry. I'll be burning the midnight oil, but I should be able to get it done."

"So we're talking tomorrow then?" Wolf asked.

He heard Garfield blow out a heavy breath. "Let's plan on late Wednesday or early Thursday."

Wolf agreed and thanked him for his extra effort.

"How's the paper coming?" Garfield asked.

"I haven't started it yet," Wolf said. "We have to do a surveillance tonight and tomorrow, so I'm planning on reading the play tonight and maybe trying to write the paper in the car tomorrow night."

"Sounds like an arduous task worthy of a modern, mythological hero like yourself."

"I'm hardly that," Wolf said with a laugh. "But I would appreciate any insight you can give me."

"Well," Garfield said. "I already told you the play is one of his lesser known comedies, and was a rather unorthodox view of the romantic situation at the time. The heroine of the play, Helena, aspires to marry a prince named Bertram, who's a bit of a cad. The situation sort of transposed the traditional romantic roles of the day, and it's resolved by her sneaking into bed with him to have sex while pretending to be somebody else. Keeping him totally in the dark, so to speak."

Wolf chuckled. "In other words, she wouldn't let him leave the lights on."

"And what fun would that be?" Garfield laughed. "I always imagined a modern version with Rock Hudson and Doris Day. But I guess that casting's a bit passé now."

Wolf didn't mention he wasn't sure who Rock and Doris were, or how they'd fit into the scenario.

The remnants of the past conversation floated into the ether as Wolf went back to the play, rereading the line and tweaking it a bit to fit his own romantic situation: *That I should love a bright particular star ... she is so above me.*

Pushing the unpleasant comparison out of his mind, he went back to the reading but was soon stopped again by another line: *The bind that would be mated by the lion, Must die for love.*

The lion ... Ironic ... Somehow he couldn't get away from that either.

He leaned back and thought about the stolen Iraqi artifact, The Lions Attacking the Nubian, parts one and two. The damn artifact that had somehow started all this. And it was also the key to the ultimate goal he sought, to be able to clear his name. But at this point he was like the play's protagonist, a commoner without resources trying to complete an impossible task where some rich and well-positioned person held all the leverage.

Once again, Bambi versus Godzilla.

Perhaps he could use that as the title for his paper.

Wolf inhaled deeply and felt the melancholy dissipate slightly, amused by the absurdity of the situation.

He was reading a play that was written over four hundred years ago and drawing comparisons to his own life in the present day.

I wonder if the Bard ever imagined that, he thought, then grinned as he mentally added, Not likely. He never heard of either Bambi or Godzilla.

It was definitely time to take a break.

He closed the book, stretched, and then slipped out of the car, walked to the parkway, and did fifty push-ups. When he got back in McNamara was awake and winked at him.

"That all you could manage?" he said.

Wolf snorted and shook his head.

"How did I let you talk me into this again?" he said.

"It wasn't that hard," McNamara said. "And besides, Manny's paying us, remember?"

"Not enough," Wolf said. "My brain's gonna feel like fried mush when I meet that lawyer tomorrow." He glanced at his watch. "I mean today."

"Yeah," McNamara said, stretching a bit. "Why don't you pass me that thermos and get some shut-eye. I'll take the next watch."

"It's empty."

"Well, in that case, let's take a drive down to Dunkin' Donuts there on the corner and get us some fresh cups. I gotta take a whiz anyway and I don't want to have any of these fine people around here maybe waking up and looking out the window and thinking there's a man wrestling with a snake out in front of their house."

"Heaven forbid," Wolf said with a grin. "After all, it's probably a very large snake, right?'

"You're damn right it is."

After getting the coffee, he managed to skim the rest of the play, and with the help of some Internet summaries on his phone and with what Garfield had given him about the play being based on a story in Boccaccio's *The Decameron*, he switched places with McNamara, fired up his laptop, and began to pound out the three-page paper that the instructor had assigned. He ended by quoting one of the final lines: *The web of our life is of a mingled yarn good and ill together ... All's well that ends well.*

But will it? He wondered about this little surveillance venture as well as his own situation with Yolanda as he saved the file.

He glanced at his watch and saw it was closing in on zero four hundred. Mac's head lolled over to the side and his breathing had the regular rhythm of sound sleep.

All's well that ends well, he thought.

———

THE MCNAMARA RANCH
PHOENIX, ARIZONA

After deciding to knock off at four-thirty, the two of them had driven back to the ranch. Wolf was in bed almost immediately and was able to fall asleep quickly. What he intended to be a solid four hours of sleep turned out to be little more than an extended combat nap as an incessant ringing stirred him awake at a resounding seven o'clock.

He blinked twice, shaking off the vestiges of sleep, and saw that it was his cell phone.

Grabbing it, he wondered if it was possibly Yolanda, but the number on the screen was blocked. The voice that spoke, however, wasn't.

"Hey, Stevie. How they hanging this fine morning?"

It was Richard Soraces. Wolf's lethargy immediately vanished.

The Devil's advocate, he thought.

"Hey," Soraces continued. "I hope I didn't wake you up. You have a late night, or something?"

"What do you want, Soraces?"

After a quick bark of laughter, the other man said, "Sorry, I had you pegged for an early riser. You know, one of those guys who's up every day at the crack of dawn putting in his roadwork."

Wolf was suddenly bothered by the mention of his routine. Did Soraces have him under surveillance or was it just a lucky guess? Regardless, perhaps it was time to take Mac up on his offer to loan him a gun to take along on those morning treks to the mountain.

"Stevie boy? You still there, man?"

"Yeah. What do you want?"

"Aw, come on. Isn't that obvious? I want to discuss a deal on behalf of my client."

"A deal? Like last time?"

"For what we discussed before in my office," Soraces said. "Oh, by the way, I don't work there anymore."

"So I've heard. And seeing as how our last venture

turned out, I can't figure out why I'm still talking to you, asshole."

"Asshole?" Another laugh. "I'm wounded. I thought we had a good, solid, professional relationship. Especially after all that good faith money I had wired to you."

"Fuck you, Soraces. Have you forgotten you tried to kill me?"

"No, no, no. That wasn't me. If you remember correctly, you were the one shooting at me."

"If I'd been shooting at you, you wouldn't be here now. And I only returned fire after being fired upon."

"Oooh, that sounds like military terminology. But that's right, you were a Ranger at one time, weren't you?"

Wolf said nothing, debating whether to just hang up.

If I do that, he thought, I'll lose the chance to figure out what his game is. He decided to wait the other man out. After a few more seconds of silence, it worked.

"So," Soraces said. "Like I told you, it's time for us to deal. That is, if we can be sure you actually have it."

"Oh, I've got it, all right."

"Well, you have to understand that after the ... disappointment that last time, there is a bit of doubt."

Wolf considered what to say. He didn't want to blurt out the name of the artifact.

It's better to be a bit vague, he thought. Just in case he's recording this.

"You know that old riddle," Wolf said. "What's rock hard and about the size of half a cantaloupe?"

Silence, then, "Okay, we're on the same sheet of music, so to speak. You've got something we want, and we've got something for you. Something that'll clear your name."

"This sounds like the same song and dance as before," Wolf said. "Which you reneged on."

"Now that's not accurate."

"The hell it's not. You talked a good game and delivered nothing."

Soraces cleared his throat. "Now look, if you think back over what actually happened, I'm sure you'll see that it was at worst, a misunderstanding. We had a deal in the works, and I was ready to abide by it on behalf of my client. Is it my fault that Cummings fellow interfered?"

The image of what had occurred in the dusty street of that deserted town danced into Wolf's memory: Soraces and the other man, the bald-headed black guy, standing over the dying Cummings with the duplicate bandito in Soraces's hands.

"Interfered?" Wolf said.

"Yeah, right. He contacted my client, unbeknownst to me and our arrangement, and claimed to be in possession of the bandito." He paused and Wolf could almost picture Soraces's cocky smile, the nonchalant shrug of shoulders. "I was then instructed to go meet him at that grimy location and negotiate for the item. It was hardly my fault things turned out that way, was it?"

"Negotiate," Wolf said. "It looked like you were negotiating, all right. A payoff with a bullet."

"Now, that wasn't me. It was the man I hired as security. Cummings tried to shoot him, and he was left with no other option than to defend himself."

"Oh, is that why he took a shot at me?"

"Sorry about that. But you'll have to admit, it was a

rather dynamic situation. I don't know his motivation for doing that, and I'm not berating you for returning fire, either. I, on the other hand, committed no hostile acts toward you, did I?" Soraces paused for a second, then jumped back in with, "So I can hardly be blamed for getting the hell out of there, can I?"

"With the bandito."

"With the *ersatz* bandito. Not very sporting of you, making a duplicate, old chum."

Wolf realized his fatigue was getting the better of him. He needed to end this quickly.

"Give me a number where I can get ahold of you and I'll call you back," he said.

"Huh-un. No can do at the moment. I'm merely trying to reestablish communication so we can complete our original agreement."

The thought of finally getting that flashdrive was a tempting one, but this guy was about as trustworthy as a cornered jackal.

"Okay," Wolf said. "I'm interested, but if we deal, it'll have to be my way, and on my terms."

"Which are?"

"I'll let you know when I work them out. Now are you going to give me way to get in touch with you, or not?"

A solid five seconds passed and then Soraces said, "Not at this time, but I'll be back in touch," and terminated the call.

Wolf stared at the lost connection on the screen and then threw the phone onto the bed. It was getting light out now as the sun was already peeping way over the mountains. He felt tired but too adrenalized to sleep. He figured he'd gotten a little over two hours in. Not nearly enough, but to try again would be fruitless. Besides, he and McNamara had agreed to get up by nine and eat breakfast together before driving downtown to meet that new lawyer.

Wolf sighed and figured he might as well do his roadwork.

———

Despite the invigorating run Wolf found the fatigue creeping up on him after eating the substantial breakfast that Kasey prepared for him, her father, and Chad. Once again, she was dressed in her crisp-looking business attire and Wolf wondered if she had another appointment at the university. Whatever it was, she didn't share her plans with either of them. Instead, she set the frying pan and hers and Chad's dirty plates into the dishwasher and told him to go brush his teeth. She started to usher him out of the room, but the boy stopped next to Wolf's chair.

"Hey, Uncle Steve," he said. "Can I take the belt to school for show and tell?"

Wolf had discovered it had been returned to his room the day before. He was about to answer in the affirmative when Kasey cut in.

"No, you cannot," she said. "Uncle Steve doesn't think that's a good idea right now."

Chad's lips curled inward, accompanying a hurt expression. He looked from his mother to Wolf.

"Aw, why not, Uncle Steve?"

Wolf was at a loss for words. Why did she make him the bad guy?

"I think it would be all right," he said. "If it's okay with your mom."

Kasey shot him a dagger's look as Chad turned to her and began an imploring series of "Can I, mom? Can I?"

"No. It's too expensive and valuable for you to take to school," Kasey said. "Besides, it's not yours. We're running late today. Go on and brush your teeth. We have to leave."

Chad's face looked pinched with disappointment as he ran out.

"Steve," Kasey said. "Please don't do that again."

"I didn't mean to—"

"I realize that," Kasey said. "But it's hard enough trying to raise my son without outside interference."

"Sorry." Wolf felt on edge, not knowing what else to say.

Her expression softened a little and she added, "I know you mean well and he's thrilled that you let him hold onto the belt, but I don't want him to get too attached to something that's not really his."

"Understood," Wolf said, and shoveled some scrambled eggs into his mouth to avoid having to say anything else.

"Hell," McNamara said. "I'd be glad to stop by his school with the belt after I drop Steve off. Maybe I'll take my shadow box along and talk to all of them kids."

"Dad, don't start. Let's just leave it alone for now, okay? We'll work something out later."

McNamara shrugged and started smearing some strawberry jelly onto his toast.

"Roger that," he said. "But he sure has taken a shine to that belt, and after all, it is something to be proud of."

"For Steve it is," Kasey said. "Not for Chad."

Kasey walked out and Wolf noticed she was wearing heels.

"Takes after her mother," McNamara said. "Anyway, it's just as well. I want to do a little shopping once I drop you off. Get some stuff for our upcoming class."

"Such as?"

"Well, since Buck's got all them nice ranges, I think I'll take some of my weapons with us so we can do some shooting. I'll want to get extra ammo. Plus, I gotta get you a web belt and a canteen, some extra mag pouches and web gear and—"

"Hey," Wolf said. "We're just taking a class, not shipping out."

McNamara held the toast in front of his mouth and grinned.

"You never know," he said, and bit off a piece of the toast.

———

Forty minutes later they were pulling up in front of the office building where the late Rodney Shemp had his office. Wolf had been there a few times before, most recently to break in and remove what he and Mac had felt were incriminating files regarding their disastrous trip to Mexico that they didn't want the authorities to peruse. The judge had appointed the Mark Edwards Law Firm as a curio amicus, a friend of the court, to review Shemp's files before turning the redacted versions over to the police department for their investigation of Shemp's murder. Everything had slowed to a snail's pace, however, mostly due to the fact that the homicide was all but cleared. A video had surfaced showing one of the South African mercenaries, who'd tried to kill Wolf, had been at the hospital masquerading as a nurse. It had definitely placed the Afrikaans in the vicinity of Shemp's untimely fall down a hospital stairwell, and the autopsy had revealed that the lawyer was, in fact, dead before he took his tumble down the stairs. The mercenary was also subsequently killed and now closing the case was all but a formality. Nobody was in a rush at this point.

"Just give me a call when you're ready to be picked up," McNamara said. "But I do expect to be introduced to this new lawyer of yours."

"I haven't hired her yet," Wolf said.

"No, but if she's half as hot as she sounds, you're gonna. If not, I might hire her myself."

He pulled up in front of the building and whistled.

"Say," McNamara said. "I wonder if that's her there?"

Wolf was already assessing the pretty Hispanic woman standing in front of the building holding a thin leather briefcase. She looked to be fairly young, maybe her mid-thirties, and her raven hair fell around her shoulders with a textured elegance complementing her light blue blouse. Her skirt was a shade darker. The triangular muscle of her exposed calves bulged with just the right amount of tension to perfectly accentuate a pair of flawless legs.

Raising a dark eyebrow, she scrutinized the Escalade, and then came strolling toward them, the obviously expensive high-heeled shoes making clicking sounds on the sidewalk.

McNamara slammed the gear shift into PARK and flipped off his seatbelt.

"Hot damn," he said. "I'm gonna get out and let you introduce me."

"I'll have to introduce myself first." Wolf was struggling to undo his own seat belt. He slipped out of the Cadillac before McNamara and stepped onto the sidewalk thinking to himself, Wouldn't it be funny as all hell if it's not her?

He smiled and so did she, exposing perfect, white dentition.

"Mr. Wolf?" she asked.

"Yes."

She extended her right hand. "I'm Delores Delgato."

Before Wolf could say he was glad to make her acquaintance, McNamara sidled up next to him with a wide grin extending his hand also.

"I'm Jim McNamara, Steve's partner." He tipped the cowboy hat he'd taken to wearing again.

Dolores Delgato smiled and shook his hand also.

"I must admit that I'm a trifle bit embarrassed," she said, turning back to face Wolf. "I was going to use Mr. Shemp's old office, but in my haste to leave my office this morning, I neglected to pick up the key from Mr. Edwards. And he's tied up in court."

"Want us to break in?" McNamara asked, the grin still plastered on his face. "We're pretty good at it."

She smiled. "I'm sure you are, but I was thinking that since it's such a nice day we could get some iced tea and sit outside at that restaurant." Ms. Delgato shrugged her shoulders and Wolf watched as the thin translucence of her blouse made a wispy sound to accompany the gesture. "I realize that sounds a bit informal, but ..."

"It sounds fine," Wolf said. He turned to McNamara. "I'll give you a text when we're done."

McNamara nodded and told Ms. Delgato it had been a pleasure to meet her. He got back into the Escalade and waved as he pulled off.

"What type of work do you do, Mr. Wolf?" she asked as they walked toward the restaurant.

"Right now I'm in bail enforcement."

Her perfectly accented eyebrow rose once again.

"Bounty hunters?" she asked.

He nodded. "Not much else available career-wise for an ex-con with a DD."

"Yes," she said. "Well, let's talk about that."

After paying for two iced teas, which Ms. Delgato insisted on doing, they sat at a wire table under the restaurant awning. Ms. Delgato set the briefcase on the top between them and took out a yellow legal pad and a ballpoint pen.

"As I mentioned," she said. "I did take the liberty of going over the file that Mr. Shemp had. It included a transcript of your court-martial." She paused and touched the top end of the pen against her perfect white teeth. "I think your military lawyer did a pretty bad job for you. About the only thing he did right was having you plead under an Alford plea. That is, allowing you to plead guilty and accept the deal without admitting guilt. It left a back door open in case we do try to appeal."

We? Wolf thought. She's already figuring on me hiring her.

Ms. Delgato must have read his mind because she

quickly placed two fingers, with well-manicured, artifi-cially-elongated, red nails, on his forearm and said, "I don't mean to be presumptuous. After all, you haven't actually hired me as of yet."

She quickly withdrew her hand, but the feel of her touch on his bare skin had felt electric. He smiled but said nothing.

"If you do," she said, pausing to take a sip from her straw. "I think I could mount a good case for inadequate defense."

Shemp had mentioned something of the sort being a possibility, but he'd also said that it would probably be a long shot ... A very long shot.

Of course, neither Shemp nor Ms. Delgato were aware of the new development and Wolf wondered how much he should tell her. Should he mention Soraces and the flashdrive? He didn't actually have it, but the phone conversation this morning was a reminder that getting it was still a possibility. And what about the stolen artifact, the Lion Attacking the Nubian? Would it be wise to divulge that to her as well? That would be tantamount to admitting that he was knowingly in possession of stolen property. Even if the communication between a lawyer and her client was privileged, she might not want to get involved in some-thing illegal.

It was almost too much to think about.

Keep it vague, he thought. It's not the right time to show all my cards to anybody.

His head was beginning to ache from lack of sleep, and he felt like a drunk trying to negotiate a circular staircase.

"Are you all right, Mr. Wolf?" she asked.

He blinked a few times trying to clear his head.

"Yes," he said. "Sorry. I had a late one last night working and didn't get much sleep."

She smiled and drank some more iced tea.

"If you'd rather postpone this to another time, when you feel better ..."

"No," he said, deciding he needed to have an attorney on retainer just to be safe, regardless of whether or not he got the flashdrive. "I'd like to hire you."

"All right," she said. "Why don't we do this ... You give me a retain today of say, one hundred dollars, and I'll get to work ordering a transcript of your trial. Then, once I've gone over everything again, we'll plan our strategy."

"Rod, err, Mr. Shemp, said it looked pretty hopeless."

Ms. Delgato's prim nostrils flared as she took a breath.

"Well, to be perfectly frank, it would be a bit of an uphill battle. But I'm not Mr. Shemp."

That was obvious. He smiled.

"Additionally," she said. "I spent four years in JAG, so I'm totally familiar with the UCMJ."

"Oh really. Army?"

She nodded. "Seven years. I enlisted and applied to OCS after MP school. They sent me through law school."

This somehow made Wolf feel he could trust her. They shared a common bond of both having served.

"What if there was something new to add?" he asked.

"New?"

He nodded, again wondering how much to divulge. "Yeah. You are aware that I wasn't able to provide a full accounting of what happened in Iraq, right?"

"Those missing eight minutes from your memory? Yes, I did read your initial CID interview and statement. It was in the discovery file. You should have requested an attorney to sit in on that, by the way. They did read you your rights before they talked to you. There's a signed right's waiver form in the file, but did you understand what you were signing?"

Wolf took a deep breath and shrugged. "Probably, but at the time I didn't think I needed a lawyer."

The perfect teeth flashed in a smile, "Mr. Wolf, Steve, you should remember that you *always* need a lawyer."

"I know that now. But I'm not talking about the missing eight minutes. I've pretty much figured out what I couldn't recall. What I am talking about is a statement, a video, by one of the men who testified against me."

The space between her eyebrows furrowed. "Statement? What do you mean?"

Again, he debated whether or not to tell her everything.

Might as well go for it, he thought. I've got to trust somebody.

He took out his wallet, removed a hundred-dollar bill from it, and handed it across the table.

"Let's make this official first," he said.

She took the money and reached into her briefcase and removed a slim laptop. "I'll draw up a receipt. In the meantime, what is it you wanted to tell me about this flashdrive?"

Wolf watched her open the laptop and press a button to turn it on.

Close enough to being official, he thought.

"I think it's what you might call," he said, "exculpatory evidence."

GRAND TETONS HOTEL
PHOENIX, ARIZONA

Soraces watched as Dirk slammed the edge of his right hand again and again against the piece of wood practicing a knife-hand karate blow. He was wearing a black T-shirt and blue jeans, and the muscles of his bare arms bulged with each movement. The board was a two-by-four about sixteen inches long and one end had a series of horizontal slits cut into the thickness running parallel to the width. Dirk had brought it back from his run to the hardware store and the methodical chopping sound was driving Soraces nuts. It was as constant and regular as a metronome. He was grateful when his burner phone rang and that Dirk stopped his activity.

"It looks like McNamara's pulling up now," Clyde Perkins said. "Wolf's saying goodbye to her."

"Did some money exchange hands?" Soraces asked.

"Yeah, but I couldn't tell how much. I'm too far away."

"Good. Keep it that way." Soraces smiled.

It looks like Wolf's got himself a new attorney, he thought. Smart move.

"Okay, she's walking away and Wolf's going toward the Escalade," Perkins said. "Want me to stay on them?"

"Yes," Soraces said. "But keep it loose. Don't let them get a whiff of you."

"I won't, as usual."

The *as usual* part had a little condescending lilt to it. A hint of acerbity. Soraces was well aware that neither of the Shadows liked to be told or reminded how to do their job, nor did they need to be. But it was all part of a master planner, an effective mission leader knowing when to keep his men on a short leash. With the Shadows, Soraces figured he could allow a lot of play in the leash, only using an occasional jerk on the line to keep things in order. Sort of like patrolling with a pair of well-trained Dobermans.

A sharp reverberation cracked the air with the abrupt intrusiveness of a gunshot. Soraces glanced over to see that Dirk had begun his knife-hand strikes again.

"What the hell was that?" Perkins asked.

Soraces held up his hand and Dirk froze, with his muscular arm cocked back.

"Dirk practicing his karate," Soraces said.

"Figures." Perkins snorted derisively. "Well, they're gonna pull out. I'll get back to you."

The connection went dead and Soraces removed the phone from his ear and glanced at the screen to be sure it had been terminated.

"What's Clyde got against you?" Soraces asked.

Dirk shrugged. "The prissy little asshole thinks I cheated him at cards."

"Did you?"

"What do you think?"

Crack!

"How about taking that thing into your room?" Soraces said. "That pounding's giving me a headache."

Without a word, Dirk got up, went to the door, and paused. "Don't forget that I need one of them debit cards to get that equipment."

"Right," Soraces said, reaching into his pocket for his long, zippered wallet. He unzipped it and removed one of the non-descript debit cards that Fallotti had given him. "Here, take this one."

Dirk turned and came back to snatch the card. He slipped it into his pants pocket and then strode back toward the door, getting in three more resounding blows as he walked.

Soraces recoiled slightly with each one.

"You might as well grab some lunch too," Soraces said. "I've got an assignment for you later. Tonight, after dark."

Dirk nodded and struck the board again. He then reached for the knob and went out.

Soraces breathed a quick sigh of relief when his large companion had left. The sharp sounds of the chopping continued with diminishing returns as Dirk, apparently, made his way down the hallway toward his room.

If the Shadows are Dobermans, Soraces thought, then Dirk's a fucking pit-bull. Or a huge Rottweiler. A god damn one-man-wrecking crew when he's turned loose.

He looked forward to seeing Dirk's ultimate confrontation with Wolf.

CHAPTER EIGHT_

OUTSIDE THE OFFICE BUILDING OF RODNEY F. SHEMP
ATTORNEY AT LAW
PHOENIX, ARIZONA

Wolf was jerked back in the seat by the momentum as McNamara sent the Escalade lurching out into traffic. Behind them a screeching of brakes was followed by the blaring of a horn. McNamara ignored it and barreled down the street.

"Let me get my crash helmet," Wolf said as he fished for the seatbelt.

McNamara glanced in the side-view mirror, scowled, but said nothing.

Wolf glanced in the back seat but saw no packages.

"You get what you needed to get?" he asked.

McNamara shook his head, still silent and brooding. He cut in front of another car to pass, eliciting another blast of a horn.

"What the hell's eating you?" Wolf asked.

"That damn daughter of mine." McNamara blew out a long breath. "You ain't gonna believe it."

They sat in silence while McNamara sped through traffic. When he didn't elaborate, Wolf chuckled.

"You want to explain?" he asked. "Or are you just going to keeping stewing and driving like a maniac?"

Shaking his head, McNamara slowed the car down considerably. The car they'd passed came roaring around, sounding its horn while the driver gave them the finger.

McNamara waved and nodded appreciatively.

"Guess I had that one coming," he said.

Wolf let a few more seconds go by figuring if Mac wanted to talk, he'd do it when he was ready. It didn't take long.

"After I dropped you off," McNamara said, filtering into a steady traffic stream. "I was heading over to that army/navy surplus store when, all of a sudden, I see the back of this attractive gal walking down the street, and somehow she looks kind of familiar. Well, I take another look as I go by and, I'll be god dammed, if it isn't Kasey."

She was dressed up pretty fancy, Wolf thought.

"Well," McNamara said. "I was gonna honk the horn, but some knucklehead swung over right in front of me and I had to jam on the brakes. By the time I got going again and started looking for her, I get stopped in traffic. But I catch sight of her and she's standing with her back to the street talking to somebody. You'll never guess who."

Again, Wolf waited, saying nothing.

"It was that god damn Franker," McNamara said.

"Franker? Special Agent Franker?"

"Yep."

They came to a red light and stopped.

"At first I thought maybe they just met coincidentally, but then she starts laughing and he's got this big, shit-eating grin on his face." He paused and frowned. "And the next thing I know, they're walking toward the outdoor seating of this one restaurant. By this time I got somebody else blasting their horn at me so I drove around the block. When I made my second pass, the two of them are sitting there at a table like two teenagers on their first prom date."

The light changed and McNamara let the Escalade roll forward.

"Well, I made another pass around the block again, and when I drove past, they were still sitting there talking and kind of leaning forward toward each other. A waiter came by and it looked like they were ordering something. Then I got your text, so I headed over here."

"And where are we going now?" Wolf asked.

"To see if they're still there. Christ almighty, you don't think he's grilling her to see what he can find out about us?"

The thought had occurred to Wolf, but he didn't say so.

"She is a pretty girl," he said. "I can understand him wanting to take her to lunch."

McNamara slammed his palm against the steering wheel.

"But why in the hell did she agree to meet with him?" he said. Before Wolf could offer any reply, McNamara said, "Okay, take a look to your right now. We're coming up on them."

Wolf looked to his right and saw them seated at a

table. Kasey's head lolled back in apparent laughter, and Franker was sitting across from her grinning like a fool.

"Looks like they're having a good time," Wolf said. "Pleasant conversation, laughter."

Mac slammed his hand on the steering wheel again as they continued past.

"Careful," Wolf said. "Either you'll break the wheel or they're going hear you and look over here."

McNamara continued down the block.

"One thing's for certain," he said. "Me and her's gonna have a little talk once she gets home."

"Mac, she's not a teenager. She's a grown woman."

"But she's still *my daughter*, dammit. And I'm not going to stand for no low-down federal agent pumping her for information." He swore. "That cold-blooded son of a bitch. FBI or no FBI, I'll take him behind the barn and beat the shit out of him."

Wolf reflected that he'd had a different impression of Franker, an almost friendly one, after the shootout in which Wolf saved the man's life with a warning of imminent danger. Franker had thanked him, and Wolf had felt that the FBI man had been sincere.

Maybe I was wrong about him, he thought, but after a deep breath and mentally assessing how pretty Kasey looked this morning, he reconsidered.

One thing was for sure, he didn't want to get in the middle of a father/daughter dispute. It was Mac's problem to deal with and, at the moment, with the fatigue creeping up on him again and another late-night surveillance looming, all he wanted to do now was go home and get some sleep.

GARFIELD AND OLLIE'S CRAFT'S SHOP
SCOTTSDALE, ARIZONA

Dirk told Charles Perkins to take another pass through the lot of the strip mall so they could scan it one more time for surveillance cameras. Seeing none, he centered his binoculars on the target. It was still light out and visibility was good without any night-vision enhancement. He adjusted the rangefinder on the apparatus, enlarging the view of the posted business hours:

Mon—Sat 1000 AM to 600 PM

Closed Sunday

Remember the Sabbath and keep it holy, Dirk thought with amusement. Solemn words to run a business by.

It was now 1745 hours.

"Okay," he said. "Pull up over there and drop me off. I'll call you when I'm ready for a pick-up. I'll be coming out the back."

"Roger that," Perkins said. He drove the nondescript white van over to the sidewalk.

Before Dirk got out he pulled on a pair of latex gloves, checked his watch, and began his count. His estimate for this one should take no longer than twelve minutes max. Well, maybe a bit more if he started to enjoy it. In any case, the risk factor was negligible. Not like the last one. He thought back to his previous mission in Caracas where he was definitely in hostile territory.

Indian country, for sure.

That's what the old Nam vets in the Agency used to call it. Hardly an acceptable expression in these politically correct times but Dirk didn't give a shit. He'd always made it a point never to be bothered by the inconsequential and was glad that he was reporting to his old buddy, Soraces, instead of some pencil-necked bureaucrat back at Langley.

He pressed one of the two buttons on his wristwatch that started the stopwatch.

The clock's ticking, he thought, and then pulled the baseball cap down farther on his forehead and canted his head downward and off to the side just in case the two shops he passed, a frozen yogurt shop and a Fred Astaire Dance Studio, had some kind of camera systems that might catch a shot of him walking by. It was doubtful, but he knew better than to drop his guard simply because this was a milk run. Any cameras would record nothing more than a big guy wearing a real loose-fitting hoodie and a baseball cap with a long bill.

A true pro never takes anything lightly, he thought. Good words to live by.

He checked his stopwatch again as he turned his hand to grip the door handle. He wore the watch reversed so that it faced the inner aspect of his wrist. Sixty seconds had elapsed.

An old, gray-haired man with circular, gold-rimmed eyeglasses stood behind what looked like a cash register from a nostalgic Norman Rockwell painting. One thing that was not nostalgic was the state-of-the-art PTZ camera that was affixed to the wall giving an unencumbered view of virtually the entire floor area of the store,

He'd have to check if it was transmitting the recording to the cloud before he left.

The cash-drawer was open and the geezer was counting the bills. He paused and looked up. "Good evening."

Dirk nodded fractionally.

There was no one else in the store, he noted, but there was a cloth curtain hanging off to the right indicating a back room. Judging from the size of this shop showroom, as opposed to his recollection of the overall width of the building from the outside, there had to be a fairly large area beyond that suspended curtain.

An office, perhaps, or a storage or work room.

Dirk bet on the last one, based on what Soraces had told him.

The old guy had made a duplicate of the statue they were after. He would need space to work.

All this for a fucking plaster bandito, he thought.

But who was he to question an easy payday?

"I'm sorry to be presumptuous, sir," the old fart said, pushing the cash back into the drawer and shoving it closed. He tried to avert attention from that movement by bringing his other hand up and adjusting the glasses on his nose. "But I was just getting ready to close. This will have to be rather quick, I'm afraid."

Presumptuous?

The old guy reminded Dirk of his seventh-grade teacher, Mr. Holt. He was always using big words and encouraging the kids to look them up when they asked what they meant. Dirk smiled as he remembered stringing a line of one-gauge fishing line across the lower hinge on the door of the classroom so that he could pull it taut just as Mr. Holt was walking in. He fell down so hard his false teeth went clattering along the tiled floor as the class roared with laughter.

"I know," Dirk said, turning toward the door and flipping a dangling card around so it displayed the *CLOSED* portion against the glass door. He then twisted the lock securing the door.

The old man's face registered concern and his right hand slowly descended toward the area beneath the counter.

Dirk quickly pulled up the front of the sweatshirt and slipped the Beretta 92F from the Velcro belly-band holster and pointed it at the old guy.

"Lift your hands above your head, real slow," Dirk said in a flat tone. "Now."

The geezer froze for a split second and then quickly complied. Dirk strode over to the register, scanning the underside of the counter. The alarm button was down a ways and Dirk didn't think the old guy had pressed it.

"Don't even think about it," he said. "Now, open the register."

"Certainly," the old guy said. "Take the money. Take all of it. I just don't want to get hurt, all right?"

"You're wasting my time." Dirk jabbed the end of the pistol against the old guy's side. He had a soft-looking body and the blow made him gasp.

"Do it," Dirk said.

The old guy's head was bobbling up and down like a yoyo. His fingers fumbled with the keys, he pressed one down, and the drawer slid open.

Dirk reached in and grabbed the cash with his left hand. It didn't look like much, but it would serve its purpose. Soraces said to make it look like a robbery.

Stuffing the money into the pocket on the front of his hoodie, Dirk then grabbed the old guy's arm, pulling him toward the hanging curtain.

"Anybody else here?" Dirk asked, keeping the barrel of the Beretta pressed into the pliant torso.

"No, no one," the old man said.

They pushed through the curtain and came into a large area with several rows of metal shelving. Each shelf was stacked with a variety of the same figurines and knickknacks that were on display in the front of the store. A special box was marked *Christmas inventory*. Another bunched-up curtain hung in front of a closed wall safe. There was a long wooden table littered with mixing bowls, bottles and cans of paint, two capped jars of what Dirk took to be paint thinner, and a variety of knives, spatulas, and paintbrushes. In the center was a partially painted plaster statue about eighteen inches high.

A Mexican bandito.

"Please," the old man said. "There's nothing of value here. Take whatever you want, just please, don't hurt me."

"What about the safe?" Dirk asked.

"It's over there. I'll open it for you. Take what you want. We don't have much money. Please."

"Shut up."

The old guy did, and Dirk felt he had total compliance but decided to allow himself a bit of fun. He forced the old man down to his knees and then released his hold on the old guy's arm.

He cowered on the floor, looking up with abject terror.

Dirk replaced the Beretta in the bellyband holster and then reached down to grab the old man's throat with his left hand. He lifted him to his feet and, keeping his fingers clenched around the jawbone, he rotated the head toward the plaster statue.

"You're going to open the safe for me, all right," Dirk said, as the latex-covered fingers sunk into the soft, compliant flesh of the old man's cheeks. "But first, we're going to talk about that."

The soft blue eyes were twin pools of sheer terror behind the convex lenses.

Dirk extended his left arm, holding the old man at arm's length while, at the same time, he straightened the fingers of his right hand and locked his thumb in place. He mentally measured the distance between himself and the bandito and then lashed out with his right hand a split second later. It was a back-handed strike and it caught the statue just under the wide brim of the sombrero. Dirk had wanted to take the statue's head completely off, similar to breaking off the top of a standing wine bottle, to create the proper effect, but, instead, the blow merely sent the entire plaster rendition flying. It crashed into a nearby shelf and knocked a dozen other plaster figures to the floor.

Mistake number one.

Bad angle for the blow, he thought, glancing at the stopwatch.

Eight minutes and thirty-two seconds.

Sloppy work so far.

This is going to take longer than ten, he thought, then smiled.

But after all, he was starting to enjoy it.

———

OUTSIDE THE RYLAND RESIDENCE

PHOENIX, ARIZONA

The street in front of the Rylands' house appeared quiet and docile under the glow of the streetlights. Wolf and McNamara had been on the job for about three hours and it was closing in on 2300 hours. Mac had hardly said two words the whole time. He'd awakened Wolf at nineteen hundred and told him they were moving out in ten. Wolf hadn't even showered. He merely slipped into his work clothes, a black T-shirt, black cargo pants, and running shoes, and trotted out to meet Mac, who was sitting in the idling Escalade in the driveway. When Wolf got in McNamara shifted into gear and took off without a word. Figuring the talk with Kasey over her luncheon date hadn't gone well, Wolf didn't inquire or push it. Mac barely said two words on the way over and they sat in silence for over an hour before Wolf decided to break the ice.

"You get any sleep?" he asked.

McNamara shook his head.

"I got a couple hours," Wolf said. "But I forgot to call Garfield about the bandito."

McNamara grunted a bit more audibly this time.

"So, you want to talk about it?" Wolf asked. "Or are you just going to sit there and brood all night?"

Again, McNamara didn't answer.

"I emailed my English paper earlier, and I don't have anything to read," Wolf said. "But I'd be glad to go over the finer points of the play."

McNamara was still silent.

"For instance," Wolf said. "Did you know that in Elizabethan times, when they did Shakespeare's plays, the audience sat so close and got so engaged that that they tended to drool onto the stage."

McNamara grunted slightly.

Wolf took this as a good sign.

"And," he continued, "that's how the expression, break a leg, came into being. The stage got so slippery that a lot of the actors fell down. If there was a lot of spit, that meant they were really fascinating the audience, hence the expression came to mean wishing them a good performance."

"Falling on their asses, huh?" McNamara said. "Now something like that might be worth seeing."

That's the spirit, Wolf thought. He decided to press his advantage, if for no other reason than to keep abreast of the ongoing dynamics between Mac and his daughter. Like it or not, Wolf was part of it. They were like family.

"Did you talk to Kasey?" he asked.

"Yeah," McNamara said. "As soon as she got home. For all the good it did."

Wolf waited for McNamara to continue and when he didn't, Wolf pressed him for more. After all, if Franker was trying to elicit confidential information about him and Mac, it was something he needed to know.

"She say what the lunch thing was all about?"

It took McNamara a few seconds to reply. He took a deep breath and then said, "It was just that. A lunch date."

"You ask her if he was inquiring about you and me and Mexico?"

"I did. That's when she got really pissed off." McNamara took in another deep breath. "Damn near exploded, saying, 'Is it so remarkable that an attractive man might ask me out on a date?' That's how she described it. A date."

Wolf didn't think it was remarkable at all, but he still was curious about Franker's true intentions.

"She was damn near yelling at me," McNamara said. "At me ... Her own father. Said I was being accusatory and not treating her like an adult. Told me to mind my own business."

Wolf pictured the scene as McNamara described it. He was glad he wasn't there, but wondered if Mac had been able to get any sleep afterward.

"It made me realize, again," McNamara said. "How little I know her, how much I missed out on. I told you before what she said, didn't I? About how I was never there for all the important things in her life when she was growing up." He continued to stare out the windshield. "I guess I never really appreciated all the stuff her mother had to go through raising her right. All them years I was away in some foreign land, fighting somebody else's war. I bet I could count on one hand all the times I was there when she needed me."

Before Wolf could think of anything to say that might comfort him a little, a faint buzzing sound, distinctive, persistent, and unmistakable, pierced the quiet night. The percussive reverberations grew louder, and it became apparent that some motorcycles were approaching.

And at least one of them sounded like a Harley.

Two discrete headlights appeared at the other end of the block and began moving toward them.

"Looks like it's show time," McNamara said, popping open the driver's door. "Let's go earn our pay."

Wolf slid out of the passenger door. By the time they'd crossed the street the motorcycles had stopped.

One was a Honda Rebel. It was solid black and looked to have a small engine, perhaps only 250 cc. The rider was a thin guy who looked to still be in his teens. He wore a pair of wrap-around sunglasses and had his hair slicked back. His facial features resembled the prom picture that Manny had shown them.

Timmy Wagner, no doubt.

The other guy was older, much thicker, and was riding a red and black Harley Fat Boy that continued to idle with its distinctive percussion. He also wore sunglasses and a blue jean jacket with the sleeves razored off. It was covered with a variety of insignias. His mange of long hair was also slicked back into a pompadour under a layer of grease. His arms were good sized, but not overly muscular, and covered with tattoos.

The two of them were talking when Wolf and McNamara walked up to them.

"Can I help you gents?" McNamara asked.

The older biker's head rotated slowly toward him, his face a mask of disinterest. He made no reply and turned back to his young companion.

"Maybe if you'd turn that damn thing off," McNamara said, "you could hear better."

He and Wolf automatically spread out, each taking the outside of one of the two motorcycles.

"These guys don't say much," McNamara said, glancing toward Wolf. "Do they?"

Wolf shook his head. Timmy's motorcycle was closest to Mac and the curb and the older biker was on the outside, next to Wolf now. He reached out and flicked the ignition off.

The biker swatted at Wolf's arm and his lips curled back exposing yellowed, crust-covered teeth.

"Don't you never touch my bike, asshole."

Wolf didn't reply, but took notice of the handle of what appeared to be a revolver tucked into the left side of the man's pants. He also had on a chrome-steel chain belt fastened loosely around his rotund waist, and the clip of a knife sticking out of his engineer boot.

"Ah," McNamara said. "Much better. Those damn Harley's do make a lot of noise. You oughta consider getting a pair of earplugs. It'll save a lot of your hearing."

"Fuck you," the biker said.

"What you hassling us for, old man?" Timmy Wagner said. "Glory's father put you up to this?"

"We're from the neighborhood welcoming committee," McNamara said. "And you ain't welcome."

The older biker seemed amused as heeled his kickstand down. Timmy shut his off as well and also got off.

"Go get your girl," the older biker said. "These two shits ain't gonna bother us none." He gripped the chain around his waist, unfastened a pair of wire hooks, and grabbed one end, letting the heavy links unfold and drop toward the street with an ominous clicking sound. "Are youse?"

Wolf wasn't about to let this pugnacious idiot make the first move, especially since he was armed. Stepping back, so the two of them were about three feet apart now, Wolf sent a quick round-house kick onto the outside of the biker's left knee. The man buckled slightly, stumbling forward, and brought the chain around toward Wolf with a whirling motion. Wolf danced away from the metallic links and they clanked onto the pavement. He stepped in again, smashing a left hook to the biker's nose, and feeling the cartilage give under the blow. The biker stumbled back and Wolf pivoted, delivering a spinning kick to the expansive gut. This sent the man hurling into his motorcycle. The big Harley careened into the smaller Honda next to it and both motorcycles crashed to the ground. As Wolf knelt beside the fallen biker, he grabbed the man's left arm with his own left hand, yanked the arm upward, and then grabbed the butt of the revolver with his right.

"Gun," he said, catching a glimpse of McNamara slamming his open palm into Timmy's face. The waspish youth took two staggering steps backward and then cradled his face in his hands.

The revolver was a small snub-nose, a belly gun, and Wolf slipped it into the lower pocket of his cargo pants. He pulled the set of handcuffs out of the case on his belt and flipped the biker over onto his stomach. After ratcheting the first cuff around the man's left wrist, Wolf straddled the rotund body, jammed his left knee onto the man's left elbow, and bent the biker's right arm around behind his back. After ratcheting the second cuff in place, Wolf began a quick pat-down search. He removed the folding knife, a wallet, a bag of marijuana, and the now-empty holster for the revolver. Putting the gun back in its sheath, he stood and removed the man's driver's license. He dropped the other items onto the prone man's back.

McNamara, already on his cell phone, walked over and took the license. His mouth twisted into a frown as his call went unanswered for several more rings.

Finally, he rolled his eyes and said, "Kase, I need you to run somebody." He waited. "Yeah, I know what time it is, but we got a situation." Wolf heard a few snatches of Kasey's voice. It sounded argumentative.

"I don't care if you were sleeping," McNamara said. "We're not and we need this. Now please ..." He waited again and pointed at Timmy. "We're bail enforcement officers, sonny boy, and I'm armed, so don't do nothing stupid. In fact, step on over here so my partner can search you." When Timmy didn't more, McNamara stomped his foot and the kid jerkily moved around the oblique cluster of motorcycles.

Wolf told him to put his hands on his head, interlock his fingers, and face away from him. After reaching up with his left hand and squeezing the interlocked fingers together hard enough to make the kid whimper, Wolf ran his fingers over Timmy's body. He found a folding knife, which he pocketed, and a bag of marijuana and some rolling papers. Determining the youth was weapon free, he pushed him away and told him to stand by the curb.

After what seemed like a solid five minutes, Kasey came back on the line and Mac read her the information from the biker's driver's license, spelling out the name Ira L. Sax.

The kid's head jerked up as the name was spoken.

A few seconds later Mac grinned and spoke softly into the phone. He then hung up and turned to Wolf.

"Looks like old boy's wanted out of Tucson," he said. "How 'bout that, Ira?"

"You don't know what you're talking about," Timmy said. "His name's Irv Bruns."

"Shut the fuck up," Ira-Irv said.

The light on the front of the Rylands' house came on and a middle-aged man in a bathrobe came hustling out the door holding a cell phone.

"I called the police," Mr. Ryland said. "Are you Mr. McNamara?"

Mac nodded and extended his palm toward Wolf.

"This is my partner."

Mr. Ryland nodded. "My brother-in-law told me about you. Thanks."

Wolf nodded back, glancing down and Ryland's yellow pajama pants and house-slippers, then at the handcuffed biker and the teenager with the bloody nose.

Looks like it was a good thing we were here, he thought.

A young girl dressed in blue jeans and an orange tank-top burst through the door and came running over to them. "What's going on? Oh, God, Timmy."

The youth stood holding his nose, the trail of blood seeping through his fingers.

The girl went to him and ran her fingers over his forehead and long hair then glared at Wolf and McNamara. "You big pricks didn't have to hurt him."

"Glory," Mr. Ryland said. "Watch your language, young lady."

"Fuck that," she said. "Daddy, you knew about this?"

Her father looked totally embarrassed as he compressed his lips and nodded.

"He brought it on himself," McNamara said. "He made the mistake of swinging on me."

"You big fucking bully," Glory Ryland said. "I hope you die."

"Glory," Mr. Ryland said. "Go in the house."

"Fuck you." She continued to rub her hands over Timmy's blood-streaked face and greasy hair.

Manny's nephew, Freddie, and a middle-aged woman appeared and moved next to the girl. "Oh, my God," she said. "Let me go get a washcloth."

"I'm okay, Mrs. Ryland," Timmy said. "Don't need nothing."

Freddie gave a quick nod to Wolf and then leaned over to try and talk to the girl, whom Wolf assumed was Freddie's sister. His thick red hair was askew and standing straight up on the left side of his head.

The four of them engaged in some kind of hushed conversation as a quick burst from a siren sounded way down the block. About forty seconds later, two squad cars, red and blue lights flashing, pulled up and stopped. An officer got out of the first one and strode over to them.

"What's going on here?" he asked.

"I'm Harold Ryland. I was the one that called." He gestured toward Wolf and McNamara. "These men are security guards I hired to keep an eye on my house. These hoodlums have been harassing and threatening my family for weeks."

A second officer approached but said nothing.

"Get out of here, you pigs," Glory yelled. "You ain't needed here."

The second cop's head jerked back a few millimeters and he smirked.

"Glory, get in the house," Mr. Ryland yelled. "Janice take her inside."

"I'm taking Timmy inside with us," the girl said, her tone brimming with defiance.

"No, you're not," her father said.

"Honey," McNamara said. "Take it from us, these boys ain't so nice."

"Fuck you," she said, her bright red lips peeling back from her teeth.

McNamara shook his head and frowned. "Now that's no way for a young lady to talk, is it?"

She gave him the finger and her mother and Freddie pulled the girl toward the front door of the house where Glory managed to stop the forward progress and grab the door jamb.

"Timmy, come on," she yelled.

"Timmy," Mr. Ryland said. "I'm sorry, but you're no longer welcome in my home. Not until you come to your senses."

"I ain't going in there anyway," Timmy sneered, his mouth twisting into a snarl, framed by a bloody mustache. "I'm staying here with Irv."

Mrs. Ryland finally managed to push her daughter through the doorway and the two of them vanished inside.

The closet cop rolled his eyes and then pointed to the handcuffed man on the ground. "I'm assuming that's Irv?"

He stooped down and picked up the holstered revolver, knife, wallet, and marijuana from the prone biker's back.

"This gun his?" the cop asked.

Wolf nodded.

"I hope you have a permit for this piece," the cop said, moving over to his squad car with the items.

"Irv Bruns," McNamara said. "AKA, Ira L. Sax.

He's wanted on an outstanding warrant out of Tucson for assault and battery and resisting arrest."

"That was squashed," Ira-Irv said.

"We'll see," the cop said, leaning down. "What's your name and date of birth?"

"I ain't gotta tell you shit," the biker said.

"I can run his plate," the cop's partner said. "I'm assuming the Harley's his?"

Wolf nodded but motioned for McNamara to hand the cop Ira-Irv's driver's license.

"This'll make it a lot easier," the cop said with a smile.

"We already ran him and discovered the warrant," McNamara said. "We're bail enforcement officers."

The other officer keyed his mic and read off the information, requesting a "Ten-Twenty-nine."

The dispatcher came back about thirty seconds later asking if he was clear.

"Ten-four," the officer said. "Go ahead."

The dispatcher broadcasted that Irv-Ira had a suspended license and the hit on the warrant.

"Ten-four," the officer said. "Confirm please."

"It's good," McNamara said. "We already confirmed it."

The cop nodded and waited. As soon as the information came back as verified, he requested a tow truck.

"Tell them it's for a Harley," the officer said.

"Aw, come on, man," the biker said. "You ain't gonna tow my hog, are you?"

The biker's voice sounded almost pitiful.

"I'm afraid so, Mr. Sax," the officer said.

"Don't call me that," Ira-Irv said. "My name's Bruns."

"That ain't your name any more than that bike's yours," McNamara said, "It was put up as collateral for the bond that was posted for you down in Tucson."

"Ira Sax?" Timmy said, his jaw hanging open. "That's not your real name is it, Irv?"

Irv-Ira didn't answer.

"I mean, that sounds kinda like a Jew name," Timmy said. His expression reflected incredulity.

Bruns's head twisted up from his prone position. "Shut up, you little fucking prick. I wouldn't even be here except for you. Now get the fuck outta here and go find Spike and tell him I need bond money." He stopped and licked his lips. "How much is the bond, officer?"

"We'll let you know as soon as we get to the station," the cop said.

"A Jew," Timmy murmured, as if in disbelief.

Wolf was amused at the kid's anti-Semitism.

Sort of like finding out the Grand Wizard of the KKK's been hiding a black face under his white hood all this time, he thought.

"What's your story about this?" the officer asked.

Timmy extended his hand at McNamara. "That guy hit me."

The cop looked askance at Mac. "That so?"

"Yeah," McNamara said. "The little twerp swung at me first."

"I did not," Timmy yelled. "You hit me for no reason."

"That's not true, officer," Mr. Ryland said. "I saw the whole thing. And I have a Ring doorbell. I have the whole thing recorded, if you want to see it."

The cop looked back at Timmy who frowned.

"Forget it," he said. "I don't wanna do nothing anyway."

The officer nodded and said, "Let me see your driver's license."

Timmy complied, going through the motions without any back-talk or reticence. The officer ran a check on him, which came back clear. He was then told to leave, with an admonishment not to return or face arrest.

"Huh?" Timmy said. "On what charge?"

"We'll think of one," the cop said.

"How about aggravated mopery?" McNamara offered. "He looks like a prime candidate."

Aggravated mopery? Wolf thought with a grin. That's a new one.

The cop smiled. "That'll do."

"Just get outta here and get ahold of Spike and tell him I need bond money," Ira-Irv yelled. "You little fucking piece of shit."

"I'll go find Spike, Irv," Timmy called out as he bent down and struggled to lift up his Honda. Wolf stepped over to help and Timmy started to say something, then relented. Wolf bent his legs, grabbed the handlebars and jerked the motorcycle to an upright position. Timmy straddled the bike and started it up. He kicked the lever up into first gear and peeled away down the block.

"You're welcome," Wolf said.

"That little son of a bitch is on a fast track to nowhere," McNamara said. "Need to serve a hitch in the service of his country."

"Probably get washed out in Basic," Wolf said.

As Ira-Irv was being loaded into the police car, the yellow, rotating lights of the tow truck appeared. Wolf glanced at the biker who looked to be on the verge of tears.

After both he and the motorcycle had been removed from the area, a quiet calm settled back over the block. Mr. Ryland walked over to them.

"I really appreciate all you've done," Mr. Ryland said, offering his hand to McNamara and then to Wolf. "And I apologize for my daughter's conduct. She's not usually like this. She hasn't been herself lately, since she got involved with that Timmy."

"Well," McNamara said. "I know how hard it is trying to raise a girl, believe me."

"We're going to be leaving for Idaho in a few hours," Ryland said. "We've made arrangements for Glory to stay with my sister-in-law for a few months."

"Maybe a change of scene will do the trick," McNamara said.

Wolf thought about advising Ryland to make sure he took his daughter's phone but decided to keep his mouth shut.

"I'll make sure and tell Manny you two did an outstanding job," Ryland said. "And I'll download that Ring video to a flashdrive for you, in case you need it."

McNamara nodded a "thanks," and they watched Ryland go back into his house.

"We gonna stick around?" Wolf said.

"For a while," McNamara said. "As the Duke once said, it looks like this little fracas is about over. But we might as well stay for an hour or so just in case. We can charge Manny a little more, and Ryland does have that Ring thing recording to give us."

Another flashdrive, Wolf thought with a biting irony. Everybody's favorite evidence nowadays. Including mine. If I ever get the one I need.

CHAPTER NINE_

THE MCNAMARA RANCH
PHOENIX, ARIZONA

The dawning of a new day brought little in the way of solace for Wolf. The lack of sleep that both he and McNamara had experienced burning the midnight oil on those two surveillances was catching up to him now and they had a lot of shopping and packing to do, Preparation for the class had eaten up both the morning and a good portion of the afternoon. By the time they sat down to dinner together, Wolf was really looking forward to turning in early and trying to get some much-needed rest. The dinner itself had been tense, with both him and Chad leery of the almost palpable tension between Mac and Kasey. Conversation was perfunctory, and Wolf felt like whenever he tried to bring up a topic to talk about, neither of them would engage.

Not that I'm the best conversationalist anyway, he thought.

An uneasiness settled over the meal, like a murky, enveloping fog. Afterward, he went back to his apartment across the way and was thrown even more off his game fielding an unexpected phone call from Yolanda. She was eager to give him an update on how her academy training was going. All the while he was listening, his heart was aching thinking how she was no longer going to be part of his life, but he didn't want to impinge upon her newfound joy and excitement.

When she'd hung up, Wolf realized he'd forgotten to check with Garfield regarding the new bandito. Knowing that the shop closed at six, and it was now almost seven, he dialed the number which immediately went to voice mail. Not wanting to leave any specific detailed inquiry, he merely said, "Hey, professor, it's Steve, just calling to see how the project was going. I'll be tied up for the next couple of days with a class, so if you can give me a call and let me know, I'd appreciate it."

He wasn't prepared for what came about ten minutes later.

The phone rang and the number on the screen looked unfamiliar. The voice was as well.

"I'm trying to get hold of Steve," a masculine voice said.

"Speaking."

"What's your last name, Steve?"

The question struck Wolf as odd, and he replied, "Who's asking?"

After a pause, the voice said, "Detective Redpath, Phoenix Police Department."

Wolf hadn't been ready for that, and suddenly wondered if this was related to the biker incident at the Rylands'. Had young Timmy pitched a bitch about his bloody nose after all? Or maybe Irv-Ira had sustained some kind of injury and wanted to blame Wolf for it?

He waited for Redpath to speak again and, finally, he did.

"Did you call the Bellows Craft Shop a little while ago?"

"Yeah, why?"

Another pause, then: "You had a business relationship with Mr. Bellows?"

Had?

That set off alarm bells in Wolf's mind.

"Right," he said. "He's working on something for me. Is he okay?"

The man ignored Wolf's question. "Working on what for you?"

Suddenly Wolf had the thought that he shouldn't say anymore. For all he knew, the person on the other end of the line could be an imposter, maybe one of Soraces's boys, trying to figure out Wolf's next move about the bandito.

But if that's the case, his tired mind asked, how did he know I called Garfield?

"Let me call you back," Wolf said and hung up.

He then went to his laptop, turned it on, and waited for the machine to boot up. When it did, he checked the number on his screen and found that it came back to Phoenix PD.

His next thought was wondering if Garfield was all right. He dialed Redpath's number and waited.

"Redpath. Investigations."

"It's Steve Wolf. We were just talking about Garfield Bellows."

"Oh, right. Thanks for calling back."

"No problem," Wolf said. "Now is Garfield okay?"

Again, he ignored Wolf's question. "Can you spell your full name for me please?"

Wolf did, irritated by the man's evasiveness, but at the same time thinking that whatever this was about, it wasn't going to be good news.

After giving the detective his information, the man said, "Mr. Bellows was murdered last night. I'm investigating the homicide."

"Murdered?" Wolf was stunned. It took him a couple of seconds before he asked, "Is Ollie all right?"

"Ollie? That's ..."

"His wife."

"Yes," Redpath said. "She's quite devastated, but all right."

"Can you tell me what happened?"

"When's the last time you saw him?"

Wolf tried to think. "A couple of days ago, maybe. No, wait, it was Monday."

"What time Monday?"

Wolf blew out a breath. "I can't remember. It was in the morning sometime. Before noon."

"And you say he was working on something for you?"

"Right. He was making a statue out of plaster for me. A Mexican bandito."

"A bandito? You mean like in a cowboy bandit?"

"Yeah. I was supposed to pick it up either late today or tomorrow." Wolf thought about their conversation about the play. "Man, I can't believe this. Can you tell me what happened?"

"What type of work do you do, Mr. Wolf?"

Again the evasiveness, Wolf thought. Ask them a simple, straightforward question, and get another question in return.

"I'm a bail enforcement agent."

"And may I ask where you were last night?"

"I was on a surveillance with my partner. Why?"

"Routine. Just trying to get as much information as I can to piece this together. What's your partner's name?"

"Look," Wolf said. "I've asked you numerous times what happened and you've been giving me the runaround. Now, please, before I answer anything more, I would appreciate knowing the circumstances. Garfield was a friend of mine. I've been straight with you, haven't I?"

More silence, during which Wolf assumed Redpath was evaluating things. Finally, the detective cleared his throat and said, "Well, since you're in the field of law enforcement, in a very loose sort of way, I can tell you at this time that it appears to have been a robbery. Person or persons unknown entered the shop, removed money from the register, forced Mr. Bellows to open the safe, and then killed him."

The thought of kindly old Garfield, who wouldn't hurt a fly, being so senselessly murdered hit Wolf again like a kick in the groin. He told Redpath just about everything he could think of, leaving out, of course, the mention of the real bandito. The possibility that it might somehow be related seemed remote if both the cash register and the safe were rifled. Wolf doubted there could have been much money in either. Certainly not enough to justify taking a man's life.

But life was cheap in these troubled times.

The conversation kept replaying itself in his mind even hours later as he tried to get some sleep, which came in fits and starts, with a lot of bad dreams in between.

———

BEST IN THE WEST TACTICAL TRAINING INSTITUTE
JUST OUTSIDE OF MESA, ARIZONA

The red warning flag flapped in the slight morning breeze in front of the pistol range the next morning. The nylon pistol belt and thigh-holster felt a bit uncomfortable as Wolf moved up to the line and waited for Big Joe Barnes to give him the signal to start. Wolf was dressed in a black T-shirt, camouflaged cargo pants, and his old military desert combat boots. At least they allowed him a distant feeling of familiarity. The timed course consisted of five barriers of varying heights. The object was to approach each one, assume a cover position, and fire two rounds at each visible target that popped up downrange. The barricades were set up so as to obscure the shooter's view of certain targets as he progressed through each station. At least one combat reload would be required.

Wolf tried to push all the unpleasantness of learning about Garfield's death out of his mind as he concentrated on the task at hand. Mac had been upset yesterday as well.

"Damn shame," he'd said. "He was a good guy."

Wolf couldn't agree more but figured there was nothing he could do about it other than accept it and mourn for the professor's passing. Their conversation about Shakespeare still loomed in his memory.

Barnes dropped his hand and Wolf sprinted to the first barrier, which was an old barrel. Dropping to one knee and crouching behind it, he drew the Berretta 92F that Mac had loaned him and squeezed off two rounds at each visible target. He then rose and ran to the next one, a stack of lumber about five feet high. Again, Wolf assumed a crouching position, making sure he kept his head below the uppermost boards in the stack, and shot at each of the other targets, which were now visible. Crisscrossing to the next stop, Wolf slid down in front of an old Lincoln Continental, positioning his legs, as best he could behind the right front tire, figuring the engine-block would offer the most ballistic protection. From this angle three of the four targets were exposed, and Wolf went down the line, from right to left, putting two more rounds in each one.

He'd been given two magazines and he'd had to start with the slide locked back and an empty chamber. The reason they'd set the prescribed number of shots the way they had was obvious. Each magazine was loaded with fifteen rounds. Not starting with one in the pipe meant he'd fired fourteen rounds thus far and the slide was still forward. They wanted you to get to the final position, which was virtually exposed, and fire that one remaining round in the chamber, causing the slide to lock back and have you suddenly realize you hadn't done your combat reload from cover where you should have.

Ain't gonna happen, he thought and pressed the magazine release button.

Wolf let the mag fall to the ground, slammed home a fresh one. Rising, he moved with all the speed he could muster to the final position, the mailbox. Wolf stopped just short of it and crouched down as best he could. He peeked around one side, fired his two rounds at the furthermost targets, ducked back and rotated, hoping he was keeping his head below the curved arc as best he could as he rotated, then leaned over and fired his final rounds.

A whistle sounded and he straightened up, wondering what his time was, figuring he'd done fairly well. But that didn't make him feel any better.

Challenging course, he thought. It had several aspects that made you think, which was always good.

Still, it was no substitute for being in the real thing. And Garfield was still dead.

As he stood there waiting for the proctors to come downrange and meet him, he evaluated his performance. He also thought about factoring in the fatigue factor and the excess baggage he was carrying. The preceding few days had been one bad development after another.

The thoughts faded from his mind as Barnes and Pete Thornton approached him.

"Good time, Steve," Barnes called out. "Sixty-two seconds. Let's see how many hits you got."

Wolf waited for Joe and Pete to join him at the targets and check the number of holes and their locations. His first shot had been from about thirty yards away and Wolf was worried he'd blown it off, which was easy to do with that first, long, double-action trigger pull. He was certain he'd hit center mass on all the rest, and the cluster of holes seemed to verify this.

"Ah," Pete said, using his pen to mark the number of hits on the target's side margin. "Looks like you blew one off."

He began tearing off pieces of masking tape.

"Yeah," Wolf said. "I figured as much."

"Still a damn good score," Barnes said. "Plus you went first."

"Always hard being the leadoff batter," Pete said, taping up the last of the holes.

Wolf watched how well Pete was able to walk with the prosthesis on the sandy ground. He'd substituted the hook-like steel apparatus today for one with a full-sized boot.

Barnes clapped Wolf on the shoulder then leaned forward slightly and whispered, "Be interesting to see how our female client does."

Buck had briefed the two of them beforehand that it was a mixed group and stressed that they should be called "clients" as opposed to "students" or "cadets."

"Remember," he said, "the object is to teach them some things, but not to make them so miserable that they won't want to come back."

The female client, Jill O'Hara, was a retired Arizona State Police sergeant and was now a supervisor in charge of security at a nuclear reactor. There was talk of closing the facility down in the next year or two, and she wanted to branch out. The performance she gave was respectable but nowhere near Wolf's time or score. Each of the other nine clients, all of whom were in some kind of law enforcement field, completed the course with a mishmash of fractured times and shooting scores. McNamara had done well, coming in tops as far as the shooting, but with a time that was thirty-seven seconds longer than Wolf's

Barnes made the signal for the last shooter to start. He seemed to exude confidence and capability as he fired his first rounds and proceeded through the course.

"That guy moves pretty good," McNamara said. "For a big man."

They watched as the guy moved with agility and grace through the various positions, taking cover and shooting with a controlled elegance. Wolf had noticed him during their easy-does-it physical training session earlier that morning. He had huge arms with bulging muscles that resembled interwoven steel cables. The man's hands were exceptionally large. When they'd stopped to do push-ups during their run, he did his with one arm, but Wolf didn't get the feeling the guy was showing off. He stayed at the back of the group, so it was more like he was testing himself.

"Shit, you got that right," Buck said. "He's almost making it look too easy."

Barnes was holding the stopwatch and clicked it as the shooter delivered his final series of shots. His dark eyebrows rose in a silent acknowledgment.

"Beat your time by two seconds, Steve," Barnes said.

"Don't mean nothing till the shots get counted," McNamara said.

"Well, let's see," Pete said as he swung his artificial leg outward and began the trek to the end of the range. Wolf marveled at how well Pete got around. He'd participated in the slow, formation PT run that they'd done shortly after the opening welcome that morning. Moreover, his attitude seemed great but Wolf wondered if the same demons that haunted his dreams visited Pete Thornton's as well.

It was hard to know who would come calling in those wee hours when it was just you and the darkness and your memories.

He thought about Garfield again.

Downrange, the big guy holstered his weapon and touched his left wrist before he began walking back toward them, not even bothering to check his hits. He paused to retrieve the fallen magazine, which he'd dropped after his combat reload and re-inserted it into his mag holder.

"Looks pretty sure of himself," Wolf said.

"What's that guy's name again?" McNamara asked.

"Dirk," Buck said. "Cameron Dirk, But he don't like to be called by his first name. 'Just Dirk,' he told me. Late comer. Just signed up yesterday."

"Where's he work?" Wolf asked.

"He's not at the moment," Buck said. "Told me he was with a couple of PMC's over in Iraq and Afghanistan and did pretty well, but with all the troop reductions he came home. Wants to start his own security company."

Dirk walked up to them now and Wolf nodded and smiled.

"Nice going." He noticed a fancy watch on the man's left wrist.

That must have been that last movement I saw, Wolf thought. He was timing himself.

"Thanks," Dirk said. "But I had the advantage of watching you guys go first."

Pete let out a yell from downrange and then cupped his hands around his mouth.

"Perfect score," he yelled. "Didn't miss none, all center mass and head shots."

"Head shots?" Buck said, extending his hand toward Dirk. "You had the best time, too, so that makes you top dog. Congratulations."

Dirk shook Buck's hand and then Mac's and Wolf's.

"Pretty impressive." Wolf extended his open palm as well. "Nice shooting."

Dirk shrugged. "Like I said, I just followed your lead."

Up close and personal, Wolf noticed two things: the man's hand had crusty, solid ridges of calluses over the huge, bulbous knuckles and along the edge of the palm. He also had strange, offsetting eyes, one blue and one brown. It gave his gaze an unsettling quality.

"And these targets ain't shooting back," McNamara said.

Dirk smiled. "True enough. You moved pretty good, too. Bet you've been in your share of fire-fights."

McNamara nodded and gestured toward Wolf. "We both have. Army. You?"

"SEALs."

McNamara raised his eyebrows. "Good outfit."

"The best," Dirk said.

"Well, for the navy anyway," McNamara said. "See any action?"

"Plenty," Dirk said. "I enlisted right after nine-eleven. Hit the ground running in Iraq, Afghanistan, and a bunch of other shitholes around the globe. Finally, decided I'd had enough of going places I didn't want to go and went private."

"A PMC?" Wolf asked. "Which one?"

Dirk shook his head. "Probably one you never heard of. Called the *Suda Americanos Vistas*. We operated in South America doing security and bodyguard work mostly for corporate executives living down there."

Wolf had never heard of them but he didn't doubt the man's credentials. The SEALs were tops. The time frame put Dirk in his late thirties, which appeared about right.

The others came over to offer their praise of Dirk as well.

"This concludes this morning's range festivities," Buck said. "Everybody report to the main classroom for a debrief and evaluation, and then we'll eat lunch."

Wolf and McNamara let the others filter on ahead of them. Dirk eyed them and then fell into place at the end of the group.

"Perfect score and the fastest time," McNamara said, watching him go. "I figured you had that one sewn up."

"Win some, lose some," Wolf said. There was something about Dirk that bothered him, but he couldn't figure out what it was. The guy was very capable and seemed self-effacing, without a hint of braggadocio. Just the kind of guy you'd want on your side when your back was against the wall.

And yet ...

———

After lunch the rest of the day's training went pretty much as expected. They did a classroom session on movement techniques, finding cover, and the difference between cover and concealment. Buck had a big flatscreen TV to show numerous real-life incidents that had either gone real good or real bad.

"The bad ones are the most informative," he said. "It's important to learn from other's mistakes."

"You want to make your mistakes here," Barnes added. "In training, so you don't make them out there."

Movement practices and room and building searches followed. These were all done with rubber blue guns, but Buck mentioned that a Simunitions training session would be down the road.

"I'll look forward to that," McNamara said.

Wolf wondered if Mac was being facetious. Having practiced with those Simunition rounds before, Wolf knew it didn't hurt as much as being shot, but getting hit certainly wasn't a pleasant experience.

I guess the best thing is to not get hit, he thought. Just like in combat.

And so it went, with the day's training concluding at sixteen-forty-five. They all went back to the main office to retrieve their cell phones and car keys.

Wolf and Mac had rented rooms with the rest of the course attendees at a hotel in Mesa, at Buck's insistence. To develop camaraderie they were all to meet for dinner every night at eighteen thirty. This emphasized team dynamics, which was a big part of the course.

"A team will always beat a group of individuals," Buck had said in his opening lecture. "No matter how talented."

To this end, he had everyone place their cell phone in a plastic basket in the office so the training would be uninterrupted by personal business.

"You'll get them back at the end of each day," Buck

said. "And then we'll all go to dinner together, which I've arranged and paid for."

After getting his cell phone back and checking for messages, Wolf saw that he had three missed calls from Manny. McNamara had five, along with a couple of texts.

"Wonder what the hell this is all about?" McNamara said, scrolling down the list.

"You going to call him?" Wolf asked.

"Yeah, might as well," he said, pressing the redial button. He placed the phone to his ear and waited. After a few seconds he shrugged and terminated the call. "Went right to voice mail. Guess it can't be too important."

Wolf didn't check his and pocketed his cell as he told McNamara that he needed to skip the dinner and go back to Phoenix.

"Huh?" Mac said. "What for?"

"I need to go check at Garfield's shop for the bandito," he said. "The cops are probably finished with the crime scene investigation there by now."

He wanted that extra edge that having another duplicate would give him, and he also wanted to convey his condolences to Ollie. He hoped that poor Garfield hadn't suffered too much and hoped Redpath would be able to track down the son of a bitch who did it. Wolf made a mental note to check on that as well.

"Yeah," McNamara said. "I guess we should go there and pay our respects to Ollie. Damn shame about him. I had Reno call his brother. Apparently, somebody beat the poor guy to death. It wasn't a pretty scene."

This made Wolf feel all the more worse. "Death never is."

"Damn straight," McNamara said. "Why is it the weak and innocent always suffer the most?"

Wolf had no reply to that. They stood in silence for several seconds, and then Wolf said, "We can see Ollie at the funeral. No sense on both of us missing dinner. We paid for it in the course fee, and if you want Buck to take you on as an instructor you should get with the program."

"I was thinking he'd take *us* on as instructors." McNamara's brow furrowed. "Unless you're not interested in doing that, but keep in mind this bounty hunting business might just be on its last legs."

Wolf grinned. Mac was still looking out for him. "We'll talk about it later, okay? Now, if you could just give me the keys to the Escalade, I'll drop you off at the hotel and be back in no time."

McNamara dug his hand into the pocket of his cargo pants and withdrew the keys.

"Here you go," he said. "Son."

Wolf's grin widened, and he was doubly glad that Kasey hadn't been around to hear her father's joking dispensation.

Wolf noticed Dirk staring at them and when their eyes met Dirk smiled and turned away.

As they got into the Escalade Buck came running over to them and waved. Wolf started the vehicle and lowered the window.

"Well," Buck said. "Whatcha think?"

"Went pretty well," Wolf said. "I learned a lot."

He was exaggerating, of course, but didn't want to tell Buck that. He seemed to know it, however.

"Don't try to bullshit the bullshitter," Buck said. "I know it was probably all a review for you."

"Oh, I've been out of practice for a while," Wolf said.

"You shot pretty damn good," Buck said. "For a guy that's out of practice."

Wolf thought about the series of gun battles he'd been in over the past few months—actually more than he'd had on his last deployment.

"If it wasn't for that Dirk fella," Buck continued, "you'd be top dog."

"Top dog in training's one thing," McNamara said. "Being there for real's a whole 'nother."

Buck laughed.

Wolf momentarily wondered about Dirk. He'd move with such alacrity that it gave the impression he'd been there as well and not that long ago.

"See you at dinner," Buck said, leaning forward slightly. "And just to give you a heads-up, I'll be having weapon's inspection in the morning, so make sure your weapons are clean and your powder's dry."

"Does a bear shit in the woods?" McNamara said.

Buck grinned again and slapped the door before walking away.

"He asked me again privately if we'd be interested in investing in this little venture," McNamara said. "So think about—"

His cell phone chimed, and he glanced at the screen and smirked.

"Manny," he said before answering.

Wolf heard what sounded like a muted, but frantic, litany coming from the speaker after Mac had pressed the button. McNamara kept issuing grunts of acknowledgment and his head jerking up and down. After a couple more minutes he emitted a final grunt and said,

"Okay, we'll meet you over there in about twenty minutes."

After terminating the call he looked over at Wolf.

"Looks like I'll be going with you after all," he said.

"Trouble?" Wolf asked.

McNamara nodded and swore.

"Glory's gone."

———

THE GRAND TETONS HOTEL
PHOENIX, ARIZONA

Soraces had just finished practicing another variation of his backhand blade toss. The ninja pen stiletto had hit the exact target that he'd set up: an apple he'd grabbed from the fruit bowl in the lobby. He'd placed it on top of the small refrigerator. The sharp pointed end sunk into the meaty part of the fruit and it pleased him. Not only had it hit exactly where he'd aimed it, he'd managed to complete the withdrawal of the blade, the cocking back of his arm, and the throw in little over a second. He was getting faster and more accurate every time.

The chimes of his cell phone jolted him out of the reverie. It was Dirk.

"What's up?" he asked.

"I'm at the hotel in Mesa," Dirk said. "We were all supposed to have dinner together but Wolf and McNamara pulled out. Something came up and they're heading back to Phoenix."

"Something came up?"

"Yeah. I overheard them saying something about

having to go see some guy named Manny regarding an emergency."

"What kind of emergency?"

"Don't know. I'm outside in the lot still. Want me to skip the dinner and follow them? That maroon Escalade stands out like an overripe tomato."

Soraces considered this, then decided having Dirk do the tail would be too risky. This could be something, or it could be nothing, but either way, he had too many pieces in place to risk exposing his overall strategy. It was like a chess match. The shadows were his king and queen's knights and Dirk his rook. Well, maybe a queen would be more appropriate for his designation, not that he'd dare call him that to his face, but it was the most powerful piece on the board. "No, go ahead and stay with the group. Ask Buck if he knows why they aren't there and see what he says. I'll have Clyde pick them up. They took I-Ten, I take it?"

"Looks that way. They just left a couple of minutes ago."

"Okay." Soraces looked at his watch. It was two minutes after five. The drive from Mesa to Phoenix was about twenty minutes or so, and Manny had to be that bail bondsman, Emanuel Sutter. Clyde knew the address.

If that was where they were going ... Have to factor in the possibility of another destination ... Again, not a significant problem. Clyde had changed cars from the once-spotted black Dodge Charger and was now driving an Avalon with tinted windows. It should be a snap for him to pick them up once he accessed the tracker information."

"How did the class go?" Soraces asked.

"Pretty much a cake walk. But it did give me a chance to get a closer look at our quarry."

"And?"

"Both competent, although McNamara is starting to show his age a bit. Wolf's good, but definitely B-team material. I can take him easy. You just say when."

"It's not about *taking* him," Soraces said. "It's about recovering an item, a very valuable item, that only Wolf knows the whereabouts of. It requires a bit of delicate planning and execution."

"So we grab him and force him to talk. What's so delicate about that?"

"There's no guarantee it would work," Soraces said. "I told you, he's tough and he's smart."

"I could make him talk."

"And we'd then have a mess on our hands to clean up. Our employer wants this handled with finesse. Brute force has failed before. Twice before." Soraces was mentally assessing the situation, shifting and arranging the pieces in his mind as he spoke. "Ideally, we need a way for him to bring us the item on neutral ground of our choosing, or better yet, totally on our turf."

When Dirk didn't reply, Soraces added, "Patience is a virtue. I've got this pretty much planned out a certain way. One that will ensure success and cover our tracks."

"If you say so." Dirk's voice had a hint of sarcasm in it.

Soraces didn't care for that, but he also knew it was in the big man's character to be a bit overbearing—a typical characteristic of the ultimate alpha male.

"Did you plant that GPS tracker on their car?"

"Yes, mother." Dirk said, his tone laced with sarcasm. "But like I told you, I think we're wasting our time."

"I'll be the judge of that," Soraces said. "And don't underestimate them. Especially Wolf. A lot of competent men have regretted taking him too lightly recently."

"I never take anybody *lightly*," Dirk said, the sarcastic lilt growing more prominent. "Not until I've finished grinding their face into the dirt with the heel of my boot."

Alpha male on a leash, Soraces thought. This was going to be fun to watch play out.

RYLAND RESIDENCE
PHOENIX, ARIZONA

It had all the earmarks of a bizarre family reunion, and then some. Wolf and McNamara had arrived at the residence to find Mr. and Mrs. Ryland, Freddie, Manny, Reno Garth, and another man in a suit who looked like a cop, along with a uniformed officer. Freddie met them at the front door and Wolf noticed the plastic frame of his glasses had been broken in the center and taped together with white medical tape like some fugitive from one of those old nerd movies. The left lens had a horizontal crack running through it. The side of his face was swollen and showed traces of a purple bruising and his lower lip was twice its normal size.

"Those assholes do that to you?" McNamara asked, pausing to check Freddie's injuries.

He nodded.

"Looks like you went down fighting," McNamara said. "When did this happen?"

"Yesterday afternoon. They jumped us at a rest stop. Took Glory. Smashed our cell phones and punctured our tires." The inside of his lip had a line of dark stitching.

"Manny called Reno when we couldn't get ahold of youse," Freddy said.

"He brought his brother over here," Freddie said. "He's a police detective."

Wolf had figured as much. Besides the marked and unmarked squad cars parked in front of the residence, he'd also seen Reno's unmistakable black Hummer.

"Lieutenant Phil Garth," McNamara said. "I know him."

Reno looked somber as he stood off to the side, leaning on his fancy cane. He gave a slight nod to Wolf and McNamara as they entered the living room. It was a large room with beige colored walls and a matching carpet. A large television sat at the far end, and next to it was a shelf with several knickknacks and miniature glass horses. There were a sofa and three chairs, but no one was seated except for Mr. and Mrs. Ryland.

Mr. Ryland's face looked in even worse shape than Freddie's. His right eye was swollen shut and both sides of his face were covered with a variety of different sized scarlet and purple lumps. He sat in a living room chair talking to Reno's brother and the uniformed officer. Manny stood on the side of the sofa, his huge body like a towering monolith, with his hand on his sister's shoulder. Mrs. Ryland's face was buried in her hands and her body jerked convulsively and her husband continued to relate the long, sad tale.

"Everything was going smooth until she insisted on stopping at that damn rest stop," Mr. Ryland said. "They were waiting there for us. We didn't see the motorcycles because they were parked on the other side, in the trucking section." His S's had an uncharacteristic lisp to them. When he paused to sigh and lick his lips, it became obvious that he was missing some important teeth in front.

"I never dreamed she'd set us up like this," he said. "I mean, after that little incident last night, she seemed to be going along with what we wanted. Said she'd go to Louise's up in Idaho so long as we promised we'd let her come home for Christmas."

"You say she was texting?" the cop in the suit asked. "Could you see who she was communicating with?"

Wolf assumed from the man's posture and question that this was Reno's brother.

"I was right next to her," Mrs. Ryland broke in, her voice sounding fragile and broken. "But she kept leaning sideways. I should've known. I should have known."

Manny patted her shoulder.

Wolf and McNamara exchanged glances.

Wolf regretted not advising Mr. Ryland to take the girl's phone last night.

"And you made out a police report with the State Police?" Phil Garth asked.

Mr. Ryland nodded. "For all the good it did. After they jumped us and took off with Glory, one of them came around and stuck a knife in two of our tires. They took our cell phones and smashed them to bits. We had to wait until someone else stopped before we could call for the police and an ambulance. By that time, fifteen or twenty minutes had gone by."

"Do you think you can identify any of them?"

Mr. Ryland shook his head and then winced as if the movement had brought a flood of pain.

"They wore masks," he said, again lisping as he said the word. "Horrible skeleton-like things over the lower parts of their faces. Even that damn Timmy, but I'm sure it was him. Glory ran right to him."

"And one of them said, 'This is for Bruns,' to me," Freddie said. "Called me a motherfucker, too."

Reno's brother nodded in acknowledgment.

"I should have known," Mrs. Ryland said, her voice a high-pitched whine between sobs.

"I called a friend of mine on State," Phil Garth said, sounding very official and reassuring. "They put out an amber alert on your daughter, and she's in the computer as a minor requiring authoritative intervention. A runaway."

"But she was abducted, I tell you," Mr. Ryland said. "They took her. That god damn Timmy was with them. That's a kidnapping, isn't it?"

Reno's brother drew his lips into a thin line.

"At the moment, let's just be concerned with finding her and getting her back," he said. "It'll be up to the State Police to determine any charges, but from what you say, your daughter was possibly complicit ..."

He left the sentence incomplete and the last word hung in the air like a bad smell.

"It was those biker gangsters," Mr. Ryland said.

"Those thugs attacked us and took out daughter. Why can't you do anything?"

"The Satan's Spawn," Manny said. "That's the group that Timmy was supposedly trying to hang around with."

"If the motorcycle gang you mentioned is involved," Phil Garth said, "they'll be checked out. My friend on State said he was aware of them. They're purported to have a club house and it's being looked at."

Manny patted his sister's shoulder twice and then cocked his head toward Wolf, indicating he should follow. Manny moved across the room with a moderately fast gait for one so large and pushed out the front door. Wolf and McNamara followed. Reno limped right behind them. The glowing porch light illuminated the area.

"Anybody got a cigarette?" Manny asked.

Wolf shook his head and looked around. None of the others had one either.

"Didn't know you smoked, Manny," McNamara said, offering him some gum.

Manny grabbed a stick, unwrapped it, and tossed the papers onto the lawn. "I quit smoking twenty years ago, but, Christ, this damn thing has started me craving something." He ran his fingers through his longish hair and shook his head.

Freddie pushed through the door and stood beside them looking expectant.

"You ask them?" he said.

Manny frowned and shook his head again. His jaws worked. After taking a deep breath, he looked at McNamara.

"What would it take for you guys to track her down and bring her back? How much?"

Wolf watched Mac's reaction. He shrugged.

"I don't know if we'd be your best choice," McNamara said. "You got the police working on it, and they're a lot better equipped than we are."

"Bullshit," Manny said. "You know as well as I do that the cops are practically fucking handcuffed. They gotta do things by the fucking book, needing probable cause and waiting on search warrants. No offense to your brother, Reno."

Reno gave a fractional nod. His face looked drawn and tight.

"Anyway," Manny continued. "My point is, we can't afford to wait. Who knows how long Glory's got before she's—" He stopped and grimaced. Freddie winced, too.

"Before something awful happens," Manny said a few seconds later.

McNamara put his hand on Manny's shoulder. "I share your concern. But the fact remains that the police have a bigger network than we do, a lot more resources, and they've got a helluva lot more intel on this biker group."

"I can ask my brother to fill us in," Reno said.

"Tell them about the cell phone, Manny," Freddie said.

"Right." Manny's head perked up. "Glory took her cell phone. Can't you guys trace it someway?"

"We can't unless we got cooperation from the cell phone company," McNamara said. "But I'm sure the police are probably already doing that."

"We are," Phil Garth said as he stepped through

the door with the uniformed officer and joined them on the cement slab that constituted a front porch of sorts.

Reno stepped up. "Phil, this is Big Jim McNamara and his partner, Steve Wolf."

Phil Garth stared at Mac. "I know McNamara. We've met."

Mac gave an acknowledging nod.

"I hope you both realize that this is a police matter," Phil Garth said. "And not some SEAL Team Six mission. You too, Reno."

His brother seemed embarrassed.

"The SEALs are Navy," McNamara said. "I was Special Forces. Army. Green Berets."

"Whatever," Phil Garth said. "Just stay out of it. And we are working that phone lead."

Manny stared at him.

"Phil, tell me that you found her," he said.

Garth took a deep breath and canted his head to the side. "Look, Manny, I came here as a courtesy because of your friendship with my little brother, but as I explained before, this is out of my jurisdiction. We gave the information to the State Police regarding the phone, and I'm sure they're doing due diligence looking into it."

Wolf felt a twinge of amusement at him referring to Reno as his "little brother." Reno towered over his brother in both height and width.

"You said 'we,'" Manny said. "What can you tell me?"

"Just that the State Police are working on it."

"Aw, dammit, Phil," Reno said. "Can't you help us more than that?"

Phil Garth rolled his eyes and took out his cell phone.

"Okay," he said. "I'll give my friend on State a call. And I've already made arrangements for a squad car to keep an extra watch on this house. If those thugs on bikes come back here, we'll grab them and shake them upside down."

He and the uniformed officer walked over to the parkway by the cars and Garth started punching numbers into his phone. Reno walked after him, his arms jerking to emphasize his words he was speaking.

The man looks by-the-book, Wolf thought. I doubt Reno's going to say anything to change his brother's mind.

"See what I mean?" Manny said. "They're moving about as fast as a bunch of turkeys prancing around the barnyard, for Christ's sake." He paused and bit his lower lip. "Look, you guys seen Glory. You know what she looks like and all. Please. You gotta go after her. Freddie, give them the phone information."

Wolf was silently glad that Manny hadn't referred to his nephew the usual pejorative nickname, Sherman.

Freddie dug a folded piece of paper out of his shirt pocket and handed it to McNamara.

"I'll pay you guys whatever you want," Manny said. "Name your price. You gotta find her."

McNamara looked at Wolf, who nodded.

"All right," Mac said. "We'll do what we can. We can work out the price later."

"Thanks, Mac," Manny said, extending his hand. "I owe you. Big time."

"Just find her," Freddie added. "Please."

"We'll do our best," Wolf said.

McNamara clapped Freddie on the shoulder and they told Manny they'd be in touch. They started walking to their car but Wolf grabbed McNamara's arm.

"Let's not rush off," he said. "Let's see if Reno's brother finds anything out first."

McNamara nodded and saw Phil Garth and Reno moving back toward Manny and Freddie.

"Okay," Phil Garth said. "They do have a lead from a phone ping and are checking it out."

"Where is she?" Manny asked, the desperation intertwined in his words.

Phil Garth hesitated before he spoke. "They didn't say. And I couldn't tell you even if I knew. It's an active police investigation and—"

"It's out of your damn jurisdiction," Manny said. His tone was harsh, but his eyes drooped with an imploring expression as he glanced toward Wolf and McNamara.

Mac nodded and slapped Wolf's shoulder, indicating the Escalade.

As soon as they got in, McNamara settled himself behind the wheel and said, "What did I tell you? That guy wouldn't say shit even if he had a mouthful." He took out his phone and started dialing. "If we're going to take on Satan's Spawn," he said, "we're gonna need some backup. Especially with little Glory involved."

"The P-Patrol?" Wolf asked.

McNamara nodded and said, "Among others." He put the phone to his ear.

"But that still doesn't—"

McNamara lifted his hand to cut him off as his face stretched into a smile and he said into the phone, "How you doing, darling?"

Wolf heard the vestiges of a sultry laugh that he was sure belonged to Ms. Dolly.

After a quick explanation of what was going on and getting an assurance that the P-Patrol was on their way from Vegas, Mac terminated the call and turned to Wolf.

"Hey, why didn't you tell me Yolanda quit the team?" he asked.

Wolf shrugged, still feeling a bit miffed about being summarily cut off before, and now feeling a renewed sense of loss regarding him and Yolanda.

"I was going to," he said. "Just didn't get around to it yet."

McNamara twisted the key in the ignition and the Escalade came to life.

"Explains why you been so damn moody lately," he said.

Wolf said nothing. He had no reply.

"So what were you saying before when I cut you off?" McNamara asked.

Wolf blew out a slow breath. Being angry at Mac was counterproductive, and besides, Wolf knew, in his heart, that the source of his angst had nothing to do with his best friend and mentor. It had to do with a beautiful lady who was out of his league, and now out of his life.

"I was saying," Wolf said, "that we still have no way to trace her. I mean, it's clear the State Police aren't going to be giving us anything."

"No," McNamara said, shifting into gear. "But I got me an idea who we might ask."

Wolf's brow wrinkled as he looked at him.

Who the hell's he talking about?

CHAPTER TEN_

THE GRAND TETONS HOTEL
PHOENIX, ARIZONA

It was closing in on eleven as Soraces listened with interest as Dirk talked ... Another adjustment had to be made on the board.

"Like I told you," Dirk said. "They came back here about twenty-hundred or so. We'd finished dinner and a bunch of us were relaxing in the bar. Wolf and McNamara found us and pulled Buck aside. I was sitting in the next booth with Jill, the chick in the class. She ain't bad looking and, man, can she drink."

He sounded a bit plastered himself, but Soraces knew that Dirk could function with deadly accuracy regardless of how much he'd imbibed. He'd proven that on plenty of ops.

"Spare me the histrionics," he said. "What did they say?"

"I leaned back so I could kind of listen in," Dirk

continued. "They said something about having to pull out of the class. So—"

"They say why?"

"I'm getting to that," Dirk said, obviously a bit irritated at being interrupted. He waited.

"Sorry," Soraces said. "Go ahead."

Dirk took an eight-count before he started talking again. "They asked Buck if they could borrow some equipment."

"What kind of equipment?"

"Night-vision goggles, and range finders. Don't interrupt me again."

"Sorry," Soraces repeated, but his mind raced. With that kind of equipment, there was something going on, all right. This could be bad for his plan. If Wolf got hurt or killed before the deal was completed ...

"You've got your own night-vision goggles, right?" Soraces said.

"In my go-bag." Dirk sounded insulted that Soraces had asked.

"Did they say anything more about what they had going? Or where?"

"Not right then, that I overheard."

Soraces contemplated this. "You said you put that tracker on their car?"

"Yeah. But there's more. After they talked to Buck, they came over to our table. I offered to buy them drinks but they declined. Then they asked Jill if they could speak to her privately. So I went over to Buck and the boys and bought another round of beers. I asked him what was going on and he said Mac and Wolf were having to pull out of the class because of some emergency. I asked him what, and at first he didn't want to say, but then said something about a friend's niece going missing. That they had to go find her and bring her back."

This jibed with what Perkins had reported with Wolf and McNamara going to the Rylands' house and meeting with the police. It was either a runaway or an abduction. If it were the latter, it would mean a whole lot of police involvement.

But then why would two private citizens, albeit bail enforcement agents, feel compelled to go find the girl? The runaway option made more sense.

"Hey," Dirk said. "You gonna reimburse me for all this shit? I had to drop a bunch of money on drinks."

"Yeah, yeah," Soraces said. "What else you got?"

"Well, after about thirty minutes Buck and the other guys leave. I was finishing up my beer and waiting for Jill to come back. I could see her and them sitting in the lobby, her talking on the phone and then writing shit down."

This is getting interesting, Soraces thought.

"So," Dirk continued, "when she comes back, I wave her over to a booth and get us another round of drinks. I told the bartender to load hers, and he must've thought I was trying to get laid, or something, cause he did. When she was primed, I asked her what was up with Wolf and Mac, and she tells me they wanted her to call somebody she knew on her old department."

"She's a cop?"

"Yeah. State Police. Retired. But like I said, she's well preserved."

Soraces filed this information.

"Anyway," Dirk said, "after another couple of drinks, she loosened up a little more and said it had something to do with a missing person investigation they were working. That's all I got out of her."

That's enough, Soraces thought. It all fit. Wolf and McNamara were heading back to Phoenix. It was time once again to rearrange a few pieces on the board.

"Want me to drop out too?" Dirk asked.

Soraces debated his possible moves, then said, "No, stay where you are for now. We don't want to create any suspicion that you were there only because of them."

"Okay. But what's the damn plan?"

"I have Clyde on them now. After they got back from Mesa, they came back to their ranch house, but the lights are still on. I told him to stay on them for the moment."

"I bet Clyde loves that." Dirk chuckled. "Serves him right. Well, maybe I'll go knock on Jill's door and see if I can get into her pants."

"I'd prefer you didn't," Soraces said. "If you want to rent a pro, that's fine. I'll reimburse you. But be discreet. Wolf and McNamara are the ones I want you to get close to, not some ex-cop, well preserved, or not."

"Ah, I need to get some sleep anyway," Dirk said. "So far I'm leading the class."

"Just stay ready," Soraces said. "I've got to work this out."

He hung up and thought about things, mentally recording what he knew, and theorizing what he didn't. An abduction ... What was it all about?

Then a variation of his plan suddenly came to him. An abduction ...

Why not? Similar to the last gambit, but different enough to be discrete ... It worked before, so why not again?

SHERIFF'S ANNEX STATION
UNINCORPORATED TOWN OF CROWN POINTS
GILA COUNTY, ARIZONA

Wolf was feeling the fatigue creeping over him again. The protracted lack of decent sleep over the past several days was catching up to him this morning like a looming set of bad debts threatening a pending repossession at any moment. And it didn't help that the air-conditioning in this box-like cinderblock building was on the fritz. Luckily, the sergeant with whom they were talking had left the door to his office half open. That helped bring in a little air from the outer reception room, but it was still unbearably hot, and Wolf was very much aware that he was in dire need of a shower. Another shower, actually, because he'd taken one after his early morning run, but he wished he'd used a double dose of deodorant. At least he wasn't the only one adversely affected by the heat. McNamara's face and neck showed ridges of beaded moisture and he'd even sweated through the open BDU blouse despite having a dark T-shirt on underneath it. Ms. Dolly, who'd presumptuously snatched a file from the stack on Hernandez's desk and was using it as a fan, and Brenda both glistened, like they'd just finished an aerobics session.

Men sweat, Wolf thought. Women glisten.

Across the large gunmetal-gray desk, the Gila County Sheriff, Sergeant Hernandez, didn't seem any more able to deal with the heat than the rest of them. His vest sat on the far edge, the stiff Kevlar panels making it look like a like a miniature tent with an embroidered badge and name plate. There were sodden expanding circles under each arm of his short-sleeved khaki shirt that threatened to encompass the bright yellow chevrons with each passing minute. Hernandez's arms looked massive and hairy, but he also had a barrel chest that didn't taper at all to a narrow waist. The rotating electric fan on the other side of the desk did little more than blow the rank-smelling hot air back in Wolf's face each time the caged blades rotated his way.

Par for the course thus far, he thought as the latest blast of warm, sweat-laden air caressed his face.

The now-depleted P-Patrol had arrived at Phoenix International Airport at 0430 hours, which was now about seven hours ago. Wolf had thought about remaining in bed when he heard the door to the ranch house open and went to the window. He saw McNamara shuffling toward the Escalade and called down to him through the open window. He seldom used his air-conditioning preferring instead the natural coolness of the desert night air.

"Want me to go? You can get a little more sleep."

McNamara glanced upward with a wry look.

"Now how would that look?" he called back. "Me asking them for help, and then not even being there to pick them up."

Wolf was wondering if Mac was regretting that decision now. He looked really worn out.

"Make no mistake," Hernandez was saying. "I got no love whatsoever for those jokers. Nor am I scared of them." The big chest puffed out slightly. "I did a tour in Iraq and ten years on Phoenix PD before I took the job out here. But even though they're low-life scum, I can't go harassing them for no reason. I got to have probable cause."

"You say you searched their place yesterday?" McNamara asked.

Hernandez nodded. "Me and two of my deputies went out there after I got the call from Detective Case on State asking us to go check. We checked the whole place out, but *nada*."

"How hard did you look?" McNamara said.

Hernandez raised an eyebrow. "Hard enough. All Case had to go on was a cell phone ping from that general area, and then nothing. No further traces. Could've been she was just traveling through the area."

"Not likely," McNamara said.

"No, but I'm a lawman. I gotta deal with facts, not hunches."

McNamara frowned. "So how'd they act? You get any indication they were hiding something?"

Hernandez shrugged. "With those kind of ass ah, idiots, they always look that way irregardless. But in answer to your question, nothing I could put my finger on. Certainly nothing to get a search warrant for. Spike, he's their leader, just sat there the whole time drinking and saying we were welcome to look everyplace even in the throne."

"The Throne?" McNamara said.

Hernandez smirked. "They got what you a brick shi —err, outhouse next to the barn. They ain't got no running water, except from a well. There's a stream running by the place."

The fan rotated back toward him and he leaned back, clasping his hand behind his head, but after a few seconds must have caught a whiff of himself and quickly lowered his arms.

"It's okay, sarge," Ms. Dolly said. "None of the rest of us are smelling too good at the moment, either. And I'm curious, too. I never seen a brick shithouse before."

Hernandez flashed a hint of a nervous smile, his face reddening, as the pungency of his body odor was again circulated by the fan's rotation.

"I sure wish that damn guy would get the AC fixed," he said. "I'm stuck in here finishing up my monthly's. It's pure misery."

"We know how it is," Ms. Dolly said with a sly grin. "Believe me."

"Did you see a Honda Fury out there by any chance?" Wolf asked.

"A Honda?" Hernandez smirked. "The only Japanese bikes they out there are in their rice garden."

Wolf raised an eyebrow. "Rice garden."

Hernandez chuckled again. "That's what they call it. All kinds of rice burners strung up on steel cables about fifteen feet above the ground. Most of them are all smashed all to hell and hung upside-down or sideways."

"The missing girl's boyfriend has a Honda Fury," Wolf said.

"Yeah, I recall Case mentioning that." Hernandez shrugged. "I don't know what to tell you. The Satan's Spawn, as they call themselves, like to come off as a hard-core motorcycle gang, but they're really just a bunch of pus—" He stopped abruptly as his eyes shot toward Ms. Dolly and Brenda again, then said, "Pansies."

Wolf and Mac exchanged a quick look as Wolf recalled what Ms. Dolly always implied what the abbreviation, P-Patrol, stood for. But it was only a lurid supposition on his part, anyway.

You ain't never met a pair like those two ladies, he thought, and then found himself thinking about Yolanda, and wondering how she was doing and if he'd ever see her again. He thought about the other romances in his own life, how he had always been the one leaving or marching off to war. Now the shoe, so to speak, was on the other foot.

"Like I said," Hernandez was saying, "they act like they're a bunch of one-percenters. Some of them even wear that patch on their colors, but deep down, they're as phony as a three-dollar bill. Just like that compliance search last night. Sure, Sergeant Hernandez, go right ahead. Search anywhere you like, sir." He stopped and wrinkled his nose. "I stay on them as much as I can. Rumor has it that they're a pit-stop for the drugs coming up from Mexico. We've assisted the DEA on a couple of raids out there but never found nothing."

Wolf wondered how hard they'd looked.

"So," Hernandez continued, "I'm stuck giving out parking tickets when they come into town here, and if I catch them speeding. And last night I cited them for open burning. They had this big fire pit blazing and I told them before, they got to have a covering of some sort to prevent the embers from floating up in the air. Like I said, they ain't as hard-core as they pretend to be. A lot of it's an act."

"Maybe they'll break a leg," McNamara said,

glancing again at Wolf. "Like they did back in Shakespeare's time."

Wolf smiled and remembered that he had to check his emails when they got back to see what he'd gotten on that English paper. Then he thought about Garfield and felt sad.

"Now I'm not saying that they're not capable of some nasty stuff," Hernandez said. "I wouldn't put anything past them, and they very well might be that pit-stop on the drug pipeline, but I've got no proof of that."

"What can you tell us about their compound?" McNamara asked.

The word seemed to cause a flicker of Hernandez's eye. "Compound? You must've spent some time in the military."

McNamara grinned and motioned toward Wolf. "Yeah, we both did."

"Well," Hernandez said after a few seconds. "They're staying at the old Basheer place. It's on the outskirts of town. You aren't figuring on going out there to confront them, are you?"

"The thought had crossed my mind," McNamara said. "Especially since you told us they were a bunch of pussies. I mean pansies."

Hernandez's head jerked as if he'd been slapped.

Ms. Dolly smiled as the lawman's swarthy face reddened.

When he'd regained his composure he said, "There's about fifteen of them, give or take a few that come and go, and that looked to be the number last night. Don't get the idea that you can waltz in there and confront them. They may not be true one-percenters, but they can be a rough bunch, especially on their own turf. They've got an enforcer nicknamed Python. Big and mean."

"We'll keep that in mind," McNamara said. "But what about this Basheer place?"

The law man trapped his lower lip between his teeth for a few seconds. "Used to be called Bootleg Basheer's. Back in the day, this whole area used to be a mining town, and when the silver ran out, things sorta dried up until Prohibition. Then this place opened up again as a booze channel, bringing it up from Mexico. Their place is one of them old farmhouses away from the main part of town. At one time it was used for sheep ranching, then booze smuggling. They're actually paying rent, so I can't just up and evict them."

"So there's probably a lot of places to hide stuff there," McNamara said.

"Yeah," Hernandez said, "there are. And we hit all of them, too. Drug sniffing dogs and all. Nothing."

McNamara grinned. "Maybe we'll have more luck."

Hernandez looked askance at McNamara, and then at Wolf. "You boys said you were friends with somebody on the State Police ... What did you say their name was?"

"We didn't," McNamara said. "She's retired, and I'd rather not bring her into this."

Hernandez raised both eyebrows. "What you do for a living?"

"Bail enforcement agents," McNamara said. "But we're not looking for any fugitive warrants now. We're just trying to locate a missing girl."

"And you're getting paid, right?"

McNamara shrugged and then nodded. "Expenses,

probably. Like I said before, this is more or less a favor for a friend."

"So," Hernandez said. "You two packing?"

Wolf was silently amused that Hernandez hadn't even directed the question toward Ms. Dolly or Brenda, both of whom had guns in their purses.

His chauvinism is showing, Wolf thought. Never assume.

"I am," McNamara said. "A Glock nineteen. Want to see my CC permit?"

Hernandez nodded and looked at Wolf.

"You?"

Wolf shook his head. "No, sir."

Keep it professional and polite, Wolf thought. Can't get in trouble that way, and Hernandez looks like the type who's easy to impress if you appeal to his vanity.

"He doesn't carry, but his whole body's a weapon." McNamara handed his concealed carry card across the desk. Hernandez studied it, then handed it back.

"Looks to be in order." He heaved a sigh. "I can appreciate you wanting to locate this runaway girl, but if you're planning on going over there to talk to them, which I wouldn't advise, you do so at your own risk."

"We're used to taking risks," McNamara said.

Hernandez's nostrils flared. "All right. Good luck on your quest, but let's get one thing straight. You see something that's a violation of the law, you call me. Understand? Do *not* try to handle anything on your own. You ain't actual law enforcement."

"Will do," McNamara said, standing. "Appreciate your time and assistance."

Wolf did the same, as did Ms. Dolly and Brenda.

As they were walking out, Wolf could hardly wait

to get back into the Escalade and turn the air-conditioning on high. A man with a garish baseball cap pulled down across his forehead was sitting in a chair next to the doorway to Hernandez's office. He had on shorts that exposed a pair of white, bony knees and he also had on black-frame glasses and a surgical mask.

That guy could be the poster boy for the stereotypical lost tourist, Wolf thought. In the age of COVID 19.

Hernandez strode ahead through the outer office and opened the door, holding it for Ms. Dolly and Brenda. They both smiled as they went out. The slender Hispanic girl in the clerk's outfit came up to Hernandez and said, "Sarge, this man's been waiting quite a while to talk to you about an incident he witnessed on Highway Seventy-two. Possible traffic violation. Insisted on waiting."

"Several violations," the man said. His voice was a wavering tenor.

Hernandez rolled his eyes and Wolf cast another glance at the concerned citizen.

The guy stood and Wolf saw he was tall and slender, with his hairless long legs extending into a pair of old-style green gym shoes below the Bermuda shorts. The baseball cap was a bright red and yellow, and the mask bulged over what appeared to be a large proboscis. The old-style glasses were perched on top of what appeared to be a big, hooked nose under the COVID mask.

That dude looks even more nerdy than Manny's nephew, Freddie, Wolf thought.

He shot Hernandez a wink for luck and followed McNamara out the door.

———

THE GRAND TETONS HOTEL
PHOENIX, ARIZONA

Soraces had been tossing his ninja blade again, more out of nervousness than for practice. The sudden departure of Wolf, before the deal for the bandito could be set up, had thrown his original strategy off a bit. And waiting always grated on him.

He flipped the knife with an under-handed toss this time. It stuck in the now perforated right side of the wooden frame of the whiteboard. The board itself had all sorts of scribbling and arrows on it in various colors. Going over to pull the blade free, Soraces noted that the frame had so many perforations it was growing unstable. He would have to switch to the other side. The bottom had a wedge-like slope to accommodate the markers, so it made a poor target for throwing, but the top portion was still unmarked.

His cell phone rang and he glanced at the screen. It was Charles Perkins.

The master's patience, he thought. It's always rewarded.

"Speak to me," he said.

"I'm in Gila County," Perkins said. Soraces could tell because his voice was an almost infinitesimal pitch lower. "Target stopped in a Sheriff's Annex Station here. Talked to a sergeant named Hernandez for about forty-five minutes."

"Any idea what was said?"

"Affirmative," Perkins replied. "I donned a disguise and listened in from the waiting room."

"A disguise? They didn't recognize you, did they?"

"Hardly." His voice sounded self-assured and totally confident. "I was doing my king of the nerds imitation. Plus, I had on one of those masks."

Soraces laughed. "Excellent. What did you find out?"

He listened as his surveillance man gave a quick, detailed summary of what he'd overheard.

So Wolf and company are about to take on some wanna-be bikers, he thought.

Not the most ideal of circumstances.

"You want me to stay on them, I assume," Perkins said.

"Right." Soraces glanced at his watch. "Maintain your distance and don't let them see you."

"I already told you, they haven't spotted me yet, and they won't."

"Take it easy. I'm thinking of getting you some immediate assistance, is all."

"Assistance? Want me to call my brother?"

"Not at the moment," Soraces said. "And let me worry about who to call."

He hung up and threw the blade at the whiteboard frame again. It stuck in the left side this time, vibrating at a perpendicular angle to the horizontal framework. He couldn't afford for Wolf to get hurt or possibly killed tangling with some biker idiots.

It's time to mobilize my rook, he thought.

CHAPTER ELEVEN

OUTSIDE BOOTLEG BASHEER'S
GILA COUNTY, ARIZONA

Wolf reapplied some of the greenish camo paint and smeared it over his face as he looked in the small mirror embedded in the passenger side visor of the Escalade. McNamara sat in the driver's seat and was using the rearview mirror. It had taken them virtually all of what had been left of the day to do their reconnoitering of the old Basheer place. It was located amongst a cluster of small hills about three miles from the outskirts of the small, unincorporated town of Crown Points. A long winding road lined with sentry-like trees on one side and a crumbling, three-foot stone wall on the other, connected to the main highway. The stream Hernandez had mentioned ran along the western section of the property and the wall had sporadic gaps in it the closer it got to the house. Fifteen Harley Davidson motorcycles were parked next to the building, all gleaming steel and leather seats. The house itself looked like it had once been a proud structure, but, now, dry rot had eroded large patches of the wall and the badly peeling exterior rested on a questionable base. A barn-like structure sat about sixty feet from the house and appeared to be in an equal state of disrepair, with weather-beaten gray boards set on top of a solid-looking cement foundation. Between the two buildings was a well-built brick structure that Wolf assumed was "The Throne." A beat-up old pickup truck and a portable gas trailer that looked like it held a couple thousand gallons, were parked in front of the barn's expansive doors. About fifty feet away a half-a-dozen motorcycles dangled from a network of chains and cables. The agglomeration was held in place by a portable winch and a massive steel bar that served as a make-shift cotter pin for the heavy chain links attached to the winch. Wolf assumed that it had to be what Hernandez had referred to as the "Rice Garden."

Most of the activity during the day had been limited to a few of the bikers stumbling out of the house to urinate or defecate in a grassy garden area adjacent to the Rice Garden.

"If they got that damn brick shithouse available," McNamara had whispered on their recon expedition as they crouched behind the stone wall about ten yards from the defecating man, "why in the hell do they keep doing their business out in the yard like that?"

Indeed, the distance seemed to be about the same but Wolf had no idea.

"What was it that idiot politician in Washington said the other night on TV?" he whispered back. "People are gonna do what they're gonna do."

And then the rain had started, and the squatting biker yelped, pulled up his pants, and ran for the house. The curtain of heavy rain advanced over the terrain like an enveloping shroud. McNamara tilted his head back and said the monsoon-like downpour reminded him of the Mekong Delta. They used the curtain of heavy rain to cover their movements through the hundred yards of thicket and back to the waiting Escalade.

"Whooie," Ms. Dolly said as they both piled into the rear seat area. "You two smell like a couple of wet dogs just coming out of the briar patch."

McNamara grinned. "You're lucky you didn't get a whiff of the other guy."

Wolf chuckled recalling the bare-ass biker running to get out of the rain.

After the monsoon passed, the trees and shrubbery glistened in the late afternoon sunshine and the area smelled almost fresh and clean. It reminded Wolf of some of the mountain patrols he'd been on in Afghanistan. Leafy and fresh smelling, but always fraught with sudden danger. After going back into Crown Points to grab some quick fast-food meals, they made their way back in the Escalade, as darkness fell. They drove with no lights and Ms. Dolly behind the wheel. The night-vision goggles sat awkwardly on her head, her red hair puffing out from under the helmet.

"These damn things are gonna take a whole lotta getting used to," she said. "Not to mention what it's doing to my hair."

"If you see another car coming with its headlights on," Wolf said, "just tilt you head back and look underneath them. Or you can flip them up."

She coasted to a lights-out stop and used the emergency brake. Across the darkened expanse they could see the lights popping on inside the house at Bootleg Brasheer's. A couple of floodlights came on in the front yard and some heavy-metal rock music began blaring from speakers set on the dilapidated, outside porch. Wolf had noticed a big generator on the west side of the old house.

"Stay in touch," Ms. Dolly said from behind the wheel, the jutting goggles making her look almost insect-like.

Brenda sat beside her in the front passenger seat.

"*Tenga cuidado*," she said. "We'll be here if you need us."

"Just shout," Ms. Dolly said, her words echoing in Wolf's earpiece.

He knew the range on the radios was about a quarter mile since there was no repeater to amplify the transmissions. Hopefully, they could stay close enough for Ms. Dolly to hear them if and when they called for the pick-up.

"You ready?" he asked Mac.

"Born ready," McNamara said. "Let's do it."

They'd both changed out of their sodden clothes and put on fresh underwear and BDUs. McNamara had his Glock strapped in tight with a low-slung tactical holster and Wolf had a large, burly bladed Coast TX395 knife in his right-side pocket that could be used for offense, defense, or just plain old tactical cutting. As the access road curved, they separated. McNamara went left, Wolf right, taking the longer trek along the stone wall and toward the Rice Garden and beyond. The low wall and the wind barrier trees afforded him plenty of cover, and, even though it was now dark, Wolf had familiarized himself with the terrain on their earlier recon. As he made his way east, running parallel to the curving wall, he tried to surmise where the girl might be. Both he and Mac were certain that she was here. And Timmy Wagner was, too. They'd both seen the remnants of a smashed-up Honda Fury hanging in the Rice Garden. The motorcycle had a new look to it, and both he and Mac were certain it was the same one they'd seen the Wagner punk riding two days ago.

But was he a punk?

Wolf thought about that as he slipped by the suspended junkyard and around toward the rear of the barn. It was certainly both possible and likely that both Timmy and Glory had been willing participants in the brutal attack on her parents but Wolf wondered if the two teenagers had bitten off way more than they could chew. Dreams of young love and rebellion might have run smack dab into a brick wall once they got here to biker haven. Wolf recalled the disparaging words Ira-Irv had used describing both Timmy and his rice burner.

What was that Manny had said Timmy's motor-cycle group called themselves?

The Lost Ones.

They were probably lost, all right. Or worse. Timmy might be planted out in the field somewhere, and Glory ...

Well, he thought. Better not try to speculate too much. Makes it too hard to stay optimistic.

In any case, he doubted that they'd discard a young female too quickly. Timmy, on the other hand, was dead weight just like his dangling Honda motorcycle.

A stir of commotion on the front porch sent Wolf to a prone position near another fracture in the stone wall.

He lifted the rangefinder binoculars to his eyes. The loud music lessened as a crowd poured raucously out the front door and down the wooden steps. The procession was led by a tall, whipcord-thin man with straggly hair and an unkempt beard. His arms, both covered from wrist to shoulder with sleeves of tattoos, were bare and he had two rather plumpish biker chicks fawning over him. Behind the trio, a huge man with grapevine muscles and a barrel chest followed carrying a large stuffed green chair that looked like it belonged in a second-hand furniture shop. The big man's arms, which were massive, were also decorated with a mosaic of inked designs.

Spike and his enforcer, Python no doubt, Wolf surmised, recalling Hernandez's descriptions.

Everyone in the group appeared to be in some degree of drug or alcohol-induced intoxication. About a dozen or so other men wearing the same motorcycle gang colors clamored down the wooden stairs, pulling and slapping at six similarly clad women, all squealing with delight. Wolf didn't see Glory or Timmy.

Spike stopped in an area next to one of the illuminated lights. It was in between the house and the barn. He said something inaudible and the group laughed. The leader waved his arms and pointed, and Python placed the chair on the ground.

"Get rid of that fucking music," Spike said in a throaty yell.

One of the other bikers turned with a stagger and pulled a gun out of his waistband. He aimed in the direction of the house and fired.

The music continued and he fired again.

"No, dumb ass," Spike yelled. "Go shut the fucking thing off."

"I'll do it," one of the biker chicks said, and started running toward the house. They were called "old ladies" or "mamas," Wolf recalled from his days of overheard conversations in the prison yard. The former meant the woman was the property of one man, subject to change, while "mamas" were fair game for everybody.

The biker with the gun squeezed off another round and the girl jumped back and screamed as the shot apparently whizzed by her.

The biker with the gun turned with a dumb-looking simper plastered across his mouth that instantly vanished as Python stepped over and delivered a swift, powerful backhanded blow to the other man's face. As the biker fell, the enforcer lurched forward and seized the gun from the crumbling man's hand.

Big and quick, Wolf thought. A dangerous combination.

"We got shots fired," McNamara said. "You got eyes on them?"

"Yeah," Wolf said, knowing his earpiece would transmit the words. "They're in the front yard acting stupid."

"Copy that," McNamara said. "You see anything of the girl?"

"Negative," Wolf replied. "But it looks like they've got something planned."

"I'll move up to where I can get a look-see," McNamara said.

"The way those idiots are shooting," Wolf said, "you'd better stay behind cover."

"Roger that."

The biker chick ran up into the house and the sound of the music lessened substantially.

Spike lifted his arms and when it seemed as though he had the group's attention he said in a loud voice, "Let the entertainment begin."

He plopped down in the unseemly green chair and Python tossed something to one of the others. It looked to be a ring of keys. The catcher and another man shuffled off toward the brick structure that Wolf assumed was the Throne. He debated whether or not to move up, and decided to wait.

About a minute or so later he was glad that he had. The two bikers who had entered the throne returned, dragging someone, a slender man, between them. Wolf brought the rangefinder glasses up once more and adjusted the zoom lens. The dragged party's head twisted to one side and Wolf caught a glimpse of his face: Timmy Wagner.

Not dead after all, Wolf thought. Yet.

He relayed this information to McNamara, who acknowledged.

"I don't like the sound of this," Mac said. "Or the smell, either."

Wolf advised that he was going to move up and did a low crawl over to the big metal poles embedded in the ground securing the winch. A shift in the wind carried the stench of human waste over to Wolf's new position, but the area directly under the suspended motorcycles afforded him an unimpeded view of the group, which had spread out into a circle. The two bikers threw Timmy into the center.

"Is this the piece of shit that betrayed brother Irv?" Spike said, addressing everyone in a resonant tone.

A chorus of boos and assents emanated from the group.

"What have you got to say for yourself?" Spike said, addressing Timmy.

The youth was crying, and his voice cracked as he made a muttering plea that he was sorry.

"Sorry?" Spike said, raising his eyebrows as his head rotated from side to side surveying his minions. "He says he's sorry."

Another chorus of boos echoed in the night.

"What shall we do with this transgressor?" Spike asked.

A unified chant from the crowd began like a mantra and grew louder and louder and it gathered intensity.

"BEAT DOWN, BEAT DOWN, BEAT DOWN ..."

Spike raised his arms again. The chant immediately ceased.

"And so, your punishment has been decided," he yelled. "Python."

The big man stepped forward and tried to seize Timmy. The youth darted to the left and tried to run, but the circle of bikers grabbed him and shoved him back toward the enormous opponent. This time Python snared an arm and delivered an underhanded punch to the boy's body. Timmy folded like a collapsible card table and sank to his knees. Python walked around and lifted a huge fist.

"Make it last awhile," Spike said.

The big man nodded and swung an open-handed

strike to the side of Timmy's head. He fell over and Python continued to walk in a circle around him.

"That boy ain't gonna last long at this rate," Mac's voice said in Wolf's earpiece.

"Your call," Wolf whispered back.

His mind raced. They still didn't know where Glory was, but Wolf felt it could be in that Throne place. If he could double-time it behind the barn without being seen, and then get into the outhouse, he might be able to locate her. But he'd seen Python toss one of the two bikers who's retrieved Timmy a set of keys. That meant it was locked. He had to get the keys first, but how?

The other, unspoken alternative would be for Mac to start picking people off. His Glock 19 had a mag capacity of nineteen, and one in the chamber made twenty. There were twenty hostiles, old ladies and mamas included, and gunning down a whole slew of people, especially the women, would not be something Mac would want to do. He was a man of honor. Plus, a mass shooting incident with a good chance of multiple fatalities, would put Hernandez on their tail. Most, if not all, of these bikers were armed, albeit probably not very effective marksmen, and none of them would probably be receptive to a call to surrender. They could try a bluff, saying that the whole place was surrounded by the Gila County SWAT team, but Wolf knew you didn't engage in a bluff that you couldn't pull off. And starting a firefight when you were facing ten-to-one odds was not a very attractive option.

But neither was watching a kid getting beaten to death, even if he had brought it on himself.

Python lifted Timmy with one arm and punched

him in the gut with the other. The youth expelled a ragged breath.

"You got any idea where they might be hiding the girl?" McNamara asked.

"Probably in the Throne," Wolf said. "But it's most likely locked."

"We need a diversion of some sort," McNamara said. "You know, I'm about twenty yards away from all their bikes. Maybe I can sneak over and disconnect a few gas lines, then toss in a match."

Before Wolf could comment, Python sent another crushing blow to Timmy's body. This time the cry was diminished.

"Wait," Spike said. "Let's bring out his little piece of ass and let her watch for a while before we pass her around."

That meant they were going to bring Glory out.

This could be the break we need, Wolf thought.

He looked over at the gas tanker and wondered how full it was. Even if it was a quarter full it would make a sizeable explosion. If he could time it with Mac blowing up the motorcycles, they might have something. He relayed his plan to McNamara, who agreed. As Wolf placed his palms down on the ground to push upward and move to the gas tanker, his fingers brushed something plastic attached by a braided leather thong to the round metal pole securing the winch.

It was a remote for the machine.

Another part of the diversion fell into place. The key would be to bring down the Rice Garden in conjunction with the two explosions. Then he could run up and grab Glory, once she was brought out. He'd have to do a quick job of convincing her, but that shouldn't be too difficult unless she'd been overcome with the Stockholm Syndrome. The sight of her boyfriend being beaten to death would probably go a long way to securing her cooperation. He radioed his plan to Mac, who agreed. Wolf removed his knife, flipped open the blade, and sliced through the leather thong securing the remote. He then pocketed it and got ready to sprint toward the gasoline tanker.

Something glinted in the moonlight, shiny in an errant patch of grass.

Wolf reached down and found an empty whiskey bottle.

Another break, he thought, making sure the bottle was intact.

"Darling," McNamara's voice said over the radio. "Get ready to pull down that road toward the fireworks when we call you to pick us up."

"Y'all gonna pop some smoke for us, honey?" Ms. Dolly's Southern twang said.

"We'll light your fire," McNamara said.

Wolf crawled past the foot-high grass and weeds by the Rice Garden. The tanker trailer was perhaps twenty-five feet away, but the ground was barren. Traversing the expanse with a low crawl would leave him too open and vulnerable. All it would take would be one of the bikers to turn and see his undulating figure and he'd be a sitting duck. But a quick sprint meant a more noticeable movement and that had its risks, too.

"Here comes the princess," Spike proclaimed. The crowd turned to see two of the bikers dragging Glory toward the semi-circle. A bunch of catcalls and whistles emanated from the group.

I'm not going to get a better chance than this, Wolf thought as he sprinted over to the gasoline tanker and slid underneath it. The gas cap was on the left side near the bottom. Wolf tapped it slightly trying to judge how full it was. The taps sounded solid which led him to believe the tank was at least half-full.

Good enough, he thought as he reached up to loosen the cap.

A steady stream of liquid began to dribble downward, giving off the unmistakable, searing odor of gasoline. Holding the empty bottle under the stream, Wolf let the gas trickle into it. When it was three-quarters full, he retightened the cap and set the bottle down. Pressing the blade of his knife into the soft, sandy earth, he then smeared dirt over the gasoline that had gotten on his hands. The underside of the tank felt solid, but not overly thick. After grinding the tip of the blade into the metal he managed to make a small hole in the surface. The noxious trickle began again in earnest, dripping down in a steady stream to begin forming a puddle on the ground beneath it.

The bikers began their chant again.

"Beat down, beat down, beat down ..."

Wolf shot a glance over and saw that Python now had Glory by both arms and was forcing her body over Timmy's crumpled form. The crowd was laughing.

Sadistic bastards, Wolf thought, determined to grab Timmy as well as Glory.

The kid wasn't an innocent, but he deserved better than that.

"Go get us another case of booze," Spike yelled.

One of the bikers on the edge of the crowd turned and started shuffling off toward the barn.

Shit, Wolf thought. The last thing I need is for him to see me.

But instead of heading toward the door, the biker kept walking and disappeared.

He must be going to the Throne, Wolf thought. Interesting.

"Sit rep," McNamara's voice asked in Wolf's earpiece.

"Almost ready," Wolf said, slicing off a long section of his BDU blouse and stuffing it into the top of the bottle. He then inverted it so that the material became immersed with fuel.

"How about you?" he said, keying his mic once more and glancing toward the barn.

"All systems are go," McNamara said. "Even found me an old paper bag I can use as a fuse."

"I've got things set here," Wolf said. "Give me about a minute or so to get around the back of the barn and up to where I can get to Glory and then when you hear the bang, light up they're bikes. I'll signal when I'm in position."

"Roger that," McNamara said.

"When they go running toward the bikes," Wolf said, "make your way to the front along the outside of the wall. I'll grab the girl and Timmy, and we'll tag up in the front drive and meet Ms. Dolly."

McNamara's chuckle came over the band as he replied, "Gonna be a pleasure. You copy, darling?"

"Roger that," Ms. Dolly said. "Sounds like you boys are gonna have all the fun, though."

Fun's got nothing to do with it, Wolf thought as he straightened up by the rear of the tanker and looked at the arena. Another round of hoots and hollers began, and he figured this was as good a chance as he was going to get. He ran for the corner of the barn. The area was dark and the ground uneven, so he slowed down a bit.

This is going to take longer than a minute, he was thinking when something cracked loudly under his foot and sent him sprawling. Wolf twisted to land on his side, holding the bottle out of way. He knew he couldn't afford to break it. Nor could he afford to damage the remote, which was in his pocket. He got to his feet, knowing he had no time to check. He wondered about the range of it now as well.

Hopefully, Murphy and his blasted law of inevitable SNAFUs wouldn't be making an appearance tonight. Now that his eyes had grown accustomed to the darkness a bit more he saw what had caused him to trip.

An old rake was lying on the ground. He reached down and grabbed it. The end attached to the metal prongs was now broken, which explained the cracking sound, but the rest of the thick wooden handle felt solid.

Carrying it like a spear, Wolf continued on his trek, rounding the first corner and then the second one. He slowed his pace now as he grew closer, going past the Throne.

Then he heard a couple of grunts and saw the biker who had gone for the booze exiting the Throne carrying a cardboard box. He was panting, like he'd just trudged up a flight of stairs, and paused, setting the box down and taking out a pack of cigarettes.

Wolf knew he couldn't afford to move up into position with that guy behind him. He looked toward the arena, saw no one looking his way, and ran to the rear of the Throne. Stooping to set the bottle on the ground, he straightened up and gripped the wooden shaft with both hands. He'd trained with the martial arts weapon, the bo, which was essentially a long wooden stick, in the army and knew it to be effective and silent.

The door to the Throne was ajar and Wolf could see light seeping through the gap between the edge of the door and the jamb. The biker stood sucking on a hand-rolled cigarette and the sickeningly sweet odor of marijuana filled the air.

Wolf pivoted and swung the staff against the biker's temple.

Smoking's bad for your health, Wolf thought cynically as the man crumpled. Turning, he caught a further glimpse inside the Throne. It contained an old, porcelain commode, all right, but there was an open trap door next to it. From what he could see, Wolf noticed that there was a set of stairs descending from the opening.

They must have been hiding Glory down in some underground room, he thought, but knew he had no time to check.

After retrieving the bottle, Wolf trotted over to the front corner of the barn and stopped. The beating of Timmy had begun again.

Wolf keyed his mic. "I'm in position. Get ready."

"Roger that," McNamara said.

His voice was a whisper.

Wolf leaned the staff against the wall and removed the remote and his lighter. After flicking the wheel and holding the flame next to the sodden material, the cloth started burning quickly. Wolf held the remote outward and pressed the activation button. The activating motor's whine was barely audible, but it was enough. Putting his thumb over the release button, Wolf pressed down and a second later the Rice Garden collapsed with a resounding thud, stirring up a cloud of dust.

All the heads in the crowd rotated left toward the noise. Wolf cocked his arm back and hurled the flaming bottle directly at the gas tanker. The shattering glass made no more than a high-pitched tinkle that was followed a split-second later by a thunderous blast as the vapors ignited. The tanker rose several feet upward, spewing flames twenty feet in the air. The crowd recoiled almost in unison and then another blast, this time from the opposite direction, tore through the night.

"Our hogs!" someone yelled, and the crowd began running toward them.

Wolf was already moving toward the arena, the staff at the ready.

One of the two bikers holding Glory turned his head just in time for Wolf to smash the end of the bo across the man's face. His nose exploded in a mist of crimson and he dropped. Wolf brought the solid portion of the staff down on the second biker's forehead and he dropped too. Python whirled and dropped Timmy, reaching down into his beltline for something.

Wolf didn't wait to find out what it was and shifted his weight, bringing the end of the bo upward in an arcing motion to catch the underside of Python's chin. He staggered back two steps, which Wolf took as a testament to the big man's toughness. He shook his head, trying to shake off the black lights that Wolf knew must be circulating behind the biker's eyes.

Been there myself, he thought.

Pivoting again, Wolf cracked the end of the staff against Python's right temple and saw the other man's eyes roll upward exposing nothing but white sclera. As added insurance, Wolf twisted and delivered another snapping blow, this one catching the huge biker on the left side of the jaw as he dropped. A spray of shattered teeth burst forth in a geyser of reddish foam as he dropped.

Although he hated to do it, Wolf hurled away the staff and grabbed Glory's arm. Her eyes flashed at him with an almost vacuous look.

"I'm going to get you out of here," he said. "Help me with Timmy."

It seemed to take a few seconds for his words to register and it flashed in Wolf's mind that it was time they didn't have.

"Come on," he yelled, as he grabbed Timmy under the arms and lifted him. "We've got to move now."

Glancing over at the conflagration of the motorcycles, Wolf saw the majority of the crowd was still over there about two hundred feet away. He slung Timmy's body over his left shoulder and grabbed Glory's left arm, pulling the girl along. After a few hesitant steps, she started moving faster and her feet fell into a consistent running pattern.

They were approaching the access road now … Perhaps only twenty yards more.

Voices, excited and yelling, sounded behind them.

Keep moving Wolf told himself. Don't stop.

He wanted to look for Mac, to make sure he was on his way too, and, suddenly, McNamara was there next to him and grabbed the girl's right arm.

"Good thing I've been doing them miles with you in the mornings," he said.

Wolf grunted in response.

They continued down the roadway. The crack of a gunshot sounded behind them.

Wolf felt no impact, but knew that meant nothing.

Another shot echoed, this one sounding like a rifle.

"Anybody hit?" he asked.

"Not so far," McNamara said, his words coming out between gasps.

Suddenly a pair of headlights illuminated about thirty feet in front of them and the Escalade skidded sideways to a stop. The front and back passenger side doors flew open and Wolf thought that no LZ chopper ever looked as good at this moment. He covered the distance in a matter of seconds and threw Timmy into the back seat. Mac was pulling Glory into the front. Both doors slammed shut and the Escalade peeled out and headed down the access road toward the highway.

"Cut the lights, darlin'," McNamara said. "We're giving them too good a target if we're lit up."

Ms. Dolly's hand moved and the view through the windshield eclipsed into blackness.

"I'm gettin' real used to these here goggles," she said. "Now I know what I want for Christmas."

"Better get that letter off to Santa then," McNamara said with a laugh.

Wolf adjusted the unconscious Timmy onto the seat and peered out the rear window looking for muzzle flashes but saw none. The twin fires on each side of the yard glowed like gigantic, flickering candles against the velvety blackness.

"We're gonna have to call Hernandez," McNamara said. "Looks like he's got another case of open burnings to investigate."

Wolf grinned.

Dirk studied the chaotic scene through the night-vision scope mounted on the rifle for a few minutes more and then flipped the safety on and got up from his prone position on the shallow hill. He took out his cell phone and punched in the number. Perkins answered after the first ring.

"What the hell's going on over there?" he asked.

"Wolf and McNamara grabbed the girl and another person," Dirk said. "A young male, from the looks of him. They should be on the highway by now."

"Anybody giving chase?"

"Negative," Dirk said, thinking that Wolf and McNamara did a fairly effective insertion and rescue.

But they're still the B-Team, he thought. If it weren't for my assistance at the end of it, that idiot shooting at them might have gotten lucky.

He slipped the rifle into its case, flipped down his own night-vision goggles, and trotted down the hill to where Charles was waiting in the Jeep. At least it was him and not his asshole brother, Clyde. Dirk smirked. It was funny how two guys who looked so much alike could be so different, personality-wise. Or maybe they weren't, who knew. But Charles always seemed like the more easy-going of the two.

At least I think it's Charles, Dirk thought with a grin. Only their mother and their hairdresser knows for sure.

It wasn't even twenty-two hundred yet so he had plenty of time to make it back to the hotel in Mesa and grab a nightcap. As he got to the bottom of the hill, he scanned the area and saw the Jeep idling about fifty yards away in a flat section between two hills. Taking out his cell phone, he scrolled to Soraces's number and hit the call button.

"What's up?" Soraces asked.

"All set," Dirk said. "Mission accomplished. Target got away unscathed, and will most likely be heading back to Phoenix with the girl."

"Excellent. Any problems?"

"Not really. I took out possible threat just to on the safe side."

"Explain."

"Just one of the bikers," Dirk said. "He was shooting at Wolf."

"Did Wolf see you?"

"Of course not. I was set up on a hill about two hundred yards away."

"Okay, good," Soraces said. "Now go back to Mesa so you can get some sleep before your class starts in the morning. And tell Perkins to stay on them, all night if he has to."

"Yes, mother," Dirk said, and hung up.

Charles was going to love that order.

Better him than me, Dirk thought.

He was getting a bit tired of Soraces's constant micro-managing. Dirk didn't recall him being this over-bearing on the missions they'd worked together in the past.

Must have a lot riding on this one, Dirk thought. Which means I'm gonna demand more money.

He slipped the phone into his pocket and continued walking as he tried to think of something pleasant. The twisting figure of the biker as the .223 round pierced the right side of his chest came to mind. He'd planned the trajectory so that the first shot struck just under the asshole's right armpit and fired twice in case the first bullet hit a rib and went off course into the lung or possibly out through the abdomen. The second shot, delivered a second later probably entered almost at the same spot. The son of a bitch crumpled immediately.

It was a work of art.

He'd saved Wolf's life, but his ultimate quarry would probably never know. Dirk chuckled. It was reminiscent of one of his favorite old James Bond movies, the one where Red Grant saves Bond during the attack on the gypsy camp.

Grant later informed him of this in the train car compartment and the look on Bond's face was priceless, Dirk thought, remembering Robert Shaw and Sean Connery.

He wondered what their confrontation in the train car must have looked like on the big screen when the movie was first released.

Robert Shaw ... What arrogance, what *savoir faire* ... The stuff that great actors and great movie scenes were made of.

It was too bad that I'll probably never be able to advise Wolf of this before I kill him, he thought. It would be fun to play Red Grant and do it right this time.

CHAPTER TWELVE

ST. FRANCIS HOSPITAL
UNINCORPORATED TOWN OF CROWN POINTS
GILA COUNTY, ARIZONA

Wolf sat beside McNamara outside the Emergency Room of the hospital in Crown Points. They were the only two people in the mid-sized room, which had three other rows of padded chairs, a coffee table with a stack of old, worn, glossy magazines, and a television set bolted high up on the wall. Jim Nabors as *Gomer Pyle, USMC*, gesticulated with ludicrous exaggeration as Frank Sutton, playing Sergeant Carter, glared back at him. The volume was only faintly audible, but that suited Wolf just fine. He was still feeling adrenalized from their close encounter with the bikers.

Satan's Spawn, he thought. Hernandez was right. They weren't so tough.

"Golooloooly," Gomer said as the laugh track

exploded with a round of hearty bellows. Sergeant Carter fumed.

Wolf wondered with amusement what old Buck thought about Gomer and his portrayal of the beloved Corps.

Either you loved him, or you hated him, he thought. And it's probably the latter in Buck's case since it made the marines look pretty bad.

Mac, however, seemed to be enjoying the hell out of Nabor's performance.

The hospital was hardly more than a big medical center but it was the only game in town. Both Timmy and Glory needed immediate care. Wolf mentioned that it would be prudent to request a rape kit be done on the girl, even though she claimed she hadn't been sexually assaulted.

"But she woulda been for sure, if we hadn't intervened," McNamara said, putting his phone back into his pocket. "Hopefully, this close call will go a long way to bringing her back to her senses."

Regardless, Wolf figured the poor girl would need a whole lot of counseling for sure. Thinking about what she'd narrowly avoided made him want to change the subject.

"What did Kasey have to say? Did you wake her?"

McNamara shook his head. "Nah, she was still up, waiting to hear from us. She was relieved that everything went okay."

Wolf didn't ask if she'd inquired about him, wanting to let things lie since a sort of truce had settled over his relationship with Mac's daughter. He figured she'd finished blaming him for everything, and he didn't want to change that.

"Made a point of asking what time we'd be back today because she's going on a date tonight," McNamara said.

That's interesting, Wolf thought, and asked the inevitable question that hung in the air between them. "She say with who?"

McNamara shook his head, his nostrils flaring. "I didn't ask her. But I should've. I'll bet it's with him."

Wolf let a few seconds pass before he spoke. "Maybe it's better to just let things run their course." He thought about adding in jest that having an FBI agent in the family might be good for business, but didn't.

"Where the hell are them gals with our damn chow?" McNamara said. "I'm hungry enough to eat a ketchup and horseradish sandwich."

Wolf was feeling famished, too. He got up to go glance down the hallway to check and got an unpleasant surprise. Sergeant Hernandez was marching through the open glass doors with a determined gait, followed by a uniformed deputy and another man in civilian attire. He was a big guy, taller than Hernandez and had an air of authority.

Another cop, Wolf thought. And from the looks of it, none of the three appeared happy.

Wolf stepped back into the waiting room and said, "Here comes trouble."

McNamara looked up. "Hernandez?"

Wolf nodded.

McNamara smiled and stood up as the trio entered.

"Well, well, well," McNamara said. "'Bout time you got here. We been waiting for almost an hour."

Hernandez glared at him. "I want to talk to you two."

"Go right ahead," McNamara said.

Hernandez stared back at him, and then asked, "I assume you two are responsible for that fiasco out at Brasheer's."

"Well, we were out there," McNamara said with a wink. "We called nine-one-one just like you told us when we saw something illegal going on."

Hernandez's mouth puckered slightly.

"So," McNamara said. "You investigate those cases of open burning?"

"Don't be a smart ass" Hernandez said. "What the hell happened up there? Looks like a fucking war zone."

McNamara shrugged. "You said we could go up there and observe, at our own risk, and if we saw any unlawful activity to call you if. So we did."

"I didn't tell you to go shooting people," Hernandez said.

Wolf and McNamara exchanged glances.

"We heard some gunshots going off, but we didn't do no shooting," McNamara said. "Like I told you, Steve here don't even carry a gun."

Hernandez glared at him for several seconds and then turned his gaze on Wolf.

"What about it?" he asked.

"It's just like Mac told you," Wolf said. "We snuck in there to observe. They were beating the missing girl's boyfriend and forcing her to watch. I overheard them planning to do a gang bang. I was afraid they were going to seriously injure or kill the boy and then rape the girl. We couldn't very well stand by and let that happen, so we created a diversion and managed to get them both out of there in the confusion."

"A diversion?" Hernandez frowned. "What exactly was that?"

"I lowered the boom on their Rice Garden, and they ran over to check it. Those bikers were all drunk or high or whatever, and *they* were the only ones shooting."

"You know anything about their gasoline tanker blowing up?" Hernandez asked. "Or their fleet of Harleys going up in flames?"

"There was quite an explosion as we were sneaking away," Wolf said. "But like I mentioned, those morons were highly intoxicated. It wouldn't surprise me if they'd left the cap off their gasoline tanker and the fumes ignited. I don't know how the motorcycles caught fire."

This was actually close to the truth since he hadn't seen what Mac had used to set off that blaze.

"In any case," McNamara said, stepping closer. "We brought Gloria Ryland here. She was being abused, held against her will, and would have been raped repeatedly by those savages, had we not stepped in and did the job you shoulda done yesterday."

Hernandez's frown deepened, his lips twisting in obvious anger.

"Not to mention the boy, Timmy Wagner," Wolf said. "He's in pretty bad shape. And, take a long look at that Throne outhouse. There's a trap door next to the toilet, and from what Gloria told us, there's a tunnel under that outhouse that leads to a large, underground storage area underneath the barn. She says it's full of bags of yellow pills—Fentanyl would be my guess. It's used to store the drugs that come along that pipeline you were talking about."

Hernandez and the man in civilian clothes exchanged a quick glance, then Hernandez stepped away and began talking into his radio. The other man extended his hand toward Wolf.

"I'm Detective Dave Case," he said. "State Police investigations. I want to thank you for rescuing the girl and the boy. And I assure you, we're working on the aggravated battery and unlawful restraint cases."

"Case on the case, huh?" McNamara said with a grin. "Well, it's mighty nice to find somebody around here who knows a crime when they see one."

Detective Case smiled.

Hernandez's head perked up and he glanced over his shoulder toward McNamara. After finishing his radio transmission, he turned and strode back toward them.

"I'm gonna need you two to come with me." He pointed toward the wall. "Assume the position."

"Huh?" McNamara said. "What for?"

"I told you," Hernandez said. "I'm investigating a homicide and you two have admitted to being armed and at the scene."

"Homicide? We didn't shoot nobody," McNamara said. "You can check my gun, It ain't been even been fired."

"Glad you're giving me that much leeway," Hernandez said with a sneer. "Now turn around and put your hands on the wall. Both of you. I ain't telling you again."

McNamara started to say something, but Wolf said, "Mac. Do as he says. He's just doing his job." With that, he turned and assumed the position on the hallway wall.

"About damn time he did," McNamara said with an accompanying snort. As he turned and placed his hands on the wall he added, "My gun's in a pancake on my right hip." The deputy removed Mac's Glock handed it to Hernandez. After handcuffing McNamara, the deputy moved to Wolf.

He felt the deputy's hands going over him in what was a pretty thorough search finding and removing his knife. The deputy shoved him forward and grabbed Wolf's left hand, ratcheting a set of handcuffs over his wrists.

"All this one's got is a knife," the deputy said.

"Well, ain't this a fine howdie-do?" Ms. Dolly said. She and Brenda came briskly walking into the room carrying two bags, each bearing fast-food labels, and a tray of soft drinks. "We save a little gal from getting gang raped by a bunch of motorcycle hooligans, and y'all are arresting the two heroes that done it."

"*Pendejo*," Brenda muttered. "*Chinga tu madre.*"

At the mention of the Spanish words, Hernandez's head rotated toward her. "You'd best watch your mouth, *Señorita.*"

"Y'all want to check our guns too?" Ms. Dolly said, holding her purse up. "They ain't been fired, neither."

Wolf rolled his eyes. This was going from bad to worse in a hurry.

"They weren't even on the biker's property," he said. "They just picked us up after we'd removed the girl and her boyfriend from harm's way."

Hernandez ripped Brenda's purse from her and then reached for Ms. Dolly's.

"You want it, all you gotta do is ask for it, honey," she said, tightening her grip and cocking her head in Brenda's direction. "And that ain't no way to treat a lady."

"If I see any ladies, I'll keep that in mind," Hernandez said. "Now, I'm giving you a lawful order to surrender your purse, *ma'am*. Or face arrest for obstructing."

"Dolly," Wolf said. "Give it to him, please. And let them search the Escalade if they want so it doesn't get towed." He glanced at Hernandez who nodded after a few seconds hesitation. "Sheriff, we're cooperating, okay?"

Hernandez held his hand out toward Ms. Dolly and she relinquished her purse. His eyes widened when he opened it and saw her big .357 Colt Python.

"Go ahead and smell it, sugar," Ms. Dolly said. "It ain't been fired since the last time I was in your fair state. And my concealed carry license is in there as well."

"*Yo también*," Brenda said. "So is mine."

As Hernandez was checking her purse Wolf said, "Sheriff, since we're cooperating, I'd like a chance to call my lawyer before any of us says anything more."

———

THE GRAND TETONS HOTEL
PHOENIX, ARIZONA

Six days cooped up in the hotel room was starting to really wear on Soraces and hearing this latest news, that

Wolf and McNamara had been taken out of the medical center in handcuffs a couple of hours ago, was like stubbing his little toe on a brick. Just when he thought he'd put all the right pieces in place for his plan to come together, something like this had to happened.

Damn that impetuous asshole, Wolf.

He poured himself another cup of coffee and dumped two packets of sugar into it. He knew he shouldn't have any this late, but sleep would prove to be elusive regardless. It always was in the final stages of setting his traps. What he hadn't counted on was this latest wrinkle.

Arrested ... Shit.

And now he'd have to take steps to deal with this.

An opponent's unpredictability is just a minor inconvenience, he thought. And it makes the game more interesting.

Before he sat down, he whipped the blade from his ninja knife and hurled it with a back-handed motion toward the whiteboard. It stuck in the top center portion, almost directly in the center, exactly where he'd intended. The board itself was a mass of drawings, scribble notes, and multicolored arrows. He looked at it with disgust and thought about eradicating the whole thing. He'd never let an operation's sketch get so widely out of control. It was a sign that he was feeling the pressure, which amused him.

Here he was in the States working on an op that involved a rich man's fancy. It was a far cry from toppling governments or removing some undesirable from the political scene in some foreign country. But all of those had been in the service of Uncle Sam. This one, which he hoped would be his penultimate retirement op, had to be handled with the utmost care to set up his fruitful retirement. Penultimate because he intended to milk Von Dien for an even bigger fee once the artifact was recovered. There was his spy pen recording to sell.

He thought about the sight of some firm, bouncing babes frolicking in some warm Caribbean saltwater. That was what awaited him on the other side. All he had to do was step over a few more bodies along with the artifact and collect his prize money. He'd be set for life.

At least this self-imposed confinement had allowed him to perfect his knife throwing once again. It was, like everything else, a perishable skill set.

After walking over and retrieving the blade, he reinserted it into the pen and returned to the table. The coffee was strong and still tasted bitter, despite the added sugar. He tore open one more packet and then stirred it with a plastic spoon. His next sip proved too sweet and he set it aside.

At least with them incarcerated, at least temporarily, it would give him ample time to head over to the pharmacy to purchase the prescription he'd had Fallotti's doctor phone in: forty-eight milliliters of ketamine and a syringe. The air transportation needed to be set up, too.

Fallotti had been skeptical about the proposal but assured him it would all be done, despite the greasy lawyer's expressed misgivings.

"A snatch?" he'd said, the skepticism evident in his tone. "You're sure that's a good idea?"

"It worked once," Soraces said. "Why not again, only with more finesse this time."

He heard the lawyer's heavy breathing.

Obviously, he's not a believer, Soraces thought.

"Listen," he said. "I told you before, let me handle this. We need to get Wolf to bring the item to us, on our home ground, and what better place than down there. He won't have any resources, no place to hide."

"Suppose he doesn't go for it? Or involves the FBI?"

"He'll go for it, if we handle it right. He won't have any choice. And we make it clear that if he does contact the feds, the whole deal's off."

Fallotti still sounded skeptical but agreed to send Von Dien's private jet to Phoenix immediately.

"So I can tell Mr. Von Dien that we can expect to see you tomorrow evening then?" the lawyer asked.

"It's after midnight now, so it'll be actually be today."

"Right," Fallotti said. From his tone, he was not amused by the correction.

"And only then if he wants to wait up for us," Soraces said.

He terminated the call and thought about checking for an update but decided not to. Nothing would happen until the morning, about eight hours or so from now. They'd call him when things broke.

SHERIFF'S ANNEX STATION
UNINCORPORATED TOWN OF CROWN POINTS
GILA COUNTY, ARIZONA

. . .

Wolf was glad they'd gotten the air-conditioning fixed. The cell was about ten by twelve with a built-in metal toilet, sink, and water fountain. The bunk was a metal slate bolted to the wall and covered with the thinnest of mattresses. There was a solid steel door with a small glass window that had a shutter on a hinge over it, and a closed slot through which food was passed. Or so he assumed. He hoped he wouldn't be in there long enough to find out, but that wasn't looking too good at the moment. All things considered; it wasn't as comfortable as the one he'd called home for four years at Leavenworth. He welcomed a chance to stretch out and get some much-needed sleep. They'd awakened him several times claiming to be doing well-being checks, and finally roused him and ushered him into another room where Hernandez and another guy, in a shirt and tie, stood on the other side of a table. Hernandez tried to come off as everybody's friend.

"Sit down, Wolf," he said, holding his big hand out toward a chair at the table.

Wolf sat.

"You already know me," Hernandez said. "This is Detective Morris."

"Can we get you something?" Morris asked. "Coffee? Soda?"

Wolf yawned and shook his head.

"I'll get right to the point," Hernandez said. "You and your friend placed yourself at the scene of a very serious crime and we'd like to hear your side of it."

Wolf nodded.

"This is your chance to tell us what happened," Morris said. "But, just like in the movies, I've got to read this to you first. I'll let you read along with me."

He handed Wolf the Miranda warning sheet and then read each point, asking him to initial them and sign the waiver at the bottom.

"I appreciate you reading this to me," Wolf said, "but I already told what happened. I'm not saying anything more until I speak to my lawyer, and I'd appreciate a chance to call her now."

Since they'd taken his watch, he had no idea what time it was, but he figured to at least leave a message.

Hernandez, who was still standing, frowned.

"So that's the way it's gonna be, huh?" he said.

Wolf said nothing.

"We ran your name, Wolf," Hernandez continued. "You served time."

"That I did," Wolf said.

"Look, Steve," Morris said. "If this was a case of self-defense, now's the time to tell us. Somebody shoots at you, you shoot back, it's all understandable."

"I didn't shoot anybody," Wolf said. "Didn't you guys do a GSR test on my hands when you brought us in here?"

Morris raised his eyebrows. "How do you know about Gunshot Residue Tests?"

"When I was in Leavenworth I watched reruns of CSI."

"So if you didn't shoot anybody," Hernandez said. "You must be saying it was your buddy, McNamara. I know you don't want to implicate those two pretty ladies, do you?"

Wolf felt a surge of panic wondering if Ms. Dolly and Brenda had been incarcerated, too.

"Look," he said. "If you're—"

He stopped. They were playing him, trying to keep

him talking. They'd Mirandized him and were now hoping to get him to say something that they could use to hold him. He was through playing their game, but allowed himself one final comment.

"None of us fired a shot," he said. "The bikers were the only ones shooting as far as I know. Now, can I please call my lawyer? I'm not saying another word until she gets here."

Hernandez and Morris exchanged glances and Hernandez stormed out of the room. Morris allowed him to retrieve Dolores Delgato's number from his cell phone and dialed the number. It went directly to voice mail, but just hearing her sultry voice on the recording put him in a better mood.

"What time's chow?" he asked Morris after thanking him for allowing the call and handing him back the phone.

"In a little while," Morris said. "Just sit tight."

The little while stretched into what Wolf figured was at least three or more hours. From time to time, he heard some raucous yelling and figured that the boys of Satan's Spawn were guests of the county as well. He wondered about the lockup capacity of the annex station. When they'd locked him and Mac up, he'd seen at least ten or twelve cells. He'd counted twelve of the loathsome bikers and six of their women. Python would probably be in the hospital with a broken jaw, and the other one he'd cold cocked at the Throne might be as well. If one of them had been shot, that brought the total down from eighteen to sixteen. He felt a surge of hope that Ms. Dolly and Brenda hadn't been incarcerated. They hadn't done anything wrong, but neither had he or Mac, and here they sat.

Well, nothing besides knocking out a couple of scumbags and blowing up a couple of things.

Open burning, he thought with a smile, and lay back down on the steel bunk to await the arrival of Ms. Delgato. I wonder if that's a fine-only offense?

———

It was mid-afternoon by the time Wolf and McNamara were released. Dolores Delgato was dressed in a navy-blue outfit with the collar of her pale green blouse artfully spread over the jacket's lapels. She stood in the lobby of the annex station alongside Ms. Dolly and Brenda. Manny was there, too. Ms. Dolly beamed as the deputy ushered Wolf and McNamara through the side door and into the lobby.

"Our heroes," Ms. Dolly said. "Free at last."

Manny struggled to lift his bulk from the bench next to the door. Despite the air-conditioning, his florid face was spotted with perspiration and the sweat had seeped through his dark blue polo shirt in several places.

"I came along in case I needed to post bond for you guys," he said, grinning.

"I knew we weren't gonna need to," McNamara said in an overly loud voice. "Once our lawyer extraordinaire got here. Much obliged, ma'am."

He grinned at Dolores Delgato.

She smiled back at him. "That's quite all right, but remember, you haven't gotten my bill yet."

"We appreciate you coming, Dolores," Wolf said. "Thanks."

She turned to him and he was once more taken by

the amber-colored eyes framed by expertly enhanced eyelids and lashes under a pair of perfectly arched brows.

"My pleasure," she said.

"She made mincemeat outta that fat sergeant," Ms. Dolly said. "Pointed out that he didn't have no reason to hold you and sent him scurrying for the hills quicker than a jack-rabbit being chased by a coyote." She paused and smiled at Delgato. "Ah, no offense, honey. Just a Texas figure of speech."

"None taken," Delgato said, then turned to Wolf. "Steve, ironically, I was going to call you. I thought we should meet and go over your case."

"You found something?" he asked.

One of the perfect eyebrows arched a few millimeters. "I was going to ask you the same thing."

Wolf shook his head.

"Well, now that we got our hardware back," McNamara said, patting his right side. "I'd like to get the hell outta here."

"Sounds like a plan," Wolf said.

"Me too," Ms. Dolly added. "But first, I think Manny has something to say, don't ya?"

Manny nodded and stepped forward.

"I owe you guys," he said. "Big time. All of youse. Thanks for saving Glory."

McNamara put his hand on Manny's shoulder.

"That's what friends are for," he said. "To count on each other when the chips are down."

Manny said lunch, now closer to early dinner, was on him.

McNamara took out his cell phone. "I'd better give Kase a call. Tell her we'll be a little late getting back. I gotta return that stuff we borrowed to Buck, too."

"Hell, she your daughter or your wife?" Ms. Dolly asked with a cynical smile.

"Well, she was expecting us early," McNamara said, sounding a bit defensive. "I just want to tell her we're on the way." He started dialing.

As they headed out the door, Delgato moved closer to Wolf and said, "I'm going to have to take a rain check. I need to get back, but call me." She handed him a scrap of paper with something written on it.

"Here, this is my cell," she said with an alluring smile. "My personal cell. The other number on the card's my business number. Call me when you have time."

Wolf nodded, put the paper in his pocket, and thanked her again. He was watching the rotation of her full hips as she walked toward a silver Toyota Camry when Ms. Dolly and Brenda came up on either side of him and grabbed his arms.

"Ain't she the hot *tamale*," Ms. Dolly said

"*Una pinchón*," Brenda said. "That's for sure."

"Yolanda know about her?" Ms. Dolly asked.

Wolf was a bit taken aback by the question. A sting of anguish and resentment swept over him as he answered. "I haven't talked to her in a while."

"Well, why the hell not?" Ms. Dolly asked. "She's sure been asking about you."

Wolf raised his eyebrows and thought that sounded a bit promising, but then reality came swinging back like a wrecking ball on a chain.

"I'm a convicted felon," Wolf said. "She doesn't need me in her life right now."

Ms. Dolly frowned. "Aw, hell, we know all about that. Mac told us you were set up."

"Yo don't think like that," Brenda said.

Wolf shrugged. "I'm sure the police department might feel differently."

"Where'd you meet that—her?" Brenda asked, cocking her head toward Delgato's Toyota, which was now pulling away.

"She works for a law firm in Phoenix," he said. "She was going over my old lawyer's files and contacted me."

"Looks like she's got more than files on her mind, honey." Ms. Dolly elevated the tone of her voice and said, "Here's my personal cell."

Brenda's full lips pursed, and she looked askance at him.

"She's not from around here, you know," she said. "I could tell by her accent."

"Accent?" Wolf said.

"Her Spanish," Brenda said. "I was talking to her."

"Too fast for me to follow," Ms. Dolly said.

"That's because she's a Puerto Rican," Brenda said. "They talk fast. Not too many of them around here."

Wolf was aware that a native speaker might be able to detect something like that, but was uncertain if it had any real significance.

"Well," Ms. Dolly said with a grin. "I guess she ain't no *tamale* after all then. But she's still pretty hot."

Maybe both of them are a bit biased against Ms. Delgato, he thought as he took a deep breath. But that still doesn't change the sad reality of things. He still had way too much negative baggage to be associated with someone who had aspirations of being a cop.

I'm not going to let my past drag her down, spoil her chances, he thought. Unless something changes.

And in his heart he knew nothing probably would.

———

THE GRAND TETONS HOTEL
PHOENIX, ARIZONA

Soraces had almost finished packing when Charles Perkins called him.

"They're still in the restaurant," he said. "The bail bondsman's with them. Looks like they're taking their sweet-ass time."

"Good," Soraces said, glancing at his watch. Sixteen-twenty-three. "Okay, stay on them. Advise me when they're heading back."

"All right, but I'm going to need to change clothes pretty soon. I've been sitting here sweating since I took over surveillance this morning. How about sending my brother to assist?"

"Negative," Soraces said. He placed the last item into the suitcase and zipped it closed. The papers on the whiteboard had been totally eradicated, and the wipe-down of this room wouldn't take him more than ten minutes. "I need him to assist me with that business tonight."

Charles Perkins grunted in weary acquiescence.

"We won't be here when you get back," Soraces said. "But your room will still be covered. Stay on them and keep reporting to me."

"And then what?" Perkins asked.

"Then you'll be coming down to join us in Belize. You did bring your special passport like I told you, didn't you?"

"Yeah, yeah. Be prepared. We were both eagle scouts." He laughed. "How come he gets to go down there with you, and I have to stay here and hold the shitty end of the stick?"

"Well, you get along better with Dirk."

"True that," Perkins said. "I'll get back to you in a couple of hours then."

Soraces hung up and looked at his watch again, doing the mental calculations. It would take Wolf and company a good two and a half hours to drive back to Phoenix even if they left immediately, and from the sound of things, they weren't even close to doing that. When he got word they were back in town, he'd give Wolf another quick call from the airport to get things moving. The timing was virtually perfect.

This was turning out even better than he'd anticipated.

Always one move ahead, he thought, as he went to the refrigerator for the vial of ketamine and the hypodermic syringe and contemplated the next step in his trap.

CHAPTER THIRTEEN_

INTERSTATE 10
JUST OUTSIDE OF PHOENIX, ARIZONA

Wolf watched the overhead road-lights glowing in the gathering darkness as he piloted the Escalade along the interstate. McNamara slumbered in the front passenger seat, having asked Wolf to be the designated driver on the way back.

He's earned the rest, Wolf thought. All of us have.

He looked in the rearview mirror and caught a glimpse of Ms. Dolly's closed eyes as she sat in the back seat, her arm around Brenda's slumbering form that was pressed against her. They both looked exhausted. The big meal and the subsequent celebratory bottle of wine probably hadn't helped. As usual, Wolf had abstained.

They were getting close to the city and beyond the guard railing periodic clusters of houses, shopping centers, and gas stations were springing up. The fatigue that had been his constant companion lately was starting to engulf him again and he was looking forward to getting back to his apartment above Mac's garage and slipping between the sheets of his comfortable bed. He was glad that Yolanda hadn't been part of the P-Patrol this time, although the thought of her soft touch brought the accompanying longing. But he was so tired all he wanted to do was sleep.

Put everything on hold, he thought. Think about it tomorrow, like Scarlett O'Hara.

Then his cell phone rang, jarring him out of his reverie.

He fished it out of his pocket and took a second to study the screen.

A blocked call ...

The last time he'd gotten one it had been Soraces.

Was the devil's advocate calling back?

He pressed the button and held the phone to his ear, cognizant that the ring tone had awakened McNamara.

"Hey, Wolf. How you doing?"

It was Soraces, all right.

"What do you want?"

"Just calling to see how you were," Soraces said. His voice sounded jovial, like an old friend just touching base. "You ready to deal yet?"

Wolf wasn't about to negotiate anything with this con man unless they were on equal footing.

"I told you before," Wolf said. "Call me back from an unblocked number and maybe we can do business. I don't deal with anybody sneaking around in the shadows."

"Maybe you should get yourself some night-vision goggles then."

The mention of the same equipment they had in the car kind of stunned Wolf. Why the hell would he mention those. It was almost as if ... He immediately checked his rearview mirror.

"I was speaking metaphorically," Wolf said. "I trust you about as far as I could throw you."

"That's unfortunate. I was hoping we might make some progress. I guess it's time for me to up the ante, eh?"

"What's that supposed to mean?"

"You'll be finding out soon enough. Honest, Injun."

"You can go to hell."

Soraces laughed. "Okay, Stevie-boy. I'll give you a call when you have more time. Maybe when you get back to the Ranch."

When you get back?

How did he know they were gone from there?

Wolf checked the mirror again.

Was it a lucky guess, or was someone tailing them?

Wolf saw nothing but a collection of headlights on the highway behind them. Early evening darkness was settling in and it was difficult to tell.

Mac picked up on Wolf's movements and glanced in the sideview mirror.

"Oh, by the way," Soraces said. "Give my regards to Special Agent Franker."

Franker?

What the hell? How did he know about Franker?

"You'd better explain what you're talking about." Wolf said.

"You haven't heard, have you? Your favorite FBI agent's in Phoenix Metro South. Intensive care. He was shot. You should give him a call. But wait, he's probably still in surgery. Maybe just send flowers. In the meantime, keep your phone on and I'll call you back in a little bit with my instructions. We'll talk then. Talk turkey, as they used to say."

"What's all this got to do with me?" Wolf said.

Soraces laughed again. "I'll be talking to you, Wolf. Probably sooner than you think. And tell your buddy to make sure and tip that babysitter real good. She's doing a hell of a job. Bye-bye."

Wolf looked at the screen.

The call had been terminated.

The Babysitter ... The words burned in his mind like a red-hot branding iron being pressed against bare flesh. A sudden, desperate thought occurred to him.

No, he told himself. It can't be.

"Was it that Soraces fella?" McNamara asked, glancing over at him.

Wolf nodded, his mind racing, not wanting to believe that what he was inferring was true.

"Who's Soraces?" Ms. Dolly asked from the back seat.

"What the hell did he want?" McNamara asked.

"Not sure," Wolf said. His mind replayed the cryptic conversation again and struggling to find the right words to say. "You said Kasey was getting ready for a date tonight. Was it with Franker?"

"Yeah, unfortunately," McNamara said, heaving a sigh. He raised an eyebrow. "Why?"

"Give her a call." Wolf was going to tell McNamara to check to see if she was all right, but it was as if he'd already picked up on Wolf's fear.

A second later McNamara's head jerked back, like he'd been smacked.

"Who're you?" he said, and put the call on speaker.

"I'm the guy who's with your daughter," Soraces said. "Now put Wolf back on."

"I can hear you, Soraces," Wolf said, feeling an immense trepidation grip his spine.

"Listen, Soraces—" McNamara started to say.

"No, *you* listen," The voice had gone from joviality to absolute malice. "I've got people watching you at all times. Pros. You'll never spot them, so don't even try. And don't even think about notifying anybody. I even get a whiff of the authorities, local, state, or federal, and you'll never hear from me or her again. *Comprende?*"

Wolf pulled over onto the shoulder of the freeway and hit the hazard lights button. Several cars whizzed past. He wondered about each one of them. They sat in stunned silence for several seconds before he reached for the phone and took it out of Mac's hand.

"Look," he said, straining to keep his voice calm and even. "This is between you and me. Nobody else. Let her go and I'll give you what you want, no strings."

McNamara reached for the phone, ripping it away from Wolf and speaking in a low, deliberate voice.

"Listen, you son of a bitch. You hurt my daughter, you even touch her, I'll track your fucking ass down to the ends of the earth and make you wish you were never born."

A low chuckle came through the dashboard speaker.

"Now that you've got that out of your system," Soraces's voice said. "Let me reiterate. Nobody has to get hurt. It's a simple exchange. A business transaction. Just follow my instructions to the letter and it'll have a happy ending." He paused and then added, "If not ..."

The silence hung in the air like an ominous cloud.

"Remember," Soraces said. "No cops. And don't try pinging this phone. It's about to become inoperative. Go home, wait for my next call."

"Soraces—" Wolf shouted.

"Bye."

The dashboard indicated that the connection was terminated.

A few more cars whooshed by slamming an air pocket against the stopped Escalade. Wolf accelerated, glanced in the mirror, and shot back out into traffic when he was sure the lane was clear.

"Oh, my God." Ms. Dolly's voice sounded cracked.

"*Madre de dios,*" Brenda said. "*Qué lastima.*"

"God damn." McNamara said, blinking away the tears. "What am I gonna do? They got my little girl."

He sounded deflated, hollow. Ms. Dolly reached across the seat from the rear passenger space and patted McNamara's shoulder. She kept her hand there on his neck.

Wolf searched for more words to say, something to give comfort and hope, but once again, came up empty. He was to blame for this. Just like with Yolanda, he brought nothing to those he cared about except negativity and sorrow.

Finally, he said, "We'll think of something, Mac. We'll get her back."

———

**PHOENIX INTERNATIONAL AIRPORT
PRIVATE AIRCRAFT HANGER SECTION
PHOENIX, ARIZONA**

. . .

Soraces removed the back of Kasey's phone and popped the battery from its holder. He then slipped it into his jacket pocket and glanced at her slumbering form in the seat across from him. The injection of ketamine would most likely keep her out for the entire flight. It was only a couple of hours, but, just in case, he looped the nylon band around her ankles, thighs, arms and wrists and secured it with a sturdy knot before buckling her seatbelt. It wouldn't do for her to wake up unexpectedly and make a run for the border, in this instance, the jet's cabin door.

At our cruising altitude of 30,000 feet, he thought, it would be rather unpleasant, to say the least.

"We're ready for take-off," the pilot said over the intercom system.

"Then do it," Soraces yelled back.

Yes, he thought, having your own private Lear Jet at your disposal was a nice convenience. First class all the way.

Across the aisle, Clyde Perkins buckled himself in and looked over at the slumbering woman.

"She's pretty," he said. "But are you sure they're going to be coming all the way down there after her?"

"Without a doubt," Soraces said. "She our assurance that they will, and also our insurance that they'll do as I tell them."

"If you say so."

"I do."

Perkins shrugged. "And that guy I had to shoot ... He's an FBI agent?"

Soraces nodded.

"I wish you would've told me that earlier," Perkins said. "I don't like the idea of shooting a fed. They take things too personally. Especially the Bureau."

"Relax," Soraces said. "And don't worry. We'll be safely out of the country shortly and once we've concluded our business, we'll collect our fat paychecks, and just fade into the sunset."

"You make it sound easy."

"It will be." Soraces suddenly felt the vibration as the turbine engines spooled up and the plane edged forward. "Once we get Wolf and his buddy down in our spider's web."

———

THE MCNAMARA RANCH
PHOENIX, ARIZONA

Soraces's second call had come about four hours after the first one. They'd all been sitting and waiting in the living room at the Ranch, him, Mac, Ms. Dolly, and Brenda.

Waiting ... and waiting ...

When Wolf's phone rang showing *BLOCKED CALL* on the screen, Wolf let it ring three times before pressing the button to put it on speaker.

"How's things at the Ranch?" Soraces said. "You tip that babysitter like I told you?"

It was an obvious ploy to let Wolf know that he was still most likely being watched.

"Let me talk to Kasey," he said.

"Ah, she's ... resting. But, I'll send you a picture if you want."

Wolf saw McNamara rising out of his chair, gearing up to yell at the phone. Wolf shook his head and held up his hand. They'd discussed earlier how they should play it. Keep cool, show emotional detachment, professionalism. In other words, don't let the other guy see you sweat. Mac's emotional state precluded him from being a part of the negotiations.

"How do I know you even have her?" Wolf asked.

"Come on, Stevie boy. Do you want me to describe what she's wearing? Maybe undress her and look for birthmarks?"

Wolf saw the tendons in McNamara's neck tighten.

"I'm still going to need to talk to her," Wolf said.

Soraces sighed audibly. "All right."

There were few a muffled sounds, and then Soraces's voice came back on the line.

"Say hello, babe," he said.

"Dad?"

It was Kasey's voice.

McNamara's mouth twisted into a scowl.

"It's Steve. Are you all right, Kasey?"

"Yes." She sounded groggy, unfocused. "I'm just—"

Soraces came back on the line: "All right, satisfied?" Without waiting for a reply, he continued talking. "Like I said, this is purely a business transaction. Here's what we'll do. Since tomorrow's Sunday, I'll give you until Monday. You bring the item to the airport where there'll be two round trip airline tickets reserved for you at the United Airlines counter. One for you, and one for Mr. McNamara. Bring your passports. The flight's to Belize."

"Belize?"

"Right, as in the Central American country of down in the Caribbean. Oh, better bring Ms. Riley's passport, too, so you can get her back across the border. The one she used getting down here has a different name on it. Once you get there, we'll have someone meet you at the airport and we can arrange the exchange of goods. I'll even toss in the flashdrive. It'll be quick and easy. I'll be glad to make some hotel reservations for you as well. Any questions?"

Wolf looked at McNamara, who shook his head, his lips drawn together in a tight scowl.

"No questions," Wolf said. "Just some statements. First, we'll make our own travel plans. Once we're down there, we'll contact you, so I'll need a phone number."

"Out of the question regarding the phone," Soraces said. "It won't do you any good anyway. But I can understand your trepidation regarding the flight and pick-up." He sighed audibly. "Look, as a show of good faith, I'll go along with the first part of it. You two make your way down here and I'll call you Monday night. Want me to recommend a good hotel?"

"Like I said, we'll make our own plans."

"As you wish. But don't even think of any outside authoritative involvement. One whiff of anything like that, and everything, and everybody, turns to sparkle dust. Get it?"

"I got it."

"Good. And just make sure you bring the real deal this time," Soraces said. "No more duplicates."

Wolf almost came back with, "There are no more duplicates," but caught himself in time.

There's no sense in divulging anything in the way of intel to this asshole, he thought.

But the fact that he'd almost blurted it out reminded him how much he was off his game. Extreme fatigue, emotional involvement, worry about Kasey, and about Mac as well, was all extra baggage he was carrying. And in combat, extra baggage weighing you down can get you killed a lot quicker. He had to get his analytical mind wrapped around this. For Kasey's sake, as well as his own. But he also knew he had to capitalize on whatever leverage he had.

"I'll bring it," Wolf said. "But I'll also bring a sledge-hammer. Any tricks, any harm comes to Kasey, anything at all, and I'll be using it to smash that little stone artifact to smithereens. You got it?"

Soraces said nothing.

"Make sure you tell that to your boss, Von Dien," Wolf said and hung up.

The four of them sat in silence in the living room, and finally Mac said with deliberation, "Those bastards are gonna pay for taking my little girl. No rule book."

"Damn straight," Wolf said, wondering if Mac was secretly blaming him for this. He didn't want to ask.

"There will be a reckoning," McNamara said, his expression austere. "And I'm looking forward to watching that son of bitch die. Real slow."

CHAPTER FOURTEEN_

**THIRTY THOUSAND FEET
SOMEWHERE ABOVE ARIZONA**

Wolf leaned back in the seat and reviewed the past fifty-seven hours in his mind. It had gone by like the miles in a marathon, the clock seeming to do double time. He estimated that he hadn't slept more than a quarter of it, and that had been in short bursts when exhaustion had overtaken him or in forced combat naps. It had been the same for Mac, who looked terrible. His face sagged with the immense weight of worry and concern. The weariness seemed like a permanent fixture inside Wolf's head, too, and each moment to maintain any clarity of thought was a struggle. Now that he and Mac were cruising at commercial flight altitude on an international Southwest Airlines flight heading south to Philip S. W. Goldson International Airport in Belize, he hoped for a chance to rest. But that prospect turned out to be problematic, if not impossible.

He'd been forced to stash the bandito in the overhead storage compartment. The bulky backpack was too large and cumbersome to try and slide under the seat. Ever since they'd removed it from the safety deposit box that morning, Wolf had kept it right by his side. Even now, within the confines of a commercial airliner, he couldn't let go of the anxiety of not having it in his direct proximity.

Separation anxiety, he told himself, allowing a bleak smile to grace his lips.

It was their holy grail now—the only thing that could secure Kasey's safety and freedom. And it was their only bit of leverage. They'd already decided that the overall operation was Wolf's to run.

"I've got too much personal involvement in this," McNamara had told him. "With Kasey being hostage, it's messing up my thinking and we can't afford any mistakes."

No mistakes, Wolf thought. Easier said than done.

He felt on the edge of physical exhaustion, but as long as he was moving he was okay. Once he stopped, the omnipresent fatigue began wrapping itself around him like an encircling python again.

A python, he thought.

Just like that idiot biker that he'd cold-cocked with the staff. He snorted at the recollection and this brought a reaction from McNamara, who was seated next to him.

"What?" Mac said. His voice was low and gravelly.

"Just thinking," Wolf said. "Trying to make sure we've got all the bases covered, for now, anyway."

"Yeah," McNamara said. "Me too." He reclined his

seat back and said, "But we'd best try to get some sleep while we can."

Wolf agreed and pushed his seat back as well, but he doubted that sleep would come. His mind still whirled with the events leading up to their trek down the jetway.

He and McNamara had both agreed that involving the authorities at this point would probably be a mistake. The feds would have little choice but to contact and work with the Belizean police agencies, and each new layer of callous by-the-book authority would lessen the chances that Kasey would be returned safely. They decided they had to do this on their own and take a more proactive stance. But that didn't mean they'd be doing it without some kind of support network.

Ms. Dolly and Brenda were the first to volunteer, but McNamara said he wanted them here to guard his grandson.

"Well," Ms. Dolly said, "at least take Brenda with you. She can pass for a local better than me. I'll stay here and watch Chad."

Wolf still remembered her attempt at some mirth: "But don't none of y'all even think about calling me grandma."

The humor had fallen flat. Mac was too worried and Wolf couldn't shake the guilt at having been the cause of all this. He felt responsible. Although he'd been dragged in through the backdoor, he'd come into Mac's life and brought nothing but trouble.

After a fitful night's unsuccessful attempt at sleep in what hours remained, Wolf and McNamara had started their own preparation. They'd made the twenty-minute trek to Mesa to Buck's and asked to borrow the night vision goggles and a few other items.

"What you need this stuff for?" Buck asked. "You just returned it yesterday. I mean, I gotta business to run and we gotta a new class coming in next week."

The haggard expression on McNamara's face told the other man it was an important and urgent request.

After hearing the dire circumstances, Buck stiffened.

"Take whatever you need," he said. "And I'm coming with you."

Despite McNamara's protestations, the former marine wouldn't take no for an answer.

"You're gonna be going down into Indian country," he said. "And I owe it to you. You saved my bacon once. Now it's my turn to return the favor."

McNamara and Wolf reluctantly agreed, with Wolf feeling a bit better after the other members of the Best in the West Tactical Training Institute also wanted to come. It was decided that Buck and Joe Barnes would go and leave Ron and Pete here to run the next class. As an unexpected benefit, Dirk, who was still hanging around the Institute helping rebuild the firing range house, also said he wanted to come. McNamara nixed the idea, but Dirk insisted.

"I'll be your ace in the hole," he said. "I been there before."

Wolf's brow creased. "You've been to Belize?"

Dirk nodded. "I taught some classes down there. Military stuff."

"You speak Spanish?" McNamara asked.

Dirk smirked, "Yeah, but they speak English in Belize. It used to be called British Honduras. The country got its independence in the eighties. The SAS still trains down there. I helped teach some of them."

Wolf was still a bit unsure about taking all of them, especially Dirk, about whom he knew little. But he'd entered the picture through serendipity and he was familiar with the terrain. And beggars couldn't be choosers.

So that was that.

First, there were three, Wolf, Mac, and Brenda, and now there were six.

Better odds, Wolf thought.

Who knew what they were going to be up against down there ... Bambi taking on Godzilla, but now Bambi had a herd with him.

Well, Wolf remembered thinking, more like a small but tough semi-herd.

After calling the hospital to check on Franker, Wolf got the FBI man's partner, Special Agent Turner. Turner was mostly unhelpful but did put him through to Franker.

"Is Kasey all right?" were his first words.

"What?" Wolf said. "Why?"

"She was with me. Now, is she all right?"

Wolf didn't answer. Instead, he asked Franker how he was.

"I'm mostly okay," Franker said. "It was a through and through. Now what about Kasey?"

"What happened?" Wolf asked, again evading the other man's direct question.

"Carjacking, apparently," Franker said. "I'd just dropped Kasey at the restaurant when this guy stepped out of the shadows and shot me. Did the police contact her?"

Wolf said nothing.

"I'm so worried about her," Franker said. "She hasn't called me. Is she all right?"

"I can't talk about that now," Wolf said and hung up. He didn't answer when his phone immediately rang again and kept on ringing. Eventually, he shut it off but felt lousy about it. He'd promised the man some answers before.

Okay, he thought. Franker will get his damn answers and if things go bad down south, I'll leave something to go on.

Wolf then spent two hours typing out a detailed letter of everything that had happened starting with the Mexico fiasco and detailing everything up to their upcoming mission in Belize. He left Reno's and the others names out of it, but basically spilled everything. He printed out and signed the copy and then put it inside an envelope, scrawling his initials over the edge of the seal. After hand-printing Franker's name on the envelope, he contacted Dolores Delgato on her personal cell. Despite it being a Sunday night, she answered with a warm greeting. Wolf asked her to meet him early that Monday morning. She agreed and they'd met at a Dunkin' Donuts shop just down from her office building. The next day, with Mac waiting for him in the parking lot, Wolf watched as she walked up casually, smiling that million-dollar smile.

She commented on how fatigued he looked.

"I've got a lot going on," he said.

She canted her head and looked at him, her yellowish-brown eyes fixed with a questioning expression.

"My," she said. "That sounds cryptic. Anything I can help with?"

He nodded.

"If you don't hear from me by next Wednesday," Wolf said, handing her the envelope. "Take this to the FBI office and leave it for Special Agent William Franker."

Her perfect eyebrows arched slightly.

"This is intriguing," she said. "Do you want to tell me what this is all about?"

Wolf mulled that over in his mind.

McNamara tapped the horn twice and Wolf remembered that they had a lot to do before their afternoon flight.

"It's best I don't right now," Wolf said, standing. He smiled down at her. "It's a long story, sort of involving what we discussed before, but I'm going out of town and I'm pressed for time."

The letter contained more details than what he'd already confided.

She smiled, placed the letter in her Gucci purse, and said, "Godspeed."

Their last stop was going to see Reno at his gym. They remembered he and Black Hercules had been taken down to Von Dien's estate a few months back, at the time of the Mexican fiasco. Both Wolf and McNamara began grilling him about what he remembered about the place.

"It's big," Reno said. "Got armed guards and an electric fence. Huge house, with a pool out back. The place is in the middle of a jungle. You gotta drive there from Belize City."

"Here," McNamara said, shoving some paper and a pen across the desk at him. "Draw us a diagram."

"Huh? What for?" His face twisted in confusion. "What's going on?"

After much hesitation, Wolf confided what had happened, figuring it might be better if somebody knew, in case things went badly and they didn't make it back.

But what came next totally surprised him.

"I'm going with you," Reno said.

"Out of the question," Wolf said.

Reno reached out and grabbed Wolf's arm. "Steve, please. I owe it to you."

"Reno," McNamara said, "this is my daughter down there. It ain't your fight."

"The hell it's not," Reno said. His grip tightened on Wolf's arm and he was cognizant of the other man's strength. "These are the guys responsible for killing Herc, ain't they?"

Wolf and McNamara exchanged glances, and then Wolf nodded.

"Then I'm going," Reno said. "I owe it to Herc, and most of all, I owe it to you two. You saved my life down there in Mexico."

After a few more minutes of silence, McNamara spoke in a low voice.

"We're going down there to get my daughter back," he said. "By any means necessary. You know what that means?"

Reno nodded. "I'm good with that. And like I said, I owe it to you."

And then there were seven, Wolf thought. The magnificent seven ... Better odds at least.

———

THE VON DIEN WINTER ESTATE SOUTH BELIZE

It couldn't have worked out better if he'd planned this new development himself. Soraces took a deep breath of satisfaction as he walked toward the library for what he hoped would be his penultimate session with Fallotti and Von Dien. Gordo, the big butler with the concealed piece, led the way.

In his original scenario Soraces had intended that Dirk would be his fail-safe figure, remaining up in Phoenix to deal with Wolf and McNamara should they not make the trek down to Belize and went, instead, to the cops. But now his rook had turned into the perfect sleeper agent.

A sapper right in their midst, he thought, smiling. And a Shadow on the same flight. Those stupid bastards don't even have a clue.

As they got to the door Gordo stopped and tapped Soraces on the shoulder before he could enter and handed him a face mask.

"*Señor* Von Dien insists," he said.

"But where's yours?" Soraces asked, allowing a little sarcastic lilt to his words and watching the huge servant's reaction.

The big man smirked and Soraces took this as a good sign. He needed to keep on the good side of the rank and file just in case Fallotti and Von Dien had some kind of a double cross in mind. He didn't think they did, but he made it a point always to consider all the moves beforehand.

More than likely, he thought, the fat, rich, son of a

bitch will be coming in his pants once he has that fucking second half of the artifact in his greedy little hands.

He slipped the mask on and went inside. They both sat at the far end of the table, the lawyer situated six feet away, the hulking bodyguard hovering over the fat Buddha's right shoulder. They all wore masks, but Soraces was sure that the rich bastard was probably frowning underneath his.

The table was long and Fallotti motioned to a chair at the opposite end.

The fucking germaphobe's so scared he doesn't want me within six feet of him, Soraces thought with amusement.

The bodyguard's light blue eyes watched his every movement.

He sat, thinking how easy it would be to repeat the practiced move of drawing the ninja blade and hurling it into the big man's eyeball.

"We'd like an update," Fallotti said.

"Of course," Soraces said. "They're on their way here with the bandito. The girl's secured in your special detention room, with a guard posted, and I've got someone watching their every move in transit."

He raised both of his eyebrows since that was the only facial gesture that would be visible over the mask's concealment.

"Here?" Von Dien said. His words sounded slightly muffled by the mask. "You're bringing them here?"

"What better place to deal with them?" Soraces shot back. "Down here where the local police are in your pocket. As soon as we get possession of the Lion Attacking the Nubian, and verify its authenticity, everything can be wrapped up with a bow without leaving a trace."

Von Dien's heavy exhalation of breath was obvious even through the mask.

"We'd prefer you to refer to it as 'the item' in these conversations," Fallotti said.

"Certainly," Soraces said, more convinced than ever that every word was being recorded by this devious rich asshole.

But that's okay, fat man, Soraces thought. I'm doing a recording of my own.

He glanced down to reassure himself that he'd activated his spy pen.

"And you're certain they're bringing the item?" Fallotti said.

"Of course," Soraces answered. "What other choice do they have?"

"Wolf was smart enough to use a duplicate the last time," Von Dien said. "What makes you think he won't try that again?"

"He knows better, for one thing," Soraces said. "And, for another, we'll have all of the principals down here as your ..." He purposely hesitated for a few beats before finishing his sentence with, "guests."

Fallotti looked at Von Dien, who made a quick nodding motion with his basketball-sized head. The lawyer turned back to Soraces.

"Very well," he said. "Keep us advised."

"I'll be glad to," Soraces said, getting to his feet, cognizant that the big bodyguard was still watching his every move.

LIBERTY CITY
BELIZE

WELCOME TO BELIZE the sign said spelling out the country's name in blue, red, yellow and green block letters.

After a four hour and twenty-minute flight, The Magnificent Seven got off the plane and tagged up outside the Custom's gate at Philip S. W. Goldson International Airport where the official seemed less interested in their lack of visas ("They are not required here, sir.") than their lack of the required 72 hour old PCR tests for COVID 19. Wolf had noticed another American on the flight from Phoenix, a tall, slender guy with a COVID mask pulled over a big, hooked nose. The man had a strange familiarity about him, as if Wolf had seen him before, but the ubiquitous fatigue prevented him from remembering where. But as tired and anxious as he was, Wolf figured that everybody was looking suspicious. The tall guy had vanished shortly after they all went through customs.

The PCR testing procedures at BZE cost them fifty dollars each, with Mac slipping the agent an extra fifty from the money belt to grease the wheels. They were, quickly, ushered to the car rental place where they found the selection somewhat limited. After a twenty-minute wait, during which time the rental agent's eyes widened when he saw McNamara pull out a stack of American greenbacks, they settled on three vehicles: an ancient, silver Toyota Camry with over 150,000 kilometers, an equally old Jeep Wrangler with no doors and a patched canvas top, and a tan Subaru Forester with an odometer showing 69,000 kilometers. Big Joe Barnes looked rather cramped as he tried to sandwich himself into the Camry, trying it out, and then opted for the open Jeep.

"At least it ain't an old Willie's," McNamara said.

Again, Wolf was glad to see the flash of humor in his friend and mentor.

Each vehicle had a GPS which the car rental agent said would guide them on the safest routes.

"You are going to Belize City?" he asked, his English tinctured with British sounding pronunciations. "I would advise you to stay away from the southern part of the city. It is a bit dangerous, especially at night."

"I've been to George Street before," Dirk said.

The rental agent's eyebrows rose like twin caterpillars.

That sounds like the place we'll have to go next, Wolf thought. After we get checked in to the hotel.

Another twenty-minute drive on a decent two-lane highway took them to a massive white and tan brick hotel located on the edge of the coast. As they turned into the drive that led to the check-in area under an overlapping canopy, Wolf turned and looked at the pristine green water that changed to a darker shade of blue a hundred yards farther out. The check-in procedures went smoothly and once they were situated in two sets of adjoining rooms in the hotel, Wolf said he was leaving the bandito with McNamara while he and Dirk went cruising for weapons.

"Like hell," McNamara said. "I should be going with you."

Wolf put his hand on Mac's shoulder. "Look, I

thought we agreed before that I was in charge of this one?"

McNamara stared at him, then nodded.

"Okay, Wolf said, "one of us has to stay with the bandito at all times. To guard it. And I've got to get us some weapons in the *mercado negro*."

"Huh?" McNamara said.

"The black market," Brenda said. "And me and Joe will go see what we can find out from the Guatemalans this *pendejo grande* uses as his servants."

"*Pendejo?*" Barnes asked.

"Asshole," Brenda said. "*Pendejo grande*, big asshole."

Barnes grinned. "Hey, I'm liking this little girl better and better."

"Don't get too attached to her," McNamara said.

"*No tenga cuidado*," Brenda said to him. "Don't worry. *Mi corazon es tuyo siempre.*"

McNamara's forehead wrinkled slightly. "Was that good or bad?"

"She said her heart belongs to daddy," Dirk said. "Always."

Barnes grinned. "No worries, Mac. My Crystal's my one and only. And I'm surprised. There's a lot of black people down here. I ought to fit right in."

"Only if you start talking with an English accent," Buck said.

"What can I do?" Reno asked.

Wolf turned to Buck. "You ever use Google Earth?"

Buck nodded. "Yeah."

"Get my laptop out of my backpack and see if you can get onto the hotel's Wi-Fi," Wolf said. "Reno, you think you can remember where that guy's estate is."

Reno tilted his head. "Maybe."

Buck clapped McNamara on the shoulder and added, "You get our knives out of the luggage, brother while I run down to the bar and get us some cold ones. Then we'll do some net surfing. Plus, we'll have three bottles to use as weapons until Steve and Dirk get back with the goodies."

"Speaking of which," Wolf said. "We're going to need some money."

"Us too," Brenda said.

McNamara nodded and pulled out a wad of bills from the money belt. He shoved them into Wolf's hand and then gave some more to Brenda.

"Just don't spend it all in one place," he said with a half-grin. "Or buy any of them expensive *zapatos*."

"The only thing I want to buy is information." Brenda smiled. "I'm glad you remember some of those Spanish words I taught you."

"I'll be needing a review soon enough," McNamara said.

More good signs from Mac, Wolf thought.

The weight of his daughter's abduction was obviously bearing down on him like a two-ton millstone around his neck. Any bit of levity was welcome, especially with their limited options.

It was time to be proactive, but they had to play it smart.

He slapped Dirk on the shoulder and said, "You ready, partner?"

———

GEORGE STREET

BELIZE CITY, BELIZE

Wolf let Dirk drive since he had a familiarity with the place. Occasional three- or four-story buildings were interspersed among rows of ragtag houses with fences made of everything from peeling white pickets to sheets of ribbed aluminum. Many of the houses were in dilapidated condition, with patches of bare wood badly in need of a coat of paint sticking out like gray scabs on an expanse of leg. Many of the shops displayed signs, some hand-painted, advertising everything from *Fashionable Clothes* to *Coca-Cola*. The Coke signs were the traditional metal signs displaying the soft drink company's antiquated emblem. Everything was in English, which seemed strange for Central America. The streets were narrow and there were a lot of people walking. Dirk used the horn frequently and drove aggressively, expecting people to get out of the way. It reminded Wolf of the driving habits of some of the GI's overseas, but since the neighborhood seemed to be getting seedier, he figured that displaying bravado wasn't a bad idea.

They passed a big fish market and drove over what appeared to be a canal. Dirk turned left and proceeded on the street that ran parallel to the water. The smell was noticeable. They seemed to be going south now and they turned left onto a street called Dean.

"This used to be the capital," Dirk said. "The south end of the city, where we're heading, is a real shithole. Lots of gangs."

They cruised past a police station.

"Looks like the cops are close," Wolf said.

Dirk snorted a laugh. "Yeah. All uniforms and bluster, but scared shitless. Most of them don't even carry guns."

Wolf figured that might be due to the British influence.

"But the gangs do?" he asked.

"Yeah." Dirk laid on the horn again causing an elderly black man to jump from the street to the sidewalk.

"No matter where you are," he said. "Those black fuckers love to walk in the fucking street."

Wolf said nothing, thinking about his own upbringing on the Rez. A lot of Indians not only walked in the street, some even fell down drunk there as well. Poverty and alcohol abuse never went well with rule-followers and caution.

Dirk hung a quick right and Wolf saw that they were now on George Street.

"Here we are," Dirk said. "It'll be getting dark soon and the scum likes to come out when the sun goes down. Let's find a place we can park and see if we can make some connections."

"Sounds good," Wolf said.

Dirk pulled into a vacant space and they both got out. The sidewalks here were made of inlaid bricks, some of which had been chipped or broken and not replaced.

They were both dressed in black cargo pants, loose-fitting BDU blouses, and running shoes. Wolf noticed that Dirk had shoved a butterfly knife into his bottom left blouse pocket before they left the hotel.

"You a southpaw?" he asked.

Dirk shook his head. "No, why?"

"I saw you put that knife into your left pocket."

Dirk's face twitched slightly with something resembling a half-smile.

"I'm ambidextrous," he said. "Good with either one." He held up his extended right hand, which looked as big as a brick. "I keep them both conditioned, but I use my right one for breaking."

Wolf had never gone in much for the karate hand-conditioning routines, like striking a *makawari* board a thousand times or plunging your finger into a basket of pebbles. The knuckles of his own hands were somewhat prominent and toughened, however, due to his work on the punching bags.

Down the block, a trio of young black guys, each wearing sunglasses and sporting unkempt Afros, leaned against a building. The sweet odor of marijuana drifted in the air from their hand-rolled cigarettes. A crude, hand-painted sign jutted out perpendicularly from the wall above them advertising *Joshua's Emporium*.

"Looks like a good a place as any to start," Dirk said.

"Judging from the clientele in front," Wolf said.

He felt the jolt of the hyper-alertness of adrenaline course through him.

"Let me take the lead on this," Dirk said. "I've dealt with punks down here before."

Wolf wasn't too keen about that idea but said, "Go ahead." It would also give him a chance to do some observation of Dirk.

The three youths eyed them as they walked up.

"Hey, *mon*," one of them said. "You looking to score?"

Dirk looked him up and down and smirked.

"Maybe," he said. "Depends on what you're offering."

The guy's lips pulled back into a grin that displayed a black lattice-work of decay curling over his remaining teeth.

"You Americans?" he asked, then turned and said something Wolf assumed was Kriol slang to his two partners.

American tourists, Wolf thought. Easy marks and lots of money. He was glad he'd brought his own Coast TX395 knife. He could flip it open using the thumb peg as he withdrew it and it looked as intimidating as all hell, but he wondered if these guys were armed.

It was never a good idea to bring a knife to a gunfight.

The young black guy turned back, his lips still framing his decrepit tusks.

"We got some dynamite Columbian for you *mon*. Really sweet." The tip of his pink tongue rolled over his thick lips. "I can get you anything you want."

"We're looking for something special," Dirk said. He paused and looked the three youths up and down. "Somehow I don't think you guys fill the bill."

The one who'd been talking pursed his lips then turned to his two partners.

"You hear *dat*?" he said in a loud voice. "We don't fill *da* bill. And all *dis* from a fucker with one blue eye and the other one brown."

The three of them started to laugh in high-pitched giggles.

Wolf and Dirk walked past them, with Wolf maintaining his usual readiness in case one of them made a move. Joshua's Emporium turned out to be a three-sided room with the fourth wall pretty much missing so that the maze of tables and chairs looked out on the adjacent street. Dirk cocked his head toward the inside and Wolf followed him in. The skinny guy who'd been vocalizing trailed behind them. The place was sparsely occupied and there was a big black man behind the bar. He grinned, his curly mustache framing his mouth, and waved his arms at an empty table. Despite the absence of a bordering outside wall, the place was still redolent of all types of booze.

"Sit anywhere you like, gentlemen." He turned and muttered something to a mahogany-colored woman in cut-off blue jeans and a white T-shirt tied under her heavy breasts, leaving her midriff bare. Wolf took notice that the abdomen had some stretch marks and loose skin, but her face was very pretty. So was her smile.

"What can I get you, guys?" she asked, stopping by the table and tilting her pelvis just enough to signal that she might also be on the menu.

They ordered two beers, "In the bottle," Dirk added.

The skinny guy pulled out a chair and sat at their table.

"I don't remember inviting you to sit down," Dirk said.

The skinny guy smiled, showing his bad teeth again.

"Come on, *mon*," he said. "You say you're looking to do business, and I'm *de mon* 'round here."

Dirk gave him a long stare, then snorted. "Yeah, right."

The skinny guy looked unperturbed. "Maybe you buy me a drink, and we can talk about what you need."

The accents and the atmosphere was almost enough to make Wolf think he was down in Jamaica or the Bahamas or, at least, what he imagined them to be like. He'd never been to either. The girl returned and set two capped bottles in front of Wolf and Dirk. She looked expectantly at the skinny guy, but before he could speak Dirk said, "Nothing for him. He's leaving."

The woman smiled and nodded. Her dark eyes widened slightly when Wolf slipped her a twenty and told her to keep the change. The sway of her full hips was exaggerated even more as she walked back to the bar.

"Hey," the skinny guy said. "How come you're being so inhospitable? Like I told you, whatever you want, Franko can get for you."

Dirk studied the skinny guy again, then reached out and curled his big fingers around the neck of the bottle, resting his callused thumb just under the rim of the cap. The big hand tightened and flexed and the cap popped off, landing on the table top. Franco's eyes widened, his glib smile vanishing.

"What's your honcho's name?" Dirk said, his voice low and gruff.

"Honcho?"

"Your boss," Dirk said. "You know, the head nigger around here."

Wolf found himself recoiling internally at the mention of the N-word, but it didn't seem to faze Franco that much. His lips closed over his teeth, then parted again with a nervous grin.

"What's his fucking name?" Dirk said.

"Bernard, sir," Franco said.

"And what do you fuckers call yourselves?" Dirk asked.

"We're the George Street Hustlers."

Wolf left his bottle capped. The last thing he needed right now was some alcohol. Dirk took a sip from his.

"Okay, George Street Hustler," Dirk said, leaning forward and putting his elbows on the table. "We're looking to buy some guns. Good stuff, not shit. You go back and tell this Bernard fella that we're interested, and we'll be here for another five, maybe ten minutes or so."

Franco kept the nervous smile on his face as he stood up, muttering a series of "Yes, sirs" and he slipped away.

"Pretty neat trick with the bottle," Wolf said. "Is that why you ordered it that way?"

Dirk drank some more and shook his head. "You never want to get anything in a glass down this way." He held up his thumb. "I've been practicing that since I was ten years old. Used to know a whore that could open them with her teeth. That was down in Venezuela."

"Never been there," Wolf said.

"You're lucky. Of course, they do have some of the most beautiful girls in the world. If you like Latinas." He brought the bottle to his lips once more and drank copiously. "They all look like Miss Universe contestants."

"So you think this Bernard can deliver?" Wolf asked.

Dirk shrugged and said, "Guess we'll find out soon enough. If he shows. If not, we go down the street to the next set of punks."

Wolf was beginning to feel like this was not only a dangerous side venture, but a fruitless one as well.

"If he shows," Wolf repeated.

"Hey, *mon*," another voice said. "I'm right here," Just chill, okay?"

Wolf turned and saw a tall, somewhat older, dark-skinned black man enter from the street and walk over to their table. He wore a baggy red, yellow, and green T-shirt and knee-length shorts. His hair was cut shorter than the other three and he moved with a bit of grace and deliberation.

"Sit down," Dirk said before Wolf could say anything.

He was a bit unsettled by Dirk's burgeoning assertiveness but decided to let it ride. The big alpha dog was champing at the bit to take over. Wolf had dealt with this type many times in the military, which was full of alpha male personalities, always wanting to show they had the biggest dick in the room. He'd remind Dirk later exactly who was in charge of this mission, but for now, he'd sit back and watch.

Dirk raised his hand and snapped his fingers. The waitress came scampering over.

"What you drinking, Bernard?"

"My usual," he said to the waitress. She gave a fractional nod and left.

"So my boys tell me you gents are looking for some hardware," Bernard said.

"Yeah." Dirk said. "Know where we can find some?"

"Exactly what kind of stuff are you looking for?"

"What can you deliver?" Dirk asked.

"Whatever you want, *mon*. Just tell me."

Dirk stared at him. "Maybe a rifle, a couple of good handguns."

"No problem," Bernard said, displaying a wide array of very white teeth as the waitress returned and set a glass filled with amber liquid and ice in front of him.

Wolf slipped her some more bills and she quickly pocketed them and left.

The three of them watched her wiggle away.

"Maybe you looking for some nice ladies, too?" Bernard said. "I can give you some fine women. Treat you like two kings."

"We'll get our own women," Wolf said, insinuating himself into the conversation. "Now let's talk time and money."

Bernard sipped his drink and then nodded. After setting the glass down on the table, he leaned forward and spoke in a conspiratorial whisper, promising to deliver what they wanted at what sounded like an inflated price. The negotiations took under a minute, and Wolf got the feeling this Bernard character was trying to get an idea about how much money they had. Finally, they settled things and the black man then removed a cellphone from his pocket and dialed a number. When he spoke into it he used a language that was full of foreign sounds and sing-song intonations. Wolf figured it must be Kriol. When he hung up he slipped the cellphone back into his pocket and flashed the ivory smile again.

"Drink up," he said. "The items are on the way."

Dirk nodded and took another drink from the bottle.

Wolf still hadn't touched his and was getting a bad feeling about this deal-to-be. Real bad but, at this point, he was on a merry-go-round that was going too fast to get off safely.

After about five minutes more, Bernard's cellphone chimed. He'd finished his drink and had started on another. He spoke into the phone and Wolf could smell the booze on the guy's breath.

"He's back with the goods," Bernard said, displaying the array of teeth again. "Shall we?"

The three of them got up with Wolf and Dirk following the slender black man outside. They both still carried their beer bottles and Dirk took another drink from his. Darkness had descended and he pointed to a shadowy expanse perhaps fifteen feet wide between two buildings. "Step into my office."

Wolf was feeling more and more that this wasn't a very good idea, but he was in the middle of it now and ultimately had Kasey's welfare to think about. If they were going to mount some kind of rescue, they needed guns. Dirk moved with the alacrity of self-assurance. Maybe it was time to let this alpha dog off the chain and see what he could do.

Dirk, apparently sensing Wolf's misgivings, asked, "You good?"

Wolf nodded, holding the bottle by the neck down the side of his leg.

This had better be quick and easy, he thought. Otherwise, we could be in a world of hurt.

The three men from before stood at the midway point between the two buildings. Franco held a box and another had what appeared to be something long and solid looking wrapped in a blanket. As they drew closer Wolf scrutinized what the man was holding and inferred that it was too square looking to be a rifle.

A three-foot two-by-four, most likely, he thought. This is probably going to be a rip.

"Dirk," he said.

But before his partner could say anything, Bernard jumped to the side and one of the skinny trio came up with what looked to be a rusty blue steel revolver and pointed it directly at Wolf. His hand shook visibly as he waved the gun back and forth between Wolf and Dirk.

Bernard reached out and Franco handed him a nickel-plated semi-auto.

Wolf surmised that it was a nine-millimeter and the design suggested Berretta or Taurus.

"Time to conclude our deal," Bernard said, flashing the smile once more. "Now give me that stack of cash you been sitting on and we'll let you two walk away."

"What about our guns?" Dirk said.

Bernard's smile flipped upside down into a scowl. "Don't you be fuckin' *wid* us, *mon*. You give us your money now, or else."

Dirk rolled his eyes and half turned toward Wolf.

"Shit," he said. "I guess we got no choice." He dropped his beer bottle.

Before Wolf could say or do anything, Dirk pivoted, driving his open left palm against the back of Bernard's gun hand. The big fingers closed over the barrel of the weapon and Dirk smiled broadly as he ripped it free and then thrust a spear-hand blow to Franco's throat. It made a popping sound similar to a chopped carrot.

Wolf didn't wait. He brought his right leg upward and around in with a crescent kick knocking the skinny arm holding the revolver askew. The gun discharged into the dirt and Wolf followed up by bringing his open hand down on top of the barrel and snatching it from the man's grip. He then pivoted and delivered an uppercut just under the chin, and the man's jaw made a clicking sound as his teeth snapped together. He folded over and collapsed to the ground. The third man ripped the blanket off what was indeed a two-by-four and stepped forward. Wolf's foot smashed into the advancing man's knee causing him to stumble forward. Pivoting, Wolf twisted his body and shot a roundhouse kick flashing upward so fast that he doubted the other man saw it before Wolf's instep crashed into the man's temple. He crumpled also.

Dirk, in the meantime, was grinding Bernard's face into the tan, stucco wall leaving the rough surface smeared with blood. Franco lay in the dirt squirming. Dirk stomped on him and then his right hand whipped out with a knife-hand to the back of Bernard's neck and Wolf heard a dull crack. Bernard fell to the ground and shook spasmodically.

"We got the guns," Wolf said. "Let's get out of here,"

In an unhurried manner Dirk picked up the nickel-plated semi-auto and handed it to Wolf. He then rolled Bernard over and began going through his pockets.

Wolf looked at the two weapons. The semi-auto was a nine-millimeter Taurus and the revolver a rusted .38 Ruger with a four-inch barrel. He checked the cylinder. Five rounds left. He didn't take the time to check the magazine of the Taurus, and shoved both guns into his waistband and covered them with his blouse.

Dirk checked each man for more weapons but found none. He then removed Bernard's shirt and stuffed his cellphone, the two beer bottles, and the other man's cellphone into the garment.

"We need to dump these in the canal on the way back," he said, handing the bundle to Wolf and reaching into his lower left pocket. His hand withdrew the butterfly knife and he swiveled it, popping open the closeted blade. "Just let me finish these fuckers off."

He stooped down and seized a handful of Bernard's hair with his left hand.

"Hold it," Wolf said, grabbing Dirk's arm. "These assholes are down for the count. And we ain't coming back here. So, let's leave them be and get out of here."

Dirk's mouth twisted into a frown. "I don't like leaving loose ends."

"We didn't come down here to murder people."

"Didn't we?" Dirk grinned. "I'm pretty sure I broke this fucker's neck."

"These guys are no threat to us anymore," Wolf said. "We need to go. Now."

Dirk smirked. "Still operating under those old rules of engagement, huh, Wolf?"

Rules of engagement ... He thought back to Iraq. Things don't always work out the way you planned.

"Let's go," he said, and headed out of the alleyway.

———

THE VON DIEN WINTER ESTATE SOUTH
   BELIZE

Soraces had grown a bit irritated waiting for the call from Dirk but it finally came well into the evening.

"About fucking time," Soraces said, making no effort to conceal his irritation.

"Relax," Dirk said. "And get ready to take notes. I had a hard time sneaking away from them."

This tripped a bit of alarm in Soraces. The last thing he wanted at this point was to have his inside man discovered.

"And just how did you do that?" he asked. "I don't want them suspecting you."

"Relax. I'm good. Now you want to hear about their plan, or not?"

Soraces took a deep breath. He had to trust that Dirk had managed to slip out of the other's presence without creating suspicion.

"Tell me," he said.

"Okay, we're set up in the Ramada in two adjoining room. Seven of us."

"Yeah, I know that. Charles told me what he saw on the plane."

"Me and Wolf went into the ghetto and got a couple of guns. A nine, with eight rounds left in it, and a piece-of-shit revolver. That one's only got five."

So, Wolf was armed but still ignorant.

"Wolf's going to be carrying the revolver," Dirk said. "They're planning on hitting you tomorrow. Early."

"Hitting us?" Soraces was astounded. "Here at the estate? Are they fucking nuts?"

Dirk laughed. "That's the plan. The broad and the big nigger went out and found a bunch of Guatemalans that work there. Your boss ain't too popular with his servants, and they sold him out in a hurry. They also spilled it about the McNamara broad being held at the estate, which room she's in, and also the lowdown on the whole security set-up there."

"They're planning an assault?" Soraces was imagining a one-sided firefight that would leave them all dead. "With two handguns with thirteen rounds total?"

"Quit interrupting me," Dirk said. "That ain't correct and I've got a lot more to tell you." After a few seconds of silence, he continued. "The way Wolf's got it figured ain't a half-bad plan. They know how a new batch of spic servants is brought in each morning on a bus, and how they're stopped at the gate and their fucking temperatures are taken. Wolf and the Latina bitch are gonna be on the bus wearing masks, like good little piss-ants, pretending to be Guatemalans. When they get up to the house, they're gonna sneak inside and go find the girl. Me and McNamara are gonna be in a Toyota Camry, and, get this, *I'm* gonna have the nine-millimeter on account of I'm such a good fucking shot." He paused to chuckle. "The two dickwads from Best in the West are in the Jeep with a chain and a grappling hook. When Wolf contacts McNamara, by text, that they've got the daughter and are en route to the front gate, we're gonna roll up and I'll take out the gate guard, if necessary. The other two will use the four-wheel-drive to take down the gate, and me and McNamara will pull on through and pick up Wolf, the Latina bitch, and the daughter and scoot."

Soraces considered this. It was bold and audacious and might, possibly, have worked, if they actually had Dirk working on their side.

But they don't, he thought.

"What about the bandito?" Soraces said. "And didn't you say there was one more of them?"

"Yeah, some big dude named Reno. Former MMA fighter, but now he's walking with a cane. He knows a lot about the estate, too."

It had to be Garth, the guy that had been recruited before.

"He's going to be holding the bandito?"

"Yeah, in the third car they rented. A tan Subaru Forester. Reno's gonna be on the outskirts with the bandito, sorta like a fail-safe."

"You sure they brought it?" Soraces asked. "You've seen it? You know what it looks like?"

"I do, and they got it, all right. In a backpack. I seen a duplicate of it, unpainted, in that craft's shop. I remember knocking it onto the floor."

Wolf must have requisitioned another duplicate, Soraces thought. This means I can't rule out the possibility that the one he brought down here might also be a fake.

Wolf had to be taken alive after they were defeated in this planned assault.

"And that Wolf gave that Reno guy a sledgehammer to take along, just in case."

The threat from before, Soraces thought.

"You hear from Lola?" Dirk asked. "She coming down to join the party?"

"No," Soraces said.

"Too bad," Dirk said. "I was looking forward to seeing her again."

Soraces said nothing to that. He didn't want to be distracted thinking about her.

Maybe this is the genuine bandito after all, he thought.

But he had to make sure, which meant allowing this

plan to appear to be completed by his opponent so he would move into the gambit.

"I say again," Dirk said. "Why not just have me slit their throats tonight and bring the damn thing to you? It would save a lot of bullshit."

Soraces weighed the offer. "No, let it play out. There's still an outside chance that this one's another duplicate. Plus, the murders of six Americans in a tourist hotel would bring too much heat. We'll deal with them quietly once we take them prisoner tomorrow, inside the estate."

"Okay, whatever trips your trigger."

"All right," Soraces said. "I'm going to make my call to Wolf now, telling him that I'll set up an exchange, the girl for the bandito, tomorrow night in the city. In the meantime, we'll let their little raid go forward seemingly without a hitch. I'll even have the gate guard leave the fucking thing open for them. The only catch will be me and the Perkins twins will be waiting for Wolf inside the main house when they come in."

"What about me?" Dirk asked. "You want me to kill McNamara and the others and just come up to the house?"

Again, Soraces considered the best options. They still had to achieve their main objective of getting the bandito, and that meant they had to maintain enough leverage to make Wolf play ball once he was in custody. The more hostages he had to play with, the better.

"No," Soraces said. "I want to keep them alive as bargaining chips, should I need them."

"Okay, sounds good," Dirk said. "And let me do that Latina bitch. I want to have some fun with her first."

"Not a problem," Soraces said, imagining Dirk

brutalizing the girl. Soraces wondered if she was pretty as he terminated the call.

Probably, he thought, although, to a sadistic psycho like Dirk, that wasn't always a requirement.

He looked around the elaborately furnished bedroom and fingered the ninja knife and wished he had that whiteboard to throw the blade at again. But then again, he'd had enough practice. Now it was time to make what would hopefully be his last Wolf call.

THE RAMADA INN
BELIZE CITY, BELIZE

Wolf tossed his cellphone down onto the bed and saw the others looking at him. He'd been thrust into the position of team leader in this situation, and he knew the stakes were high. Still, he felt a certain responsibility for causing a lot of the hardship and this had turned into his last remaining chance at some achieving some form of redemption. Gone was his hope to find the flashdrive and clear his name. Getting Kasey back safely was all that mattered at this point.

"Soraces says he'll call tomorrow night with the instructions for making the exchange," Wolf said. "But we'll have Kasey back before that."

"Maybe we can negotiate then for that flashdrive, Steve," McNamara said.

"Let's not worry about that," Wolf said. "Kasey's our sole priority at this time."

McNamara looked old and worn down, and Wolf

knew it wasn't only from the fatigue of operating on little sleep for the better part of the last week. The concern for his daughter was taking its toll on him. Hopefully, in about twelve more hours it would be over, and Kasey would be safe. But he knew they couldn't afford to drop their guard.

McNamara nodded. "But just the same, we're down here, and I'm getting mighty sick of just sitting back and taking hits. These fuckers are gonna have to pay, one way or another."

Wolf said nothing, letting the tension slowly dissipate. He knew Mac wanted a reckoning. So did he, but, in the grand scheme of things, they were way overmatched. Stealth and a quick, in-and-out op were their best chances.

Our only chances, he thought. We're still a herd of Bambi's baiting Godzilla.

"Okay," he said. "We'd better try to get some sleep, but I want two-man guard duty in four-hour shifts, and everybody up and ready to go by zero five hundred. Brenda and I need to get dropped off at the pick-up point in the Guatemalan section by zero six-thirty."

"Guard duty?" Reno said.

"Right. We've got to operate under the assumption that Soraces might know, or try to find out where we are. We can't afford to take the chance that he might send somebody after us."

"An old army proverb," McNamara said. "Never get caught with your drawers down."

As Wolf was making the assignments the phone in the hotel suite rang, shocking everyone.

Wolf immediately was on guard again as he picked up the receiver.

"Mr. Wolf?" a British sounding voice asked.

"Yeah."

"This is P. D. Jeeves at the front desk," the voice said. "There's a man down here in the lobby causing a bit of a ruckus. He's being quite adamant about going up to see you. Naturally, we haven't told him your room number."

Could Soraces have found them so soon? Had he sent somebody? But why would they announce themselves?

"And he asked for me by name?" Wolf asked.

"Yes," Jeeves said. "He's a bit of an unruly chap, but doesn't seem all that threatening. In fact, he appears to have been injured. His left arm's in a sling."

"A sling?" Wolf's mind raced. "He give a name?"

"Just a moment."

A muffled sound came over the phone, accompanied by the sound of Jeeves saying, "Oh, dear."

"Wolf?" the familiar voice said. "It's Franker. We need to talk."

CHAPTER FIFTEEN_

JUST OUTSIDE OF THE VON DIEN ESTATE
BELIZE

The bus trundled down the highway and then slowed to make what Wolf assumed to be the final turn onto the winding road that led up to the estate. It was very uncomfortable inside the bus and the lowered half-windows seemed only to let in more of the hot, tropical air without creating any kind of refreshing current. The fatigue factor had grown exponentially. He'd never, in his wildest dreams, figured on Franker making his way down here. He recalled the FBI man's steely resolve when he'd gone down to meet him in the lobby the previous night.

"What the hell are you doing here?" Wolf had asked.

"I intend to ask you the same question," Franker

said. "You got no right keeping me out of this. Where's Kasey?"

Wolf took a deep breath and ushered him over to a set of empty chairs surrounding a small table in the far corner of the massive lobby. Franker looked like he'd been through the wringer and traces of pain showed on his face as he moved.

When they sat, he leaned forward, grimaced and tried to hide it, and then said, "Where is she?"

"First, you tell me what the hell you're doing here? How the hell did you find us?"

"I'm in the FBI, remember," Franker said. "It's what I do."

"Come on," Wolf said. "You bring Bureau boys with you?"

Franker shook his head. "I ran the flight manifests for your names, which gave me the destination. Then I did a credit check to pinpoint the hotel. Now it's your turn and I'm not taking no for an answer."

Wolf studied the man. Involvement of the Bureau at this point would definitely make things worse. Right now, Wolf and company were operating under a different set of rules of engagement, as Dirk had said. They'd already technically committed more than a few illegal acts. That wasn't something that a straight, by-the-book federal agent could tolerate. Not to mention lying to the FBI was what put him on thin ice before.

"Look," Wolf said. "There are things going on down here that you can't be a part of. Rules are getting stretched. The situation is—"

"Bullshit," Franker said. "Tell me, and tell me now, or I swear I'll knock your fucking head off."

Wolf felt like saying that the guy didn't look like he could break an egg, but his raw emotion was obvious.

It looks like love, Wolf thought.

"All right," Wolf said. "But first, you got to tell me. Are we on the record here?"

Franker frowned. His head shook slightly.

"I checked myself out of the hospital," he said. "Took emergency medical leave from the Bureau. I knew when you were stonewalling me that something had happened to Kasey. And it was my fault. I should have been able to protect her." He stopped talking and his lips compressed inward. Tears glistened in his eyes and his head bowed. "It was my fault. I should've done more."

"You did all you could," Wolf said. "These guys are pros, and they came at your blindside. No way you could've prevented it without dying in the process."

Franker looked up at him, the tears more noticeable now.

"I'm ready to do that," he said. "If that's what it takes. I want to help get her back. Just tell me what you need me to do."

And so Wolf did. A slight change in his plans had Franker teaming with Reno in the third car holding the bandito.

One guy with a bum leg, Wolf thought, and the other with an arm in a sling and a condition of the heart. Crunch time.

He felt a copious amount of sweat running down his sides from his armpits. He wondered if it was due to the lack of air-conditioning inside the bus or the pending raid. Brenda was beside him, her dark hair pulled back and pinned up inside a confining piece of multicolored cloth. The moisture had collected on Brenda's upper lip and neck as well, but she still looked elegant. Everyone had a mask either in their laps or dangling from one ear but nobody had them on at this point, except Wolf. The chatter in low murmurs of rapid Spanish buzzed through the other workers. Wolf wondered if it was about him or Brenda and strained his ears to try and catch some discernible phrases. From what he could gather, the two *llegados* seemed to attract little notice. Their confederate, a heavyset woman named Rosa, had been paid off quite handsomely for getting them on the bus and was making more money than she would in a year doing the grunge work for Von Dien.

Wolf resisted the temptation to speak to Brenda. They'd decided to sit next to each other but not to say anything that could indicate familiarity. He'd hoped to talk to her before they'd gotten on the bus back in the Guatemalan section. Wolf had wanted to ask her about Yolanda. Her previous comment about Dolores Delgato, along with Ms. Dolly's quip, had given him a flicker of hope that maybe there was still a chance for the two of them after all. But, he'd pushed all thoughts about that possibility out of his present state of mind. There'd be time enough for that kind of speculation once this mission was completed, once Kasey was safe.

It had been the same during his deployments. Thinking about home, about sweethearts left behind as they got ready to climb in a Humvee or go into the ville and start kicking down doors.

You always wonder about who you left behind, he thought, and looked out the window to catch his first glimpse of the Von Dien Estate. They were approaching a large gate that was fastened between two stone pillars. Big signs were attached to the gate that spelled out warnings in both English and Spanish about not trespassing or touching the fence.

Electrified fencing, Wolf thought. Just like Reno had advised.

He used his thumb to send Mac the message that they were approaching the gate, then slipped the phone into his pocket. The revolver was pinching his groin at the moment, secured by a Neoprene belly band.

No tough guy in the world's gonna search me there, he thought.

It was a funny but true line from an old movie that he'd seen. He couldn't recall the name of it, but he remembered it had brought a laugh.

The bus's brakes squealed to a halt and the gate slowly slid open. Two uniformed guards, both wearing holstered side-arms, waddled up to the bus and the driver hit the lever opening the door.

"*Las tempaturas,*" one of the guards said, holding up one of those gun-like thermometers.

Wolf wondered if the ambient heat and humidity would affect his reading.

The guard with the thermometer began the checks. The bus was pretty full and the process took several minutes. When the guard got to Brenda and him the man's eyes widened and a smile stretched his lips.

"*No te veía antes,*" he said as he held the gauge in front of her face and pressed the trigger. "*Muy bonita. Cual es tu nombre?*"

Brenda said nothing.

The guard took a few more seconds to admire her,

then looked at the reading and said, "*Trenta y seite. Pero eres muy caliente.*"

"*No molestala,*" Rosa said in a sounding harsh tone. "*Eres mi sobrina. Es casado y esta embarazada.*"

Married and pregnant, Wolf thought as he watched the guard recoil slightly. I'm going to have to tip Rosa another twenty once this is all over.

If they got out of it.

The guard murmured an apology and flicked the device at Wolf. He then did a cursory job on the rest of those in the back of the bus.

After finishing he walked back up the aisle to the front, turned, and announced in a loud voice, "*No olvidense las mascaras.*"

He and the other guard stepped off the bus and the driver closed the door.

As the bus rolled forward Wolf glanced out the window. The guards were standing off to the side smoking with the gate standing open. Maybe the lazy bastards were going to leave it open for the bus's return trip out with the night shift.

It would be nice if we could hitch a ride on it, Wolf thought. With Kasey.

He whispered this to Brenda, who nodded.

The roadway wound past an expansive green lawn, punctuated by artfully trimmed bushes and artistic flower gardens. There was enough yard work here to keep a lot of gardeners busy. Then he saw the mansion. Reno had said it was big, and the satellite views that they'd gotten from the Internet hadn't done it justice.

It was two stories of solid red brick spreading out on either side of a triangular peak in the roof that was braced by four huge, white pillars. A massive fountain bubbled water from a stone statue in front of them. Sets of twin windows with gables were on both sides of the triangular peak and Wolf noticed that one of them had bars. According to Rosa, that's where *la mujer americana* was being kept under lock and key.

He nudged Brenda slightly and she made a fractional nod of acknowledgment.

The plan was for her to go in with the rest of the housekeeping staff as soon as they debarked from the bus. The men were mostly assigned to do the yard work, but Wolf intended to break off from them as quickly as he could. Brenda would text him when she was at the rear door so she could admit him. From there, they'd make their way upstairs with Brenda carrying a sack with a dress for Kasey to put on, along with a rag and black wig to cover her red hair, once they got into the room. It depended if there was a posted guard or not. Rosa had said there was, but since the door was locked and the room was on the second floor with barred windows, the guards were not very diligent unless Gordo, Von Dien's *mayordomo*, was around. According to Rosa, he was a bit of an overbearing bully and carried a gun. She also mentioned that there were a couple of Americans staying there as well. One was an *abogado*, a lawyer, who'd been there for months. The other was a thin, surly man who treated the women, the prostitutes they brought in, very badly. He'd even manhandled some of the prettier servants from time to time.

That has to be Soraces, Wolf remembered thinking.

One of his regrets was that he wouldn't be able to settle the score with that asshole.

Keep your eye on the ball, Bambi, he told himself.

Worry about evening things up later. Much later, when Kasey's safe.

The bus pulled past the four pillars and eventually came to a stop at the edge of the big structure.

The servant's entrance.

Everyone stood up and began putting on their masks as they shuffled toward the door. The pervasive scent of body odor hung in the air. Everybody seemed to be sweating as much as he was.

As he stepped off the bus, the bubbling noise of the fountain was audible. One of the security guards shouted for everyone to keep moving, men this way, women that way. He and Brenda split up and she headed for the house. He followed the group of men who kept moving toward a section of smaller brick row houses in the back. Glancing around, Wolf searched for the security guard who'd been directing them and saw that he was with the women, talking and laughing. As the group of men continued their march, Wolf slowed his pace until he was the very last in line. As they veered off to go to the row houses, he darted between one of the bigger trees and a stone statue of a man holding a flute with misshapen goat-like legs.

A satyr, Wolf assumed remembering Pan from his lesson in mythology.

A trio of massive, humming air-conditioning units and a generator were next to the house and Wolf moved there next, darting between the huge metallic cylinders and the brick wall. He had to step over the series of hoses that ran from the machines to the edifice.

He crouched down and waited. The procession of workers continued toward their destination. No one seemed to have taken notice of him.

Just like escape and evasion training in the army, he thought.

It was easy going so far.

Almost too easy.

After doing a few quick peeks he straightened up and moved with steady, but not rapid assurance toward the corner of the building. He walked rather than ran, figuring that a running man might attract undue attention.

His cellphone vibrated in his pocket and he glanced down. A text from Brenda: *At door*

When he got there, he saw it was ajar. He pulled it open slightly and slipped inside. The coolness of the air was almost chilling, but it served to stimulate him a bit. The room was a large kitchen storage area. Rows of utensils hung on holders on a stainless-steel counter along with pots and pans and several stoves and refrigerators. Brenda was standing there with the sack of clothes. She slipped her phone into her pocket and pulled her mask away from her face.

"We can go through there," she said, pointing to a door on the other side of the room. "There's another room and then the stairway's beyond it. I'll go first, text you if it's clear. Remember to keep your mask on."

She adjusted hers back into place and they went to the door. Brenda pulled it open and slipped through. Wolf kept it open a sliver and watched her progress. The room she'd entered appeared to be some kind of museum room or something.

The text chimed: *Venga.*

Wolf slipped into the room and saw her exiting at the far end. He quickly followed.

It was the size of a banquet hall and filled with

paintings, statues, and a huge glass case. Something caught his eye: one of the figurines on a top shelf. It was a fancily chiseled half-circle of stone with a familiar, intricate design. Inside the hollowed-out portion, the creamy lining had two smaller, intricately carved black onyx figures of a man and a big jungle cat, a lion, but this rendering of the big cat had no mane.

A lioness, Wolf thought, attacking a Nubian. My portion's other half.

Another text came: *Clear*

Brenda was mixing Spanish and English, he thought. She must be nervous.

They were supposed to use only Spanish as part of the masquerade.

Wolf walked out, scanning for people, and then looking toward the ceiling.

His heart froze.

The black plastic globe of a pan-tilt-and-zoom camera was mounted on a bracket on the far wall.

If someone was monitoring the surveillance system, it was only a matter of time before they spotted him, and Brenda as well.

Crunch time exacerbated, he thought. Better to keep moving than be spotted sneaking and hiding.

If someone did pick him up on camera he wanted to appear as legitimate as he could. He reached down and picked up a small decorative table. Carrying it in front of him, he continued through the dining room and into a long hallway. At the stairway Brenda caught sight of him and stopped.

"*Qué pasas aqui?*" she asked, staying in character and speaking in Spanish.

"*Las cámaras,*" Wolf said. "*En el cielo.*"

Her astuteness and street smarts showed when she just smiled and nodded and didn't look around.

"*Venga con migo*," she said, and headed up the stairs. *Come with me*, in case someone was listening.

Wolf followed carrying the table like a dutiful assistant to *la criada bonita*. Hopefully, if anyone had picked them up on surveillance it would look like he was doing something for her.

They made it up the long staircase with no problem. Wolf noticed a black metallic rail on the wall side with a carrying car at the top.

Von Dien must have an aversion to stairs, he thought.

He wondered about his faceless foe. No pictures existed of the man that Wolf could find, other than some from thirty years ago. Those showed a pear-shaped man with a huge head and perpetual scowl.

Ironic, Wolf thought. That somebody born into such riches couldn't find something to smile about.

Brenda continued up the stairs and turned left at the landing, looking like she knew exactly where she was going. Wolf followed trying to adopt a desultory posture—the bored, obedient drudge.

Just another lackey carrying furniture up the stairs ... Hopefully, whoever was watching would see it that way. He immediately looked up and scanned the area. PTZ's were at both ends of the upstairs hallway.

Brenda turned left and headed down the hallway. Wolf did the same. To his surprise an empty chair sat next to the solid-looking door at the end of the hall, but no guard.

That could mean a lot of things, he thought. It's shift change, for one thing.

Or maybe the guy was off getting something to eat or going to the bathroom.

They went down the hallway at a brisk pace and Brenda stopped and tried the knob. It made a clicking sound that told them it was locked. Wolf was estimating the chances of taking it out quickly and quietly with one or two kicks and decided that it would be very problematic, not to mention noisy. Instead, he set the box on the chair and took out his knife. The hinges were on this side, which meant that the door opened outward. The easiest way, not to mention the quietest, would be to remove them.

"Steve, *mira*," Brenda said.

A key hung on a hook next to the door jamb.

It makes sense, he told himself, not wanting to believe it, yet it made sense. If the guard or someone had to open the door in an emergency, they would want to be able to do so quickly.

Yeah, he thought. Easy. Almost too easy.

His worry-quotient elevated, but he grabbed the key and shoved it into the lock. It twisted and the sound of a deadbolt sliding out of the jamb was evident.

He pushed the door open and stepped inside whispering, "Kasey?"

She came at him fists raised and he reacted quickly enough to grab her, then her eyes widened, and her head jerked with recognition.

"Steve, what?" she said.

She was wearing an orange cotton jumpsuit and no shoes. Her hair looked flat and greasy; her face devoid of make-up.

"Never mind that," he said, choosing his words carefully. In his mind, he'd rehearsed what to say and how he might communicate the urgency of the situation. "We're here to get you out. Take that orange thing off and put this on." He motioned to Brenda who opened the cloth sack and handed her the dress.

"They took everything," Kasey said, grabbing the garment. Even my shoes."

She unzipped the jumpsuit and yanked it off. Wolf saw that she had nothing on under it. She turned away from him and stepped into the dress they'd brought.

"Here," Brenda said, stepping over to help her zip up the back. "We've got a wig to cover your hair. And tie it on with this scarf."

"Is Bill all right?" Kasey asked. "They shot him."

"He's fine," Wolf said. "And he's here. I'm going to text your dad to get ready to pick us up out front. But, we'll still have to run the gauntlet to the front gate."

He took out his phone and typed in, *popping smoke.*

"I don't know the grounds at all," Kasey said. "They've kept me locked up in here the whole time. They brought in a bucket so I could go to the—"

She stopped but Wolf got the idea. He slipped the phone back into his pocket.

"Bastards," he muttered and peeled away the Velcro to pull out the gun. "Come on. Let's move."

Kasey tucked her hair under the sheaf of black hair and Brenda helped her tie the scarf around it. Wolf went to the door and pulled it open a sliver. The hallway was still empty.

With a little luck, he thought, we can make it out of here.

"There's cameras everywhere," he said in a low whisper. "Walk fast but don't run. We don't want them to see anything out of the ordinary."

"Yeah, right," Kasey said with a sarcastic lilt to her voice. "Like the three of us walking down the hallway isn't out of the ordinary?"

Wolf felt both amused and irritated.

The same old Kasey, he thought. Always critical, always sarcastic. But at least she hasn't lost her spunk.

He stepped out into the hall and motioned for them to follow.

The three of them walked briskly toward the stairs.

Still no sign of any guards.

No sign of anyone, Wolf thought.

Strange, but he didn't want to look a gift horse in the mouth.

When they got to the base of the staircase the main floor was still deserted. Wolf debated whether to make a run for the front doors and keep going, or sneak out the back and go around the way he'd come.

Hopefully, Mac and the boys had taken out the main gate and would come roaring down the driveway for the extraction.

Hopefully, he thought, and took out his cellphone again.

Suddenly, two doors opened across from them. A big swarthy looking guy in a black butler's uniform stepped out leveling a shiny semi-auto at Wolf. He grinned. Two men, looking incredibly alike, exited the second door. One was holding a Glock, and the other had a yellow and black gun of some sort.

The yellow and black gun popped sending a spray of minute confetti into the air in a cloud and Wolf felt twin bee stings on his chest and then a paralyzing pain. He literally could not move but was aware that he was sinking toward the floor. The pain continued and one of the men stepped over and kicked the old revolver from his grasp. Wolf could see, but he couldn't move and what felt like an electric glove enveloped his body. The mask made it almost impossible to breathe. He was cognizant of men huddling around them, grabbing Brenda and Kasey.

The pain stopped and Wolf ripped off the mask and took a deep breath.

Taser, he thought. Shit.

"You enjoy the full ride?" someone asked. The voice had that all too familiar ring to it.

Soraces.

A setup. They'd been watching and waiting the whole time.

So much for the best-laid plans.

But then he realized that Mac and the others were probably barreling toward the house. When they didn't see Wolf and Kasey and Brenda out there maybe they'd try to break in. Or run.

No, he thought. Mac wouldn't run. He wouldn't leave us.

There was going to be a shoot-out. There was going to be blood.

Wolf felt some strong hands grab him and lift him up effortlessly.

It was a big blond guy who looked like Dolph Lundgren from that old Rocky movie. The guy stepped away and Wolf saw a fancy looking gun in a holster on his belt. It had a red-dot sight attached and the extended cam of a silencer stuck out the bottom of a pancake holster. A Japanese *tanto* knife was in a sheath on the other side.

Soraces stepped forward and grinned.

"You've still got those prongs embedded in your chest, Wolf. Charles here can give you another fifty thousand volts with a flick of his finger, so don't try anything."

Wolf could feel the two fish hooks sticking into him, one in his left pectoral muscle and the other in his right outside oblique.

He needed to knock at least one of them loose. He also had to figure out a way to warn Mac.

If he could.

As if reading his thoughts, Soraces said, "Don't fret about your other buddies, pal. They'll be joining us momentarily."

What the hell did that mean?

Then the front door opened and McNamara, Buck, and Joe Barnes came trudging through, their hands on their heads. Dirk followed behind them holding the captured Taurus nine-millimeter. The grin on his face told Wolf everything.

"Sorry, Steve," Buck said. "I shoulda known there was something funny about this guy."

Dirk cuffed him on the back. "Shut your fucking mouth."

"You son of a bitch," Wolf said. "How much they paying you to sell us out?"

"Oh, he and I are long-time friends," Soraces said. "Along with these two handsome gents." He gestured toward the two other men, who looked extraordinarily alike.

Wolf saw their identical hook noses and realized that he'd seen one or the other of them before: once at the sheriff's substation in Gila County and once on the plane coming here. He'd been totally outclassed in this one.

Bambi was about to be crushed by Godzilla.

A crafty Godzilla and his minions.

Dirk shoved Barnes into McNamara and the three of them stopped about ten feet from Wolf and the others.

"They've got some banged-up FBI agent with the other guy," Dirk said. "Give me his phone and I'll go up to the main gate and text them to meet me. That way they won't suspect anything. I'll ice 'em both when they pull up and bring you the bandito."

Wolf felt a sickening feeling in the pit of his stomach. Reno and Franker would be driving into a death trap. He'd been outsmarted again. Badly. But he still had one more hand to play.

"Listen, Soraces, we can still deal. If anything happens to us, any of us, there's a letter in the hands of an attorney back in Phoenix that'll blow the lid off you and this whole operation."

Soraces laughed and reached into his pants pocket, withdrawing an envelope and Wolf recognized his handwriting on the front of it.

"You talking about *this* letter?" Soraces raised an eyebrow and studied Wolf. "Don't be too shocked. Lola, aka Dolores Delgato, overnighted it to me the same day you gave it to her."

"She's worked with us before," Dirk said.

"True that," Soraces added. "She specializes in making fools of gullible idiots like you."

Gullible doesn't adequately cover it, Wolf thought.

He felt like he'd just been kicked in the balls.

Soraces had been one move ahead every step of the way.

The big blond guy held out his hand.

"Give me your phone," he said. His words had a heavy German accent.

Wolf hesitated, but not wanting to get incapacitated by another Taser blast, handed the big man the cellphone. He tossed it to Dirk, who caught it.

"Gimme another gun, will ya?" Dirk said. "This one's a piece of shit."

"Clyde, give him your Glock," Soraces said.

The one twin's face twisted into a scowl.

"Why *my* gun?" he said.

"Because I said so," Dirk said. "Don't get your panties in a bunch."

Clyde glared at him then strode over and handed Dirk the pistol.

"Thanks, Clyde," Dirk said and stuck the Taurus into his waistband.

Clyde's face twisted with a look of disgust.

"Go do it, dammit," Soraces said. "It's almost checkmate. All we have to do is verify that that's the real bandito."

"Yeah, yeah," Dirk said, moving toward the door, opened it, and left.

So he's worried about a duplicate, Wolf thought. Maybe I can buy us some time.

"You really don't think I'd be stupid enough to bring the real one down here," he said. "Do you?"

Soraces's head turned, but before he could speak another voice intruded.

"Dammit. You guaranteed me that this one would be the original."

Everyone turned toward the waddling figure that approached. He was perhaps five and a half feet tall and almost that wide. He wore a blue terrycloth jumpsuit and his body jiggled with each step. His head, which was as big as a regulation basketball, was wrapped in an elaborate looking mask that looked almost like a mutilated gas mask. Another man was with him wearing a blue cloth mask. His dark hair, tinged with gray, was slicked back.

"Where are you masks?" the waddling man shrieked. "None of you are wearing any. Put them on now. Immediately. Hans, see to it."

He has to be Von Dien, Wolf thought.

The other resembled the pictures he'd seen of Fallotti, the lawyer.

The big blond guy who'd picked Wolf up stepped over and lifted his hands to pull a mask up over his prominent jaw, momentarily exposing his right side to Wolf.

With the opening there, Wolf moved, yanking the one prong out as he made his grab for the big man's gun. The big guy whirled, reaching down, but it was too late. Wolf smashed a hard left to the big man's kidney as his fingers grasped the weapon. He twisted and pulled, shouting, "Get down!"

The big man's elbow struck Wolf's right temple and he reeled. The black dots swarmed in his eyes, blocking out the light for a split second, then vanished.

Close, Wolf thought. But no cigar.

He fired two rounds into the big man's back, then brought the weapon up and shot the heavyset Guatemalan butler just under the chin. Each round made a plunking sound. The man's mouth gaped, releasing a torrent of blood. Wolf then turned the gun toward the first twin who was still squeezing the trigger of the Taser. Wolf's next shot hit him squarely in center mass. As he twisted and fell, his brother rushed forward, his face an angry mask. Wolf stepped to the side, pivoting, and fired again. The back of the second twin's head exploded outward, framed by a crimson halo. He dropped face-down to the floor.

Wolf saw that Mac and the others had hit the dirt as directed. So had Brenda, but Kasey was still standing.

Wolf started to yell at her when the giant rose up and lunged forward, holding the *tanto* knife. Wolf used his left palm to strike the back of the huge man's hand, pushing the knife away. The sheer momentum of the huge attacker drove Wolf backward and he went down on one knee. The giant started to swing his arm back to deliver a back-handed slicing blow with the knife, but Wolf elevated the barrel of the pistol and squeezed off two more rounds. He was point-shooting, but even without proper target acquisition the second bullet struck home going up through the huge man's throat. He collapsed like a six-story building imploding.

Wolf took three stumbling steps to regain his balance and whirled only to see Soraces behind Kasey, his left arm crossing diagonally across her breasts, his fingers entangled in her hair. His right hand held what looked to be a long, thin blade against her right carotid.

Wolf leveled the gun at him and said in as guttural a tone as he could manage, "Let her go."

"Huh-un," Soraces said. "Me and her are walking out of here. Unless you want to watch her bleed out?"

McNamara rose to his feet.

"Take the shot," he said.

Wolf's breathing was ragged, and he wasn't sure he could hold the gun steady enough to do it. The heavy sound suppressor attached to the barrel felt like it weighed a ton. Soraces seemed to sense Wolf's hesitation.

"Besides, Stevie boy," Soraces said. "I'm your only hope of getting that recording that'll clear your name. Let us walk outta here, and I'll let her go and book. I'll contact you later about the flashdrive. I can care less about this prick's stupid artifact."

Wolf was suddenly cognizant that Von Dien and Fallotti had vanished. More adversaries might be on the way. He tried to regulate his breathing, to steady his hand.

"He's lying," McNamara shouted. "Take the damn shot. He'll kill her otherwise."

Other voices chimed in but, to Wolf, they were a cacophony of indecipherable noise, like the thunder of a waterfall. Only one stood out as clear as the pealing of a church bell.

"Take the shot, Steve."

It was Kasey.

The red dot magically appeared, centered on Soraces's forehead, and Wolf's finger gently stroked the pistol's trigger. The plunking of the round, the sudden burst of smoke from the end of the barrel, all seemed to unfold in exaggerated slow motion.

Soraces's mouth opened to form an O and his head jerked back, a small, neat, round hole appearing just under his right eye socket. A red mist momentarily blossomed around the back of his head and the fingers holding the blade went slack. It fell away from Kasey's neck and she collapsed, too. Wolf was immediately worried that he'd somehow harmed her. He rushed forward and collided with McNamara who had rushed toward his daughter, too. Wolf went sprawling and threw out his left arm to catch himself. He heard a distorted voice now. It was Buck's.

"Dirk's still out there. He'll kill Reno and that FBI fella when they pull up."

Wolf was steady on his feet now and he went to the fallen blond giant and rolled the body over. The pale blue eyes stared upward under half-closed lids and a trickle of blood spilled from the patted lips and wound down over the lantern jaw. Wolf bent down and grabbed the two fresh magazines out of their holders.

"I'll get him," he said. "You guys grab some of these weapons and clear the building. We've probably got some more security guys to deal with."

"And we gotta find that fucking Von Dien," McNamara said, getting to his feet.

"You've got to save Bill," Kasey yelled. "Please."

Wolf went to the door and saw the Camry parked way up the drive at the main gate. It was perhaps fifty yards away. Far enough that Dirk probably hadn't heard the commotion, and especially not the subdued sounds of the sound-suppressed gunshots.

Wolf saw the crowd of Guatemalans congregating by the bus about thirty yards down the drive. He ran to the vehicle, pushing his way through and pushed the driver away from the doors.

"*Qué pasa?*" the man said.

Wolf held up the gun and said, "*Salga.*"

The group of them scattered like leaves thrown into a strong wind.

Wolf climbed the three steps, plopped down into

the driver's seat, and twisted the key in the ignition. The bus's engine rumbled to life. Shoving the gear shift into first, Wolf popped the clutch and the elongated vehicle lurched forward. He twisted the wheel, steering it toward the road, grinding over some decorative stones along the fountain. The engine squealed and Wolf realized he needed to shift into second. After slamming back the shift lever, the bus accelerated, the engine still giving off a high-pitched whine. The pistol was in his right hand. It was a Walther. Wolf hit the ejection button and saw the mag drop and inserted a fresh one.

Combat reload, he thought.

The front gate was perhaps fifty feet away now. Up ahead he saw Dirk standing there next to the unoccupied Jeep and Camry. He turned slightly and motioned emphatically at the bus to turn away.

He must think I'm the Guatemalan Express, Wolf thought, and stomped on the accelerator

The Subaru was turning through the open gate area. Dirk waved casually and moved toward it. As Wolf drew closer he saw that Dirk held the Glock out of sight, down by his right thigh.

He continued toward the Subaru, then his head bobbled a bit and he glanced over his shoulder.

Something must have registered with him this time because he whirled and brought the Glock up in a firing stance.

Wolf instinctively leaned to his right just as the windshield spider-webbed in front of him.

Two rounds whizzed by him.

The bus was maybe twenty feet away now, barreling forward like a fullback toward a defensive goal line stand.

Another spider web cracked the windshield and Wolf felt a star-scatter of glass sear the left side of his face. He'd blinked just in time. Yanking the lever to open the front doors, Wolf leaped out of the seat. The bus continued forward, and Wolf jumped through the open doors as the crunching sound of metal striking metal reverberated as the bus smashed into the Camry. Wolf tried to stay on his feet, but the momentum was too great. He took a stumbling step forward and tumbled onto the asphalt about fifteen feet away. Rolling, Wolf extended the Walther and frantically scanned the space between the underside of the bus and the asphalt.

No sign of Dirk's feet.

Wolf's mind raced as he scrambled to his feet.

No cover where I'm at, he thought, but did Dirk go left or right?

The natural tendency would be to favor the side of his dominant hand, but he remembered Dirk saying he was ambidextrous. He also might have the combat savvy not to do the most obvious. It was a toss-up.

But he hadn't seen the other man's legs at all under the bus. If Dirk were moving to his right, they should've been visible. Wolf was rotating his body toward the front end of the crushed Toyota when a lambent shadow dappled the ground in front of him. Whirling and elevating the Walther, Wolf caught sight of the burly figure, silhouetted by the sun, coming over the elongated roof of the bus.

Wolf fired without aiming as the dark figure disappeared.

He's got the high ground, Wolf thought, and darted

back into the bus, raising the Walther and firing up through the roof.

Two perforations appeared in the metal. Wolf heard a scrambling sound and then two loud shots from above. Twin beams of sunlight burrowed through a pair of ragged holes in the bus's ceiling, the rounds ripping the fabric of a nearby seat. Wolf fired upward again, adjusting his aim in a desperate guess of his adversary's movement.

A pair of feet smashed onto the metallic hood, then Dirk sprang off to the side. He landed with a cat-like grace, bringing the Glock upward and firing three rounds. Wolf returned fire, sending three rounds of his own through one of the side windows, the glass fracturing in several places.

I've got the high ground now, he thought, and saw Dirk's face twist into a grimace. He staggered back a step, like he'd been punched, then brought the Glock up again.

Wolf centered the magical red dot on Dirk's broad chest and double-tapped two rounds, then elevated it and sent a third one between the space separating the blue and brown eyes.

Dirk's head snapped back. A second later his legs folded like an accordion and he collapsed to the ground.

Wolf approached with his pistol at the ready, but saw there was no need.

The Subaru pulled up and jerked to a stop. Reno was driving and Franker held the backpack with the bandito.

"Where's Kasey?" Franker yelled.

"Up in the house," Wolf said.

The Subaru took off. Wolf checked the Camry. It

was totaled, but the Jeep still had the key in the ignition. As he drove to the mansion he saw the Subaru jerk to a stop in front and Franker got out and ran inside leaving the passenger door open. Reno limped after him. When Wolf got there he glanced inside the vehicle and caught sight of the overturned backpack and the leering grin of the bandito, which had slipped partially out.

Siempre con una sonrisa en la cara, he thought. Always with a smile on his face.

Buck came running out with a frantic expression on his face and started running toward the far corner.

"Buck," Wolf called. "We got any security guards lurking?"

"Nah, they gave up their weapons and are now supervising the looting," Buck said. "But Von Dien and that other fella are getting away."

Then Wolf heard it: the unmistakable chopping sound of spinning rotors slicing the air.

He looked up and saw a sleek white and blue helicopter rising upward as if being manipulated by some omniscient puppeteer. Wolf strained to see who was inside but couldn't tell. The chopper swung upward going over the roof and hovered momentarily as it crested the tops of some of the more distant trees. He and Buck ran around the side of the building hoping at least to get off a couple of parting shots.

But it was too late. It was way out of effective pistol range.

"Shit," Buck said. "Too late."

Wolf felt deflated. The devil who'd orchestrated all this mayhem, all the unnecessary deaths, was getting the last laugh after all.

The helicopter was achieving some height now,

escaping the perimeter of the trees and the high, cyclone fencing, a diminishing shape against a cerulean sky.

Then, a trail of smoke arched upward on an intercept course and a second later the helicopter burst into a fireball and descended in a rotating dive into the jungle canopy.

Wolf saw McNamara walking toward him, a thick barreled weapon that almost looked like an M3 MAAWS anti-tank weapon resting on his shoulder.

"Look what I found hiding in the woodshed," Mac said, holding the weapon up for Wolf and Buck to see. A wisp of smoke still trickled from the back end of the over-sized barrel.

"That an M-Three?" Wolf asked.

"Nah. One of them old Carl Gustof Recoilless rifles. Five-hundred-yard effective range. Always wanted to fire one of these antiques." Mac's grin was wide. "I told you there'd be a reckoning, didn't I?"

Wolf felt a wave of relief. It was over.

"Nice shooting," Buck said.

"And that ain't all," McNamara said. "Show him, Buck."

"Oh yeah." Buck held up a pen and smiled. "This is one of them spy pens. I sell them at the Institute. Don't know what's on it, but maybe it'll be something you can use, Steve. That Soraces guy was a snake, but I can't see him carrying one that wouldn't have something good recorded."

He handed the pen to Wolf. He put it in his pocket and looked at Mac.

"We better beat feet out of here," he said. "Somebody's probably gonna come to check on that crash."

"I got big Joe and Brenda doing some quick clean up," McNamara said. "They gotta be about finished so I agree. But I wish I could take this baby with me." He patted the gun.

Shakespeare said it best, Wolf thought. All's well that ends well, but then he thought of something else. Something that needed to be returned ... To Iraq.

"I gotta get something," he said, and trotted back into the house.

THREE WEEKS LATER
THE MCNAMARA RANCH
PHOENIX, ARIZONA

As the mid-morning sun hung above the mountains, Wolf and McNamara carried the last of the boxes containing Wolf's possessions down to his Jeep.

"You sure you want to keep this thing?" McNamara asked, cocking his head toward the restored bandito statue which sported more cracks and a fresh refilling of plaster. "After all the trouble it caused you?"

"Why not?" Wolf said. He placed his box into the back section and turned to gaze down at the bandito's smiling face. "We've run a good course together."

He took the last box from McNamara and shoved it into the vehicle as well. It held his laptop and a couple of books.

"You never did tell me how you did on that school paper," McNamara said.

"I aced it. Thanks to poor old Garfield."

"Yeah, shit. He was one of the good ones." He took a deep breath. "You gonna be staying with Yolanda?"

"That's the plan. For the moment, anyway. We're going to see how things go."

"Well, she's one fine lady, that's for sure." McNamara laughed. "Like I said before, you'd best be careful or you'll find yourself getting serious with that little gal."

"The verdict's not in on that yet."

"Well, you know you'll always be welcome back here."

"I appreciate that, Mac," Wolf said. He lowered the back window and slammed the tailgate. "But it's time for a change."

McNamara raised his eyebrows. "Well, I'm hoping that high-priced lawyer can do something to get your name cleared up with what he's got to work with on that spy pen recording. Now that we've settled most all of this other business."

"You and me both," Wolf said.

McNamara canted his head back and squinted at him. "So, you thinking about taking Ms. Dolly up on her job offer?"

Wolf smiled.

"I haven't thought much beyond the next few weeks. Like you said, it depends on what Mr. Taylor can do. He seemed pretty optimistic once he saw that video from the spy pen."

"Hell," McNamara said. "He should. It's what they call exculpatory, ain't it?"

"That's a pretty fancy term. Maybe you should take up practicing the law."

"Maybe I will," McNamara said. "You know, I never did use my GI Bill benefits. And depending on how this bail bond reform bullshit they're pushing turns out, the bounty hunting business might be over with. Trackdown, Inc. will be a thing of the past." He turned and glanced at the ranch house. "Guess I might as well start thinking about selling this place, too. It's gonna be way too big for me with you, Kasey, and Chad all leaving."

"Chad'll still need a place to come visit his grand-pa," Wolf said.

"True enough." McNamara snorted and shook his head. "Damn, that thing with her and Franker running off together knocked me for a loop. I mean, who'd a *thunk* it?"

"He turned out to be a decent guy. Try to be happy for her."

"Yeah," McNamara blew out a heavy breath. "At least he's got a steady job. And he's riding the crest of the wave after turning over those stolen artifacts." He shook his head. "Imagine all this bullshit over a couple hunks of old stone and carved onyx."

"Well, he'll be out of our hair for good now. I know he definitely doesn't want to piss off his new father-in-law."

"He better not," McNamara said. "Of course, him and Kasey are already on my list for taking off on their honeymoon and leaving me to babysit,"

"Who you kidding? You're loving it."

"Yeah, I guess I am at that."

They both laughed.

"Tell Chad goodbye for me," Wolf said.

McNamara nodded.

Wolf stepped over, opened the passenger door, and pulled out his championship belt. "Here, give him this."

"Your belt? No, you already give him plenty setting up that college trust fund, Steve."

"He likes it so much," Wolf said with a shrug. "And who knows? Maybe I'll find the time to win another one down the road."

McNamara nodded. "It'll be kept in a place of honor, on the mantel right next to my shadow box."

Wolf was feeling the twinge of immense sadness creeping over him.

Mac shouldered the belt and sighed. "Well, with Trackdown, Inc. kinda hitting the skids, I can always pick up some extra money teaching for Buck at the Best of the West. It'll give me some gambling money when I come to visit you and Ms. Dolly."

Wolf grinned.

"Best be careful," he said. "Or you'll end up getting serious with that special lady."

"That sounds familiar." McNamara laughed again, but this time Wolf thought he could hear a note of sadness mixed in with the mirth. "Guess this is it. Been here before, many times, but this time's really hard. And special."

Wolf felt a lump forming in his throat as he extended his hand. "Mac, thanks for everything. You literally pulled me from the brink, brought me back, and gave me something to live for. A new start. A new life."

"Aw, shucks. Don't be giving me more credit than I deserve now."

The handshake turned into an embrace, which

culminated with McNamara's big hands slapping Wolf on the back.

"We've run a pretty good course together too," McNamara said. "Ain't we?"

"Damn straight," Wolf said. "All the way."

You can't go home again...

Ex-Army Ranger Steve Wolf is wondering just that after receiving a desperate call home from his mother. His younger brother, Jimmy, is in trouble.

As Wolf heads back to North Carolina to set things straight, he realizes that things have changed—and not for the better. The name of the town is different, a recycling plant has replaced the old textile factory, and a new off-reservation Indian casino is the main attraction. To top it off, the bitter stench of a burgeoning crystal meth problem is hanging over the area, and Wolf's brother is heavily involved in the distribution process.

Jimmy and his friends have also secretly concocted a dangerous plan to rip off a violent drug kingpin. And Wolf's best friend and mentor, Jim McNamara, is working down by the Texas/Mexico border and is unable to offer his expertise.

Standing alone, Wolf is forced to confront the ghosts from his past as well as a host of new and vicious adversaries, and—in a last-ditch battle to save his brother—Wolf races against a ticking clock to avert the impending carnage from destroying the only family he has left.

AVAILABLE NOW

Michael A. Black is the author of 36 books and over 100 short stories and articles. A decorated police officer in the south suburbs of Chicago, he worked for over thirty-two years in various capacities before retiring in April of 2011.

Black holds a black belt in Tae Kwon Do from Ki Ka Won Academy in Seoul, Korea. He has a Bachelor of Arts degree in English from Northern Illinois University and a Master of Fine Arts in Fiction Writing from Columbia College, Chicago.

Black wrote his first short story in the sixth grade, and credits his then teacher for instilling him with determination to keep writing when she told him never to try writing again. He has since been published in several genres including mystery, thriller, sci-fi, westerns, police procedurals, mainstream, pulp fiction, horror, and historical fiction. His Ron Shade series featuring the Chicago-based kickboxing private eye, has won several awards, as has his police procedural series featuring Frank Leal and Olivia Hart.

Black writes under numerous pseudonyms and pens The Executioner series under the name Don Pendleton. He is very active in animal rescue and animal welfare issues and has several cats.

www.MichaelABlack.com.